FOUR DAYS IN JUNE

Iain Gale has strong Scottish and military roots. He is the Editor of the Scottish National Trust magazine and Art critic for *Scotland on Sunday*. He lives outside Edinburgh and is working on a second novel.

Visit www.AuthorTracker.co.uk for exclusive information on Iain Gale.

D0733890

IAIN GALE

Four Days in June

A battle lost, a battle won, June 1815

HARPER

Harper
An imprint of HarperCollins*Publishers*
77–85 Fulham Palace Road,
Hammersmith, London W6 8JB

www.harpercollins.co.uk

This paperback edition 2007
1

First published in Great Britain
by HarperCollins*Publishers* 2006

Copyright © Iain Gale 2006

Iain Gale asserts the moral right to
be identified as the author of this work

A catalogue record for this book
is available from the British Library

ISBN-13: 978 0 00 720104 4
ISBN-10: 0 00 720104 4

Typeset in Sabon by
Rowland Phototypesetting Ltd, Bury St Edmunds, Suffolk

Printed and bound in Great Britain by
Clays Ltd, St Ives plc

This novel is entirely a work of fiction.
The names, characters and incidents portrayed in it,
while based on historical events, are
the work of the author's imagination.

To the memory of
George Gale
and
Giles Gordon

CONTENTS

PROLOGUE

A hundred days

They had thought him broken. Believed that they had vanquished forever the tyrant who had laid Europe waste for two decades. But he had proved them wrong. Had, in an unguarded moment of that first spring of peace, slipped the bonds of his captivity and returned to France. Had raised again the eagles and the empire and readied himself for battle.

So now the redcoats waited and watched and guessed how he would come to them. The generals, the captains and the men. Men who had thought their soldiering days were past. Who, depending on their rank, had seen their futures now lived out in riding to hounds or gambling in St James's or spending hard-earned booty in the taverns and whorehouses of Liverpool and London. Men from the shires and men from the hard north. Highlanders and farmers' boys and thieves and petty felons. Soldiers all.

Men who had fought this irksome man through eight long years in Spain. And with them now the new blood. Callow privates and pale young subalterns, drawn by the promise of an unexpected last chance to find glory and fortune in Boney's wars. Others came to swell their ranks: Germans, Dutch and Belgians, and on their flank a huge army of Prussians, all of them equally determined to finish now a job they had thought long done.

Together they waited and they watched. And the summer grew strange and unsettling, the days drifting between hot sunshine and heavy rain. In the fields the rye and wheat, still green in ear, stood shoulder high. And the redcoats and all their allies grew restless and longed for him to come.

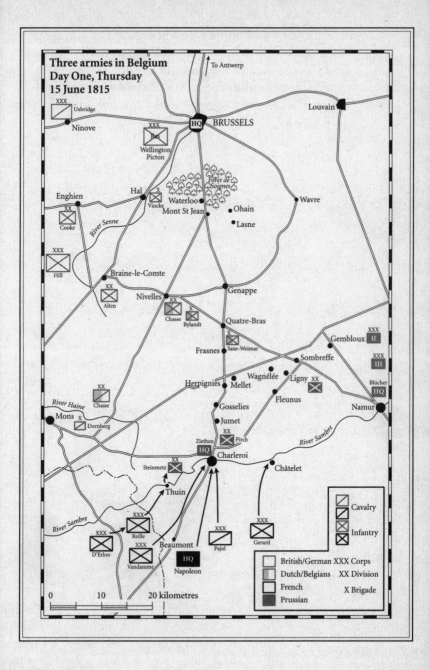

**Three armies in Belgium
Day One, Thursday
15 June 1815**

To Antwerp

XXX Uxbridge
Ninove
BRUSSELS HQ
Louvain
XXX Wellington Picton
Forêt de Soignes
Enghien
Hal
X Vincke
Waterloo
Ohain
Mont St Jean
Lasne
Wavre
XX Cooke
River Senne
XXX Hill
Braine-le-Comte
XX Alten
Nivelles
Genappe
XX Chassé
X Bylandt
Quatre-Bras
Gembloux
XXX II
XXX III
X Saxe-Weimar
Frasnes
Sombreffe
Blücher HQ
Wagnélée
Ligny XX
Herpignies
Mellet
Fleunus
XX Chassé
River Haine
Gosselies
Jumet
Namur
Mons
X Dornberg
Ziethen HQ
XX Pirch
River Sambre
Steinmetz XX
Charleroi
Châtelet
Thuin
XXX Reille
XXX Pajol
XXX Gerard
River Sambre
XXX D'Erlon
Beaumont
XXX Vandamme
HQ Napoleon

0   10   20 kilometres

Cavalry

Infantry

British/German XXX Corps

Dutch/Belgians   XX Division

French

X Brigade

Prussian

DAY ONE

Thursday
15 June 1815

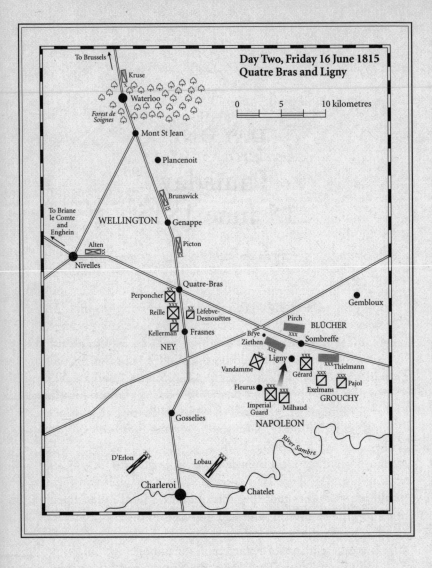

Day Two, Friday 16 June 1815
Quatre Bras and Ligny

0   5   10 kilometres

To Brussels ↑
Kruse
Waterloo
Forest de Soignes
Mont St Jean
Plancenoit
Brunswick
To Briane le Comte and Enghein
WELLINGTON
Genappe
Picton
Alten
Nivelles
Quatre-Bras
Perponcher
Reille
Lèfebve-Desnouëttes
Gembloux
Pirch
BLÜCHER
Kellerman
Frasnes
Brye
Sombreffe
NEY
Ziethen
Ligny
Thielmann
Vandamme
Gérard
Exelmans
Pajol
Fleurus
Milhaud
GROUCHY
Imperial Guard
NAPOLEON
Gosselies
River Sambre
D'Erlon
Lobau
Charleroi
Chatelet

ONE

Charleroi, 3.30 a.m.
Ziethen

The man was terrified. Ziethen was not surprised. The only penalty for desertion was death, and he had gambled his all on making a desperate rush through both his own lines and the enemy pickets. By some miracle he had not been shot. To risk death; to betray your country. It was a strange courage. A courage born of cowardice. He did not look like a coward, this Frenchman. And he did not look like a hero. Or for that matter much like a soldier. On his head was the familiar black shako, with its brass plate bearing the raised number 13. The 13th Regiment of Line Infantry. Ziethen tried to place it. Which corps? Which brigade? Who was facing him down there across the river? No matter. They would get that from him later. He remembered the 13th, though. As heroes – of Austerlitz, Eylau, Wagram, Borodino. He had even crossed swords with them himself – at Auerstadt. But this man was not the Frenchman of 1806. The French who had marched into Berlin a month later, to Prussia's everlasting shame. This, thought Ziethen, was a different sort of Frenchman – shambolic.

He was unshaven. Three days, Ziethen guessed. His uniform was principally a filthy long brown overcoat, albeit with the familiar dark blue jacket beneath. His frayed yellow collar and tattered red and yellow epaulettes testified to his élite status as

3

a voltigeur – a sharpshooter. *Élite?*, thought Ziethen. He had thrown away his musket. He was still laden down, though – with four days' bread ration and extra cartridges – necessitated presumably by a lack of adequate transport. If this was all that Napoleon could throw at them they had nothing to fear. Secretly, though, the general knew that he was fooling himself. This sad man was not typical. That was why he was here – in the sombre, provincial dining parlour of Ziethen's requisitioned headquarters on the outskirts of this godforsaken Belgian town. This fool. This brave coward. This deserter. He would not fight. But he was the exception. There were other men out there, beyond the river, and they, Ziethen knew, were different. They were hardened, they wanted to fight. And they were filled with hate. Hate for the Prussians. Hate for men like him.

There was food on the table, and a bottle of local wine. He had been about to eat when they had dragged the wretch into the room. Conscious now of the Frenchman'eyes, focused on the thin chicken leg in his hand, Ziethen threw the bone into the fire and, somewhat obviously, he realized, wiped his greasy fingers on the scarlet turnback of his own dark blue coat.

The Frenchman took off his shako, revealing lank, greasy hair. He spoke. But the accent was too provincial; the words too garbled. Ziethen's Chief of Staff, the laconic, educated von Reiche, managed a rough, staccato translation:

'He says, sir, that he is from the 13th Regiment of the Line. From Count d'Erlon's corps. That they have been camped for some days near Beaumont, to the south west of us. His whole regiment was there – three battalions. Around 1,200 men, he thinks. But some have left – like him. Some of his friends. And some have died. They came there from Lille. He says that to reach our lines he had to walk ten kilometres. It's another ten to here. He came through what he thinks was another French corps. A lot of men. Perhaps 20,000. All arms. He saw infantry, many cannon, lancers, chasseurs. One of his friends was shot, two others captured by the gendarmes. He says it was very frightening. He does not want to fight. He says that he would like to help, sir.'

The Frenchman smiled, feebly. Since yesterday Ziethen had expected something to happen. But up till now just where it would come had been unclear. This man was all that he had hoped for. But could he be trusted? He desperately wanted to believe so. Outside there was a heavy mist. His pickets could see nothing. Even the keen-eyed Hussars of his own old regiment, the 4th, had returned with no information. Anything would be of help. He tried to interpret the news, to ignore the Frenchman's terrified, plaintive gaze.

'Get him a drink.'

'General?'

'A drink. Get the man a drink. Wine. Water. Get him a cup of water. And a chair.'

A guard produced a battered tin cup; water was poured. Ziethen picked up the wine and poured a little into the water. A grenadier brought one of the few chairs which had not been taken by the owners of the house or broken up by his men for firewood. The Frenchman sat down, took a long drink and forced a smile. He was sweating. From outside the window a sudden burst of laughter and the sound of a smashing bottle made the man turn his head. Below in the courtyard Ziethen's junior officers were enjoying themselves. Trying to forget the dawn; the battle they knew must come.

'Ask him what Napoleon is doing now. Where is he crossing the river? Is he concentrating his men in one place. Is he coming here? To Charleroi? Ask him.'

The Frenchman looked worried again. He answered the questions quickly. Too quickly? Ziethen tried to gauge his reaction, his honesty.

'He says that there are rumours. That Napoleon has sent to Paris for Ney. That the Belgians in Wellington's army will desert and side with the French. That Wellington will abandon Brussels and make for the coast.'

Ziethen had heard the rumours too. There were always rumours before a battle. He was more concerned with the reliability of the information which might win them the coming battle. So he humoured the man; allayed his fears; gave him confidence, and more wine and, little by little, learned through the garbled reports that the Emperor had issued the order to march towards the Sambre. Then his tone changed. A final test.

'Why did you desert?'

The Frenchman swallowed hard and began. He had no love for the Emperor. For France, yes. But Napoleon? He spat at the floor. He had lost three brothers in the past ten years' fighting. He was a farmer, from Normandy. Not a soldier. He had two sons. He wanted peace. His eyes filled with water.

Ziethen smiled. It was good. This was no rehearsed deception. And it made sense. The Emperor was about to attack – at Thuin. He intended to concentrate one wing of his army. An entire wing, aimed here. Towards Charleroi. It would hit Steinmetz's brigade head on. Napoleon planned to split the allies before they could join forces. Then he would destroy them in detail. Little by little, with his classic strategy of the central position. It was brilliant. Obvious. Dangerously simple. All he had feared. Ziethen needed to move quickly. Blücher would act, would march to the battle. Of Wellington he was not so sure. Wellington, the hero of Spain, with his ragbag army of British, Dutch, Belgians and Hanoverians. How would they behave when faced with the might of the Empire? Would they stand? Oh, Wellington wouldn't cut and run. But would he come to their aid? There was no time to find out. If Napoleon was to be stopped the Prussians at least would be ready for him.

'Reiche. Send a despatch to Field-Marshal Blücher. Tell him that Napoleon is about to attack me at Thuin. Make sure that

6

the message gets through to Lord Wellington. Oh, and this time don't forget to copy it to General von Gneisenau. We wouldn't want to upset the delicate etiquette of the high command, would we?'

He and Gneisenau had never got on. Ziethen hated the jumped-up Saxon, with his clever army reforms and the deft political manoeuvring that had raised him to Army Chief of Staff. And he knew that Gneisenau loathed him. That he had attempted to block his appointment as corps commander. But Papa Blücher's word was final. Now he would repay the old man for his confidence. As Reiche hurried from the room, Ziethen turned to the captain of the guard.

'Now take this fellow outside and give him something to eat. Then tie him up, and if he tries to run, shoot him.'

As the Frenchman left, Ziethen wondered, as he often wondered, how Napoleon had ever achieved the marvels of the past fifteen years. The French did not make war like Prussians. They had no code of discipline. Too often he had seen soldiers whose dress had almost rivalled that of his recent guest. They were badly drilled and often poorly led. But these were the men who had conquered Europe, who had not so long ago controlled an empire which had stretched from the coast of Spain to the Russian steppes. It had been Napoleon's vanity that had undone them. Just as his ego had been the making of France, so it had been her downfall. But the fact was they had done it. And despite all that he knew and all that he had seen, Ziethen still wondered how.

Some men spoke of ten years of war, some of fifteen. But Ziethen had been fighting this war, fighting the French, for a quarter of a century. He had been there as a young hussar officer at the storming of Frankfurt. There at Valmy in 1794, when Napoleon had been merely Buonaparte, the precocious young Corsican Colonel of Volunteers. He had seen a ragged French revolutionary army throw back the mighty Prussians and had known at that moment that his life would be spent in defeating them. At Jena-Auerstadt in 1806 he had earned command of his regiment. Then had come promotion to the staff. The memories came fast. The faces. The dead friends. Names. Voices. Their peculiar laughs. Their eccentricities. They came as they came often to him in the dark, silent hours. Their names. Their faces. Most of all their voices.

The sounds of the camp were suddenly split by distant gunfire. A low rumble. Ziethen listened more closely. Cannon. Six-pounders. Regimental artillery. The guns which in the French army alone accompanied every corps, making it into a self-contained army. That would be Thuin. The French bombardment before the attack. Naturally he would obey Blücher's plan to the letter. Would pull his men back here – to Charleroi – a slow retiral to protect the bulk of the Prussian army which would gather at Sombreffe. His outposts at Ham and Thuin would have to be sacrificed to delay the enemy advance. No unit was to support them, no one to go to their aid. They were expendable. Treskow's cavalry would have to cover them. The Prussians would be overrun. His own old regiment would suffer. But there was no alternative. Ziethen knew that if he fell back too slowly he would be surrounded, too quickly and he would allow a swift French advance to engulf not only him but the entire wing. And then Fleurus would be perfect for a limited defence, perhaps even for Blücher's battle. He had reconnoitred it only this past week. Knew the land, the gully, the woods to the rear.

It was of course painfully familiar terrain. The place of another battle. Almost twenty-one years ago to the day, when another French army had broken the 50,000 allied troops of Austria, Britain and Hanover, before taking Brussels. Many soldiers would have taken it as a bad omen. Ziethen touched the black Iron Cross which hung at his neck. Had he been a superstitious man, which thank God he was not, he would have regarded it as a talisman. Which, of course, he did not. Still, he touched it, felt its reassuring coldness. Remembered what it stood for. The blood. The screams of the wounded. The dying. The noise. The smoke. It was as clear in his mind as if it had been yesterday. Haynau. Two years ago. The great plain of Leipzig. He had been awarded the Iron Cross – 1st Class. Gneisenau, naturally, had been made a count. But now was not a time to open old sores. Now was a time to act. A time to fight. A time to hate.

TWO

Brussels, 5.00 p.m.
De Lancey

She was exquisitely beautiful. A somewhat girlish face, full-lipped and with huge saucer eyes, and serene beyond her years. There had been other women, of course. Such women as Spain could boast. But Magdalene – Magdalene was everything that he wanted, all these long years.

She was a Scot. Her father, Sir James Hall, farmed at Dunglass, near Berwick, on the coast. Nine thousand acres with at its heart Sir James's great new house in the eccentrically fashionable Gothic taste. It had first struck De Lancey as being more oppressively gloomy than one of Mrs Radcliffe's novels. But if Magdalene loved it, then so must he.

It had not been at Dunglass that they had met, but in Edinburgh. At a winter ball, on a chill December evening, in the city's Assembly Rooms. There, beneath the light of 500 candles, spinning across the floor through the cream of Edinburgh's society, he had seen her. A face so new, yet so familiar. The shock. Had caught it reflected in her own eyes. Had stopped. Had apologized to his angry partner. Had carried on the dance – clumsy, unthinking. Thunderstruck. Like a blow on the back, a fall in the hunt.

They had talked. And danced, he seemed to remember. And, after the dance, De Lancey had walked through the dark, pre-dawn streets, back up the hill to the Castle, his head filled with visions of Magdalene.

A month after they had met he had received his knighthood. Invited to Dunglass by way of celebration, he had walked with her into the gardens. That little Eden. And it had been there, in that earthly paradise, beneath the oak tree under which her mother had loved to sit during those years while Sir James had been abroad, that he had proposed to Magdalene. And she had accepted.

'We will always be together, William.'

'More than that, my darling. I shall never leave you. Never.'

The wedding had been a small affair. A bright, crisp Scottish April morning, only two months ago now. Their church, the tiny kirk of Greyfriars in the heart of old Edinburgh, had been bedecked with branches of blossom and sheaves of daffodils. And, although its architecture was less ornate than he might have liked, the preacher, a Mr Inglis, a regular firebrand, had married them with the utmost eloquence. It was, he felt, true to the spirit of the age. A marriage of intellect and beauty. He recalled her sisters – their pretty, sprigged muslin gowns, their giggling at the advances of his brother officers.

Afterwards they had travelled to Dunglass, as husband and wife. And then ten days of perfect bliss. How he loved her. And in the gardens again, where the spring was everywhere, she had turned to him, her beautiful eyes filled with the need for assurance.

'We shall never be apart.' Almost a question now.

'Never. My dear, darling Magdalene. I shall never leave you.'

Their time had been brief, though, and continually subject to interruption by one of her family. He had not minded, such was his happiness. And her father had opened his mind to so many new things.

Sir James had introduced him to an entirely different way of looking at the world. Had taken him to the cliffs on which

Dunglass stood, towering above the waves. Had shown him the rocks. Had told him their secrets. Of the formation of the earth. Of sandstone and schistus. Of the immeasurable force which had torn asunder the then so solid fabric of the globe. And there, in that instant, high above the waves, he had felt himself transported back to a time when the rocks on which he stood were yet at the bottom of the sea. A topsy-turvy time before time. Before revolution and war had blighted the perfection of the earth. His mind had seemed to grow giddy, looking so far down the cliff – so far back into the very abyss of time. He had felt himself on the brink of some great realization. And then Sir James was talking to him. 'It is, as Hutton says, that we can find no vestige of a beginning to the world – no prospect of an end.' No end. World without end. He had felt suddenly light-headed. Had seen how his own reason was taking him further into something perhaps than his imagination might care to follow. Had felt an intimation of something like . . . eternity.

Before he lost himself entirely in that vortex, Magdalene was there. Come, she said, to 'rescue' him from her father. And later, when he had told her of his fascination with what Sir James had said, she had taken him to show him the 'museum of stones' – stones which she herself had gathered on the nearby beach below the cliff. And then they had climbed down and she had kissed him on that narrow strip of pebbles – there below the cliff. Had made him close his eyes as she stooped to pick something up and then pressed into his hand one particular stone. Quite small, pale golden-yellow, marbled white. Then she had whispered into his ear, her voice barely audible – soft, against the rolling of the waves.

'Forever.'

He felt the stone again now, its cool roundness, tucked away as it always was, in the pocket of his waistcoat. Ran it between his finger and thumb. Stones. Stones of an incredible age. Stones that seemed to echo the sense of permanence of his new family.

Stone on stone, through the generations, he thought. The Halls had their own vault, made from local sandstone, in the parish church – their church. Stones which somehow echoed his own need for a sense of permanence. His need for Magdalene. Like the stones, she was immovable. Utterly dependable in a world in which too often he had seen friendships vanish into atoms before him in the flash and thunder of gunfire. Magdalene, like the stones, was eternity.

And so it was that, together, as husband and wife, they had travelled to London. Wellington had asked for De Lancey particularly as his Quartermaster General – *de facto* Chief of Staff. It was not quite the post that he had wanted – a colonel on the Staff. But it was an honour, and he was happy to go. To be in at this final reckoning with Boney. And though it was only an acting post while they waited the arrival of Sir George Murray from military operations in Canada, here at last seemed to be the path to promotion for which he had looked so long.

At the end of May he had arrived in Brussels. It was only a week now since Magdalene had joined him – for what had proven to be the most wonderful seven days of his life.

He was only required to attend the Duke – 'the Peer', as De Lancey and his brother officers liked, with respect, to call him – for one hour a day, and from their grand lodgings in the house of the Count de Lannoy, on the Impasse du Parc by the Parc Royale, they had taken daily promenades about the town.

De Lancey had delighted in showing his young bride the wonders of the continent – almost as much as he enjoyed showing her off to the many beaux and beauties of British society who had crossed the Channel in expectation of the coming battle. But the couple had avoided all the dances and formal dinners, preferring to spend their time together, alone.

Even this evening they had spurned an invitation to a ball being held by no less than the Richmonds. The Peer, he believed, proposed to attend. Such appearances were vital for morale, and he was well aware that Wellington relished the attention of the ladies. But for his own part De Lancey had contrived the clever excuse of a small private dinner with his old friend Miguel d'Alava, from which he knew he would be able to steal away early to rejoin his wife. Now, having dismissed his valet, Jervis, for the evening – the servants too would have their dance – he was beginning to regret his generosity. He fumbled with his coat.

'Damn these medals.' He had never been good with intricate things. 'My darling. Do help me, please. These confounded decorations. How does one put them on?'

She took his Knight's Cross – along with the other shining gold and silver circles and crosses – the material proof of his bravery, and with her tiny hands began to pin them on to his coat. As she did so she gazed up at him. Those eyes.

'Tell me again, William, about Talavera. And Bussaco. About how our boys came up over the ridge and chased the Frenchies down the hill. And of Badajoz. Oh, how I love that tale. All those poor, brave boys of yours in their hopeless attacks on the ramparts. And then the glorious victory. And the Peer in tears. And all the tragedy. Do tell me, William. Oh, what it must be to be a soldier!'

'It is not quite the grand thing that you imagine, Magdalene. Mostly it is spent in marching. And waiting. And when the battle does come it is the most terrible thing you have ever seen. But it is glorious. Perhaps the most glorious thing a man can know . . . apart from love.'

'Oh, William. Do you suppose that I might see a battle? Might come with you? Some wives do. Mrs Fortescue told me that the wife of Quartermaster Ross of the 14th has been with her husband on many of his campaigns, these full ten years, and that she fully intends to be with him in the coming battle.'

'Magdalene. Dear, darling Magdalene. You are not the wife of a quartermaster. I am the Quartermaster General. A colonel.'

'But I should so love to see you go into action, William.'

'I have told you before, my darling. I do not "go into action". My action is all about taking and giving commands. I shall be with the Peer throughout the battle. By his side. Issuing his orders. That will be my "action".'

'But I do so want to see your brave boys finish Bonaparte at last. It will be the last battle. Everyone says so.'

'I daresay that in that one thing at least "everyone" for once is right, my darling. One last battle.'

She hugged him, smiling. 'Is he really as awful a monster as they say, William? Have you seen him? Papa says that at Brienne he was really a very quiet little schoolboy. Very kind-natured. Clever. Good at snowball fights, he says.'

'Your father, darling Magdalene, with respect, did not know the Bonaparte that we play with. The man is a tyrant. We presumed that we had rid the world of him. And now he has returned. He was not satisfied with an honourable peace. He still desires to have the world. To possess our world. Your world. He would reduce free-born Britons to slaves and put the world in chains to his own despotism. He proclaims his cause as freedom, but it is no freedom that I know: the freedom for which we fight. If you had seen, Magdalene, the things that I have seen. Terrible things. In Spain. Things done in his name. You would not talk of schoolboys and snowballs. He is a tyrant, Magdalene. A curse. An evil. And now we must silence him. Forever.'

'I . . . shall not ask again, William.' She let him go.

'And I am sorry. I did not mean to become so passionate.'

'You know, William,' clinging once again to his tall, strong frame; stroking his back with her hand, pressing her leg against his own; touching the forelock of his thick, dark hair; running a finger down the length of his side-whisker, 'it is never in my purpose to cool your passion.' She looked him straight in the eyes. Smiled at her handsome soldier.

'Magdalene. You quite disarm me.'

15

'Oh no, William,' letting go again, turning away, then back to look at him. Shamming coyness. 'It is quite the contrary. You know, when we were first introduced I was quite intimidated by you. You had taken Edinburgh by storm. The talk of the town. So dashing. My . . . rambling soldier.' She giggled.

'Magdalene. Please. I am a soldier. I am an officer. I do command men.'

She smiled again. Through half-lowered lids. Played with the pale green silk bow of her low *décolletage*. 'Well, then. Am I not also yours to command? Command me.'

Of course he had been late for dinner. Had arrived flushed, unsettled. The crumpled necktie told its story. D'Alava had not minded. He had known De Lancey for some years now. They had served together against the French in the fight for his homeland. Had ridden together with their friend Wellington. He knew too that he had only recently been married. And at a time when this day might be your last on earth, there were surely more important matters than social punctuality. Besides, he enjoyed the Englishman's company. And De Lancey, in turn, relished the lack of formality of d'Alava's house. Had become used to its like in Spain. Was his own man. Hated the pomp of the court and the garrison officers' mess. Preferred the relaxed atmosphere of campaign life, where one night might bring an inn for a billet, another an open field. And this was as close as he could find to it. This, and the unexpected joy and daily novelty of his life with Magdalene.

'But William, tell me.' The genial, balding Spaniard flashed his dark, almost black eyes at his old friend, grinned and took another sip of the heavy red wine which he had brought here in no little quantity, from his own estates in Navarre, when appointed Spain's Ambassador in Brussels. 'You of all men have the Duke's confidence . . . even above me. How does he intend to deal with Bonaparte?'

'You know, Miguel, as I do, that my Lord Wellington is

never quick to explain what he intends on the battlefield. Why, in the campaign of Salamanca, you will well recall, he did not vouchsafe any plan of execution, even to Sir George Murray. He is expert, Miguel, at keeping us all in the dark with regard to his intentions. He will sit at table with the General Staff and fill their heads full of humbug as to their dispositions. And then, not twelve hours later, will instruct me to issue an order which will march the brigades in quite the opposite direction. What we do know is that when Bonaparte moves on to the offensive – as move he will – we, the British and our Dutch and Belgian allies, are his most likely target. We are merely waiting for him to play his hand. You know that when the Peer met with Prince Blücher last month it was agreed that the two armies should support each other and that the crucial axis of communication was to be the road from the Prussian army – at Sombreffe – to ourselves, around Nivelles.'

'Yes. Of course, William. I am well aware of all this. But what will he do, d'you suppose? The "monster", as all your pretty ladies here in Brussels like to call him. Wellington is obsessed, is he not, with the idea that Bonaparte intends to turn his right flank – to cut his communications and his escape route to the sea, at Antwerp? But what, William, if he is wrong? I think that your line is too extended. Let us say that he is wrong. That Blücher is the first to be attacked. Think of it. How will you ever move fast enough to help the Prussians? I do not think it can be done. And so . . .' He made a forward gesture with his hands, as if pushing between two objects. '. . . You are split in two by the French. And then . . .' He clicked his fingers. '. . . One . . .' And again. '. . . Two. I think that what we have here, my dear friend, is a simple conflict of interest. And I am wondering whether your good friends the Prussians – Prince Blücher and Count von Gneisenau – will share my opinion?'

'Wellington will honour his word, Miguel. You know that. He will march to Blücher's aid.'

'But with what, William? With what? This army of twenty nations? If anyone is aware of the fine fighting quality of the British it is I. You and I, we remember Badajoz, Salamanca, Vitoria. But this army? Wellington himself has called it "infamous". For every British soldier you have I hear that there are two Germans, Dutch or Belgians. Half of your army is German. Fine men of course, the King's German Legion. They fought well in Spain. But William, what of the other Hanoverians? The militia? Peasants, farmers. And one third of your men are Netherlanders – most of whom, you will not deny, wearing the same uniforms with different hats and under different colours, were only a year ago fighting loyally for Bonaparte!' He slammed his fist hard down on the table.

De Lancey leaned forward in his chair. 'I cannot deny what you say, Miguel. But let me apprise you of some other facts of which you may be unaware. At this moment we have 95,000 men in the field; the Prussians no less than 130,000. We have more cannon than in any previous campaign and no want of ammunition. Do you know that the Peer has been in command of his "infamous" army a good two months and that during that time he has been careful to reorganize? Do you know that in every division, save the Guards, the Duke has taken care to mix the British battalions with veteran redcoats of the German Legion? Do you know that even in the Guards' division he has specifically commanded that the three younger battalions should be stiffened with one of old sweats from the Peninsula? Do you know that in every brigade which contains inexperienced British troops, fresh from the shires, he has placed proven battalions of German regulars? And do you know that he intends to keep any doubtful elements of Belgians and Dutch well in the rear? No, Miguel. This army is not quite the flummery you might suppose it to be.' De Lancey sat back. Smiled. Sipped his wine.

'William. Dear friend. Do not agitate yourself. Be sure that I have great faith in Wellington. But what I am concerned with is how he will use his force.'

'That all depends upon Bonaparte. And we shall soon enough know that man's intentions. You may know that for over a month now our friend Colonel Grant has been busy behind French lines gathering intelligence, just as he did so well in Spain. We know that Bonaparte has assembled a sizeable army – around 200,000 men. And that perhaps 125,000 of them are directly before us on the border. What we do not yet know is quite where they will attack. It might be at Mons. Or at Tournai. Or at Charleroi. Once we do know that, then will be our time to act.'

'But Wellington, you know well, William, prefers to defend. That is his skill. And here is the problem, my friend. Prince Blücher – Marshal "Vorwärts" – likes to attack. It is all very fine for Wellington to draw his supplies from the coast. But Blücher must pay to supply his army. Can you imagine what it is costing him now, just to sit on his arse?'

De Lancey, for once, was silent. Knew of old that this was mere teasing. That both men believed that their mutual friend, their commander, the hero of Spain, the toast of Europe, would be victorious. They were simply playing the same games that they had before every battle in Spain. Nevertheless the conversation had stirred some genuine worries, and it disturbed De Lancey to realize that he was concerned. He stared thoughtfully at his plate, took another sip of wine and, having considered his words, smiled before opening his mouth to reply.

As he prepared to do so, the double doors of the dining room opened and d'Alava's butler came quickly to the table and cupped his mouth to his master's ear. D'Alava spoke. 'It seems that you have a messenger, De Lancey.' He grinned. 'He has come . . . from your wife.'

Spotless and gleaming, a young pink-cheeked British

aide-de-camp was shown in, sword clattering, spurs ringing on the polished wooden floor. He handed De Lancey a note. D'Alava laughed and thumped the table with his fist.

'So, my dear William. You see? You are away for only one hour and already your lovely wife has need of you. Ah, my friend. What it is to be young and in love.'

De Lancey unfolded the piece of parchment. Read it quickly. Rose to his feet. Turned to the aide: 'Wait.' Then to d'Alava. 'You are sadly mistaken, señor. I assure you, this is no message from my wife, but an urgent dispatch for the Duke of Wellington. I am afraid, my dear Miguel, that here is an end to our delightful dinner.'

'Can you tell me?'

'It is from Berkeley, our man at the Prince of Orange's headquarters, at Braine-le-Comte. It seems that at noon today the Prince's office received information from General Dörnberg that Bonaparte had crossed the frontier. But the Prince was not there to receive it. He was here, in Brussels, making a report of "light gunfire" to be heard in the direction of Thuin. And, as a consequence, no one thought to take any action on Dörnberg's message – for over two hours. That is, until Berkeley happened upon it. Miguel, we have lost two hours. Bonaparte is at Charleroi.'

'God help us.'

'I must go to Wellington. Adieu, Miguel. Thank you again for your hospitality. Until we meet again.'

'On the field of battle, William.'

Their handshake – wonderfully un-British, thought De Lancey – had become for both more than a gesture of farewell. It was a symbol of faith in their mutual survival. Just as it had been before Salamanca, Badajoz, Vitoria.

De Lancey turned and walked quickly to the door, closely followed by the aide, and out into the candlelit hall, where the clatter of the young man's spurs changed to a brighter note as they rasped on the black and white marble of the chequerboard floor. At the door De Lancey turned again and raised his hand in a final farewell.

'Till the battle, Miguel. Then we shall know the true mettle of this army. And so shall Bonaparte.'

Smiling, he turned through the door and walked out into the warm evening. Outside, at the foot of the steps, the aide was waiting, holding his horse by the pommel of its saddle. Without a word, De Lancey, who had arrived by carriage, took the reins and hoisted himself up. Sensing that this was hardly a time to protest, the aide let go his mount and, saying nothing likewise, De Lancey urged the handy little chestnut off along the street, quickly breaking into a canter. His speed alarmed several of the promenading couples, sending them back against the shuttered windows.

It was not far to the house that Wellington had taken – an imposing ten-bay mansion, set back from the Rue Royale, to the west of the Parc. De Lancey pulled up the horse, leapt from the saddle, leaving it untethered, and rushed past the redcoated sentries, through heavy oak doors, across the court-yard and into the house.

He found the Duke still seated at the dinner table, on which, although the dishes had been removed, there yet remained eight wine glasses and a half-full decanter of port. Everywhere – across the table, the chairs, the floor – lay papers. Maps, plans, orders of battle, reports. Wellington did not look up, continued to read.

'General d'Alava was well?'

'Quite well, sir. He sends his warmest regards.'

'Oblige me, De Lancey. That piece of paper. There. Yes, that one. A despatch from General von Ziethen. Read it, please.'

'Sir, I myself have come with a despatch.'

'Quite so. Quite so.' Wellington looked up. 'And I presume I am correct in supposing that it will tell me that Bonaparte has attacked the Prussians . . . at Charleroi?'

'Yes sir. But how . . . ?'

'Read Ziethen's despatch. Go on.'

De Lancey picked up the folded piece of parchment, and opened it. It was brief. A pointed cry for aid. The Prussians had indeed been attacked, at Thuin. Which would indicate that the initial French objective was Charleroi.

'It is as we thought, your Grace. The secondary French plan. Bonaparte intends to push between us and the Prussians. To destroy first their army and then our own. In detail.'

It was just as d'Alava had predicted. Driving a wedge between the two armies, snuffing out first one, then the other.

'Sir, we must act. What do you intend? We should surely alert the First Division. Call the reserve to arms. What are your orders, sir?'

'My orders, Sir William, will be made plain by and by. It is not my intention, however, to amuse Bonaparte's many spies and other fine friends in this city by running around Brussels like some dumb-struck virgin on her wedding night. Besides, I believe it may be a feint.'

In the wall directly behind Wellington a door opened in the panelling and six men entered. Staff officers. A gracious welter of red, blue and gold. Fitzroy Somerset, the Duke's secretary; Sir Alexander Gordon, his principal aide-de-camp; George Lennox and George Cathcart, more aides; from De Lancey's own office, Alexander Abercromby of the Guards; and George Scovell. Wellington addressed them, without turning his head from his papers.

'Ah, gentlemen. To work. There is much to do.'

Half an hour later De Lancey, still riding the aide's horse, pulled up outside his own house. Inside he found his staff – a dozen young men, junior officers mostly – all crowded around his young wife. They were by turns garrulous, detached, flirtatious, earnest. These were his chosen ones, the men who would carry the war and word of how to wage it to every brigade, every battalion. Will Cameron, young Ed Fitzgerald, Charles Beckwith in his distinctive rifleman's green, James Shaw, the hero of Cuidad Rodrigo. Seeing him enter, their laughter stopped.

'All right, gentlemen, as you were. The world is not yet come to an end. Magdalene, my dear, I am sure that you will forgive us if we make our headquarters in the dining room. Charles, ensure if you please that any messengers know to wait in the drawing room. Magdalene, my sweet, we shall need some sustenance. Perhaps cook would prepare us a little supper and a sufficient quantity of green tea. I suspect that we shall be on this business the entire evening.'

He sensed disquiet. Smiled.

'No, no, gentlemen. Do not be alarmed. Rest assured that you will – all of you – be able to spend some time at the Duchess's dance. Indeed the Commander-in-Chief himself has commanded it. All will go ahead as planned. William, be a good fellow and go and seek out Mr Jackson. More than likely you will find him walking alone in the park.'

His comment about the contemplative Jackson served to lighten the mood in the room.

'And Edward, take yourself off and see if you can run to earth one Colonel Meyer, of the 3rd German Legion Hussars. His men are to be our couriers and escorts for the night.'

As the young men left to go about their errands, De Lancey began to feel the burden of his position. He realized that whatever should soon happen on the battlefield, this would most likely be for him a defining moment. It was his reponsibility to ensure that everything worked perfectly, otherwise disaster would ensue. It was he who would guarantee that every one of the troops of the allied army, some 95,000 men, would arrive at precisely the destination for which Wellington intended them, at precisely the correct moment. And that when they arrived they would be provided with the right equipment, and the right ammunition, in sufficient quantity.

Flashing him a nervous, sweet smile, Magdalene left to consult with the cook. De Lancey walked to the dining room, extracted from his soft leather valise the sheaf of order papers which Wellington had given him and laid them on the table before him. Other officers began to arrive now. William Gomm of the Coldstream, together with Hollis Bradford of the First Guards, both fresh from a shopping expedition, laden with bundles of lace; George Dawson of the Dragoons and Johnny Jessop of the 44th. And other, younger men, captains mostly – and now the lieutenants, Peter Barrailler and, at last, Basil Jackson, who had been discovered, as De Lancey had predicted, sitting in the Parc, reading Byron. Sixteen assistant quartermasters general; twelve deputy assistant quartermasters general. His military family.

Within minutes the room had become a scene of frenetic activity as the staff set about their business. Maps appeared from cylindrical carrying cases and were spread on the table to show the better of the roads and the capacity in tonnes of every bridge – and whether it was suited to taking artillery or cavalry. And around the long table the officers took up their stations, became in effect so many clerks, writing out in neat copperplate, in duplicate, every one of the Duke's orders:

Dörnberg's cavalry, to march upon Vilvorde;
Uxbridge's cavalry, save the 2nd Hussars, to collect at Ninove;
The 1st Division to collect at Ath and be ready to move;
The 3rd Division to collect at Braine-le-Comte;
The 4th Division to collect at Grammont;
The 5th Division, the 81st Regiment and the Hanoverians of the 6th Division to be ready to leave Brussels momentarily;
The Duke of Brunswick's Corps to collect on the road between Brussels and Vilvorde;
The Nassau troops to collect on the Louvrain road;

The Hanoverians of the 5th Division to collect at Hal and
to march tomorrow towards Brussels;

The Prince of Orange to collect, at Nivelles, the 2nd and
3rd Divisions under Perponcher-Sidletsky and Baron
Chassé;

The artillery to be ready to move off at daylight.

In effect the entire army was being placed in a state of
readiness to move. But, as far as De Lancey could see, no
unit had actually been ordered on to the offensive. Caution.
Wellington was waiting. Would not move directly to help the
Prussians. Did not believe that it might not be a feint. But
what if d'Alava had been right? Equally, Wellington might be
correct.

The French might intend to move against his right. But De
Lancey also felt a sense of unease. He decided that the following morning, before the army moved off, he would send
Magdalene away – to Antwerp, safe from the threat of what,
to both he and the Spaniard, now seemed to be the obvious
direction of French attack.

For over two hours the staff scribbled and copied, blotted,
folded and sealed; sent the messages into the anteroom to the
waiting Hussars and filed their duplicates at the end of the
table. And all the time De Lancey pored over the maps;
occasionally, noticing an anomaly, changed a route, recalled
an order. And all the time Magdalene and the servants brought
tea in pots and urns and whatever supper cook had been able
to find for the officers – toasts and savouries, mostly. Not
much was eaten, for no sooner would there be a slowing-down
in the work than De Lancey, remembering something else,
would call for a change of route, or issue an entirely new
order.

It was past nine o'clock when they finished. And then, with
hardly a moment's pause, every one of the junior officers
assembled at the end of the dining table, to be entrusted in

turn by De Lancey with one of the duplicate orders. It was a practice which had proven its worth in Spain. How many times had a courier fallen from his horse, or been delayed by some unseen hazard? A second copy of every order was now to be delivered by 'hand of officer'. And, like the originals, every one was to have its own receipt, from the hand of its recipient.

Check and double check. It was the only way, thought De Lancey. And he hoped to God that he had got it right. Had made no mistakes. That nothing would go wrong. For, whatever the virtue of Wellington's strategy of caution, were anything to go awry in its execution, and if as a consequence of it the battle were to be lost, he knew that there was only one man in the entire army on whom the blame would fall.

THREE

Gosselies, 8.30 p.m.
Ney

The evening, which he had hoped might offer a little relief from the heat of a long day, was proving oppressively warm, its intense humidity hinting at the possibility of a coming storm. Michel Ney, Duc d'Elchingen, Prince of the Moskowa, tall, barrel-chested, strikingly handsome in the gold-embroidered, dark blue coat of a Marshal of France, stood alone in the garden of a shell-damaged cottage on the edge of the town of Gosselies and looked to the north. Through his field telescope he scanned the sun-dappled fields of tall rye and wheat which stretched out towards Brussels and the waiting enemy. Behind him, tethered to an apple tree, grazing placidly, stood the horse he had bought two days ago from his old friend Marshal Mortier on his sick bed in Beaumont. Mortier, the veteran of Friedland, Spain, Russia, Leipzig, struck down now, at this time of greatest need, not by an enemy musketball but by an attack of sciatica. Well, they were none of them young any more.

An officer appeared at his side. A junior aide-de-camp. Chef de Bataillon Arman Rollin. Ney spoke.

'I see nothing, Rollin. No one. You think?'

'I can see no movement, sir.' Ney dropped the spyglass from his eye.

'No. Why should there be? Of course they're not here. They're further north. And to the east. Oh, we've found them all right, Rollin. But we have not yet brought them to battle. And that is what we must do, eh?'

But how? And with what? Ney was not yet sure exactly who it was that he commanded. Had not seen many of them. On paper he had a third of the army. In the field, he stood here at the head of a corps, II Corps, General Reille's. But as to the rest of his command – he was beginning to wonder quite where it was. He thought of historical precedent for his predicament. Scanned his mind for the many military theorists of whom he had made a study – Frederick the Great, Caesar, Gustavus Adolphus, Turenne, Alexander. Could find little to help him. Perhaps Frederick's invasion of Bohemia – a divided army, two wings. With what result? The battle of Lobositz. But had he kept his army intact Frederick could have marched on Prague and walked straight in. An opportunity lost. Ney prayed that they had not just made the same mistake with Brussels.

The marshal had staked everything on rejoining his Emperor. In truth it had not been hard to desert the Bourbons. His wife had been treated abominably by the ladies of the new Royalist court. His return to the eagles was inevitable. But there had been moments. In particular that embarrassing reconciliation in the Tuileries, with Napoleon making Ney pay for his previous defection and all his grand utterances in favour of the new monarchy. The agony of contrition. Particularly before his fellow generals. But then – silence. The Emperor had not rewarded him for his renewed loyalty until two days ago, when a letter had arrived at his château at Coudreaux, near Châteaudun, summoning him to the army. They had met at last at Avesnes. The Emperor had embraced him, had clapped his personal aide, Colonel Heymes, on the back. They had all joked and smiled. And over a long, relaxed dinner their friendship had resumed.

They had spoken of the old days. Of Friedland, Eylau, Borodino. Not, predictably, of Spain. And then it was that he remembered just how much he loved that man. How long he had loved him. How he would have done anything for him. Still would. They were the same age and for the past twenty years their fates had been intertwined.

A sergeant-major under the last King Louis, by 1794 Ney has risen to major in the Republic, received the first of many wounds and by the age of twenty-six was colonel of his regiment – the 4th Hussars. By 1797 Ney was a general de brigade.

It was Napoleon, though, who had made him. Created him first, in 1801, Inspector-General of all France's cavalry. In May 1804, on the day after Napoleon had been declared Emperor, he had made Ney a marshal. Four years later he was a duke. His service in Russia, commanding the heroic rearguard on a retreat that had cost the lives of half a million men, had earned him the unique title 'Prince de la Moskowa'. And Ney knew himself to be a 'prince among men'. Knew that his presence on a battlefield could inspire men to undreamed-of feats of bravery. That his name alone could win a battle.

It did not surprise Ney that no mention had been made that night at Avesnes, or since, of the fact that before his return to the fold Ney had sworn to Louis XVIII that he would bring Napoleon back to Paris 'in an iron cage'. That was all in the past now. There was a war to fight. A war to win.

The following morning, with no horse of his own, Ney had followed the General Staff to Beaumont in a peasant cart. And then at Charleroi, only this afternoon, a smiling Napoleon had given him command not of a mere corps but of the entire left wing – more than a third of the army. And in addition, to his amazement, the light cavalry division of the Garde – the finest cavalry in the world. His orders were merely to 'go and drive the enemy back along the Brussels road'. Jubilant as a child, Ney had taken Mortier's horse and ridden fast to join Reille's II Corps at Gosselies. And so here he was, standing with the few staff he had as yet assembled, on the rising ground above the little river Piéton, looking north.

Ney felt energized, more alive in fact than he had in years. Yet he was also more than a little alarmed. He had been given no specific insight into the Emperor's plans and had had no time to formulate his own, to conduct any reconnaissance, even to meet his own staff. He knew most of them, of course – d'Erlon, Piré and Lefebvre-Desnouettes he had served with in Spain. But Reille was known to him only by hearsay – as the Emperor's former aide. And within Reille's corps was a wild card. The Emperor's brother, Prince Jerome, the now ex-King of Westphalia, had been given a division – the largest in the army. He had a reputation for rashness, and Ney was anticipating problems.

He had left his own personal aide, his old friend and confidant Heymes, at Charleroi, to improvise the rest of the headquarters staff and follow on as he could. He knew that he must win this battle, this war. For if he lost, if the Emperor fell again, then his fate could only be a dawn appointment with a firing squad.

And things were not going according to plan. Despite the vagueness of the Emperor's orders, one thing which had become clear to Ney from even a cursory look at the map was the strategic importance of a small crossroads astride the roads from Charleroi to Brussels and Namur to Nivelles. This junction, the village of Quatre-Bras, must, he felt, be taken by nightfall. But here at Gosselies he was still some 8 kilometres short of it, confronted by a force of uncertain number and with no way of achieving his primary objective.

'We must consolidate, Rollin. We must push further. Establish the extent of their forces.'

'Quite so, sir. But it is getting late and our men are tired and widely dispersed.'

He was right. The sun was sinking. It had been an exhausting day. And not without its flashpoints. Ney's first action on assuming command had been to send one division of Reille's corps to the north of the town to repel a Prussian attack. They had inflicted reasonable casualties and captured a dozen regular infantry, who revealed that they were part of Steinmetz's brigade, Ziethen's corps.

That had been at 5.30. Three hours ago. Quickly, Ney had divided his men, sending Girard's 7th Division off in pursuit of the Prussians, who halted to the north east, at Wangenies. Just over an hour ago he had sent off General Lefebvre-Desnouettes and the Garde cavalry to reconnoitre around Frasnes. Now he held in his hand the report from Colbert, flamboyant colonel of the Garde's Polish lancer squadron.

They had met 'some resistance' from within the farm buildings at Frasnes but had found no one beyond there, at Quatre-Bras, and had returned to the main force. Ney had immediately moved off a battalion of infantry to Frasnes and soon ejected the enemy. He was unclear again, though, as to exactly whom they had encountered and in what numbers. He looked at the report. Green uniforms, red facings, black busby. He showed it to Rollin.

'What do you make of that?'

'Nassauers, sir. Grenadiers. Wellington's men.'

'What do we know of them? What unit? See if you can find out.'

So. He had found Wellington's advance guard. If that was what it was and nothing more. Even as he waited for more details a courier pulled up with another note, direct this time from the hand of Lefebvre-Desnouettes.

Monseigneur.

Frasnes we found occupied by around 1,500 infantry and eight cannon. Not those from Gosselies. These men are under the Duke of Wellington's orders. Nassauers. The Prussians from Gosselies have gone on to Fleurus.

Tomorrow at dawn I will send out a reconnaissance party

to Quatre-Bras, which will occupy that position. I believe that the Nassau troops have now left. The peasants have told us that the Belgian army is in the vicinity of Mons and the headquarters of the Prince of Orange at Braine-le-Comte.

It was somewhat garbled. But Ney thought that he understood what was meant. The Prussians had, as expected, retreated not towards Brussels but eastwards, in the direction of Fleurus, where their main army was evidently assembling. And Wellington? Wellington was somewhere to the north.

He was haunted by the man. Had encountered him first in Spain, at Bussaco. And just as Spain had been Wellington's triumph, so it had been Ney's undoing. The only smear on an unblemished military career. Massena's fault. And then, amazingly, Ney had happened upon the Duke while out walking with Aglaé a year ago, in the Bois de Boulogne. Some months later he had made a now embarrassing outburst against Wellington in the Tuileries – bombast, and what amounted to a challenge. The words rang in his ears:

'Let him meet us when luck is not in his favour. Then the world will see him for what he is.'

Perhaps now, at last, they would discover the truth of that boast.

Tonight, however, it was too late to move. Past nine o'clock. Desnouettes was right. The morning would do. The Nassauers would have run off with news of their encounter and Wellington would surely be hurrying to consolidate around Brussels. What to do? He thought of his mentor, Baron Jomini, France's master tactical theoretician. Tried to imagine what he would do in such a situation.

Ney decided to pull back the infantry to Frasnes. He had heard firing from the direction of Gilly. That surely must be Napoleon engaging the Prussians? It was more imperative than ever now that his own force should remain secure. Besides, if his staff were to be believed, his men were dropping with fatigue. They had been on the march since three that morning. He considered his position. Napoleon and the right wing were on his flank, engaging the Prussians. His own command was strung out across more than fifteen kilometres, between Marchienne and Frasnes. The heavy cavalry under Exelmans was near Campinaire, and some distance behind them came the rest of the army. Yes. It was time to rest.

'Dinner, sir?' It was Heymes, at last, arrived from Charleroi.

'Of course. Dinner. Where?'

'A house, not a hundred metres away. In the Rue St Roch. The only place still occupied – with food and a fire. We could walk there.'

'Fine.'

The little house looked out of place amidst the debris and chaos of war. A fairy-tale house – smoke at the chimney and flowers around the door, which was open. Ney entered and found inside a family, neatly turned-out and drawn up, almost as if for inspection. He felt faintly embarrassed. Smiled. Heymes spoke.

'His name is Dumont, sir. He's a clerk in the town. His wife. Their children.'

The couple looked terrified. The children less so. Four boys, thought Ney. A curious coincidence. He looked for a moment. The woman was pretty in a charming, petit-bourgeois way. Not like his own Aglaé. Her husband looked sound, if somewhat round shouldered, with an air of indignant confidence. He was no soldier, though.

The boys were roughly the same ages as his own. Good-looking too. He compared them – Napoleon, twelve, Louis, eleven, Eugene, now seven, and young Henri, just three. He thought of them all at Coudreaux, where even now Aglaé was perhaps helping their cook with the supper. The vision led him into foolish thoughts of their life together and everything with which they had been blessed over the last thirteen years.

They had met through the Empress Josephine, who, much taken with Ney, had begun to matchmake immediately for her young friend, pretty Aglaé Auguié, whose father had been one of Louis XVI's finance ministers, and whose mother, in that vanished other-world, was lady in waiting to Marie-Antoinette. As a child she had survived the Terror and her mother's suicide, precipitated by the execution of the Queen. Ney loved her for it. For her bravery. But more than this he loved her for her beauty – physical and spiritual. He touched his breast pocket, felt inside the shape of the miniature of her portrait by Gerard – the companion to his own.

He thought of their Paris house at the height of the Empire. Of his apartments overlooking the Seine. Of rooms crammed with mirrors, Aubusson tapestries and crystal chandeliers. Of the paintings – he had a particular taste for seventeenth-century Flemish art. Of his library, with its volumes of Racine, Rousseau and above all military theorists. Of their lavish candlelit receptions, thronged with painters, musicians, writers – Gros, David, Girodet, Gerard, Spontini, Gretry, Stendhal, Madame de Staël.

He found that he had been gazing blankly at a crucifix on the wall and turned again towards Dumont's four boys. Wondered when again he might give his two youngest piggybacks around their farmyard. Thought of their future together. All the pleasures that lay in store. Of taking them fishing; hunting wild boar; helping with the harvest. Then, becoming suddenly and unpleasantly aware of his own mortality, of the possibility of there being no future, he cast the vision from his mind. Smiled. Waved his hand towards the uncertain Belgian children.

'Please, please. Do not be afraid. Thank you for your hospitality. Please just behave as you would normally. Pretend we are not here. Ignore us.'

Absurd, of course.

Food arrived. Bread, cheese, bacon, wine, brought in by the

lady of the house. The servants had fled. Ney gave her a smile. Rollin entered.

'The Nassauers, sir. We believe them to be part of Wellington's 2nd Division; Perponcher's men. The Prince of Saxe-Weimar's brigade. They might be part of a force as strong as 8,000. But I have to say that we believe it probable that they have now rejoined the main army.'

'My thoughts exactly. Thank you. Join us?'

Local wine. Thin and lacking substance. What he would give for a good glass of Calvados. Noticing a flute hanging on the wall, he turned to his nervous host.

'You play?'

'A little, sir. When I have the time.'

'I too. When I have the time.'

He laughed and thought again of home. Of Aglaé at the piano and of himself struggling with the flute. He thought of her sweet voice. Her taste for Italian arias. *Don Giovanni.* That divine duet – '*La ciderem lamano*'. He began to hum the melody.

Dumont's house, he thought, was the epitome of petit-bourgeois – safe, dependable. And now, as Ney relaxed into a reverie, it took him back further to another, similar household, many years before. To a cosy parlour in the Saar where a father, a barrel-cooper by trade, would speak in German and French of the virtues of France, the glory of battle. How he had been proud to fight for King Louis against the Prussians. An image came to him of a small boy, ruddy-faced and with bright blue eyes, who, having listened spellbound to tales of war, had pursued his dreams of glory into the *Song of Roland*, the tales of Charlemagne, his knights, another empire. An image of a hot-headed boy of eighteen who had gone against his father's wishes and joined the army. The army of France in whose ranks his German accent had quickly disappeared and in whose service, in the uniform of a hussar, a quarter of a century ago, he had first ridden to glory. So long ago.

Mozart's aria was going around and around in his head. So too was an unpleasant thought which had come to him as he ate. Why should the Nassauers have rejoined the main force? What if they were still there at the crossroads? What if the cavalry reports were muddled? It happened. Might they not mean that the enemy had left not Quatre-Bras – which he saw now was the key to the road, and the flank – but merely Frasnes? Looking out of the open window Ney saw that, although night had fallen, the street was still well illuminated by the cold light of a full moon. He stood up.

'Heymes, my horse. We will ride to Quatre-Bras. I cannot rest until I see for myself our precise position.'

'Sir, it's dark. Surely?'

'The moon will suffice. Monsieur Dumont, thank you for your hospitality. I believe that a bed has been arranged for me here? You are very kind. Madame.' Giving a quick bow he left the house.

Outside, with Heymes and the two aides, Ney mounted his waiting horse. With a small escort, found grudgingly by a half-troop of the First Chasseurs, they rode in silence the few kilometres to the crossroads. At Frasnes Ney caught the familiar stench of a recent battle – putrefaction and powder-smoke. Trotting along the street they passed occasional groups of Garde cavalry – chasseurs and lancers – some snatching what sleep they could, others eating, drinking, talking. The marshal and his party went unremarked.

It was ten o'clock when they reached the French advance lines, to be greeted by a single sentry and a somewhat startled Lieutenant of Lancers. Quickly the little group dismounted and walked towards the front. Through the darkness, across the fields, Ney could see the fires of the enemy pickets. He counted them. Swore quietly. No. The Nassauers had not left. Were still here. Encamped in fact, it seemed, in some force. To his left Ney could see the bulk of a large wood and in the centre and on the right the dim shapes of three sizeable complexes of farm buildings. The crossroads itself lay straight ahead. It looked, as he had supposed it might, ominously like a highly defensible position. He began to run through the dispositions of his troops.

'Rollin, where is Bachelu's division?'

'Two kilometres to the east, at Mellet, sir.'

'And Prince Jerome?'

'Ransart, sir.'

'And Piré's cavalry?'

Another aide: 'At Heppignies, sir.'

'Count d'Erlon's corps?'

'His headquarters have been established at Jumet, sir.' Rollin again. 'But half of his divisions are strung out along the route, one at Marchienne, another at Thuin. Jacquinot's cavalry we believe to be somewhere near Binche.'

Ney sighed. 'And Reille?'

No one was entirely sure where the rest of Reille's corps was. Ney swore again. Audibly now. He realized that he could not after all afford to rest. He would himself ride at once to Charleroi. Must attempt to glean more precise directions from the Emperor. Must be allowed to know more detail of his plans. His mind was addled, confused. The ride there and back would clear his head. Without a word, he walked back to his horse and remounted.

'You have the time, Heymes?'

'10.30, sir.'

It would be close to midnight before he reached Charleroi. It was going to be a long night.

FOUR

Brussels, 1.30 a.m.
De Lancey

De Lancey sat at the unfamiliar bureau of his borrowed office in the house near the Parc and rubbed at his face and eyes. It had been a frantic evening. Unpleasantly warm for the time of year. At around nine o'clock a message had arrived from Blücher telling Wellington that he was now *en route* to Sombreffe and preparing to face Bonaparte there. Another came an hour later, from General Dörnberg, commander of the Hanoverian cavalry and senior intelligence officer at Mons. Still nothing though from Grant. Dörnberg reported that there were no enemy directly before him. In his opinion the entire French army was now focused on Charleroi. But surely, thought De Lancey, this was old news? The French might by now be long past Charleroi. In effect they were, all of them, chasing shadows.

Wellington, however, had at last seemed sure that he knew what Napoleon intended. Shortly after ten he had sent for De Lancey and given him his 'after orders' – a common practice. De Lancey had found the Peer in blue velvet carpet slippers, a silk dressing-gown over his shirt, preparing for the ball already in progress in the Rue de la Blanchisserie. The Richmonds had taken a house in the Rue des Cindres and in this small street to the rear the Duchess had found the perfect venue for their dance – the workshops of a coach-builder. That afternoon the old carriage works had been cleaned by a fatigue party of defaulters and decked out with all the frivolity of an English village fête. Reports of the spectacle had been coming to De Lancey for the past two hours as his officers, beginning to return from their various dispatch rides, had managed brief sorties to the gilded assembly. No sooner had they gone though than he had been compelled to summon them back to deliver these fresh orders personally.

The 'after orders' were clear enough: The 3rd Division would continue from Braine-le-Comte to Nivelles. The 1st Division, the Guards, was to move at once from Enghien to Braine-le-Comte. The 2nd and 4th Divisions were to move to Enghien, as was the cavalry.

De Lancey detected a general sense of urgency, but realized that the Peer remained convinced that the real French threat was to his right wing. He was pondering the probability of this when, quite unannounced, out of breath and without knocking, Will Cameron burst into the room.

'What the deuce? Will?'

'Sir. More intelligence. I come directly from the ball. From Lord Wellington himself. The French have taken Charleroi, sir. Even now are marching on Brussels. Their pickets have been at Quatre-Bras. The message was timed at 10.30, sir. It comes direct from General Rebecque. The Peer has left the dancing, sir. We are to order a general state of readiness.'

'What news from Grant?'

'None, sir. Only this from Rebecque. And direct from the front. The ball is finished, sir. Officers are to return to their units. We are to prepare to advance.'

'Calm yourself, Will. If the Peer has not yet received news from Colonel Grant, he will not order a general advance.'

'No, sir. Yes. I mean. Quite.'

'We will merely proceed with the after orders that he has

already issued – a concentration upon Nivelles. Unless he gave you to understand otherwise?'

'No, sir. That is indeed his intention.'

'Well then, I suggest that you find yourself somewhere to catch a few hours' sleep. You will certainly be needing them in the coming days. Take one of our rooms. Goodnight, Will.'

'Thank you, sir.'

After Cameron had left, De Lancey looked again at the map – the old, inaccurate 1790s survey of the area by Ferraris and Capitaine – spread out on the table in the centre of the room. It was still just possible. A feint. He understood Wellington's caution. What if he was right and Napoleon had called his bluff? Intended to divert the Anglo-Allied army to the east and then turn its flank? He walked towards the door, intending to find Magdalene and possibly a few hours' rest. As he went to turn the handle, however, the door flew open and he came face to face with General Dörnberg, behind him an aide. Both of them hatless, dripping in sweat, reeking of horses and brandy. The general was in a state of some distress.

'My God, De Lancey. I have come from Mons. Oh God, De Lancey. What have I done? How could I have been so foolish? We must go at once to Wellington.'

In the entrance hall of the house on Rue Royale most of the evening's candles had already been extinguished. In the half-light they were greeted by Wellington's secretary, Fitzroy Somerset, still fully dressed. De Lancey spoke quietly.

'Somerset, we must see his Grace. Immediately. We have grave news.'

Without a word, Somerset hurried them along the dark corridor and up a long flight of steps to the Duke's bedroom. Entering before them, a few seconds later he showed them both in. Wellington was sitting straight up in bed. He fixed De Lancey with a hard stare.

'Well then, gentlemen, what is it?'

Dörnberg spoke. 'Your Grace, I am afraid that I have been terribly amiss. I am aware that throughout the day you have sent me constant reminders that, should I hear from Colonel Grant or his agents, I should waste no time in at once letting you know. I am afraid, sir, that I have not done so and have only now realized my grave error.'

Wellington said nothing. Dörnberg continued: 'It is now clear to me, sir, that yesterday, at about midday, a report which I assumed had simply come to me from a commonplace French Royalist agent was in fact from an agent of Colonel Grant himself. In consequence, sir, I sent you an edited version. I see now from his agent's description of the dispositions of Bonaparte's troops that they were without doubt heading directly for Charleroi. For the *chaussée* running between our-selves and the Prussians – the highway into Brussels.'

Dörnberg stared awkwardly at the floor. Wellington took in a deep breath. Said nothing to Dörnberg but turned to De Lancey.

'Quatre-Bras, De Lancey. You will order the entire army to collect on Quatre-Bras.'

My God, thought De Lancey. You have been caught out. D'Alava was right. Bonaparte has fooled you and even now is closing with the Prussians while we are too extended to offer any immediate help.

They left Wellington to sleep, Dörnberg calmer now. Chastened, reprimanded, conscience salved. They rode back to De Lancey's house, and for the first time since he had arrived in Brussels the Quartermaster General began to worry.

Outside the De Lancey house Dörnberg bade goodnight and rode off to alert his officers. The lights were still lit and Magdalene and the staff all quite awake. For, although the dawn was not yet risen, in the past hour all Brussels had come to life. She met him in the doorway.

'Oh, William, you must come and look. It is so exciting. So glorious.'

Taking him by the hand, like an eager child on Christmas morning, she led him up the great staircase, into the drawing room and out through the open window on to the balcony.

All across the city drums beat an insistent and cacophanous stand to. Bugles called. Looking into the street he saw soldiers of all ranks, all regiments, spilling out of their billets, some with their erstwhile hosts, a few carrying children high on their shoulders. All was a clatter of soldiers, officers, horses, gun carriages, wagons.

The sky, catching the first rays of dawn, bathed the marching figures in a strange pale light, giving them an unearthly pallor. The morning was a cool and refreshing contrast to the stifling humidity of the previous day and, his tasks finished for the time being, the army about its business, De Lancey too felt refreshed and allowed himself a moment of relaxation as the couple watched in awe as the spectacle unfolded before them.

At first it seemed very solemn. Picton's division, Kempt's brigade first, the regiments marching past in column of threes. He saw the 32nd, the men looking exhausted rather than jubilant. No drums played, merely the fifes whistling the plaintive tones of an old march, 'Guilderoy'. A sudden fear welled inside him. Not for himself, but for Magdalene. She would go to Antwerp. Certainly. But he realized now that he was leaving her as he had promised he never would.

Then the mood changed, and momentarily his fear passed. Another regiment, the 28th, appeared in swaggering style, their band playing 'The Downfall of Paris', the old Revolutionary air, the 'Ça Ira', the tune that the British had stolen from the French and renamed, the tune which had marked the redcoats' progress to victory through Spain and into France. And after them came a regiment of Highlanders, swinging down the street, heading for the Charleroi road. By their kilts and the

42

deep green of their facings and their regimental colour, De Lancey recognized them as the 79th, the Camerons.

'There, Magdalene. Look. Your countrymen.'

'Oh, William. How bold they look. How very fierce.'

As they passed below the little wrought-iron balcony their pipers struck up the regimental march, and she gave a little jump. And then a huge smile. Tears began to run from her eyes. She looked at him. Pulled him down towards her. Held him as tight as her pale, thin arms could manage. Gently, De Lancey placed his own arm about her waist and ran his hand up her back.

After the Highlanders came the Rifles. Unusually towards the rear of the column. Not for long, he thought. 'First in, last out' their motto. Even as he looked, their pace began to quicken. Once on the open road they would open up to double time – light infantry pace. No band for them. Instead they were singing, 'The girl I left behind me'.

And with it his fear returned. Magdalene alone. Without him. Perhaps forever.

'Oh, William, I shall never forget this moment.' She pressed closer to him. Turned again towards the endless column of marching men.

De Lancey followed her gaze and lost himself in the spectacle. Soon. It would be soon now. He felt the thrill rise within him. Soon they would find Bonaparte. And then a battle. Silently, he watched the men file past and prepared to say goodbye.

DAY TWO

Friday
16 June 1815

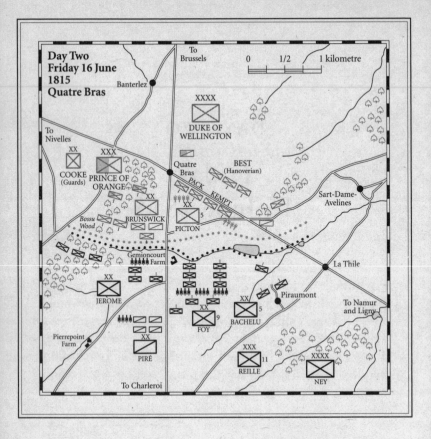

Day Two
Friday 16 June
1815
Quatre Bras

To Brussels

0   1/2   1 kilometre

Banterlez

XXXX
DUKE OF
WELLINGTON

To Nivelles

XX
COOKE
(Guards)

XXX
PRINCE OF
ORANGE

Quatre
Bras

BEST
(Hanoverian)

Sart-Dame-
Avelines

PACK   KEMPT

XX
BRUNSWICK

XX
5
PICTON

Bossu
Wood

Gemioncourt
Farm

La Thile

XX
JEROME

Piraumont

To Namur
and Ligny

XX
FOY
9

XX
BACHELU
5

Pierrepoint
Farm

XX
PIRÉ

XXX
REILLE
11

XXXX
NEY

To Charleroi

FIVE

Braine-le-Comte, 9 a.m. Macdonell

Slowly, and with carefully measured pace, he rode the big grey horse up the cobbled main street of Braine-le-Comte. Ahead of him the way was blocked by a jubilant crowd – peasants, townspeople and soldiers, in British red and Belgian blue. Some civilians, smiling broadly, made effusive gestures, offered bottles of the local schnapps. A few of the soldiers accepted. Belgians rather than British, he presumed. A group of children had begun to run alongside him, half-skipping, half-marching, singing in French:

> 'Dansons la carmagnole,
> Vive le son, vive le son
> Dansons le carmagnole
> Vive le son du canon.'

Macdonell recognized the song of the French Revolutionary Republic. No more dangerous now than a children's rhyme. He smiled at them, then looked up at the high windows of the thin, red-brick houses which lined the street and out of which people were now leaning, straining to catch a glimpse of this moment in history which, without warning, had overtaken the drab existence of their little town. They were women mostly, of all ages and stations, shouting unintelligible flatteries, waving lace handkerchiefs or lengths of orange silk. More scraps of orange material of all sorts were pinned up all along the street – on the walls, signposts, trees. Orange. National colour of the Kingdom of the Netherlands and as close to an expression of loyalty as these people could find for the strange red-coated soldiers who had come to 'save' them from the little man whom some still called 'the monster'.

Macdonell looked as if he might manage the job on his own. Blue-eyed and with a shock of wavy, fair hair, Lieutenant-Colonel James Macdonell had been a professional soldier in the army of King George for more than a score of his thirty-seven years. A soldier ever since that day in 1794, when he had left Oxford and the unsatisfying indolence of his studies to join the Highlanders.

At six foot three inches, half a foot above the average, he sat tall in the saddle, his stature increased all the more by the high, false-fronted black shako, with its gold and crimson cords, shining brass plate of the Garter Star and spotless red and white plume. At his side, in its black leather scabbard, hung a straight-bladed infantry sword – 32 inches of tempered Sheffield steel.

As he continued along the street, Macdonell's gaze was caught by the dark eyes of a particularly pretty local girl who had come to smile at him from the balcony of a second-storey window. Out of courtesy and intrigue, he smiled back. Then, lest his men should notice, although they were some distance to the rear, he looked away. And in doing so he began to pay closer attention to the people pressing around him – their clothes the long blue smocks of farm labourers. There were women in long-eared caps and thick petticoats. Hard-featured, heavy-set, peasant stock. They had come into town, he imagined, to see the English march through. To welcome him and his men as liberators. Not since Spain had Macdonell received such a hero's welcome. And this time he had not yet even helped win a battle. Had not yet killed a single Frenchman. They had come too, he quickly realized, with an eye to a little business. For apart from the schnapps he could now see that they had come with cheeses, sides of ham, sausages, live chickens, bread, dark-looking beer. Dangerous place for an army, he thought. He saw too that, beyond the crowd, the main street of this, the key town on the advance of the Anglo-Allied army, through which many units, he presumed, were to pass that morning, had become quite impassable, blocked with wagons – civil and military – in a tangle of transport and manpower which could only be left to the provosts and Scovell's staff cavalry.

Macdonell turned his horse and trotted her quickly back down the street, towards the waiting head of the column, left in the charge of young Gooch. He liked the boy. One of the battalion's more promising ensigns. He'd joined the colours three years ago, just a year after Macdonell himself had transferred into the regiment.

'Mr Gooch. We'll stop on the east side of the town, away from the main street. Move the men off, if you please. Down that street. Over there. Oh, and send a runner to Colonel Woodford. Tell him that the route through the town is blocked to all troops and suggest he call up the provosts.'

'Very good, sir. Sar'nt Miller, have your men right face and double into the fields. Oh, and find me the colour sar'nt.'

'Sir.'

Miller, five foot eight of solid muscle and solid good sense, twice Gooch's age, turned to the ranks. Raised his voice. Changed its tone. 'Number one section. By the right. Right turn.' A crash of boots coming down in unison – grinding leather and hobnails on the cobbles. 'Forward march.'

With a swinging, rhythmic action, led by Miller's men, the two light companies of the 2nd and 3rd Regiments of His Majesty's Foot Guards moved off the main road leading into the town of Braine-le-Comte and down the side-street which led up towards the rising ground of the surrounding fields. Macdonell and the other mounted officers went with them. Reaching the open country he gently urged his horse over a low hedge before dismounting and handing the reins to his soldier-servant, Tom Smith, who, as ever, had materialized silently at his side.

Lush country this, he thought. Very different to Spain. Villages and farms in all directions. Fields rich with crops – wheat, rye, hops. Here and there the top of a steeple, just visible over the gently undulating ground. The roads, though, were not so good. Worse in fact than the Peninsula, were that possible. Uneven surfaces and in bad repair. And now made no better by the rain which had featured on and off throughout the early morning. There was too a sense of neglect about the countryside. Of resignation to forever being in a state of disruption. A sense of a land which, over the centuries, had become accustomed to being no more than a corridor for so many armies. Not just those which had fought here these last twenty years, but the armies of Marlborough's time and, even before then, those of the old kings of the Middle Ages. This was history-book country. Nursery names – Crécy, Oudenarde. The land was inured to the passage of men. Men on their way to die. It was a land scarred by death and, Macdonell reckoned, would long remain so.

He shivered.

'Colour Sar'nt Biddle.'

He or Miller never seemed very far away.

'Sir?'

'Make sure that the men get something to eat. And that they're fit to march.'

The men could really suffer on these roads, he thought. Of course their shoes were nothing like the sandals and rags to which some, even officers, had been reduced in Spain. And, since Brunel's business had taken over the footwear provision, gone too were those ridiculous shoes with the clay insoles, bought in their thousands in a contract which, all knew, had been designed merely to line the pockets of those charming commissary officers at the Horse Guards. Shoes which would disintegrate with the first few drops of rain or on crossing a single stream.

Even so they had come eight, perhaps ten miles already this morning. Smith had woken him at Enghien, long before dawn, with the movement order on Braine-le-Comte. By 4 a.m. they had been *en route*. Macdonell counted himself fortunate. Some of the officers had managed no sleep whatsoever, having come directly from the grand ball held the previous evening in Brussels by the Duke and Duchess of Richmond. Although invited, Macdonell had chosen not to attend. Oh, he loved to dance. But his way was real dancing. Highland dancing. The dancing in which he delighted back home at Invergarry. Anyway, this was no time to be dancing. And to prove it, George Bowles had come rattling back from Brussels at 2 a.m. to join the route.

Dear George. Six years his junior. A Wiltshire squire's son and ever the dashing, dandy captain of Number Seven Company. Macdonell caught sight of him now, riding off the road, still clad in his elaborate full dress uniform. And he knew that George was not the only officer on the march that morning dressed in muddy dancing pumps and white hose. But it had not been with the expected tales of amorous exploits that George had returned to camp. As luck would have it he had far more piquant news. He had discovered what they were to do. How they were to be engaged in the coming campaign. And before they had set off that morning he had promised Macdonell a full explanation of what had now brought them to this sodden field after five hours on the road.

As the men unslung their hard, wooden-framed back-packs, removed their battered shakos and prepared to brew their tea, Bowles approached Macdonell, dismounted, leading his horse. He was looking, evidently, for his servant and his baggage which had been strapped, as Macdonell's was, to a single mule – the transport allowance of every field officer of the Guards. Bowles saw the big Scotsman and, having hallooed him across the field, came shambling over – a difficult feat in his improbable court dress – through the mud and trampled crops.

'James. James. Have you seen Hughes? Where's the man gone? I must have my valise. Look at me. This ridiculous costume. And it's utterly ruined. Another visit to my tailor.'

For once he did not exaggerate. His white silk stockings hung in a sodden, crumpled mess, leaving a gap of bare leg below once-white breeches. On his feet he wore a pair of what had been dancing pumps, one missing a gold buckle.

'Well, George. You know as well as I do that what pleases the ladies in the ballroom will not suit you for dancing along the road towards the French. And no, I have not seen your man. But now do tell me, as you promised last night. Continue your account, and I myself promise that I in turn will lend you a pair of my own grey overalls.'

'In your debt, James. Once again. In your debt.'

They were old friends. Had served together through Spain. This was not the first time that one had come to the other's rescue.

'And yes, you are quite right, James. I was with the Peer last night. We were at supper at the Duchess's ball when the Prince of Orange, our dear "slender Billy", entered the room and spoke a few words in his ear. Wellington told him to go to bed. To bed, James. I heard him myself. In full view of the General Staff. "Go to bed," he said. And d'you know what the sprat did? He went to bed. Straightway.

'Well, we sat on. For a half hour. And then Wellington turns to Richmond and declares that he thinks that he himself will go to his own bed. Well, James. I knew what was up and I was having none of it. And sure enough. For no sooner had our old commander made his goodnights and left the ballroom than, as if by some prearranged sign, there was a general exodus of all the senior staff – Daddy Hill, Picton, Kempt, Ponsonby, Uxbridge. Some officers too had already begun to make their own farewells – or I dare say their arrangements for the night, so to speak. But James, I stayed, for I was determined to know more. And sure enough, ten minutes later my good friend Richmond appears from within the house, across the yard from the dancing room, and beckons to me. The Peer, it seems, had asked him for his best map of the area. "Well, George," says he, "he laid it on a table and, standing before us all, declared as cool as you like: 'Gentlemen. Napoleon has humbugged me, by God. He has gained twenty-four hours' march on me.'"

'James, Bonaparte has attacked at Charleroi and driven back the Prussians. The battle is on. I tell you, we will not rest here, but must march on – to Nivelles. And then further still. To a crossroads – Les Quatre-Bras. That is where Wellington first intends to hold the French. We have a march ahead of us and a battle at the end of it.'

He paused. But only briefly.

'More than this, though, James. And here is the real route of our destiny. Richmond showed me the map itself and the place on it where the Peer had placed his mark. Had dug it in hard with his thumbnail. It is a long ridge, James. A ridge. Barossa over again. He had seen it, ridden the very ground, he told Richmond, not a year ago. He had marked it out and had the engineers draw up a map of it and kept it in his mind. A ridge. It is to the north of the crossroads. Runs in a line below a road between two villages. That, my friend, is where Wellington intends us to defeat Bonaparte. Between those two villages – Genappe and Waterloo. I cannot find the latter one on the map, but I am sure that is the name Richmond gave.

'And now, James, if you please. The overalls.'

As Bowles was speaking, Macdonell had been turning over the earth at his feet with the end of a stick. Had drawn, in effect, his own small map of the country described. He stared at it and wondered. Will this indeed be our destiny? My destiny? Will it end there? Will I end? Will we prevail? He looked up. Threw down the stick. Rubbed the earth plan away into the ground with his boot.

'Ah yes. The overalls. Quite. Well, all in good time, George.'

Bowles frowned. Could see what was coming.

'You see, George, you shall have your overalls – just as soon as Smith has found my own valise. You shall have them then. As promised.'

Bowles smiled. 'James, you quite outdo me. I swear we shall yet turn you from a heathen Highland savage into a Guards officer. I wonder whether you've not been taking lessons from Mackinnon.'

Macdonell too was smiling, thinking. If you but knew, dear boy. I was taking lessons in guile from my father's ghillie when you were still in the womb.

Bowles continued: 'Very well, James. I await your signal.'

He bowed – quite aware of the absurdity of his dress – in an exaggerated ballroom gesture, before leading his horse further into the temporary camp. Macdonell, catching the smile passing over Biddle's face, straightened his own. Watched as his friend stumbled across the field. Could still hear his voice as, walking away, he passed the small, huddled groups of men: 'Hughes. Hughes. Dammit. Where is my damned valise? Confound the man. Hughes.'

Macdonell covered his smile with a hand. 'Colour Sar'nt. Be ready to stand the men to. I expect an order within the half-hour.'

So this was it. Merely the start of a gruelling march. And then not one, but two battles at the end.

'Tea, sir?' It was Miller, with the offer of a steaming brew in a dented tin mug.

'Thank you, no. But thank you, Miller.'

Gooch appeared again. Eager. Shining. Agitated.

'Colonel. Is it true, sir? Have the French really attacked?'

'My dear Henry. If they have, they have not attacked us. They have not attacked here. Why don't you go and find yourself some breakfast? You're going to need it. I believe that Sar'nt Miller here knows the whereabouts of some good eggs and coffee.'

The sergeant nodded: 'Sir.'

'And don't worry, Henry. You'll find the French soon enough.'

Or they you, he thought. Better look out for that one. Over-keen. Might find himself on the wrong end of a bayonet. Macdonell sat down on a tree-stump by the low hedge at the roadside, looked at his men. His family. His life. A good life. A warrior's life. What other life could there be for the son of a Highland chief? His was a family of warriors. Hadn't his grandfather, Angus Macdonell of Invergarry, been slain by the English at Falkirk in 1746, fighting for the same Jacobite cause to which his brother Alasdair now drank bucolic and secret, sentimental toasts? Wasn't his brother Lewis a captain in the 43rd? Hadn't another brother, poor Somerled, named after the Lord of the Isles, perished from fever in the West Indies, an officer in His Majesty's Navy? Why, even his late brother-in-law Jack Dowling had been a soldier. A Peninsular man like himself. Jack had died in Spain.

Two minutes' rest, Macdonell decided. He pulled down the brim of his shako and closed his eyes. Of course he had not always been with the Guards, although his countrymen accounted for a good portion of their officers, as they did throughout the army. No. His first commission had been with the Highlanders. He still felt a keen attachment to his own regiment – the 78th – and to all those who went into battle wearing the kilt.

He recalled his days as a new lad of that great regiment. The thrill of donning for the first time the plaid; the feather bonnet. But for all their fine appearance they had seen little action and his real apprenticeship had been in the cavalry. For nine years he had served in the 17th Light Dragoons. Had learnt the skills of swordplay. No great need to learn. He had always been a fine fencer. Had won the praise of his tutor at Oxford for his prowess in the *salle*. The cavalry had taken him from Ostend to the West Indies. But the Highlanders had always held his attention, and when in 1804 the 78th had formed its second battalion he had transferred back as a major. Had had his portrait painted in Edinburgh to commemorate the event. How his brother, with his love of the pomp and swagger of Highland chieftainship, had loved him for it; and had envied him.

What years those had been. What soldiers to command. Ross-shire men mostly, and hardly an English speaker among them. He recalled the training ground at Hythe. The English drill sergeants, powerless to command the 'Highland savages' and his own gentle commands in his native Gaelic which had moulded the company into the fighting unit he had taken into battle. They would have followed him anywhere. To Hell itself. Had followed him within two years to Sicily. Into the French lines at Maida in that glorious charge which had brought him the Gold Medal, the army's highest honour. He had addressed them afterwards, in Gaelic:

'*Tha mi a'creidsinn, a chairdean, gu bheil subh sgith.*'

For the medal was not his, but theirs. And the following year they had gone with Macdonell to India. Discovering with him the mysteries of that beautiful and hellish continent. Returning home with them, he had marched into Edinburgh as their lieutenant-colonel.

There had been tears, a lament for the pipes composed in his honour – 'Colonel Macdonell's Farewell to the 78th' – when, four years ago now, he had transferred from the old regiment into the Guards. It had been inevitable. The brilliance of his military masters never ceased to amaze him. What officer, he often wondered, had put him and his Highlanders – the heroes of Maida, fighting men to the last – on garrison duty in the island of Jersey? Macdonell was a leader, a warrior. Not some clerk. His men had no alternative save to languish in their new role. But, for all his regimental loyalty, Macdonell had been damned if he would suffer the same fate. The exchange of a captaincy in the Coldstream with a callow youth who preferred the comforts of home to the rigours of campaign had cost him the not inconsiderable sum of £3,500. And, thanks to the Guards' curious system of 'double-ranking', his new role still held the equivalent status of lieutenant-colonel in the eyes of the line regiments.

And so he had gone to Spain. Many of the officers and men he saw around him now, chattering, dozing in their weary little groups in this sodden Belgian field, Henry Wyndham, his second-in-command, George Bowles, Miller, the Graham brothers, Josh Dobinson, Motherly, Kite, Fuller, were those whom he had led for two years in the Peninsula. Led through a maelstrom of regimental battle honours – Salamanca, Vitoria, Nivelle, the Nive. They were good men. Not Highlanders, mind. But good, sound fighting men. English, mostly. A few Irish, like the Grahams – though not as many as filled the ranks of the line regiments. They were men like Dan Perkins, the son of a Yorkshire sutler, with a grip like iron and tenacity to match. Men like 27-year-old John Biddle from Worcestershire, his colour sergeant and trusted friend who, with nine years' service behind him in the battalion, had taught Macdonell the ways of the regiment in the very direct manner that his brother officers never could. There were others, too. New men, brought in from the militia to make up numbers. But, thanks to the attentive ministrations of Battalion Sergeant-Major Baker, they had quickly been assimilated into the regimental family. Macdonell cared for them all with a paternal affection – strict yet compassionate. And they in return were prepared to do anything he ordered. He was their 'chief' now. They his 'clan'. Their loyalty was unto death.

He opened his eyes. Looked at the men again. Thought to

himself what a very different sight they presented this morning to the public image of a Horse Guards' review. Their clothes were largely those with which they had been issued two years back, and their service was beginning to tell. They had not been home since the end of the Spanish war and their famous scarlet coats, once vivid, had faded to a dull brick-red, too often patched and made good. The long-awaited new uniforms had still not arrived, and when they at last met the French it would be like this. Macdonell himself had been fortunate enough to have ordered a new service coat from his tailor in St James's. It had arrived only last week. Scarlet with blue facings, edged in gold lace and with two heavy gold bullion epaulettes. He had also managed to get a neat new shako direct from Oliphant's. In effect, he thought, with his grey overalls still missing, forced into white kerseymere breeches and tassled hessian boots, he might look rather too smart. Too tempting a target, perhaps, for a French sharpshooter.

At least he knew that, if they could not parallel his own sartorial pose, his men would do everything else they could to make him proud. Would, if they had half a chance, whitewash their cross-belts to a parade-ground brilliance; polish their brass; hone their leather. More than this, though, they would make him proud of them as soldiers, doing what they were trained to do: kill Frenchmen. He knew that in the heat of battle, when lesser men were panicking, losing their minds if not their lives, his lads would still be standing firm. Two ranks of muskets, spitting smoke, flame and a three-quarter-inch round lead ball. And then, when they had stopped the enemy in his tracks, as they had so many times before, they would follow up with the bayonet. And as for him, thought Macdonell, well, if that Frog sniper hit his mark, then that would be his fate. He was in the business of death and knew that one day it would come looking for him. His duty was to lead from the front. If necessary to fall at the front – as he had seen so many of his brother officers fall, all too often and too closely, in Spain, Sicily and India. Merely duty.

He stood up slowly, straightened his shako and turned to Biddle, who was hovering, alert, close by. 'What's our strength, Colour Sar'nt?'

'This morning, sir, one hundred and ninety-three men, sir, all told. Including that is yourself, sir, and the two colonels, Captain Moore, Captain Evelyn, Captain Elrington and the ensigns, sir – Mister Gooch and Mister Standen.'

In normal circumstances Macdonell's command – No. 1 Company – consisted only of his own junior officers, Tom Sowerby and John Montagu, ten NCOs and some 100 guardsmen. Ten such companies formed the battalion – Second Battalion, 2nd Coldstream Guards, under Colonel Alexander Woodford. For the last year, however, while the battalion had been stationed here in the Low Countries, Macdonell had been its temporary commanding officer. It was perhaps on account of this responsibility, he supposed, together with his impressive service record, that he now found himself, for the duration of the campaign at least, moved to command of the battalion's Light Company. And more than this, to the command too of the Light Company of the 3rd Scots Guards, who drew their recruits primarily from his native country. In all, nearly 200 men.

Good to be leading Scots again in what he believed would be the final conflict of these long and bloody wars. Of course they were not, most of them, Highlanders like him. Many originated from Edinburgh and Glasgow. A few were borderers. There were some, though, whom he knew to understand the old tongue. MacGregor, for instance – that big sergeant-major of the 3rd Guards, with the huge grin and hands like spades. Macdonell closed his eyes, and, leaning back against the hedge, attempted to catch a few moments' rest. Good to lead Scots again. Back where he had started. Full circle.

SIX

Quatre-Bras, 11 a.m.
De Lancey

He took a sip of coffee and winced. The brew, which he had accepted gratefully from George Scovell and of whose origins he had thought it best not to enquire, was stronger than that to which he was accustomed and uncommonly bitter. Still, it was fulfilling its purpose. Twice in the last hour he had felt his eyes begin to close. The strain of the previous evening and a profound lack of sleep were starting to tell. It had been 7 a.m. before he had despatched Magdalene, her groom and maid, to Antwerp. He was content at least with her safety, having already made provision for her to be cared for there by Captain Mitchell of the 25th, the Deputy Assistant Quarter-master General to the city. He took another sip of the thick brown liquid and rolled it around in his mouth. He knew of old, from so many mornings in the Peninsula, similarly heavy-lidded under a Spanish sun, that if only he could keep awake until midday he would be able to function till nightfall.

De Lancey had left Brussels at 8 that morning, reaching the Quatre-Bras farm close on 10 o'clock. He and Wellington had ridden hard down the main road from Brussels, their advance party composed only of Somerset, Müffling and a half-troop escort of Life Guards. The remainder of the Duke's staff

60

– some forty officers, including their friend d'Alava, had followed close behind. They had been greeted by a suitably aggressive picket of green-coated Nassauers, Prince Bernhard of Saxe-Weimar, his superior General Perponcher and the Prince of Orange, all still jubilant at having held off what purported to be a sizeable French force. Of that force, however, there was as yet little immediate evidence. In fact Saxe-Weimar and Perponcher had gone against Wellington's express directive to collect on Nivelles. Securing the authority of the Prince of Orange's Chief of Staff, the enigmatic and talented General Constant-Rebecque, and in the knowledge that they might be hopelessly outnumbered, they had decided to stand at the crossroads. Naturally the Peer had not thought it politic to mention the fact this morning. For it was just possible, thought De Lancey with wry amusement, that Rebecque's direct disobedience of an order from the greatest military mind on Earth might have saved the entire campaign.

De Lancey sat astride his horse at the centre of the highest point of what would be, when the army finally arrived, the Allied line. Following Wellington's example he was clad in a dark blue civilian top-coat, rather than the regulation red tunic. What need had either man for show? Wellington might wear red and gold for parades at the Horse Guards, but in battle he preferred the plain clothes which told his men that here was a man of sober mind and quiet sensibility. The sort of man whom they knew they could trust to win a battle.

Like Wellington too, and the entire General Staff, De Lancey wore a simple black bicorn hat, fore and aft. He had also, since the last years of the Peninsular campaign, taken to imitating Wellington's habit of strapping a change of clothes to the back of his saddle, and, in place of a pistol holster, a pen and paper, with the addition of a bulging map case and a deep morocco leather document wallet. He reached into it now, pulled out a small field telescope and brought it to his eye.

This was good ground. He was aware that there was not a

pronounced reverse slope – the Peer's preferred defensive ground – behind which to shelter an army from the enemy's gaze and cannon fire. But it was a good position all the same, its virtues evident on this still, fine morning. Via the small circular lens he traversed the field, moving slowly from the left, along the line of a wood and a lake, through the small village of Quatre-Bras itself, with its few whitewashed houses around the key road junction, to the mass of a larger wood, marked on his map as the Bois de Bossu.

To the left the ground was open, laid mostly to cereal crops, which now stood impressively high. So high, he thought, that within one such a field it might be possible to hide an entire battalion. In the distance, though, on rising ground stood a farm – Pireaumont. In the centre ground lay another, Gemion-court, with its high walls an ideal strongpoint. It was imperative that they should seize both before the French. In the far distance, beyond the Bossu wood, De Lancey could make out a third and fourth defensive structure, the two farms of Pierrepont. These too should be occupied by the Belgians before it was too late. A voice from his side made him take the glass from his eye.

'No Crapauds yet, De Lancey?'

It was Alexander Gordon, one of the Duke's aides and a close friend of both men, along with Fitzroy Somerset, the latter's hooked nose and angular features giving him the absurd appearance of a diminutive Wellington.

'None, I'm afraid. That wood may be good cover, but it makes it damnably hard to see who we're fighting.'

'Well, I am beginning to wonder,' said Gordon with a knowing smirk, 'exactly where the Prince's "French corps" might be.'

'I did hear a little popping musketry,' interjected Somerset.

'Ours or theirs?' asked Gordon.

'I . . . I couldn't really say.'

De Lancey smiled. 'Muskets or not, I can feel them there.

Our reports suggest an entire corps. Perhaps more. Reille or d'Erlon. Probably under Ney. Cavalry too. We've had sightings of lancers.'

Gordon shuddered. 'Well, we'd better make damned sure that our own cavalry are here before they do attack.'

Somerset spoke again. 'I believe that the Prince has told his Grace that one of his Dutch cavalry brigades is on its way from Nivelles, even now.'

Gordon, unimpressed, sighed and looked despairingly to De Lancey. 'Where is Uxbridge and the English cavalry? Do we know?'

'On his way to Nivelles from Braine-le-Comte. Or so I've told the Peer. I had supposed that he might arrive here early in the afternoon. But I'm beginning to wonder whether perhaps I haven't been a little hasty.'

Before leaving Brussels Wellington had asked De Lancey to draw up a detailed list of the exact dispositions of the army. This, after some deliberation, he had done, basing it on the orders he had sent out the previous evening. In his haste, though, and amid all the chaos of packing and getting dear Magdalene safely off to Antwerp, he was uncertain as to whether he had been thinking of the Duke's first or second set of orders. It gave the impression of the army having advanced somewhat further east than in fact it had. He was far from happy with the document.

But he felt that he and the Peer had such a degree of understanding and such was the exigency of the hour that it would suffice. He had presented it to Wellington at 7.30, just as they were setting off, explaining its meaning as they moved out of the city. It was not, he had emphasized, quite as precise as he would have wished, but it did, he believed, convey the situation well enough. The Duke had been satisfied. But still De Lancey couldn't help but feel that he might have committed a grave error. His troubled reverie was disturbed by voices. Somerset and Gordon had reined their horses round to greet the approaching figure of Wellington and some twenty of his staff. Spotting De Lancey, the Duke rode closer.

'A good position, De Lancey. Is it not?'

'Indeed it is, your Grace. Not ideal, perhaps, but I believe that we can make it do.'

'My only concern is the speed with which the rest of the army will reach us. I have not been in such a very unpromising situation in the matter of reinforcements since, when would you say?' He paused. 'Well, I will tell you. Fuentes de Onoro. Portugal. Four years ago. You recall, William? We were a divided force then. Outnumbered and over-extended. But we beat them, gentlemen. And so here we are again. And we can do so again. Can we not, gentlemen? What have we exactly? Somerset?'

'Our current strength comprises Prince Bernhard's 2nd Brigade of Dutch and Belgians, your Grace. That is the 2nd Nassau infantry of some 2,800 men and the regiment of Orange-Nassau, numbering perhaps 1,500. They have been here since yesterday and early this morning were reinforced by the remaining units from Baron Perponcher's division. That is Bylandt's brigade of Dutch and Belgians, your Grace. Principally militia. In total I believe that we can currently field some 7,500 men. With eight cannon.'

'And when might we expect to see the first of our own lads? What of Picton? De Lancey. Your report.'

'As I said, your Grace, I believe that the reserve will be in Genappe by noon. They will be the first to reach the field. Perhaps by two o'clock, your Grace. The cavalry should not be far behind.'

'Well, we shall see. In any event I must send a despatch across to Blücher. He must have my assurance. We cannot afford to have his generals persuade him to turn. Without him, gentlemen, we are lost. We must persuade Prince Blücher that we shall soon be in a position to come to his aid. And to judge from your note of this morning, De Lancey, I see no reason to suppose otherwise.'

De Lancey opened his mouth to suggest that the memorandum had not been entirely accurate, that perhaps the British and Allies might not be as close to them as the Peer imagined, but quickly decided that it would be better to say nothing. If the Prussians felt reassured, if they stood and fought, with or without Wellington, then they all had a chance. He nodded.

'Quite so, your Grace.'

Wellington called for an aide and began to dictate: 'To Field-Marshal Blücher, at Sombreffe:

'My Dear Prince,

My army is situated as follows: Of the corps of the Prince of Orange, one division is here around Frasnes and Quatre-Bras. The remainder at Nivelles. My reserve is on the march from Waterloo to Genappe, where it will arrive at noon. The English cavalry will at the same hour be at Nivelles. Lord Hill's corps is at Braine-le-Comte.

I cannot see any great force of the enemy in front of us and await news from your Highness and the arrival of troops before I decide on my operations for the day.

'Conclude, "Your very obedient servant". The usual form.'

He turned back to De Lancey. Smiled. 'I think that will do it.' Then to Somerset. 'That farm, Somerset. The central position. Make sure that we hold it. Tell the Prince of Orange it is vital to the battle. Send down . . . a battalion of Nassauers. And Somerset, make sure that he covers the two farms further forward, to the left and right. And now to business. What new intelligence have we of the French? Scovell, come and tell me what you know while I tour the lines. Gentlemen, will you join us?'

Reining his horse down the slope behind the Duke's party, towards the thin line of blue-clad Belgian infantry, De Lancey felt more keenly something which he had sensed immediately on first arriving at the crossroads. Now, he thought, I am at the centre of the world, the vortex into which events are being drawn. More than ever before, I am standing on the edge of the precipice. Nervously, he touched the reassuring coolness of the small, round stone in his pocket. All over Belgium, he thought, thousands of men are marching directly towards this curiously insignificant place, with its farms and its woods and its strangely shaped lake. Are marching towards the coming battle. Marching towards their fate. Towards death. Marching directly towards me.

SEVEN

Braine-le-Comte, 12 noon
Macdonell

Macdonell was awakened by a respectful cough. He had been dreaming. Running through a stream of cool water in the shadow of friendly purple mountains, dappled with Highland sunshine. Opening his eyes he found instead only the florid face of Sergeant Miller.

'Begging your pardon, sir.'

'Sar'nt?'

'Galloper, sir. From General Cooke, sir.'

Macdonell stood up, brushed his jacket, straightened his shako. Saw before him a boy of perhaps seventeen, in the ornate uniform of the Life Guards – Grecian helmet, high collar. The courier began to speak, stammering the orders out with a slight lisp.

'The general's compliments, Colonel, and would you move your men to the right and around the town and back on to the road. We proceed in the direction of Nivelles.' And then, slightly embarrassed to be giving his superior officer an order: 'With the greatest of haste, sir, if you please. You are the vanguard of the entire division.'

Macdonell nodded.

The aide coloured, nodded uncertainly in return, pulled round his horse and galloped away.

'Sar'nt.'

'Sir.'

Miller moved quickly. Some of the men had overheard the orders and, even before the sergeant had barked his commands, were already beginning to pack up. Swearing; fastening buttons and packs; scratching; stamping tired feet; shaking limbs. If the job was to be done they might as well get on with it. Quickly they transformed from a resting rabble into a smartly formed-up unit of recognizable platoons and companies.

It was midday. The sun was high in the sky. For three hours they had sat here. Such delays were nothing new to Macdonell. But surely, if George Bowles were to be believed, haste was of the essence. Someone – from his broad Devon accent and tuneful baritone, Macdonell guessed it to be Tarling, the company bard – began to sing:

'Her golden hair in ringlets fell, her eyes like diamonds
  shining,
Her slender waist with marriage chaste, would leave a
  swan reclining.
Ye Gods above now hear my prayer, to me beauteous fair
  to bind me
and send me safely back again to the girl I left behind me.'

Biddle roared: 'That man there. Who gave you permission to speak?'

'I was singing, Colour Sergeant.'

'I don't care if you were playing the bloody piano, Tarling. No one ordered you to sing. Get fell in. I'll tell you when you can sing.'

Still dusting themselves off, straightening their kit, the Guards gradually regained the Nivelles road and fell into step. It was drier now and, as they marched, clouds of yellow dust began to rise from beneath their feet. There was no more singing, just the tramp of leather and the repeated clank of wooden canteen against bayonet. The marching soon regained its regular motion. Seventy paces to the minute. Regular and steady, thought Macdonell. None better. He noticed now that there were fewer civilians on the road. Houses too were more obviously deserted. Signs that they were nearing the battle. Sometimes, from one of the few cottages still occupied, small children would venture out, sent to offer bread or fresh eggs to the sergeants. Macdonell, usually strict in such matters, turned a blind eye. It was freely given and he knew that Biddle and the other sergeants would ensure that all the men who deserved to would have a share.

It was early afternoon when at last they reached Nivelles. They came smartly to a halt. Macdonell could hear the guns now. How far away, he wondered. Five, ten miles? Ours or theirs? Corporal James Graham approached him, brushing dust from his tunic.

'Sure, sir, that'll be all for the day now from the good general. Do you not think?'

'It is not my place, or yours, Corporal, to think about orders. But d'you hear that?' He indicated the direction of the gunfire. 'No. I am very much afraid that we have not seen the end of the road today. Look to your fellows if you would. Put them at ease.'

He was wise to rest them. It was a full ten minutes before he saw the young aide riding up. Redder in the face than ever, but more assured now.

'Colonel Macdonell, sir. You are to advance into the town. If you please. Colonel Woodford's orders, sir. And would you be so kind as to ascertain as to whether the town is held by the French, sir.'

Macdonell loosened his sword belt. Prepared to draw. 'Have them untie ten rounds, Colour Sar'nt.'

Biddle turned to the company. 'Ten rounds and look to your flints.'

Nervous hands fumbled with the strung-together cartridges, making ready for combat.

Macdonell began to act with automatic ease. This was his natural state. 'Officers, to your companies. Bayonets if you please, Mr Gooch.'

He heard the familiar clank and scrape of barrels as 200 17-inch triangular blades were slotted into place. Macdonell drew his sword. Rested it flat against his right shoulder.

'Follow me.'

They advanced 200 yards. A too familiar eternity. Waiting for the flash of the first enemy musket from behind a wall or through a window. The flash. The scream. But none came. And then they were in the town. There was no firing. No French. Merely a mess of abandoned possessions and confused local civilians, none of whom seemed sure of what to do. In the gutter to his right, sitting up against a wall, Macdonell saw his first Allied casualty of the campaign, a captain of Belgian militia. His grey trousers were covered in blood. He had been shot through the calf and the tourniquet improvised from his orange sash seemed to have staunched the bleeding, which had already stained it a deeper red. As Macdonell looked at him he smiled and spoke softly. 'Hurry on. It does not go well for us.'

Macdonell said nothing. Hoping that the men had not heard the Belgian's halting English and ignoring the alternately ecstatic and bewildered civilians, he led the two light companies along the street and within a few minutes had arrived at the end of the town. He gave the order to return bayonets to scabbards and sent a runner back to battalion headquarters to report that no contact had been made with the enemy. To his surprise, the man returned almost immediately with the order to stand down. As the light companies moved off the road and once again began to unshoulder packs and prepare their rations, Macdonell heard again, quite clearly, the sound of gunfire. Surely this was no time to make camp?

He was on the point of riding to the adjutant to enquire of the decision when past him, at full pelt, coming from the direction of Quatre-Bras, rode two men on foam-flecked horses. One he recognized as George Scovell, of Wellington's staff, the other as an officer of Scovell's cavalry staff corps – Wellington's messengers. A few minutes later they rode back and, to his surprise, straight up to him. Scovell addressed him:

'Colonel, you are to proceed immediately in the direction of Les Quatre-Bras. Lord Wellington's forces are engaged in battle and you must join them with all speed. On arriving on the field you will see that the French have the object of gaining a large wood to your right. This is the Bois de Bossu. Should they do so they will hold this road and with it our flank and the key to Brussels. You must at all costs prevent this being done. The light companies will be the first to arrive. Yourself and those of the First Guards. You must hold the wood until relieved by the remainder of the division. Is that clear?'

'Quite clear, sir. You may depend upon it.'

Without another word Scovell and his companion turned and were gone.

Macdonell gave the order to march and once again, and with an audible collective groan, the campfires were extinguished, the half-cooked rations abandoned.

Back on the road, leaving the town behind them, the division continued to advance in the direction of Quatre-Bras. It was mid-afternoon now and the shadows were growing longer. With every step the guns grew more clearly audible, bringing a new urgency. And with it, Macdonell knew that among the new recruits, at least, there would come an unwanted sense of unease. He turned to Gooch, who was riding immediately behind him.

'Mr Gooch, send word to Colonel Woodford. Beg to suggest to him that it may quicken our pace were he to have the music strike up.'

And so, to the strains of the march from Mozart's *Marriage of Figaro*, only recently adopted as the new regimental quick march, the Coldstreamers again began to move. Now though, as Macdonell had anticipated, they had a fresh spring in their step. The open road ran on before them. Turning on a sudden whim he looked to his rear.

Beyond his own two companies, beyond Dan Mackinnon's tall grenadiers, came the entire division, a great, dust-shrouded, red, black and grey snake, stretching away into the distance, punctuated at regular intervals by stiffly saddled officers rising high above the ranks. Just visible near the front, behind No. 4 Company, waving in the breeze, he saw his battalion colours. Those three sacred, six-foot squares of crimson silk: the colonel's colour with the Garter Star; the lieutenant-colonel's, with the Union flag; and the major's, with its blazing stream of woven gold. The honour, the spirit, the soul of the regiment. They had carried them to Egypt, to Talavera and Barrosa – through the battles whose names they now bore – and then on to Salamanca and Vitoria. Soon they would carry them to Quatre-Bras and deep into the darkness of Bossu wood. Then they would find the French.

EIGHT

Ligny, 3 p.m.
Ziethen

Even here, on the rising ground, high above the village of Ligny the atmosphere was oppressively humid. It was not so much the weather, although the sky looked set for a storm, but the intense heat and smoke and the cloying smell of gunpowder produced by the battle which had raged for almost an hour now on the plain below. It had started, as they always started, thought Ziethen, with three shots fired by a single French battery, timed at regular intervals, and sounding, as von Reiche had once remarked to him, like the opening notes of an opera. He knew what would come next, and soon the valley had filled with the music of the French regimental bands. He recognized one old favourite: 'La victoire en chantant'. Within a few minutes, however, the instruments had been drowned by the crack of musketry and the thunder of cannon fire.

The opening moves had come shortly after 2 o'clock. Ziethen, along with Gneisenau and Blücher, had watched with interest from their hilltop vantage point on the heights above Brye as French cavalry, Dragoons by the look of their crested yellow metal helmets, had galloped towards their left flank. It was evidently a feint, though, or a holding action, for no sooner had the Prussians begun to plan a response than two French infantry columns had emerged from the wood behind

73

the village of Fleurus opposite them, where Napoleon had established his own command centre, and begun their steady march down the hill.

The Prussians waited, behind the limited cover of their defensive position. On Blücher's orders, Ziethen had drawn up his I Corps, the front line of the Prussian army, in a long 'S' shape, ranged 10 kilometres in a string of hamlets which ran along the course of a stream, the Ligne. It was a good defensive feature; its pleasant banks – lined with willows, alders and brambles – were naturally marshy and would be impassable to infantry under fire. The French would be channelled on to the four bridges across the Ligne. Forced into bottlenecks, which, if the Prussians used their time carefully, raking them with cannon and musket fire, would soon become crammed with enemy dead and dying.

On the right, in the houses of Wagnelée, La Haye and St Amand, Ziethen had placed Steinmetz's dependable Brandenburgers and Westphalians and Jagow's crack 29th Infantry. In the centre, around Ligny itself, the largest of the villages with two farms, a church and a walled cemetery, and in Potriaux and Tongrinnelle, stood Henckel's 19th Regiment and the remainder of Jagow's men. Here also was Krafft's brigade, detached from II Corps. The left flank and the farming settlements of Boignée, Balatre and Bothey were held by Carl von Thielemann's III Corps. The reserve cavalry, Uhlan and Landwher lancers mostly, Blücher had positioned in a hollow behind Ligny. Pirch's brigade stood just behind the commanders, on the heights of Brye.

The second line of II Corps had arrived at midday and fallen into its pre-ordained supporting position on the forward slope of the high ground along the Nivelles road, centred on Sombreffe. In all Blücher's men numbered around 84,000. Yet, as Ziethen was well aware, they were barely enough for such an extended front. This was nevertheless the plan which had been prepared and agreed upon by the General Staff a month

74

ago. And as such it must be adhered to. Their precise positions, though, thought Ziethen, were not as had been prescribed – on a north–south axis. Napoleon's direction of attack had forced them to wheel ninety degrees, with their forward positions now taking the form of a vulnerable salient. It was far from ideal.

As much had been evident two hours ago to Wellington, who had ridden into the camp with a small escort of his staff, and gone largely unrecognized by the majority of the Prussian soldiers. The Duke had been greeted by Colonel Hardinge, an amiable officer of the English Guards, attached to Blücher's staff, whom Ziethen had come to know and admire over the past few days. Taken by Hardinge to Blücher, Wellington had climbed with him, and Gneisenau, Ziethen and von Reiche, to the top of the windmill that stood high above the village, affording a wide view of the plateau below. The Prussian commander was unsettled. Ziethen knew that he had a recurring problem with his back. He had been on horseback since dawn and would doubtless be in a bad mood. He was clearly beginning to feel his seventy years. And Ziethen had also noticed an alarming stiffness in his commander's legs as they had climbed to the top of the mill earlier that morning.

Back at their makeshift observatory, they had stood in silence as, revealing nothing, Wellington surveyed the positions. Ziethen had met the hero of Vitoria only once before, last year, in Vienna. He admired his composure. With such coolness he might almost have been a Prussian officer rather than an Englishman. It was this, perhaps, along with the value of his word and his effect on the morale of troops on a battlefield, which he knew Blücher most valued. Gneisenau of course was another matter. Had it been up to him, the Prussians would not now be acting in concord with the English, but would have waited for the promised Austrian army to arrive. But that, they all knew, would have been too late. And so, reluctantly, the Chief of Staff had bowed to the wishes of the Field Marshal. This morning he stood at a little distance from the rest of the party, absorbed, apparently in his own observations.

At one point von Reiche had become excited, spotting on an opposite slope a group of French officers, with among their glittering finery a little man in a drab grey coat. He'd turned to Gneisenau: 'Bonaparte, your Highness. It's Bonaparte.'

The Chief of Staff had put a field-glass to his eye. Even Blücher had looked. The Duke alone had continued his inspection in silence, before at length turning to Blücher. Why, he asked, had he not made use of the reverse slope? Surely the Prussian reserves would take a pounding from the French guns? Ziethen had relished the Field Marshal's reply: 'My men like to see their enemy.'

At length, as they were about to descend from the tower, Gneisenau, ever distrustful, had asked the Duke if he would send at least a division as quickly as possible along the Namur road, towards the Prussian lines. Again Wellington had remained silent. And then, pretending to ignore the request, had spent some time with Hardinge, poring over Blücher's maps. Nevertheless, before riding off, he had finally offered his assurances that he would come to their aid – providing of course that he was not attacked himself. A conditional promise. Better than none, thought Ziethen. Although within the hour he had cause to doubt his conclusion.

The first great attack had come in three huge, extended columns, each with a cloud of skirmishers in front, which had smashed their way, without waiting for a covering cannonade, through the four-foot high corn towards St Amand and Jagow's 29th Infantry. The Prussian artillery had done dreadful work among the French, scything into their ranks. And still they came on. Once at the village Jagow's 2,000 men had poured volley after close-range volley into the front ranks. Yet still they came. It had taken no more than fifteen minutes for the French to drive the beleaguered 29th out of St Amand.

This success seemed to be the signal for a wider attack, as the other villages came under a withering fire from, he estimated, at least 100 French cannon. In La Haye, Steinmetz had attempted a counter-attack and moved his brigade reserves against St Amand to bolster the decimated but unbroken 29th.

Where, though, was Wellington? Perhaps, he thought, Gneisenau's fears were not groundless. About one thing, however, the Duke had been right. The French artillery had been raking the reserve lines for almost an hour. Firing high over the heads of the front line, their ricocheting cannonballs had taken a terrible toll of II Corps. Surely the English would hear that? Surely they must march to the guns? Quietly, Ziethen cursed Gneisenau for his damnable ability to be right.

A roundshot, whistling a little too close over his head, *en route* for the reserve, brought Ziethen back to the present. Peering ahead, into the valley, he could see, across the entire front, dense columns of French pressing home their attack. Reports were coming in from all sides.

A messenger rode up. One of Jagow's aides, sent from the bloodbath at Ligny.

'Herr General, Major-General Jagow begs to inform you that he is facing renewed attacks. He estimates over 10,000 French infantry. He requests reinforcements, sir, but asks me to inform you that he will hold till the last man. He is even now exhorting his men to die for the Fatherland.'

'Tell him I can promise nothing. I have no more troops in reserve and the whole of II Corps is under heavy fire and unable to manoeuvre. No. Wait. Tell the general. Tell him that something . . . someone . . . some men will be with him soon. Tell him to hold on.'

Another rider. This time from Steinmetz. He recognized him. Captain Werner. His face black with gunpowder. A sword cut across his chin.

'Herr General. Major-General Steinmetz begs to inform you that he has taken more than 2,000 casualties and has been forced out of the village, sir. St Amand is lost. He requests further orders, sir. Shall we counter-attack?'

Ziethen thought for a moment.

'No, Werner. Tell the general to regroup. To form up before the village. To consolidate whatever remains of his brigade. Tell him that I'm coming. That I'm bringing reserves. Tell him to wait for my arrival. Understand?'

With St Amand gone, their right flank and with it their link with Wellington would be seriously threatened. This had not been part of the master plan. Incredibly, although they must outnumber Napoleon by 10,000 men, they were losing the battle. Ziethen was haunted by memories of Jena. Disgrace. Humiliation. But this was a different army. It was also different, though, from that which had crushed Bonaparte at Leipzig. It was hard to believe how quickly last year the General Staff in their wisdom had disbanded that army. Hard too to credit the short time it had taken to assemble the one now suffering so badly. Young and green, it had been well drilled and disciplined to react like the modern army it must be. But it was still an army constituted for the most part from conscripts and militia. He only hoped that what it lacked in experience it could make up in determination. So far, at least, it seemed to be holding.

Riding around the base of the windmill, Ziethen searched for Blücher, but found only Gneisenau. Surly. Frowning. A cannonball had cut his horse from under him. He rounded on Ziethen.

'Well, my dear count. What of this? You will no doubt recall that I advised you that we should not stand here. That we should retire on Liège. Tell me, General von Ziethen, where do you suppose, at this moment, is the Duke of Wellington?'

Ziethen did not rise to the bait, but remained set on the matter in hand.

'Sir, I must find Marshal Blücher. We must reinforce the right flank. Both St Amand and La Haye have fallen. We must retake the villages. If we do not we are lost. Our flank will be turned.'

'Prince Blücher is down in the valley.' He gestured towards Ligny. 'He is doing what he does best. Inspiring men to fight for their country. I am in command.'

'Then, your Highness, you must decide. Have I your permission to send in a brigade of II Corps?'

'Count von Ziethen, you are aware that I do not believe that Wellington will come to our aid. But you and I must agree that there is no point in our sacrificing the army. We cannot afford to risk being taken in the flank. Yes, the villages must be retaken. Do what you have to.'

Ziethen called an aide. 'Send this to II Corps.

'To Herr General von Tippelskirch, 5th Infantry Brigade. By order of Count von Gneisenau, you will advance to the outskirts of the village of St Amand where you will reinforce General von Steinmetz. You will take the village and hold the position at all costs. Cavalry will be in support.'

As Werner rode off to deliver the order, Ziethen looked again across the valley. Clouds of dense white smoke enveloped the battlefield, along the length of the stream. As ever more wounded emerged dazed and bloody from its depths, so further reinforcements were pressed forward out of sight, to plug the new gaps in the line.

Howitzer shells were falling in the villages, in Ligny in particular, setting houses on fire. In the few brief lulls in the firing, Ziethen could hear the frenzied screams of the wounded trapped inside. He imagined them – boys mostly, dying so horribly in their first, their only battle.

Another rider delivered a hand-written note from General Henckel. There was hand-to-hand fighting in the streets of Ligny. Every lane, even the gardens, was choked with the dead. And all the time it seemed that, inch by inch, the French were gaining ground. In the fields behind him, the greater part of II Corps stood in its positions on the forward slope, pinned down by the French artillery. Unable to reinforce the line.

For an instant the smoke grew less dense and, noticing a gap, Ziethen rode 100 yards forward down the slope and put a telescope to his eye. Bizarrely, he was able see quite clearly. Down in Ligny a brigade of French infantry was moving in to the attack. He saw them break into a charge, some of them peeling away down a hollow track across which Jagow's men had dropped felled trees, farm machinery, furniture, pews from the church. Faced by this tangle, the French came to a halt. For a moment. Then the press from behind, the sheer weight of numbers, began to push the front ranks forward, crushing them against the makeshift barricades, moving them by force of human bodies. Trampling over their own men, they reached the church. Without warning, as Ziethen continued to stare, from behind the walls of the churchyard, from the cover of tombstones and from windows, Jagow's infantry opened up. Perhaps twenty score of French fell at once. He took the telescope away. Wiped the dusty lens, looked again. Saw yet another French column rush into the town and towards the church. This time they were met with bayonets.

Ziethen gazed in unconcealed horror at the ferocity of the fighting. Men were firing into each other at close range. Blowing off pieces of their adversaries. Leaving smouldering black powder marks around the wounds. He saw French and Prussians alike fall by the score. Saw, quite clearly, a young Prussian grenadier use the butt of his musket to beat out the brains of a voltigeur before he too was cut down by the slashing sword of a French officer. Who in turn was shot point-blank through the mouth. A sergeant of chasseurs was beating the bloody head of an already dead Jäger rifleman against the wall of the burning church. Never, in twenty years of soldiering, could Ziethen remember witnessing such basic, primeval violence.

For a moment the French appeared to falter. And then another officer, a full colonel, rode up and rallied them and, although he could hear nothing above the din of battle, Ziethen could see the blue-coated infantry shouting, mouthing oaths to the glory of their Emperor, before they disappeared into the madness of the mêlée.

Drained, he dropped the glass from his eye. Stared in silence. If they continued to fight like this, surely the French would win against any odds. Gneisenau must commit the entire reserve. Bring them down now, never mind the cannon fire. Ziethen raised his telescope again. Swung it round to the left of Ligny and across the stream. A glint of brass caught his eye. Cannon barrel.

He called to von Reiche. 'Do you see that?'

There was no question about it. Artillery. He counted more than ten batteries. Heavy guns manned by men in peaked bearskins, being moved up towards Ligny. Bonaparte intended to reduce the village to rubble. And after that he would be free to swing those twelve-pounders around and enfilade either wing of the Prussian army.

All they could hope for now, it seemed, was to hold out until nightfall brought an end to the fighting. Then perhaps the survivors might join with the English tomorrow.

In the sky the storm clouds were gathering, steadily growing heavier. Where in God's name, he wondered, was Wellington? And then, remembering his promise to Jagow, Ziethen set off, back up the hill, in search of the reinforcements.

NINE

Quatre-Bras, 3.45 p.m.
Ney

He sat on Mortier's old horse, in the centre of the line, by the wood behind the little whitewashed farm, and stared at the pall of white smoke rising from the crossroads. Ney knew that he must work to calm himself. Wasn't Aglaé always telling him so? He must control his temper. But, he reasoned, General Bachelu had been asking for it. Of course it was true that the high crops might conceal more of the enemy. There were always hidden dangers in battle. So why, he had asked him, had Bachelu ever become a soldier? Was he afraid? Ney had to admit it was a bit severe. More than that, it was unfair. Unjust. Ney bit his lip. Knew that the only reason he had treated the general so badly had been his own frustration. His orders from the Emperor had only arrived late in the morning, delivered in person by Charles de Flahaut. It was good to see the handsome young general. A reminder of happier times. Flahaut was the lover of Hortense de Beauharnais, the Emperor's stepdaughter, and had been Aglaé's favourite singing partner in so many concerts at their Paris home. Ney had always been a little jealous.

It was a short message. Ney was to engage the English at once. Take the crossroads. But it had not taken him long to realize that, if he were to safeguard his flank, Bossu wood must also be secured. A frontal assault on the wood? Reille advised caution. Instead, Ney had decided to attack the Allied left. To make for the Namur/Nivelles road and to take it at the hamlet of Paradis. That done, he calculated, the Dutch would be forced to abandon the big wood to save their own flank. There would not be, as the Emperor had demanded, some daring *coup de main*. The only way to beat Wellington at this game, Ney knew, was to muster his men and simply press the Allies into the ground by weight of numbers. A mass attack in the old style. Of course the French would take casualties. But d'Erlon's corps would be here soon to exploit the gap, and after that the way to Brussels would lie open. It was a brilliant plan. Worthy of the Emperor.

It had, however, taken the remainder of the morning to manoeuvre into position. Twenty thousand men had moved from column of route to column of division and finally into column of attack. Twenty-four battalions, each of them with a frontage of sixty men and nine ranks deep. At length, it was not until 2 o'clock, far later than Ney had originally intended, that he had sent them in.

Bachelu needn't have worried. His division had simply walked through the handful of Dutch skirmishers. A thirty-gun cannonade had knocked out one Dutch battery in spectacular fashion, blowing up an ammunition caisson and sending men, parts of men and horses and shards of wood flying thirty feet into the air. True, Foy's division over on the left had been harried by the remaining Dutch guns, but another barrage soon silenced them. Then Foy's men had pushed into the edge of the wood, forcing back the Nassauers. Within an hour Ney had advanced 1,000 yards. On cue, Jerome's division had arrived.

Looking through a field-glass at the crossroads, Ney had also noted the arrival among the Dutch of fresh, green-coated troops. More Nassauers. Running, curiously, into position. It was of no consequence. What was important was to take the crossroads before Wellington was able to deploy his English.

The central farm, Gemioncourt, was held in force. Ney moved quickly. Sent in four of Foy's regiments to the assault, supported by Piré's lancers. As they moved relentlessly forward, a rider approached the marshal from the direction of Paradis. A dust-covered captain of infantry.

'Captain Letort, sire, of the 3rd Line. From Colonel Baron Vautrin. I have urgent news. The English, sire. They're on the road. At Paradis and at the crossroads.'

'Impossible, Captain. I can see no redcoats. Where are they?' Ney peered through his telescope.

'Not redcoats, sire. Riflemen. And believe me, they're there. In the Bois de Cherris.'

Of course. Those running, green-coated infantry who had reinforced the Dutch skirmishers. Not Nassauers at all, but English riflemen. Raising his glass again, Ney tried to make them out, but the smoke was now too dense. He swung the telescope round to his left and instantly knew the report to be right. There in the middle distance, behind the thin hedge which flanked the road, was a line of red. Redcoats, their black shakos ranged in four ranks, under fluttering regimental colours – one dark blue, the other the cross of the British Union flag. Beyond them he saw others. Men in skirts. Highlanders.

Now Ney began to sense the danger. Now at last he had to acknowledge that this was no Dutch provincial general facing him out there across this shallow valley. This was Wellington, the master of concealment. For all Bachelu's fears, the cover of the crops did not concern him so much as what lay beyond. Who knew what troops the English commander had now behind the crossroads? This could be Bussaco again and, if he were to be honest, Ney knew that somewhere out of sight, probably on the slight reverse slope to his rear, Wellington was massing a considerable body of infantry.

He turned to Reille, sitting silently on his horse, a few paces behind him. 'The English, Reille. Wellington. You remember Bussaco? No, no. Of course. You weren't there.'

'Sire.'

The general was quiet. But Ney remembered Bussaco. Foy too. Would never forget it. Five years ago. The early morning mist lifting over a wooded hillside. His own VI Corps advancing in two massive columns, into what he had assured them was a retreating enemy. Advancing under light cannon fire to the crest of the hill. And then the shock. The two English battalions that had appeared from nowhere, delivering volley after unforgiving volley into their ranks. Sending the survivors hurtling down the slope in panic. Coming after them with the bayonet. There had been riflemen there too. Short swords screwed to the barrels of their guns. By 8 a.m. it had all been over. After Bussaco nothing had been the same. Wellington.

'You see, Reille.' Ney was suddenly animated. 'At this moment Wellington will be manoeuvring his men out of sight. Behind that slope. Well, we are wise to his game, Reille. And we still outnumber him.'

Even as he spoke a great cheer went up from the centre of the line. Foy's men had taken Gemioncourt.

As they emerged into the open ground on the other side, however, Ney saw a mass of cavalry move across the field towards the right. Sky-blue hussar uniforms and what looked strangely like green-clad French chasseurs. Dutch cavalry. They spurred headlong into Foy's emerging infantry, managing to ride many down before they were able to form rallying squares. Within minutes, though, he could discern on the left the distinctive helmets of their own lancers. They took the Dutch in the flank, causing havoc. Men pulled back on their horses, tried to run. Turned, only to meet more lancers behind them. The Dutch Hussars and light dragoons wheeled about in disorder. Tried to find a way out. And then they were all streaming back up the road, the lancers hard after them. He saw more Dutchmen fall. Taken not by lance but by musketry.

Mistaken by the redcoats, he realized with grim amusement, as they had been at first by him, for French. Rollin rode up.

'Sire. Prince Jerome has advanced into Bossu wood, on a line with the farm, sire, as you ordered.'

'Good, Rollin. That's fine. Fine. Any news of d'Erlon?'

'None, sire. But we know that he has left Jumet.'

Ney grunted. Where was I Corps? Jumet? D'Erlon was not even at Gosselies. Still, despite the presence of the English, things were going well. Jerome it seemed had taken almost half of the wood without firing a shot. Was ready to attack. Ney rode towards the left of the line, trailing in his wake his string of officers. As he approached Bossu wood, scattered shots began to ring out from the Allied skirmish line. He ignored them. Until one caught his horse square in the neck. It crumpled beneath him, trapping a booted leg.

'Rollin, Heymes. Get me out. Help me.'

The two aides dismounted and rushed to Ney. Pulled him from beneath the dying animal. A fresh horse was brought up, the second he had purchased from the stricken Mortier.

Winded, bruised, Ney paused briefly before mounting, then continued towards the wood. He must take Bossu wood. Take the wood and he would be able to turn Wellington's flank.

'What troops oppose us in the wood, Heymes? Do we know?'

'As far as we can tell, sire, just the Belgians. We have seen only blue coats, sire. No red.'

What was Wellington playing at? He had positioned his veteran English units on his left flank, and left only the half-trained, skittish Dutch militia to defend this key position. Foolish. He had made a fundamental mistake. And Ney would make sure that it was fatal.

Reaching the flank of Jerome's column he rode between the trees, his new horse nervously picking its way through the undergrowth. Reckless in the face of enemy skirmishers and much to the concern of the staff, he removed his hat and waved it in the air so that the men could see his face. His voice rang clear through the wood.

'The Emperor will reward any man who will advance.'

It was the old slogan. The words of Austerlitz and Wagram. Ney repeated them over and over again, circling his hat in the air as he rode the length of Jerome's extended front line of cheering, blue-coated light infantry. He turned and rode back to rejoin his staff. Reining in towards Jerome, Ney caught a glint of something on his right, deep in the wood. Looking again, he saw a body of men crouching in the scrub, perhaps 200 yards away. Enemy skirmishers. But instead of blue coats they wore black. Brunswickers. Germans. What an assembly was this army. Brunswickers. A little better though, he presumed, than the Belgians. It would be harder to clear the wood. And, as Jerome sent his division crashing into the trees, Ney realized that he had now committed his entire force. There was no reserve. Where was d'Erlon? He swore.

'Sire?'

'Nothing, Rollin. Nothing. I see that the Duke's German friends have come to help the Belgians. Where is d'Erlon?'

'We believe him to be just south of here, sire. Perhaps near Frasnes.'

He was about to ask more precisely where, when an orderly rode up with a despatch from Napoleon. It was timed at 2 p.m. Written by Soult.

Attack whatever force is before you. After driving it back you will turn in our direction to bring about the envelopment of those enemy troops which I have already mentioned to you.

'Those enemy troops'. The Prussians, he presumed. So the Emperor had decided to crush Blücher first before turning on Wellington. Here then was a very different plan from that which he had first understood. Nevertheless it was the

87

Emperor's. It would work. The only way to honour it now though, Ney saw, was to take the crossroads. And to do it quickly. He continued to traverse the field from west to east. His right flank was looking increasingly vulnerable.

The redcoats whom he had seen earlier, lining the road, seemed to be here in greater force. And, as he watched, that worrying red line began to move forward, through the shoulder-high rye. Close to the shallow stream which ran to the lake it stopped and, with an enviable precision, sent a volley crashing into the head of Bachelu's columns. As the French staggered to recover, the redcoats followed up with a bayonet charge. Slowly, Bachelu's men gave fire and pulled back, leaving the ground to the English.

Ney, seeing an opportunity, called to an aide. Pointed towards the redcoats. 'Have Maréchal de Camp Pellitier train his artillery fire on that English line. And order General Piré to move his 6th Lancers up towards it. They should take with them Captain Gronnier's horse artillery. Tell him to unlimber at . . . 200 yards.'

That would break them. The threat of cavalry would force the English, and that Highland regiment he had noticed, into square. Then the artillery would cut them to pieces. He looked over to the wood. A stream of blue-coated fugitives fleeing towards the Allied lines indicated that the Belgians and Dutch had begun to crack. The black Brunswickers had also left the trees and were advancing purposefully towards Gemioncourt. As Dutch reinforcements moved into the wood to relieve their beleaguered countrymen, Jerome's light infantry seized their chance and, rushing forward and with a great cry of 'Vive l'Empéreur', took the vacant ground.

At precisely that moment the remaining battalion of Jerome's infantry, positioned at the near edge of the wood, opened fire on the exposed Brunswickers. Ney saw that Pellitier had also now, on his own initiative, brought his cannon to bear on them. From the rear of the Brunswick corps a detachment of black-uniformed cavalry appeared, led by a senior officer, his rank evident from the staff who hovered around him. They rode straight for Jerome's men, but before they were able to make contact another volley rang out. The black-coated officer went down, followed by a score of his hussars.

Looking again to his right, Ney observed the lancers going about their bloody business. To his dismay the Highlanders had not formed square and he saw the lethal spear-points of the cavalry break in among them. There would be no need now for artillery. Seeing the carnage, the other redcoat battalion had already begun to retire, back to their starting position. As Ney looked on, Gronnier's horse artillery came galloping full pelt across the field before him and, with a speed and precision worthy of a Sunday afternoon review, unlimbered their four six-pounders and went into action against the Brunswick troops – with canister. A minute later the men in black were running pell-mell back towards the crossroads.

Wellington's centre was wide open. Now, thought Ney. Now was the time. He saw Rollin, remounted after losing his own horse. Called him over. Quickly dictated a single line to d'Erlon.

General. Do not lose a moment. Bring me I Corps.

'Go. Find him. Bring him here. Now.'

One push would do it. But he needed d'Erlon. Rollin was not 100 yards away when his horse crossed paths with the figure of de la Bedoyere, making for the marshal. The young general rode up to Ney.

'An order, sire. From the Emperor.'

Ney took the folded parchment. It was an unsigned note, in pencil. It bore no time, but he seemed to recognize Napoleon's hand. It ordered d'Erlon to march with his corps at once towards Ligny. To fall on Blücher's right flank. De la Bedoyere spoke:

'I trust that you will forgive me, sire. I have already taken the liberty of enforcing the order myself. I passed General d'Erlon on the way here. He is at this moment marching on Blücher.' He smiled at Ney. The marshal spoke softly.

'You have what? You have ordered General d'Erlon where?' His voice rose alarmingly. De la Bedoyere stopped smiling. 'Forgive you? Forgive you? What have you done? How dare you. General d'Erlon's corps is my command. I have ordered him here. Here. With him here we can crush Wellington. Where is he? Where is d'Erlon?'

'Sire, the Emperor expressly informed me –'

'Informed you? You, boy? I'll inform you, boy. I'll tell you. I know what the Emperor wants. He wants me to kick Wellington's arse. And then he wants me to march to him and to do the same to Blücher. That's what the Emperor wants. And to give it to him I must have d'Erlon. Here.'

De la Bedoyere said nothing. He had gone quite pale. For a moment he stared at Ney. Then he reined his horse around and rode back to Fleurus. He was not quite out of sight when another officer rode up. Even in his rage, the marshal recognized him. Colonel Forbin-Janson, of Soult's staff.

'Sire, I come with a message from the Emperor.'

He was in the motion of producing a despatch from his waistcoat pocket when he added something that Napoleon had told him to say in person. 'He, the Emperor, sire, begs me to inform you that you are to finish the business at Quatre-Bras, without further ado. His words, sire.'

Ney looked incredulously around at his staff. Tried to meet their eyes. Heymes and Flahaut looked down at their reins. The marshal's cheeks, already red with the heat of battle and his annoyance with de la Bedoyere, now deepened in tone to a livid purple. Looking away at the horizon, he opened his mouth in a scream which even on the battlefield was audible at 100 yards. An animal noise of pure rage. Gradually it subsided. Ney clenched his fists. Finally he turned on the colonel, able at last to articulate his fury.

'His words? His words? You bloody imbecile. You idiotic, pompous ass. His words? His words? I don't need bloody words. Not even the Emperor's bloody words. I need men. I need d'Erlon. What do you mean, "finish the business"? Without d'Erlon "the business" as you call him – Wellington – is going to finish me. Tell him that, you stupid ass. Tell the Emperor that unless I have reinforcements it won't be the English but me that'll be finished. Tell him that.'

Forbin-Janson was staring – at nothing. Unable to speak.

Ney began to calm down. 'I'm sorry, Colonel. What I should have said was, "Please inform his Majesty of exactly what you have seen here." Tell him that I am opposed not by a token force, but by the whole of Wellington's army. That I am even now, I suspect, outnumbered. That I will nevertheless hold on despite this and despite the fact that General d'Erlon has not yet arrived. As he has not yet arrived. As he is at this moment marching ... elsewhere, I am very much afraid that I am unable to promise his Majesty any more than this. Tell him that.'

Embarrassed, confused, the colonel, red-faced and wide-eyed, saluted, released his hold on the now forgotten despatch and rode away.

Ney was confused. What now were his orders? There was only one course of action. To follow his instinct. It told him that he must defeat the English. And to do that he needed d'Erlon.

A third horseman appeared among the staff. Delcambre, Chief of Staff to d'Erlon, and with him a bewildered-looking Rollin.

'Marshal, I have to inform you that General d'Erlon is, at the Emperor's request, on his way to Ligny.'

Ney groaned. 'I know that, you fool. Don't you know that

91

I know that? Now let me tell you what to do. Listen carefully, Delcambre. Do not mistake my words. This is what you are going to do. You are going to ride back to General d'Erlon, wherever he might be – on the road to Ligny, or on his way back to Paris. And you are going to bring him back here. To me, Delcambre. Bring him to me. And then together, Delcambre, you, me, General Reille and General d'Erlon, we are going to smash the English. Then we will all go to Ligny. Do you understand?'

'Sire.'

'So do it.'

As the colonel galloped away on his thankless mission, a roundshot, fired by a troublesome, newly-arrived battery of English horse artillery, came flying towards the hill, headed directly for the group of staff officers around Ney.

It hit the earth just before the marshal's horse, bounced up and seared a bloody channel straight through the animal's belly. The horse reared in agony, tossing Ney off to one side, before toppling over and away from him. The cannonball continued to ricochet, taking a leg off one of Ney's junior aides and going on past the staff to disembowel a young lieutenant of Foy's infantry.

Cursing, Ney got to his feet. Heymes trotted up, holding the reins of a fresh horse which fifteen minutes earlier had belonged to a major of chasseurs who, as he explained to the marshal, 'no longer had need of it'.

This moment, Ney knew, was the crisis of the battle. If only he could act now, play for time, while d'Erlon was coming ever nearer, Wellington would be defeated. He looked for precedents. Alexander? Frederick? But his fuddled mind found none. He tried to rationalize. To consolidate what men he had.

All three divisions of infantry were fully engaged in holding the line. Of his lancers, one regiment had been mauled in the aftermath of the engagement with the Highlanders. The other, though, was relatively fresh. And then there were the heavy cavalry. He thought of Borodino. Of Murat and himself, wild with battle, at the head of a horde of cuirassiers. Borodino. There for the first time his bold initiative had won in the face of the Emperor's indecision. It could happen again. Cavalry. Cuirassiers. Looking about, he found Heymes. Shouted across to him through the din of cannon fire.

'Take a message to General Piré. No time to write. Tell him, from me, the 5th Lancers must ride directly into the centre of the Allied line. Attempt to pierce it, to enable General Kellerman to exploit the breach.'

Turning in the saddle he found Kellerman, uniformed as was his custom in the half armour of a cuirassier, in conversation with Rollin.

'Kellerman. Your cuirassiers. You're ready?'

'Sire. I have only one brigade. The rest of my men remain in reserve. I'm not sure, sire, precisely where –'

'I don't care how sure you are. Do you understand? You charge with whatever you have. You get your men, Kellerman, and you ride against that infantry.' He was pointing now. Straight at the centre of the Allied line. At the redcoats. 'You ride against them and you ride them down. Crush them. Go. Now!'

The general left in search of his one brigade. Ahead of him Ney could see Piré's lancers already riding into three incredulous regiments of redcoats – one in kilts. He saw Scots and English officers pointing in alarm. Saw the sickening looks of realization as it quickly dawned on the redcoats that they had been caught. Saw two battalions hurrying to form square. The other had no time. He saw the lancers riding round and round, taking their time to choose their targets, as cool as a hunting party, pigsticking. Caught in the open, the defenceless infantrymen tried to parry lance with musket and soon saw with horror the futility of their attempts to stop the inevitable. It was quickly over, the destruction of a battalion.

And now, on his left, Kellerman was underway. Ney felt the earth tremble as the 500 armoured cavalry on their shining black horses switched from trot to gallop. At their head, sword raised high, next to Kellerman, rode their commander, Baron Guiton, the hero of Eylau. Unstoppable, the dazzling blue and silver juggernaut rolled smack into the red line, and disappeared in a cloud of white smoke. It was hard to make out from here exactly what was happening. And then, as the smoke drifted, Ney saw a small miracle. What had been a battalion of redcoats in square was being cut to pieces by cuirassiers. One Frenchman had seized an English colour – a sheet of green and gold silk – and was carrying it back to the lines.

Another British battalion had been forced sideways by the shock of the charge; driven into Bossu wood and on to Reille's waiting infantry. Ney saw Kellerman himself, surrounded by a troop of Guiton's men, at the junction of the crossroads.

By God, he thought. We've taken the road. With cavalry alone. He had known it was possible. Now all that he had to do was to support them with infantry and the day was his. Where was d'Erlon? This was the moment. Now. Only now. Not to act now and it would be gone.

And, all too soon, it was. Within minutes, when Ney looked again at the crossroads, he saw two fresh red-coated battalions move methodically across the field and towards the cuirassiers. As they changed formation from column into line, another British horse battery opened up. And as they did so, Kellerman wheeled round and found another target. A second battalion of Highlanders. This time, though, there was no momentum for a charge. The cuirassiers approached at no more than a trot, and at thirty yards out the first Scottish volley stopped them in their tracks. Enfiladed now by the English on their flank, the French cavalry began to retire. Slowly, they came back towards the lines. Riding and walking. In twos and threes, mustering in bloodied troops and squadrons. And with them, out of the smoke, came Kellerman, unhorsed and holding on by his hands to the bridles of two horses. He was not wounded, but had suffered a badly sprained ankle.

Ney knew now that the moment had passed. Refused to admit it. Looked around. The bulk of his staff, it seemed, had just melted away. Killed, wounded or unmounted. Rollin was clutching a bloodied arm. Heymes, though, was still up with him. And Flahaut. Where was d'Erlon? But in his heart, he knew that it was too late. That I Corps were still on the march. Caught somewhere between here and Ligny. Caught between two battles. Between two sets of orders. Caught between two commanders. It was up to him now to finish this business. He was hatless, and soon horseless again as his third mount of the day now panicked, unseated him and ran off into the Allied lines. Ney prepared to advance on foot. He wiped his forehead with his hand. Closed his eyes. When he opened them, staring for a moment towards the ground, he saw in the mud the unexpected whiteness of a piece of paper. He bent to pick it up. Could barely make out the smudged words: 'By hand of Colonel Forbin-Janson'. It was from Soult. Timed: 'Fleurus 3.30'.

Marshal,
    I indicated an hour ago that the Emperor would attack at 2.30 the position between St Amand and Brye. At this moment that action is taking place. His Majesty has instructed me to inform you that you must manoeuvre immediately edgewise to encircle the enemy's right flank and fall upon his rear. If you act vigorously the Prussian army will be lost.
    The fate of France is in your hands.

The fate of France. Ney smiled. Closed his fist around the paper until it was a tight ball. Then, thrusting it into his pocket, he raised his sword and marched alone towards the front of Foy's skirmish line.

TEN

Ligny, 6.15 p.m.
Napoleon

From the observation platform, built that morning by the engineers of the Garde around the upper storey of a windmill high above Ligny, the Emperor gazed out in silence across the smoking valley. He was becoming irritated by a straggling lock of hair which had stuck to the beads of sweat coursing down his face. He pushed it aside and scratched at his forehead, before returning his hands to their habitual position, crossed behind his back, hard against the tails of his green coat. He pulled them tighter together, turned quickly and walked back inside the mill. Five staff officers sprang to attention. Grabbing a piece of paper from the sheaf which lay ready on a millstone, Napoleon took a pencil and wrote on it one word, 'Marbais', underlining it ten times with frenzied strokes, before pinning it to a low beam.

'Marbais, gentlemen. That is the key to the battle. At precisely seven o'clock this evening Count d'Erlon's corps will arrive on the field of battle, between Marbais and Wagnelée, to our north west and strike directly into the right wing of the Prussian army.'

Soult, as ever, was on hand. 'Sire. If Count d'Erlon carries out your orders to the letter, then surely the Prussians are lost.'

Napoleon, not bothering to reply, looked down at the

white, flour-coated boards of the mill. Well, of course Soult was right, with his irrelevant, sycophantic comment. It was a brilliant plan. Blücher was beaten. And now was the time for the *coup de grâce*. D'Erlon and the Garde would attack together. The one on the flank, at Wagnelée, the other directly into the centre. A battering ram and an iron glove to smash the Germans. Forever.

Walking out from the mill on to the platform, he was hit by the blanket of heat which rose from the conflict below, which had been raging since the early afternoon. He looked out across the plain. Noticed that the Prussians were man-oeuvring to their right, weakening their centre. That would do. The right was strong. Vandamme secure at St Amand.

He was not, at first, aware of the arrival directly below him of an officer of chasseurs who, dismounting, ran to the slim wooden stairs and climbed to the platform. Seeing Gourgaud, the lieutenant saluted and began his desperate message.

Without dropping the glass from his eye, Napoleon gestured to the staff colonel. 'Let him through, Gourgaud. Bring him here. What news?'

'Sire. Belgians. On our left, sire. I come from General Vandamme at St Amand, your Majesty. We are about to be attacked.'

Napoleon lowered the telescope and looked more closely at the agitated young man. 'You're sure? Sure that they're Belgians?'

'A large body of troops, sire. Perhaps 20,000 of them. In dark blue, advancing upon our flank.' He pointed in the direction of the Roman road to the south west.

Napoleon walked round the platform, to the west side of the mill. Was it possible? Had Wellington managed to break free from Ney? He peered again through the telescope. Kept it to his eye for a full minute.

The man was right. There was no doubt about it. There it was, on his left flank. A long, dark column of marching men.

In effect they were moving not into, but actually behind his flank. Making directly for the Imperial headquarters.

He tried to estimate how many. Perhaps 5,000 visible in the vanguard? They must be Belgians. Even at this distance the column was too dark for English red. And they could not possibly be d'Erlon's men. They would be in entirely the wrong place. Some 5 kilometres too far south. Napoleon looked away and walked over to the map which lay, weighed down by stones, on a large, up-ended wooden barrel. Whoever they were, they were heading for the village of Wagnée.

He froze. Looked up and absently out into space. No. It was ridiculous. Absurd. But in war anything was possible. Particularly the ridiculous. Could it be? De la Bedoyere himself had taken the message to Ney ordering d'Erlon to march on Wagnelée and Marbais. Had written it himself. But what exactly had he written? Might it be possible that, in his haste, the young general had written not Wagnelée, but Wagnée? Of course it was possible. Damn this hot, damp country, with its vile Flemish names. Wagnée. Wagnelée. Gosselies. Herpignies. He looked again at the map. It was more than possible. It was certain. Napoleon put the cool brass rim of the telescope back to his eye. Looked more closely. Saw the square of a regimental colour floating above the column. Tried to make out detail. A tricolor. The glint of an eagle. There was no need to look again. They were French. D'Erlon. He snapped the telescope shut. Turned to the staff.

'French. They're French. It's d'Erlon. Soult, tell me, what in God's name is d'Erlon doing heading for my left flank? Where are his scouts? Why has he sent no advance warning of his arrival? Are all my generals incompetent? Must I do everything personally?' He brought his fist crashing down on the makeshift map table, sending the stones flying 'Gourgaud. Corbineau. Send an aide to observe the head of column. I need immediate confirmation that it is d'Erlon.'

There was no harm in making sure.

No sooner had the courier left, along with the confused lieutenant of chasseurs, than another messenger reined in his horse below the mill. An infantry lieutenant this time. Gourgaud motioned him to speak.

Napoleon stared at him. What now?

'Sire. General Vandamme begs to inform you that his men are becoming increasingly perturbed by the presence of the unidentified column advancing on his left, sire. He asks for reinforcements, sire. Otherwise he will be forced to abandon his position at St Amand.'

Napoleon shook his head. 'Very well. Gourgaud. Have someone find General Duhesme. Tell him to take the Young Guard and move across to reinforce St Amand. And make certain that whoever takes the message tells General Duhesme, from me. From me. I am giving him a chance to re-acquaint himself with this ground. Tell him that if he does as well here today as he did on this same battlefield in 1794 then we will all breakfast in Brussels. And for God's sake, Gourgaud, tell Duhesme to tell Vandamme not to panic. They're French troops advancing on him. It's D'Erlon.'

Pray God, he thought, that it *is* d'Erlon. For if it's Wellington, we're done for.

Nervous now, Napoleon walked back inside the mill. He sat down for a moment on the millstone. Folded his arms. Closed his eyes. Tried to focus his mind. They are waiting for me, he thought. Waiting for my orders. For my miracles. They know that I will win. But do I know it? Can I be sure? Have I over-reached myself? Am I too old? A sudden tiredness descended upon him, along with a creeping nausea. He crossed his arms tighter. Willed it away.

Around him, the generals, the orderlies, the courtiers, marvelled at the Emperor's composure. At his ability to relax at this, the most crucial moment of the battle. What a man. Not a man, surely, but a god.

A slight cough. Napoleon opened his eyes. Gourgaud.

'The scout, sire, has returned with news of the column. They're French, your Majesty. It is d'Erlon, sire. You were right.'

Of course it was d'Erlon. And he was heading for their flank. De la Bedoyere must have caught him already on the road. No time to change routes. Take the quickest. That was fine. Improvise. Sound generalship. No need now to send him further orders. D'Erlon was no fool. He would know to continue along the Roman road. Napoleon rose and walked across the room to where a second map had been set up on a block of stone. He marked d'Erlon's current position with his thumb. Traced its route towards him. That would bring him on the field at the little village of Trois Barettes. Well, that would do. He would not surprise the Prussians – who must also have seen him – but he would still threaten their flank. They would have to deal with him. It was good enough.

And there was now no need to wait for him. Napoleon had had enough of this bloody slogging match. Enough of 'Papa' Blücher. He turned to Soult.

'We'll finish this business now. With the Garde. Drouot?'

The tall, impeccable Garde commander, amicably nicknamed 'the sage', a veteran of twenty-two years, moved forward from the crowd of officers. Pulled his lame leg to a painful attention. 'Sire?'

'Now's the time. Move the Old Garde, grenadiers, chasseurs, directly into the attack. Desvaux. Where is Desvaux? Someone. Gourgaud. Lannoy. Someone. Go and find Desvaux and tell him to open fire with the Garde artillery in . . . ten minutes from now. Tell him nine batteries, twelve-pounders, six-pounders. No, not the horse batteries. He should send those into the attack. The others to fire directly into their centre. Tell him. Go. Go.'

The officers dispersed.

Walking out on to the platform, back into the searing heat, Napoleon looked down at the path that his 'invincibles' were to take. The rise in the land would hide them, even their tall bearskins, from the Prussians until it was too late.

Looking further across the valley now he could see more activity in the Prussian lines. On the left he saw a body of cavalry move towards St Amand, supported by what looked like an entire brigade of infantry. So Blücher was committing his right to a counter-attack. Surely, now was the time. The air was extraordinarily still. For an instant he found it hard to breathe. Loosened his collar. The moment passed.

Directly over the battlefield, in what seemed a curious micro-climate, fuelled in part by the smoke of the battle, heavy, black storm clouds had gathered. Yet despite the heat and the alarming, stifling moment, Napoleon began to feel himself calming. Body and mind back in control.

'Gourgaud. Send half of the Garde light cavalry, the red lancers, directly towards St Amand to support the Young Garde. And Domon's chasseurs.'

That would deal with any new threat.

He turned to Gérard, commander of IV Corps, who was hovering by his right hand, awaiting his orders to support the Old Garde. Smiling, Napoleon pointed to the central hillside, now entirely empty of Prussian troops. Covered only with corpses.

'Look, Gérard. You see. Now they are lost. Blücher has committed his reserve. There is nothing to stop us.'

As he spoke, as if in agreement, the clouds above opened at last with a great thunderclap and warm rain began to pour down on the two armies.

A moment later, theatrically on cue, the fifty-four cannon of the Garde artillery opened up on Ligny. Desvaux, observing Napoleon's instructions to the letter, was pouring his fire directly into where Blücher's line was at its weakest. It was the old way. Pound away at one point and then, when it's good and weak, pound some more. And Napoleon was aware that somewhere in those crackling, molten ruins, alongside the

101

Prussian dead and dying, lay French wounded, among French corpses, all of them now being ripped to pieces by their own artillery. Well, that was war. It was too bad. They would die for their Emperor. They understood. He reached inside his coat and produced the snuff-box. Taking a pinch he applied it to his nostrils with a slight sniff and replaced the little tortoiseshell coffer. He turned to his left, took from another pocket the cologne-soaked handkerchief and held it to his nose.

'I tell you, Gourgaud. There is nothing like a grand battery, sixty, eighty, a hundred guns. Twelve-pounders if you can get them – a real cannonade – to make your enemy shit in his pants. And then,' he smiled, 'then he really does have no stomach left for a fight. Eh, Lannoy? Moline? Eh, Resigny? No stomach. Ha.'

Pleased with his joke, Napoleon laughed to himself. The four aides knew to join in.

From behind the Emperor an unrelated peal of laughter erupted simultaneously from a group of orderlies. Napoleon turned, suddenly stony-faced.

'You might be a little more serious, Saint-Denis, when you are surrounded by so many brave men killing each other.'

Silence.

Napoleon looked up at the rain and then down, and across the valley. 'Now, we move.'

The group descended from the platform.

'Come on. Come on. Find my horse. De la Bedoyere.'

'The general is with Marshal Ney, sire.' Gourgaud.

'Of course. Yes, of course. You're right.'

A green-liveried equerry brought up Marengo. Napoleon mounted the beautiful white horse, startlingly bright amid the darkness of the battle. Quickly now, followed by his un-shakeable tail of officers, he rode for high ground. To a spot where he could be seen clearly by the Garde who, even as he arrived, had begun to file past their Emperor.

They came on in two columns, the left made up solely of grenadiers, the tall 'grumblers' of his army. Veterans to a man, heroes of ten years of battles, with their earrings, moustaches and flour-whitened hair, their height emphasized by the prized tall black bearskins. On the right marched a mixed column: more grenadiers, chasseurs and the gaudily dressed 'marines', most of whom had never seen the sea.

Above the tumult of the guns, their cries of allegiance rang out. 'Vive l'Empéreur', 'Mort aux Prusses'.

Napoleon was surrounded by the men he had made. Soldiers and officers. He saw Friant, the son of a furniture-polisher, who had risen from sergeant-major to command four regiments of Garde grenadiers, and Morand, the former lawyer and an Egyptian veteran, also now a general, of chasseurs. Poor, ugly Morand, whose face had been so badly disfigured by a shell splinter at Borodino that it was said that any woman to whom he made love could not bear to look at him and begged him to take her from behind. Napoleon smiled at the thought. Here too now, smiling back at his Emperor, came Petit, whom only last year in the courtyard at Fontainebleau he had left in tears as he prepared for exile on that execrable little island. Well, they would not have the opportunity to do that to him again.

His vengeful reverie was interrupted by a flash of steel-grey tunics on his right and the tumbling rush of ammunition caissons and limbers, which announced the artillery train of the Garde, hurrying their light guns up to the assault.

It took a full twenty minutes for all the columns to reach the front line. Once there, though, their momentum carried them quickly down the slope towards Ligny. Twenty thousand men, in five regiments, constantly under fire. The two Garde columns flowed around the burning village, one to each side. Between them the mass of IV Corps hit it square on. They were flanked by cavalry. On the left the huge, bearskinned grenadiers à cheval of the Garde, with their massive, jet-black horses and the helmeted green and gold Garde dragoons, who still bore the title of Napoleon's dead empress. On the right rode the 3,000 cuirassiers of Milhaud's corps. All came on relentlessly, regardless of the ferocious Prussian fire, thrown point-blank into their faces. Sabres gleaming, bayonets promising no quarter, the French fell upon what remained of the Prussian centre.

This, thought Napoleon, was how it should be. This was war. War on his terms. War without limit. Alexandrine war. Caesarian war. His mouth was dry. Parched with excitement. His body deliciously alive with sensation. Also, to his delight, he realized that, as so often at this point in a battle, he had an erection. Amused at his own predicament, he sat perfectly still and watched the bloody drama unfold.

In Fleurus the church bells tolled seven, their low tone blending with the music of the grenadiers' band who propelled the last battalions into the mêlée with the strains of the 'Chant du Depart'. And then followed them into the flaming, shattered remains of what five hours earlier had been the village of Ligny.

Steadying himself on Marengo, who had shied, uncharacteristically, at the close passage of a roundshot, Napoleon watched absorbed, electric with tension, as his columns reached the Prussian lines. Saw the impact as their huge impetus pushed the Germans physically backwards up the hill. Now all the French were across the stream. He looked with pride as the Garde moved swiftly from column into line, ready to bring as many muskets as possible to bear on the enemy. Officers ran in front barking orders, twirling their swords in the air, urging the men on. On the right he watched a Prussian cavalry regiment appear from nowhere and make for two battalions of the grenadiers. With one double wheeling action the veterans transformed their line into a hollow square. The cavalry, seeing the bearskins, reined in, turned and fled.

Napoleon clapped his hands. Without shifting his gaze from

the carnage and spectacle before him, he addressed his aides; not in the voice of the Emperor, but with the victory crow of the playground general.

'Look. Look at them all. Aren't they the finest in the world? My children. What can stop them? What will stop us? Now can you see? Now do you see how to win a battle?'

ELEVEN

Quatre-Bras, 6.30 p.m.
Macdonell

They had been marching for fourteen hours. Had covered, he estimated, at least twenty-five miles. Since they had regained the road, past Nivelles, Macdonell's place at the front of the long, weary column had been taken by the light companies of the First Guards. By way of a diversion he had temporarily left his men in the charge of Henry Wyndham and ridden up to join the commanding officer of the new vanguard, George Fraser, Lord Saltoun, a fellow Scot and his exact equivalent in rank and command. Saltoun, seven years his junior, was an amiable man and the two had much in common. Like Macdonell, Saltoun had originally served with a Highland regiment – the 42nd, 'Black Watch', before transferring into the Guards. The two men rode together now, exchanging pleasantries and observations, although both knew that this was merely to disguise the inevitable apprehension which marked the approach to battle.

Having covered the health of several mutual friends at home in Scotland and the merits, on a Highland estate, of replacing tenant farmers with sheep, as Macdonell's brother Alasdair was at that very moment in the process of doing at Invergarry, their conversation had moved on to fishing, about which Macdonell was passionate. In the Peninsula, in the many breaks between engagements which made up most of a soldier's life, he had revelled in the variety of fish to be found in the Spanish rivers. Not only salmon and trout, but mullet, barbel and rock-fish.

Saltoun was currently reaching the end of an extended appraisal of the sporting glories of his estate, a substantial acreage near Fraserburgh, on the Aberdeenshire coast, with at its heart the ancestral seat of Philorth Castle.

'When this business is done, James. When we have disposed of Boney and his cronies for good and are back at home in Scotland for a while, you will come and stay with me at Philorth and I will show you the finest salmon fishing in all the country. We shall fish the Don and the Dee and I dare say even, if you will, my own modest Loch at Strathbeg.' He laughed. 'I know, of course, that you consider me the lesser fisherman.'

Macdonell began a half-hearted objection. Saltoun waved his hand.

'No, no. I'll not hear your protests. I am resolved. You will see for yourself.'

Macdonell smiled. 'Perhaps, Saltoun. And I'm always happy to accept an offer of a day's sport. But, with my brother's permission – though he is no fisherman – I shall return your invitation. And then you'll join me at Invergarry and we shall see quite how true your boast might be. I know of a spot on a high bank, above the river Garry. The air has a particular freshness. That's where we'll make our camp. Then I'll take you down across the rocks, to where the river crashes like a mill race, roaring down the four miles to Loch Oich. And then, my dear Saltoun, then you will see how to cast into a fast river. That's where you really have to work a fly. There you must "strike the rise". If you do not, all is lost. Timing, Saltoun. It's all about timing. Now that's fishing. Real sport.'

Saltoun laughed and shook his head.

His junior officers, riding to their right and left, smiled at the gentle rivalry of the two men, envying the colonels their apparent composure. For their own thoughts were far from anything as peaceful and mundane as salmon fishing. Their heads were filled with the horrific images which they had encountered, continued to encounter, over the last few miles, as they passed the streams of wounded British, Dutch, German and Belgian troops, flowing back along the road towards Nivelles. Some were on foot, others, too badly mangled to walk, travelled in commandeered hay wagons, drawn by oxen and driven by sullen peasants.

As the officers rode on, the sound of the guns grew ever nearer. The regimental music had long since ceased and with it had gone the jaunty spring in their step. It had been replaced by a new haste, spawned by a real sense of urgency. Apart from the guns, the only noises were once again the tramp of marching feet, the clatter of horses' hooves, the jangle of their harness and the dull, rhythmic clank of bayonet on wood.

Rounding a bend in the road, Macdonell saw ahead of him the houses of what he guessed must be Quatre-Bras. On his left he discerned a body of men. Belgians, by the look of them. They were sitting down. Evidently awaiting orders. Over on the right he could see the outline of a large wood, stretching off to the south for perhaps over a mile. That would be the Bois de Bossu. Their objective. As they approached the village he caught on the air the unmistakable stench of a battlefield, bringing back countless memories, and with them conflicting emotions of exhilaration, sorrow and fear. Near the crossroads the men began to pass the first bodies. Men who, sensing the hopelessness of their condition, had crawled away from the fight to die in peace at the roadside. There were more wounded too. Men of all arms and nations. English, Scots, Nassauers, Belgians, Dutch, Brunswickers. It was not a pleasant sight, and Macdonell knew that, for many of the younger men in his command, officers included, this would be their first encounter with the blood of a battlefield. From behind him he heard

Miller bark a reprimand as some of the raw recruits threw up at the roadside. Being himself largely inured to the sight, however, he was more interested in attempting to identify from their uniforms which regiments had already become involved in the battle.

It appeared that the reserve had arrived some time ago, such was the evident extent of their losses. He saw men of the 69th, dead and wounded. Lying on his back, face frozen in a contented smile, was the corpse of a private of the 28th, still wearing his distinctive stovepipe shako. There were Highlanders here too. Macdonell startled a wounded sergeant of the 92nd, nursing a maimed hand, with a word of encouragement in Gaelic. On another body, lying face down in the ditch, he could make out the kilt of the Black Watch, Saltoun's old comrades. He was about to point this out to his companion when both men noticed a group of horsemen hurrying towards them along the road. At their head rode a distinctive figure, clad in black with an extravagant fur-trimmed pelisse and an outrageously plumed bicorn hat. There was no mistaking the Prince of Orange. At his side Macdonell recognized his chief of staff, the renowned General Rebecque. The Prince rode hard up to Saltoun, whom he had decided was the senior officer. He wore an expression of unconcealable jubilation and spoke in the stilted, staccato court English of European royalty.

'Gentlemen. Your arrival could not be more timely. Attack. Attack. You must attack. Waste no time, sir. Drive your men into the wood. Take the wood. Attack the enemy.'

Saltoun, casting Macdonell a sidewards glance, was sanguine in his reply. 'Of course, your Highness. Of course we will attack. But with the utmost respect, sir, where exactly are the enemy?' With a gesture of his hand, Saltoun continued: 'You know Colonel Macdonell, of course, your Highness? Of the Coldstream.'

The Prince looked at Macdonell. Tried to place him. Failed.

Nodded politely. Turned back to Saltoun. 'Why, they're in the wood of course. Can't you see? It's full of the French. Look. Can't you see? They're everywhere. You must attack.'

The Prince was becoming agitated now. Impatient with this coolly obsequious English aristocrat. Rebecque frowned. Pursed his lips, embarrassed by his commander's outburst before two senior officers of the British army's élite. Men whom he knew must be veterans of the Peninsula. The Prince continued.

'Colonel, I order you to move your men into that wood at once. If you will not undertake it, then I shall find someone who will.'

It was too much for Saltoun. A slur on the brigade. Macdonell too felt the injury. Bristled with anger at this disagreeable young man, whom political necessity had dictated should be their corps commander.

After a short pause, Saltoun spoke. 'Very well, your Highness. As you order. We shall attack the wood.' He turned to Macdonell. 'Colonel Macdonell. Would you oblige me by returning to your command and following us into the wood. My own light companies will lead the way, followed by Colonel Askew with the battalion companies of the First Guards. May I suggest, Colonel Macdonell, that you skirt the edge of the wood and take the French in the flank, at its far end?'

Macdonell nodded. Amused at this new formality, adopted for the benefit of the royal presence, he matched it. 'Indeed, my Lord. That would seem to be a prudent decision.'

Saltoun turned back to the Prince. Extended his arm in an extravagant gesture which might, by an older man, have been interpreted as sarcasm. 'I trust that will suffice, your Highness.'

Orange, either unaware of the amusement he had caused, or choosing to ignore it and evidently satisfied that his orders were being obeyed, merely smiled. Then, without another word, he turned his horse and took his staff off, back down the road to Quatre-Bras.

Saltoun stiffened. 'A sprat, James. We've nothing more than a sprat to command 30,000 men, and among them the finest infantry in all the world. A puppy to give us orders. "Attack the wood at once." Oh, how I do not envy the Peer. Give me a company. A battalion, even. But an army, with Orange as my deputy? Oh no. Not for all the world.'

Leaving Saltoun, still cursing, to organize the invasion of the wood, Macdonell rode back down the marching column until he found Wyndham, riding with Robert Moore at the head of the Coldstream light company. He smiled at them. Turned to the ranks. 'Colour Sar'nt Biddle'.

'Sir?'

Macdonell pointed towards the trees of the Bois de Bossu. 'We are ordered to attack that wood. We will move along its northern edge, to the flank and rear of Lord Saltoun's light companies, who will assault it directly. The men have time to check their flints and untie ten rounds. Captain Moore, have the company officers assemble on me.'

Turning his horse, Macdonell rode off the road into the fringes of the wood. The two companies followed, in extended order. A distance of at least a yard between each man. His company commanders and their subordinates rode up. Charles Dashwood of the Scots Guards with George Evelyn and young Standen behind them, Wyndham, Moore and Gooch. He nodded a greeting.

'A few words now for the men, before we go, I think, gentlemen. Do you not?'

Macdonell turned back towards the assembled rank and file of the light companies, drawn up now, at their sergeants' orders. He felt it important that he make some sort of gesture as he prepared to lead his combined command for the first time into battle.

'Now, my lads. You can see what we have to do. Never forget that the eyes of your country are upon you. Be steady. Be cool and be firm in your action. This wood must be ours this day. The battle depends upon it and Lord Wellington knows that he can depend on us. Many of you know me. Have served with me before. Many of you, however, do not. I must ask you to trust me. And you may surely trust in one thing, my boys. You are his Majesty's Foot Guards. You hold the right of the line. And by the end of this day you will hold the wood. Now, let's be at them.'

A great, ragged cheer went up, followed by a few scattered shouts of 'huzzah'. And then they were about their business.

This was what the light companies knew best. This was why they were here, in the vanguard of the regiment. Here in this wood. It was one of the few good things to have come out of the American war. The creation of just such units of light infantry, trained to fight in conditions precisely like this. In America they had learned how to beat the rebel woodsmen at their own game, and for the last ten years, in the same way, they had beaten the French. Macdonell realized of course that there would always be a place on the battlefield for the devastating firepower that only a mass volley from a densely packed block of troops could bring – that after all was what won battles. Nevertheless he could not help but wonder whether one day this would not be the way that all fighting was done. With soldiers treated as independently motivated individuals. Every man a skirmisher. Sir John Moore had understood how that might work. Had questioned Dundas's ludicrously rigid rule book, by which Britain's infantry were to move by eighteen manoeuvres alone. Moore had looked at the lessons of the American wars and drawn up his own system for the training of light troops. His teachings were embodied in a treasured pocket-sized volume of hand-written notes that Macdonell reckoned his most valuable possession. Quicksilver remarks made by the much-mourned general and painstakingly recorded by the young Macdonell while training under Moore with the 78th at Shorncliffe in 1804. These past ten years it had been his daily reading. His bible and his prayer-book.

Since then, the Guards had led the way with a light company, and every battalion in the British army had followed. Hand-picked men from every regiment, chosen for their athletic ability and their marksmanship. But also for their self-sufficiency. And then there were the light regiments themselves. And the rifles. He respected too the way that in all the light units discipline was maintained less by the lash, which ruled throughout the army, than by respect, duty and pride. Although in the Guards, of course, as much was already understood.

He observed the men with pride now, operating as true light infantry. Making use of cover. Working in pairs. The one giving covering fire while the other advanced. Macdonell called to a familiar figure who was pressing forward on foot just ahead of him. James Graham.

'Corporal. Stay close to me.'

He would need his own covering man. He looked to his left and saw that Gooch too was pressing on, covered by Miller. Slowly, the two companies worked their way, inch by nervous inch, along the edge of the long wood. At first, as they moved forward, they did not encounter much evidence of the enemy. Working his horse through the scrub, among the smoke and heat, Macdonell was surprised by the smell of freshly damp leaves. It triggered thoughts of similar summer days in Glengarry. Of precious moments, with a fowling piece in his hands, Alasdair Macdonald, the young ghillie, at his shoulder, treading gently through the undergrowth in search of pigeon, snipe, teal and mallard. Remembered too the swarming midges. For a moment he saw himself standing at dusk, before the peat fire of his bedroom in the castle, scratching at the great red insect bites on his legs and arms. Tried to remember too the pleasant after-dinner fug, down in the lodge among the keepers, savouring the pale amber of their local whisky – a drink eschewed by his brother at the castle's dining table. He recalled the sound of flocking geese as they flew across the

113

lowering sun. But the image merely jerked him back to reality. For there was no birdsong here. The wood was entirely empty of wildlife. Already seasoned by death. Men had been fighting in this place all day.

His horse shied over a body. Looking down he saw a Belgian officer. A young man, his head very nearly severed from his body; a gaping, ragged hole in place of his neck. A shell burst, he presumed. As if in answer he heard the splintering of wood from up ahead, where Saltoun's men now led the way, and the anguished cries of the first English wounded. A French battery on the rising ground above the wood had observed the Guards' advance and timed its fire with cruel accuracy. As the Guards moved forward, the shelling became heavier. Macdonell recognized at once the staccato mutter and fizz of the spinning six-inch iron balls as they flew high above his head. Within seconds the wood was a storm of flying timber, as the bursting shells sheared great splinters off the trees. Still advancing, Macdonell's men began to encounter Saltoun's dead and wounded. Injured guardsmen came staggering out from the trees to their left, supporting each other, some cheering their comrades on. Coolly objective in the unreality of action, Macdonell noticed that many of the casualties seemed to have been caused not by the pieces of shell, but by shards of wood, splintered from the trees, some of them as sharp and as long as sword blades, many still embedded like stakes in their unlucky recipients.

There was more firing now, to his left, musket shots, as the First Guards' battalion companies and grenadiers began to close with the French.

An ashen-faced young captain of one of the light companies of the First, Ellis, rode out from the depths of the wood. Careered towards Macdonell.

'Sir, have you seen the Prince? For God's sake, sir, do send a runner. I beseech you. Find the Prince and tell him to order Colonel Askew to cease his fire at once. He is firing directly to his front. But not on the French. He is firing into his own men. On us.' And with that he was gone. Back into the darkness.

Macdonell acted at once. Had Biddle find a messenger. But not to the Prince, that would have no effect. He'd send the runner directly to the colonel of the First Guards.

Ahead of him, the Coldstream light company had now moved properly into the wood. From necessity, as the brush became thicker, the men were forced out on to one of the many cleared rides, cut through the wood in more peaceful times, for the pursuit of game. Even on this long summer evening the light was poor this deep in the wood and, whatever the Prince had said, it was not easy to see their enemy. Macdonell wished, as he often did, that his men had the advantage of the rifle regiments, uniformed in dark green rather than their gaudy scarlet and white. They were sitting targets for the French tirailleurs, whose own dark blue made them far less distinct against the foliage. Of course both sides were armed with muskets, notoriously inaccurate at more than eighty yards. But in sufficient numbers, even in skirmish order, their fire was still lethal. If they could close with them, though, take the bayonet to them, then Macdonell knew the Guards would sweep the French from the wood. They could see them now. Through the trees. Masses of blue, discernible by their only clear feature, the absurdly tall wagging shako plumes of yellow and red. He could see them darting about. Dropping to take cover in the ditches, or behind rocks and bushes. He heard the crack as their muskets spat flame into the darkness. The swoosh of the musket balls scudding past his face. He caught Graham's voice swearing, frustrated by the lack of vision. The corporal was close beside him now.

'Wouldn't you say so, sir, that this is a terrible place? I was just saying to my brother. God, but you can't get a clear view of the beggars.'

'Quite so, Graham. But you can certainly hear them.'

With his words a flurry of musket fire tore at the already

ragged leaves on a tree above his head. Graham ducked as the balls smashed into the trunk. And as both sides now exchanged fire, the white smoke from the muskets decreased the visbility even further. It was like fighting in a dense fog, crowded with unseen obstacles. Hard to tell the men from the trees. The officers of course were easier to spot. And they began to pay the price.

Foolish, thought Macdonell, to remain up here on his horse. But it was his duty. To lead. To inspire the men with his coolness. The smoke had made it unclear as to just how far ahead of them the French were.

And now, as the two sides realized their closeness, the fight became a game of man against man. Suddenly, from out of the smoke a swarthy, mustachioed tirailleur appeared before Macdonell, in the act of reloading his musket. Macdonell raised his sword. Brought it whistling down, through the shako and into the head. The man fell, clutching at his cleft face. Screaming, gurgling through an agony of blood. A moment later, over to his right, Macdonell saw Graham run his bayonet clean through another Frenchman, who grasped in vain at the barrel. The Irishman punched him away. Withdrew the bloody blade, moved on, workmanlike as ever. Still the shots rang out. Musket balls flew around his head as the French demonstrated their reluctance to give an inch of this hard-won ground.

At least the cannon had stopped now and Macdonell's horse was more sure footed. Its fear of bodies now gone, it advanced steadily over the lumpen shapes in blue and red uniforms, lying together in oblivion. Among them he noticed one of his own men. Tried to recall his name. Stevens? One of the new intake. Lincolnshire lad. Poacher, he thought. Dead poacher now. Hole through the throat, crusted with dried blood.

The wounded were still moving past him. Walking and crawling. But the further he pushed into the wood he was encouraged by the growing numbers of French dead. Mounds of dark blue. Crumpled heaps of men. There was no doubt. Little by little they were pushing them out. Clearing the wood. Must be almost an hour since they had started. For a moment the smoke cleared and he thought that, perhaps 200 yards up ahead, he could see more light. The far edge of the wood.

Still around him came the crunch and splinter of timber and leaves, as musket balls crashed into the trees. And the less frequent, duller thud as they hit a human target. There was cheering from the front now. The First Guards must have reached their objective. Or at least had pushed home a bayonet charge. Still he could see nothing. Below him a Frenchman suddenly thrust up with a bayonet. It missed him, and his horse, embedded itself in a saddle bag. As the tirailleur struggled to release his musket, Macdonell raised his sword, but before he could bring it down the man fell. Shot through the heart. He looked around. Saw Graham. The barrel of his musket smoking. A great grin across his face. Macdonell touched the peak of his shako in thanks and turned back into the mêlée.

A red-coated soldier came running towards him, jumping over boulders and scrub. A lieutenant of the First Guards. Bloody face. Broken sword. White breeches spattered with gore. Couldn't place him.

'Colonel Macdonell, sir. Lord Saltoun's compliments and we have taken the far end of the wood. He asks you, sir, if you would be so good as to direct your men in a movement towards the left.'

'Consider it done, Lieutenant.' Macdonell wheeled in the saddle. Found Robert Moore: 'Captain Moore, I would be much obliged were you to find Colonel Dashwood and ask him to move his company over there.' He pointed. 'Towards the far edge of the wood. I want to sweep this area clean of the enemy. You understand? Wyndham, take Colour Sar'nt Biddle and half the company and cover the track to our right. I intend to take the centre.'

'Very good, sir.'

Ducking now to avoid the low branches as he walked his horse deeper into the wood, Macdonell found his face level for a moment with its mane. Caught the distinctive smell. Horse sweat, powder smoke. Death. As the smoke cleared, the full fury of the engagement became apparent. The floor of the wood was carpeted with spent musket balls, jagged pieces of shell, shakos – French and British – discarded and shattered muskets. And with them the bodies of the dead and dying. He passed a tirailleur, barely alive, sitting on a tree stump, clutching his stomach. He had been bayoneted just above the diaphragm. Blood covered his blue coat and vest. Trickled from his mouth. He looked up at the passing English officer, for an instant caught his eye and then slowly looked away, off into the distance, waiting for release.

Then, without warning, the shooting became less intense. The last French just melted away. A few turned to give covering fire. He glimpsed the falling, scarlet form of one unlucky guardsman, caught in the closing rounds. And then he was there. At the edge of the wood. Looking out on to a scene of utter devastation. The ugly remains of a day's battle.

Under a pall of dirty grey smoke, the bodies of the dead, the dying and the wounded covered the field. Maybe as many as 2,000, thought Macdonell. All nationalities. All uniforms. And with them the larger, more motionless forms of dead horses. And parts of horses. And those not yet dead. Some of the beasts were lying on their backs, rolling in agony. Others knelt on stumps of forelegs, whinnying pitifully. Through the carnage, badly wounded men slowly dragged their broken bodies to whichever side seemed to offer most safety. And beyond the bloody mess he could see the two lines facing each other. The red, green, blue and black of the Allies and, opposite, the dark blue of the French. Colours still waving over their heads. Officers riding up and down both lines. Yelling encouragement. Sergeants barking orders. Keeping formation.

Looking over to his right, Macdonell saw that Saltoun had advanced the First Guards up a small hill beyond the wood, to a farm complex. They seemed to have taken the buildings. But then he saw the red and grey figures running back down the hill, and behind them more English guardsmen, in orderly ranks now, but still clearly withdrawing. And then he saw why. Over the crest of the hill came a body of cuirassiers. He could not guess how many. The First Guards were making for the cover of the wood. He reckoned they would manage it. Sure enough, just moments before the cavalry hit, the last redcoats found cover. The front ranks of the cuirassiers, unable to curb their momentum, went crashing into the hedge of bayonets among the trees. A small group of the French, however, seemed adamant in their pursuit of two mounted figures, officers who had yet to make the safety of the wood.

Macdonell recognized one as Saltoun, the other as young Hay, another Scot, the son of the Earl of Errol and General Maitland's personal aide. Not quite eighteen, he was considered, by common agreement of his peers, the handsomest soldier in the army. He was also thankfully, thought Macdonell, given his present predicament, an expert horseman. Only three days before Hay had won a steeplechase at Grammont on this very same horse, if he was not mistaken. Miss Muzzy, he'd christened her. A fine-looking grey mare. George Bowles had lost a sovereign in a wager. Mackinnon, as was his way, had made twice that sum.

Macdonell watched, fascinated, as this new, spontaneous horse-race unfolded. Saw Saltoun make the wood. Jump the short hedge that marked its western limits and land safe among his men. He looked back to the chase. Grinning hugely, Hay was now clearly enjoying his moment of celebrity every bit as much as any field day out with the hounds. The men were cheering him on now. Urging him with laughter towards the safety of the wood. The little thoroughbred, part Arabian by the look of her, was easily outpacing the lumbering black chargers of the three remaining cuirassiers who came on behind him. The Frenchmen hadn't a chance.

Hay rode straight at the hedge, with a jockey's eye, and set his horse to jump. And then. Unthinkable. She pulled up. Stopped dead before the short, dense wall of gorse and elder. Turning her to try again, Hay, no longer laughing now, seemed just for an instant to sit straight up in the saddle. His eyes shone with surprise. Then with terror. The shot, from a cuirassier's carbine, had caught him square in the chest. His horse began to run, shaken into panic. And then, with the flopping-headed, grotesquely supported body of the young ensign stone dead in the saddle, still clinging to the reins, she leapt the end of the hedge and crashed solidly, bloodily, into the astonished Saltoun. In an instant, the sudden silence which had descended on the battalion was broken as another shot rang out from the ranks of the light companies and the cuirassier too fell dead to the ground. Two corporals ran to disentangle the dead boy from their shaken commanding officer.

Macdonell sat motionless. Took off his shako and mopped his dripping brow. Ran his hand across his face and through his hair. Rubbed at his eyes. 'Why?', he wondered. What cruel God had sentenced young Hay to this ridiculously unlucky death, in his first action? For all the killing Macdonell had seen, this surely came closest to a real tragedy. A truly senseless loss.

The moment soon passed. Never ask why, he reminded himself. Never in battle. The only answer to that question lay in madness. For there was no answer. If you were going to die that day there was nothing you could do about it. Except fight.

Macdonell replaced his hat, reined his horse round and shouted back into the wood. 'Colour Sar'nt Biddle?'

He took out his pocket watch. It was nearing eight-thirty, but the sun had not yet set. And there was still much for them to do before the day was out. Biddle was with him.

'Colour Sar'nt. Stand the men easy. Five minutes' rest. And

120

take a roll-call, if you will. Have you any notion of our losses?'

'Hard to say, sir. It was that dark in there. And those Frenchies don't like to give you a moment to look. Mind, sir, I did see Beckey hit. Tarrant too, I think. We'll go back in for the wounded, sir.'

'I saw a few go down. That new lad. Stevens.' He paused. Collected himself. 'Well, let's get on with it, Colour Sar'nt. Can't delay.'

'I'm sorry, sir. About the young Lord. Bloody waste, if you don't mind my saying so, sir.'

'Just so, Colour Sar'nt. Although I do seem to recall you once telling me that there was no such thing as waste in war. Only winners and losers.'

Biddle laughed. Nodded. 'I'll see to the men, sir.'

'Four minutes, Colour Sar'nt. No more. Or I dare say that his good Highness, the Prince of Orange, will be wondering where the deuce we've all got to.'

DAY THREE

Saturday
17 June 1815

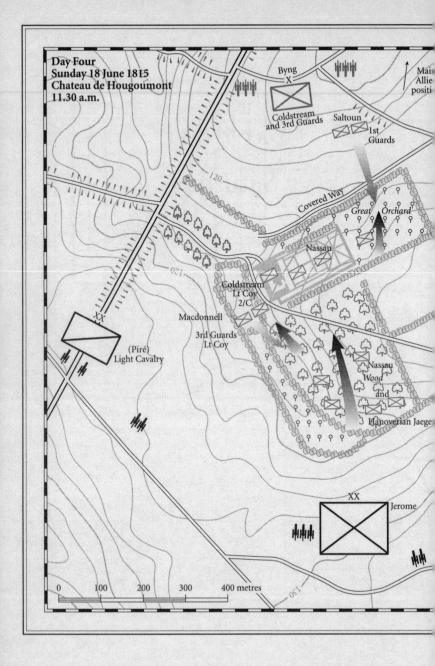

Day Four
Sunday 18 June 1815
Chateau de Hougoumont
11.30 a.m.

Byng
X
Coldstream
and 3rd Guards

Saltoun
1st
Guards

Main
Allied
positi

120

Covered Way

Great Orchard

Nassau

130

Coldstream
Lt Coy
2/C

Macdonnell

3rd Guards
Lt Coy

XX
(Piré)
Light Cavalry

Nassau
Wood
and

Hanoverian Jaeger

XX
Jerome

0   100   200   300   400 metres

130

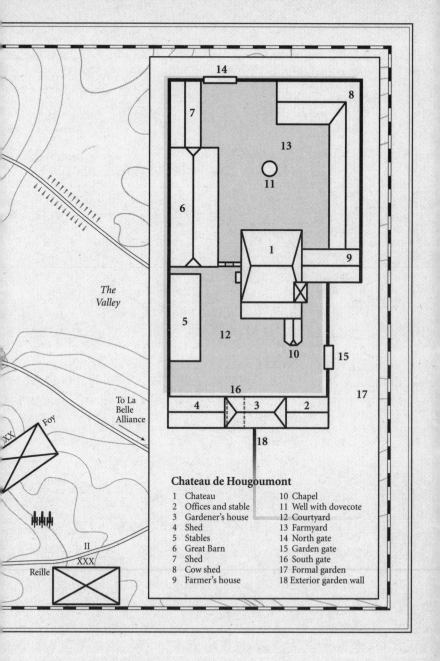

Chateau de Hougoumont

1 Chateau
2 Offices and stable
3 Gardener's house
4 Shed
5 Stables
6 Great Barn
7 Shed
8 Cow shed
9 Farmer's house
10 Chapel
11 Well with dovecote
12 Courtyard
13 Farmyard
14 North gate
15 Garden gate
16 South gate
17 Formal garden
18 Exterior garden wall

The Valley

To La
Belle
Alliance

Foy

XX

II

XXX

Reille

TWELVE

Quatre-Bras, 10 a.m.
De Lancey

Dawn had come up fast, casting its raw, unforgiving light over the bloody field. On the high ground, behind the angle of Quatre-Bras farm, De Lancey sat astride his horse and rubbed a hand wearily over his forehead and eyes. He had spent a restless, uncomfortable night, billeted with Wellington and the majority of the staff in a squalid little red-brick inn, the Roi d'Espagne, at the village of Genappe, two miles to the north. Fully awake by five and anxious to know both the full extent of the carnage and the state of the troops, he had risen quickly and ridden in Wellington's wake to the site of yesterday's action. Now, positioned at the centre of the Allied line, he put his spy-glass to his eye and looked down the road into the shallow valley beyond the crossroads.

There on the left lay the farm of Gemioncourt, focus of the bitterest of the fighting. The landscape around it had changed in the twenty-four hours since he and Wellington had first stood here. There were curious new features. Small hillocks and mounds of blue, green and red. Shapes which had once been men. Occasionally one of them moved. For the wounded were still lying there, mingled with the dead. Among them he discerned the bent-over forms of a few peasants. Looters who, despite the continued presence of the two armies, felt it worth the risk to walk the field with the slow pace of avarice, stripping, tugging and cutting their precious booty from those who no longer had need of it. From time to time a single pistol shot sounded another death knell for any wounded wretch foolish enough not to give up his earthly possessions without a struggle. De Lancey watched as, closer to the Allied lines, blue-clad Horse Guards, the provost's men, manoeuvred their mounts carefully among the barely alive and the corpses, intent on preventing such heathen practices. Watched as they drew their pistols to pronounce a cool summary execution on any looter unfortunate enough to cross their path.

De Lancey moved his glass slowly along the length of the Allied line. The positions of the forward units remained precisely as he had ordered them in the new day's orders, written out the previous evening in the inn at Genappe. The troops were to stand their ground and place picquets to their front. The Nassauers and Brunswickers he had kept in the far wood. The Guards he had ordered to bivouac to the north of the crossroads, but they were to leave their light companies at the very front of the position, as a rearguard. Having done with the orders, he had written a short letter to Magdalene and despatched it to Antwerp. A simple note to ease her mind. He was well – unhurt. They had given the French a licking, but would fight another, greater battle very soon. She should not worry on his account. He was constantly by the Peer's side. Victory, he assured her, would soon be theirs.

But De Lancey knew in his heart that this was very far from the truth.

Even before he had been dressed, Wellington had sent Alexander Gordon galloping off to find Blücher at Sombreffe. Gordon had found nothing but the French. Eventually, though, he had stumbled across General Ziethen at Tilly at the head of a rearguard, desperately organizing picquets to warn him of the approach of the French.

It had been an hour since Gordon had returned with his

findings. The Prussians had been soundly beaten. There were distressing details. Poor Henry Hardinge, their liaison officer, a genial guardsman, had been maimed. His hand, crushed by a stone thrown up by a roundshot, had been amputated on the field. The whole affair had been desperately bloody. The French too had suffered. But Napoleon's army remained intact and a very real threat.

Now the main body would rejoin the wing he had left at the crossroads. Then they would see a battle. And so the Prussian army, what was left of it, was falling back on Wavre. In truth De Lancey had not known where it was before looking at a map. And once he had found it, the dispiriting news of its distance from their position filled the assembled officers with a terrible gloom. No one spoke. Wellington had grasped the table. At length the oppressive atmosphere had forced De Lancey out into the morning light, to horse and to his present position. His present inaction.

Blücher was retreating. With immediate Prussian help that morning, he thought, the Peer might yet have moved on to the offensive. Now, though, there was no alternative but for the British and their allies to pull back. If they remained here they would be dangerously exposed. Encircled. That, he realized, had ever been Bonaparte's intention.

Yesterday's engagement had been precisely the confusing and unplanned affair he had feared. Not least because he had witnessed its opening. This morning Wellington had concluded that a mere despatch to Blücher would not do. Had deemed it necessary to discuss the situation face to face. And so, shortly after eleven o'clock, they had set off for Sombreffe. De Lancey, Wellington, Somerset, Dörnberg and much of the staff, accompanied by a half-troop of life guards. *En route* the Peer had acquainted him with the need to agree on a course of action. The need for Blücher and himself to have absolute confidence in one another. But his words served only to amplify De Lancey's concerns over what he knew had been his ridiculously over-optimistic predictions of the army's estimated time of arrival at the crossroads. By the time they reached the Prussian picquets, De Lancey was consumed with worry. More than ever convinced that he had made a catastrophic blunder.

Moreover, their journey had taken very nearly two hours.

Passing with remarkable ease through the Prussian lines, they had found the General Staff established below a windmill, overlooking the field of battle. Hardinge had led them to the brow of the hill, where Blücher stood looking out across the two armies on the plain below. After a brief greeting they had climbed the mill steps and there, across a map laid on the old grinding stone, for almost an hour the two generals had spoken, interrupted from time to time by their staff. Bizarrely, they had conversed in French, for neither spoke the other's language. There had been demands from the Prussians. In particular from Count von Gneisenau, whom De Lancey knew did not trust the British. Might there be, Gneisenau suggested in his irritating, half-mocking way, perhaps a division available to aid the Prussians? To De Lancey's great relief Wellington had said nothing. But then. Just as they were leaving. Calamity.

The Peer had turned to Blücher and with smiling sincerity had assured him that by two o'clock he would have sufficient forces to be able to attack. De Lancey winced. He knew it to be impossible. The British and their allies were strung out from Nivelles to Quatre-Bras.

Naturally, given that assurance, the old man had decided to stand and fight. Wellington's parting words came back to him now with an awful clarity: 'At four o'clock I shall be here.'

De Lancey knew in truth that this could not, would not, be done. That Wellington's promise to reinforce the Prussians had been founded on his own misplaced optimism. On his own well-intended deceit. He had in effect forced the Peer to break his word.

The thought sat heavy on his conscience as he looked out again across the field of Quatre-Bras, taking in the pathetic rise and fall of the wounded. The piles of dead. What, he wondered, had his part been in the death that lay before him upon this field and across at Ligny? It was being said that the Prussians had lost 15,000 killed. How sensible a decision had it really been to stand and fight when the Allied army was in reality, as only he knew, hopelessly spread out across the Belgian countryside?

By the time they had returned from Blücher it had been half an hour after three. They had heard the battle long before they saw it. Almost as soon as leaving Sombreffe. Had ridden into the very heart of a savage cavalry action. Extricating himself from this immediate danger, Wellington had realized almost at once that he had not a hope of keeping his promise. That less than half of his army was yet assembled, and not one full brigade of cavalry. The reports had confirmed their peril. The first attacks had come in at two o'clock. The Prince of Orange (God help them) had assumed command. Unsurprisingly, the French had propelled the Belgians from their advanced positions. Shortly before their arrival, however, Picton's men had begun to appear from the north. Quickly, together with the Hanoverians, the 32nd and the First and three battalions of Highlanders had formed a sound front line. But bad news came in equal measure. The road from Nivelles was blocked with baggage. The 3rd division would not be there for another hour at the least. The Brunswickers had been badly cut up and were now leaderless, their commander-in-chief, the Duke of Brunswick, having been mortally wounded by a musket ball through the stomach. The 69th, to their shame, had lost the King's colour.

By the end of the day the Allies had taken 5,000 casualties. The French, he was informed, a little fewer. While the Belgian light dragoons had done deadly work on the Crapauds, at any one moment there had been barely 2,000 Allied sabres on the field. By the time the battle had ended, further slaughter made impossible by the failing light, barely a third of the Allied army was anywhere in the vicinity of the field. Not once had they had sufficient men to stage anything like a full counter-attack. At last, towards seven o'clock, the Guards, arriving from Nivelles, had taken the woods.

Whatever account he had sent to Magdalene, this was no victory. Oh, they had held the French. But by their inaction and lack of troops they had also allowed Blücher to suffer horribly. De Lancey knew that they would never be forgiven that broken promise. He had heard already that Gneisenau was actually suggesting that the Prussians abandon the British and head east. Fortunately Blücher seemed to have prevailed. And so it was that now they too would have to pull back. It was not a retreat but a tactical withdrawal. All around him the army was beginning to retire, as the Duke had indicated, back along the same road down which it had so lately come. Company by company. Troop by troop. But now there were no skirling pipes, no fifes and drums, no bugles or flags. Just an exhausted river of humanity. Muttering, joking, groaning. Wondering where on earth in this godforsaken country old Nosey now had a mind to take them.

De Lancey knew.

Wellington was familiar with this ground. Had ridden it only last year, taking along with him a colonel of engineers, one James Carmichael Smyth. It was Smyth's map that De Lancey now carried in his valise. It had arrived yesterday, at the height of the battle, being momentarily misplaced when the messenger's horse had gone missing in a vegetable field. It had soon been recovered and Wellington had presented it to him shortly after the early-morning briefing. Before doing so the Peer had marked on it a line. It defined a ridge some ten miles to the north. A ridge punctuated by walled farms and bordered on both left and right by forest and rough ground. It was, as anyone could see, the perfect defensive position. The ridge straddled two roads whose junction formed a letter 'A' with, at its apex, the hamlet of Mont St Jean. Before it lay three farms, a château and a small cluster of houses at a crossroads with the ironic name of La Belle Alliance. For he was aware that by that evening they would be more than seven miles from their Prussian allies. Seven miles of the most difficult terrain the country had to offer. Yet here it was, seven miles from Wavre, that the Peer intended to stand. Here, to Mont St Jean, that Blücher must bring the vital reinforcements. And it was to Mont St Jean that De Lancey knew he should already be making his way this morning. With him would go his staff, each of them charged with carefully guiding into its pre-allocated position every brigade of the army, directly as it arrived from the march.

There was but one provision. If Blücher was unable to provide them with even a single corps in support, then Wellington had stated that he was prepared to abandon this new position. If Blücher did not come across, they would sacrifice Brussels to the French.

De Lancey looked to his right. A few paces away, his officers had now stopped talking among themselves and begun to look towards him; patting their restless mounts as, sensing the feelings of their riders, the horses showed their own impatience and anticipation. One moment more, he thought. Almost said it aloud. Allow me but one moment to gather my thoughts.

He closed his eyeglass and returned it to the leather holster on his saddle. But he continued to stare out across the ghastly field, and suddenly felt quite alone. A universe away from any sense of belonging. Away from anywhere he could call 'home'. Away from the army. Away from the pretty house in Brussels. From Dunglass and from Edinburgh. Away from his childhood homes in Yorkshire and London. He was overcome by a sudden craving for that security. By a yearning to visit his mother once again in her little house in Colchester and by a sudden pang of loss for his dear, sweet father, dead these past seventeen years. And it occurred to him now how fast his own life had gone. Seemed hardly a moment since he had left Harrow for the light dragoons. For Holland, Madras, Calcutta, where he had first encountered Wellington. June 1797. A supper party thrown by Will Hickey to honour the King's birthday. He recalled the imposing presence of this man not eight years his senior and yet so impressively confident. Lieutenant-Colonel Arthur Wellesley, commanding officer, 33rd Foot. And so, by fate, their careers had marched hand in hand. Through Portugal and Spain they had soldiered together. Friends, though never equals. Through six bitter years of campaigning. Through the hell of Talavera, Bussaco, Fuentes, Badajoz and Salamanca, they had pushed the French back beyond their borders. And as his own glory had increased, so Wellington had faithfully ensured that De Lancey too received his share. At last, in the victory honours came his reward. A knighthood.

Yet now even the Peninsula, for all its memories, all its nightmares, seemed to De Lancey, as he looked with tired eyes across the bloody landscape, so distant as to be unreal. He was alone. And yet he would never be alone again. He put his hand in his pocket and grasped the little, round pebble. Felt its smooth, cold purity. As soft and cool as her pale, downy skin.

'De Lancey?'

He dropped the stone quickly, felt it fall back into his pocket. 'Your Grace?'

He had not noticed Wellington riding up. Wondered if he had seen his consternation. Wondered just how aware he was that it was he, his comrade of two decades and countless campaigns, who must bear the blame for yesterday's débâcle. For their losses. For the Prussians' defeat as they waited and suffered at Ligny for the promised British reinforcements which he had known could never arrive in time. Wondered, too, when such was the surrounding cacophany of marching feet and hooves and jangling harness that a rebuke would have gone unnoticed, whether now at length the Peer would reveal the extent of his anger. Waited for the thunder.

'De Lancey.' Wellington spoke with a calm, soft voice. 'Surely, you are late? Why do you delay? It will not do for you to arrive in the rear of the army. You are Quartermaster General, are you not? It is to you that the army looks for its direction. Its dispositions. You have the map?'

'Sir.'

'Well then, be off man. Outride the army. You and I have no time to ponder such scenes as this.' Then, in a quieter voice. 'This is no time for regret, William. Make yourself of the moment. Do not lose an instant.'

And, pulling gently on Copenhagen's reins, he turned the horse and was gone as silently as he had arrived. There was no reproach. No words of accusation. No thunder, thought De Lancey. Merely this: 'No time for regret.' That and a look of such piercing, accusatory directness as he had never, in twenty years of friendship, seen in the General's eyes. He knew.

THIRTEEN

Quatre-Bras, 2.30 p.m.
Napoleon

The British had gone.

The Emperor picked savagely at the loose skin of his right index finger, digging the sharp yet carefully manicured nail of his left thumb into the soft flesh until the pain made him wince. He didn't need any spyglass to see beyond the road. Beyond the farm, to the eloquently empty fields. Beyond the hedgerows, across the road and to the left it was not hard to discern the blue coats and fur caps of the English Hussars. The rearguard. But of the rest of Wellington's army, nothing now remained here.

Save the dead. He turned from the view, frowned and stamped his foot with the frustration of a spoilt child. He slammed his right fist into the palm of his left hand. Gnawed at his lip, imagining, with rising fury, how it must have been. How, not believing his good fortune, Wellington must have moved his troops back with such care. Must have replaced each front-line battalion with another, until at length he had only a skeleton line facing the French. And then that too would have gone, melting into the landscape and away up the road to Brussels. And so, an entire army had slipped like dust through his fingers.

And no one here had done a thing. He was surrounded by

blind fools. And the greatest of them all was nowhere to be found. Where in Hell's name was Ney?

'Gourgaud. De la Bedoyere. Where is Marshal Ney? Someone find me Ney.'

That had them scurrying. They sent an aide off down the road to Frasnes.

Napoleon turned to look to his rear, to where the battlefield opened out into a little valley. Fewer corpses here than at Ligny, he thought. But the stench was equally unpleasant. He pulled the cologne-soaked handkerchief from his pocket. Pressed it to his nostrils. Inhaled. Tucked it away and tried, from the positions of the dead regiments, to piece together the progress of Ney's battle. What had happened here? Where was the evidence of victory? He sat down at the small campaign table and chair that had been set for him at the side of the road. Around him the officers of the General Staff formed a circle of quiet discussion.

He had arrived here half an hour ago. In silence, ascending the hill which carried the road from Marbais, still out of sight of the armies. Had been surprised by the lack of noise. No guns. No musketry. No clash of sabres. Over the crest he had found himself not, as he had imagined, in the midst of an attacking French army, but in a no man's land between Ney's troops to his left and on his right Allied cavalry. On closer inspection it became clear that his infantry were not marching to the fight, but sitting down to eat their lunch. It was the final act of a farcical morning whose progress was mocked by the weather. From a fine dawn it had grown overcast, with dark, almost black clouds, their hard, gunmetal edges defined against a clear sky. He felt them press down upon him, amplifying the overwhelming lethargy that had slowed his every step since waking. Lying in the little folding bed he had wondered at first whether somehow during the night he had become paralysed. For thirty minutes he had hardly been able to move. His sleep had been torture. In the darkest hours, clammy hands tearing at the bedsheets in spasms of agony, he had at length been obliged to summon Dr Larrey and his personal physician, Lameau.

It seemed that the haemorrhoids in his anus had prolapsed. Were being strangulated. Perhaps, suggested Larrey, the Emperor would not object to a little soothing ointment? Some leeches? Hot towels?

By morning, however, the pain had still not yet subsided, and only at nine had Napoleon been in a condition to board his coach for the field of battle. Although he had soon changed to a horse after the rutted road began to jolt his delicate body even more than a saddle.

It had been a relief to walk the field with Grouchy. But all the time he was plagued by indecision. Should he take the bulk of the army after Blücher and end the Prussian threat forever? But that would leave Ney with Wellington. Did he attack Wellington himself? And if so, then how many men to send with Grouchy to hold Blücher? Above all he had to know what Wellington and Blücher intended. Reports were coming in that the Prussians were making for Liège. If that were so then they seemed to be abandoning Wellington. But was it true? Surely he must know? In the old days would have known instinctively. But this morning that seemed so very long ago.

Would the Prussians turn and stand? Come to Wellington's aid? Another report of Prussian troops seen at Gembloux suggested that this too was a possibility.

At length he had decided. He would split the army. Unorthodox? Maybe. It was something he had always, always argued against. But then he had not conquered Europe by being orthodox. He would split the army. Grouchy would take Gérard and Vandamme and part of Lobau's VI Corps. Infantry, cavalry, artillery. Almost a third of his entire force. They would pursue Blücher. His army was already half beaten. They could not hope to destroy him, but could certainly prevent him from coming to Wellington's rescue. He himself would go to

Quatre-Bras and deal with Wellington there. That would be his headquarters.

Surprisingly the normally subservient Grouchy had protested. Had had the temerity to object. He had told him. Had made it perfectly clear. Ordered him to pursue the Prussians. To keep at them. Keep his sabres up their arses. But now, this.

Where in God's name was Ney? At midday, shortly before setting off for the crossroads, he had sent a simple order to the marshal. 'Attack the enemy at Quatre-Bras.' What had he been doing? Why had he not attacked? Where was he? And where was Wellington? As if in answer the group of officers around him parted and two immaculate chasseurs à cheval of the Garde Imperiale appeared, preceded by their equally flawless officer. Each of the men had a tight hold of one of the arms of a struggling young woman.

'What's this?'

'She's English, sir. We captured her on the field, attempting to rob the dead. She was with the army before they left. Says that Wellington has retreated north.'

She was disgustingly filthy, this English *vivandière*. But under that grime his seasoned eye could still discern a hint of youthful beauty. What was she? Nineteen? Twenty? Nice tits. Pretty mouth too.

Napoleon smiled at her. A momentary rush of sexual arousal held his rising temper in check.

Catching his gaze, she grimaced. He waved his hand and the chasseurs relaxed their grip.

'Ask her where. Where's he gone?'

She spoke no French and her English – a broad Tyneside accent – was almost unintelligible. But eventually they got it. He'd gone north. Towards Brussels. Some of his men she thought were headed for Nivelles. She'd heard names of villages. Genappe, Waterloo, Mont St Jean. That was all she knew. Could she go now, because she was nursing a baby and it needed its milk?

The Emperor smiled. Yes, nice tits. He waved his hand towards her captors. 'Let her go. See that she is fed and give her a few sous. Gourgaud. See to it.'

The staff closed around him again. Napoleon rose to his feet. Smashed his clenched fist down on the table. His face, which while the camp follower had been talking had remained quite blank, now a vision of rage. 'What is it? What must I do?' He growled the words from deep within. The aides and generals cowered before him. 'When I rose this morning the British were here. I ordered Ney to the attack. I myself brought the reserve here to support him. And now this harlot tells me what none of you have the guts to say. They've gone. Gone? How can they have gone? And where is Ney? Shit! Shit! Shit!' He slammed his hand down hard again making the little table jump. 'Why am I surrounded by idiots? I came here expecting a battle. Expecting a victory. I find nothing but idlers and fools. Find me Ney.'

Two officers left the group in search of the errant marshal. Napoleon rubbed his face hard into his hands. Ney is losing me this war, he thought. Has lost me three hours. How do I get back three hours? What magic can even I work that will turn back time? Three hours. That would be more than enough time for Wellington.

He rose and pushed through the crowd to reach the road. Over on the other side of the *chaussée* he saw that the green-jacketed 7th Hussars had recently made camp. Their commanding officer was sitting on a tree stump, eating a sausage. Napoleon shouted to him.

'Marbot. Come here.'

The man rose. Saw his Emperor. Threw away the piece of meat and, still hatless, clutching his scabbard to his side, doubled with difficulty across the rye, which had been flattened by the recent battle to a slippery carpet of matting. 'Sire?'

'Marbot. Take your regiment and find Marshal Ney. Tell

him to report at once to me here. At once. To me. At Quatre-Bras.'

'Sire.'

Leaving the colonel to goad his Hussars into action, Napoleon turned to d'Erlon. 'France has been ruined, d'Erlon. Ney may have lost France for us. Go, my dear general. Place yourself at the head of your cavalry. Ride up this road and press the English hard. Do not allow them to regroup. Give them no respite. No quarter.'

Then: 'No. Wait. I'll join you.'

He turned back to the staff. 'Gourgaud. Marchand. My horse.'

Within moments Desirée, the little grey Arabian mare, was picking her way through the corpses and the abandoned weapons. They were cuirassiers mainly here, he noticed. Men from the brother regiments of the armoured giants on black horses who now followed him up the cobbled highway from the crossroads. Shafts of sunlight began to penetrate the gloom. He quickened the pace from trot to canter. Mounting the crest of a plateau he was met by the sight, perhaps 1,000 yards away, of a troop of enemy horse artillery. Saw the guns spit flame and smoke. And in the same instant, with a thunderclap and a lightning flash, the heavens opened. The British roundshot landed far short of their target. Bounced towards the French and carried on with less force before nevertheless still finding some unfortunate victim in the rear. The rain, though, came down like canister fire. Within a few minutes the ground on both sides of the road had become a muddy quagmire. The cavalry began to slow its pace and to cluster unsteadily towards the roadside. Looking behind him Napoleon could see that the infantry had stopped altogether.

Well then. That settled any chance he might have had of surrounding the British rearguard. He could not use cavalry over fields like this. Could only pursue on the road. He looked about him. Saw men up to their knees in mud. Cannon and wagons sinking into the filth.

141

He wiped his dripping face with both hands. Allowed them to linger there. Pulled at his cheeks and rubbed his eyes. A clamour of hooves and the jingle of horse harness back along the road made him look up. Marbot. Someone had found Ney. The red-headed marshal greeted him with a friendly smile. It soon vanished. Napoleon spoke. Quietly at first.

'You ignored my order to attack. Tell me why?'

'I . . . sire. My letter. I sent you a letter not four hours ago. I have carried out your orders to the mark. I have been waiting for you, for the reinforcements, before attacking.'

The Emperor began to raise his voice. 'Attacking? Attacking what? Attacking whom? Look over there and tell me what you see. Who were you going to attack? The English have gone. Wellington has gone.'

As if to qualify his words another salvo of cannon fire came rolling in. Around them the horses shied.

'Sire. I was waiting.'

'Waiting? Waiting for me? You have been waiting for me?'

'I had the entire British army before me. What could I do?'

Napoleon stared at him. Looked away. Turned back. Quiet again. 'Excuse me. I do beg your pardon. I had assumed that you were Ney. The hero of Elchingen. The last Frenchman on Russian soil. The Bravest of the Brave. But I must be mistaken. For if you are Ney then you are not the man whom I used to know.'

He paused. Then: 'You fool, Ney. Didn't you even think to send out a patrol? Didn't you even think to try to find out what Wellington was doing?'

Ney's face was growing redder by the moment. 'I . . . I was waiting for you, sire.'

Without a word, Napoleon turned his horse. Rode away from the crimson-faced marshal. Nothing for it now but to lead them himself. Lead the pursuit from the front. As he had done in the early days.

With his bodyguard of chasseurs following close behind, he

placed himself at the head of the column. Already his grey coat was heavy with water and the familiar hat was beginning to lose its shape. It was vital now to do something to impress the men. He cantered. A mistake. Great God, the pain in his arse. Carrying on, regardless of the pain, he ground his teeth and gripped hard on the leather of the reins. At length he reached a company of horse artillery. His arrival took its commander, a young, ruddy-faced captain, completely by surprise.

'What's your name?'

'Captain Bourgeois, your Imperial Highness.'

'Well, Bourgeois, come with me. And bring your guns.'

Napoleon turned and rode faster, still in excruciating pain, just ahead of Bourgeois and the limbered guns which careered up the road behind him, past the Guard, past d'Erlon's infantry, on the heels of Jacquinot's green-coated lancers. He pulled up on the brow of another hill. In the distance, at perhaps 800 yards, he could see again quite clearly the British guns, also limbered up now and with them a sizeable body of British light cavalry. Before a valet could help him, he was off his horse and stumbling into the mud. Quickly he recovered. Straightened his coat as he walked. Found the captain, already unlimbering. 'Quite right, Bourgeois. That will do well. Unlimber here. And quickly now. I need rapid fire in the direction of that cavalry. There. Look. Range. Seven hundred and ... eighty yards. Minimum elevation. Fire as you will. Let them know we're coming, Bourgeois.'

Into the mud he went, pursued by the floundering staff. Walked up to where a corporal was busy traversing one of the cannon.

'Come on, come on, man. They're the British, can't you see? Fire at them.'

And so the Emperor moved on. Through the rain, from gun to gun. Aligning each of them himself with an expert's eye. He was back at Toulon again. Back with the guns. Young.

Grouchy would take care of the Prussians. Now, at last, he

was determined to meet this Wellington on his own terms. He knew that Blücher would not be in time to help this great British general. Knew it. Soon they would see who was master of the battlefield. Now, for just this one last time, he appealed to Dame Fortune to smile on him. Soon, he promised her. Soon there would be peace. But first, there was Wellington.

FOURTEEN

Above Hougoumont, 7 p.m.
Macdonell

Rain and mud. Nothing but rain and mud. They had come to this place late in the afternoon. An exhausted column of red-coated infantry. All day long they had covered the army's retreat. For, whatever the Peer's plans, it was as a retreat, Macdonell had no doubt, that their current situation would be reported. Even now in Paris, he supposed, freshly printed bills were being pasted on the walls, proclaiming the news of Wellington's defeat.

Macdonell ran his hand across the stubble on his chin and, as his men appeared otherwise occupied, permitted himself an indulgent scratch just below the whiskers. He would make sure that he shaved before the coming battle. There had not been a moment to do so that morning. He had been awoken by Smith as usual at 5.30. But no sooner was he half-dressed than the order had come to stand to arms. For four hours the men had stood in line while, to their front, the French did nothing. Did not even break camp. Indeed, from what Macdonell could see they had done no more than cook and eat their breakfast.

And there they had left them. Without a shot being fired in anger, Wellington's army had finally moved off at around 10 o'clock, but it had been another four hours before the tail of the huge Allied force, Macdonell's light companies among them, had finally begun to leave the bloody battlefield around the crossroads. At last they had been told to halt.

They were the final element of the brigade to arrive, here in Wellington's chosen position. But where exactly? On the right of the line, he knew, and on rising ground. Macdonell peered down at his feet. Within the thick, red-brown mud he could make out the crushed remains of a harvest of young beans, churned by the wheels, hooves and feet of the division now encamped above them on this long hill. Directly to his left, so he understood from one of his corporals, stood Peregrine Maitland's 1st Guards. The main body of the brigade was encamped behind him. Now perhaps, he thought, there would be a brief moment of respite. He stood a little distance away from his men. Alone. Close to a hedge, slightly out of earshot of a group of quietly spoken junior officers and farther still from the party of sergeants from the brigade's two light companies, who stood talking and laughing, away from the other ranks.

A few of the men had begun to make campfires and now were working in pairs, pitching their blankets as makeshift tents. This was unique to the Guards. Two ordinary regulation blankets, but each sewn with a button and loop so that they could be buttoned together and pitched on bayonets, making a reasonable field billet. The old sweats hadn't bothered. Macdonell's fellow Peninsular veterans knew the man they liked to call 'old Nosey' too well to be caught out. Had learned too many times how the Duke had an irritating habit of making you move just when you'd got settled. So they'd held off from erecting or improvising any form of shelter for the night and were sitting on their packs in the downpour; smoking, chatting, laughing. Macdonell envied them their simple, fatalistic good humour. They were here to do a job. And to do it well enough to be proud to talk of it at the end of the day. Should they be killed or maimed? That was merely an anticipated though unlonged-for possibility of their profession. They sat on the sodden ground and drank their strong tea and lit their temperamental, damp pipes. And laughed.

And all the while the water continued to run in clear streams from the peaks of their oilskin-covered shakos and clung to the tufted wool of the white-fringed epaulette wings which marked them out as men of the élite companies. One man, despite the rain, pulled from his pack a tin whistle and struck up an air. A few of the others joined in. The lyrics Macdonell could not make out, but it was a pleasant, infectious little jig. Irish, he thought. He began to tap his foot, but his reverie was soon interrupted by the arrival of a horseman.

'Colonel Macdonell, sir?'

A courier. An eager young sprat, as sparkling and shiny-new as if he had just come from parade at the Horse Guards. A vision for the ladies, in scarlet and blue, topped off with a great, lace-trimmed dragoon shako.

'Sir?'

'My Lord Wellington's compliments, sir, and he would be very much obliged if you would kindly take the light companies and move them directly down to the château? You are to occupy the buildings, sir. Colonel Saltoun will accompany you on your left, towards the orchard. With the light companies of the First Guards. You will, er . . . await further instruction. His Grace asks . . . if you please, sir?'

Macdonell smiled at the young man, noting both his embarrassed uncertainty as to how to conclude his message and his all too evident pride and excitement.

He took his gold watch from his waistcoat pocket. Flipped open the lid. It was 7 o'clock. There were, he surmised, perhaps two more hours of daylight. He turned towards the lowering sun. Spoke without looking at the aide de camp.

'Thank you . . . sir. You may inform his Grace that Colonel Macdonell will act on his word, instantly.'

As the young messenger turned his horse, Macdonell barked

in the direction of the chattering NCOs. 'Colour Sar'nt Biddle.'

A figure snapped to attention and left the now silent huddle.

'Colour Sar'nt. Have the men stand to. We are to move down to the château. What is our current strength?'

'Seventy-nine men, four officers including yourself, sir, myself and three sergeants, sir. Five corporals and the bugler, sir. Now I'm not so clear as to the state of our men from the 3rd Guards, sir, but the latest reckoning is around ninety other ranks and four officers, sir, including Colonel Dashwood.'

'Thank you, Biddle. You may move the men off.'

Well, thought Macdonell, perhaps at least for some of them this would mean that their last night on earth would be a dry one. He looked towards the château. It seemed a fine establishment. A group of some half-dozen substantial buildings, enclosed within a high red-brick wall, with a good-sized barn and what appeared to be intriguingly elaborate formal gardens. He called for his horse, mounted and began what proved a difficult 500 yards down the hill.

Those men who could do so fell into a column of threes on the road and then turned left on to the drive. No more than a dirt track, it was nonetheless still better than the sodden surrounding fields. For the rain had turned the ground to little more than mud, and the soldiers, laden with pack and musket, soon found themselves sliding down the slope. They fared barely better on the flat. Macdonell saw one man, a lad from the 3rd, boldly attempt to jump a watery ditch, only to slip backwards under the weight of his pack and fall into it up to his shoulders.

Looking back up towards the twinkling fires of the lines it was possible from here, even in the evening light, to appreciate the nature of Wellington's position. The army was encamped on a ridge, running as far as the eye could see, perhaps more than a mile and a half. A ridge. The Peer's favoured defensive position. A ridge behind which he would conceal his men and make Napoleon guess as to where and how many they might be. But Macdonell and his men were not to be upon that ridge. Nor behind its sheltering brow. They were to be here; wholly one third of a mile from aid. Macdonell had a sudden, keen sense of isolation. Pictured himself riding to an island in a sea which tomorrow would surely be an ocean of French blue. Without betraying his flush of anxiety, he turned back to the château and continued towards the gate, noticing as he passed a round pond and beyond it the defensive potential of a sunken road, perhaps thirty yards from the garden boundary, shaded by an overgrown hedge. The drive split into two here, one fork, the better maintained, curving along the side of the buildings, past a kitchen garden towards what Macdonell presumed to be the main entrance. He continued up the lesser path and passed between two heavy wooden gates fixed with massive iron hinges to stout columns of red brick, linked above by a thick wooden beam. Beyond lay a cobbled courtyard, perhaps 50 feet square, with, in the centre an attractive covered well topped with a dovecot. Before him, up a slight incline, stood the mass of the château itself, a two-storey structure constructed, like the rest of the farm, from the local red brick, but in this case clad in white limewash. Directly to his right was a huge barn of the sort used for storing grain, and adjoining that a small cowshed.

Here then was the farm.

Dismounting, Macdonell handed his horse to the ubiquitous Smith and noticed, standing to his left, a group of British cavalrymen. Light dragoons in blue, with bright buff and yellow facings. Close by, two of their officers stood in conversation. Noticing Macdonell, they stopped talking and one advanced towards him, hand on his sabre hilt.

'John Drought, sir. Lieutenant, 13th Light Dragoons.'

He had a soft, southern Irish accent. His men, perhaps a half-troop, Macdonell now saw, were positioned on foot at key points around the walls, their carbines held in readiness for any attempt by the French to rush the position.

'Welcome to Hougoumont, sir. We arrived here shortly after midday to claim the farm and I can report that to date we have received scant attention from the French. The farm, as you'll see, sir, is in two halves. Here we are in what you might call the service area, and there beyond that small gate is the smarter part. This here is the main house. The château, they call it. There's a large garden to our right, and beyond that an orchard. The front is heavily wooded. That we perceive, sir, is the direction from which the French will make their attack.'

'Thank you, Drought. We'll take over from you now. But feel at liberty to remain here as long as you wish. Your men may make their billets in the barn. They'll find the Guards pleasant enough company.'

'Thank you, sir. Indeed my orders from Major Boyse are to remain here until first light. So by your leave I will set about settling my men and the horses. I wish you a pleasant evening, sir.'

As the young cavalryman walked away, Macdonell began to assess what he had taken on. By Drought's reckoning the more formal area of the complex lay beyond a small door in a brick wall. He walked up to it, pushed it open and found himself in another yard with ahead of him an elaborate gate-house and on his left a small chapel, attached to the château itself. Instantly the reason for his being here became apparent. This was no mere farm. It was a fortress, with inner and outer defensive positions, the advantage of height in at least two vantage points, several areas in which he could establish a sweeping crossfire and even a large well that would enable him to withstand hours of siege. It was clear that Wellington had placed him here to create an impassable strongpoint which would counter any notion Napoleon might have had of turning the army's vulnerable right flank and cutting off the Allies from the sea.

And with his realization came another, more sobering thought. The awareness that it was just possible that the whole battle would hang on him and how he acquitted himself here. In this farm. Hougoumont. For the coming night and day Hougoumont would be his universe.

'Sar'nt Miller.'

'Sir.' The man appeared, at the double.

'Sar'nt Miller, post picquets along those walls and in the upper floors of the buildings. I'm going to take a look around.'

Already walking away from them, he called over his shoulder to the officers who had followed him down to the château, at the head of the ragged column.

'Dashwood, Wyndham, Evelyn, Gooch, you others, come with me.'

As they caught him up, Macdonell began to walk the position, taking in every potential strongpoint and weakness with the now instinctive eye of a man who had spent his life preparing for this moment. He walked into the space below the gatehouse and pushed hard at the closed and barred main southern gates. Firm enough, but best to be sure. Drought was right. This was where the French would try first.

'Barricade this gate. Use everything you can. Wood. Barrels. Anything.'

He turned to his second-in-command, Henry Wyndham, plucked from the sixth company. Dependable Henry. With only a year's service behind him, still a Peninsular veteran.

'Henry. Take Gooch and our light company and occupy the buildings. The château, that house beside it, the stables and the three structures along this front. In particular we shall need a constant garrison above these gates. Make sure that every window is filled at all times by at least two men. When one has fired, the other will take over, and so on. I want an unrelenting fire. Have the men enter the attics and knock holes in the roof. We must direct as much fire as possible at the enemy before he reaches the walls. And you'll need to place some men in the farmyard. Our own flank is by no means invulnerable.

'Dashwood. Your company will fortify the garden and the

immediate grounds as best you can. You might want to place some men in the kitchen garden, just outside the large barn. They'll come round that way. You won't be able to hold them, of course. Just let them know you're there. And don't worry about your left flank. Lord Saltoun will be in the orchard. Just concentrate on the garden. We can't allow them to break through there and come round in our rear. And we'll need to keep the north gate open for as long as we possibly can. It's our only supply route.'

The young officer saluted and hurried off to gather his command.

Macdonell turned to the fourth officer in the group, George Evelyn of the 3rd Guards. He was about to assign him a command when he was interrupted by the arrival of a civilian. It was a man, in early middle age, dressed somewhat bizarrely in a green formal coat, plum-coloured velvet waistcoat, high-buttoned linen trousers and clogs. Clearly a rustic. The man began to address him in rushed and garbled Walloon French. Macdonell smiled and signalled him with his hand to slow down. Gradually he began to understand. This was the gardener. Monsieur van Cutzem. Macdonell noticed now that hiding behind him was a young girl, no more than ten years old, holding on to his coat. She, he presumed, was the man's daughter. The gardener continued. At some length. The owner of the château, a Chevalier de Louville, had not lived here these past ten years. He lived now at Nivelles. His tenant, a farmer named Du Monsault, Macdonell thought he said, had left some days ago, taking with him all his possessions and the other staff. His own wife, it seemed, had also gone to safety and he too had meant to go. He had stayed behind only to lock up and to ask them to please be careful of his garden. He had tried that very afternoon to leave. To take his daughter Marie to safety. But now the roads were blocked with soldiers and carts and guns. Now it was impossible. Too late.

He stopped and shrugged. Smiled pathetically. Might he, he

152

wondered, be of any assistance? He did not care much for the French. He wasn't bad with a gun. Could shoot rabbits. One thing he begged. Could the esteemed general please instruct his men not to destroy his garden? It had taken him twenty years to create. It was his life's work.

Macdonell smiled back. Felt truly sorry for this victim of fate. Of course, he assured the gardener in halting French. His men were not vandals. But he must also understand that this was war, that things would be . . . lost. Changed forever. But, he assured the bewildered man, he would do his best.

Macdonell's courteous smile hid his displeasure at this unwelcome complication. Civilians. By the end of this fight, he thought, you will be lucky if the house is still standing, man, let alone your precious garden. Lucky too if you and your pretty daughter both are any more than corpses. Looking over the man's shoulder he summoned one of the soldiers busily barricading the gate. 'Corporal Henderson.'

The man dropped the huge barrel he had been manhandling and hurried over across the yard, his ill-fitting shoes slipping on the shiny cobbles.

'Henderson, do me the service of placing yourself with these two good people and ensuring that no harm comes to them. In the absence of the owner they are our hosts and we no more than their guests. The chapel would seem to be a good enough refuge. And Henderson, I shall hold you personally responsible should anything go amiss.'

'Sir.'

Macdonell smiled at the gardener and stretched out his arm towards the grinning corporal, happy to have been selected for this less arduous task.

'Monsieur, my corporal will take good care of you and your daughter until the present danger is past.'

That at least was one problem dealt with. He walked away from the gatehouse, back towards the entrance to the formal garden. Through a side gate, beyond an elegant balustrade, lay a perfectly laid-out parterre. Macdonell was beginning to admire it and again about to summon Evelyn when he was disturbed by the sound of gunfire. It was coming directly from his front. From the orchard. He saw puffs of white smoke. Clearly Saltoun had found the enemy. The shots were moving now, out into the wood. The French appeared to be falling back. He was unable to see a thing, but could hear muffled commands and shouts. At length he found George Evelyn.

'Evelyn. Take Standen and twenty men from Captain Wyndham's company and report to Lord Saltoun in the orchard. I presume that that commotion was the sound of his men succeeding in driving off a French reconnaissance party. If that is indeed the case take your men and form a forward picquet in the woods. Just to the west of the orchard wall. Ensure that nothing of the sort should happen again tonight.'

'Sir.'

So that was Evelyn accounted for. And Standen. Macdonell looked about him. Only Moore left of his own officers. And Elrington from the 3rd. Everywhere men were working at the walls, coats off, sergeants and corporals barking out orders. It was good to have beaten off that scouting party. Should give them the chance to work unimpeded. He doubted whether the French would try the same thing again tonight. It must be clear by now that he and his men held the château. It was too late to contest.

As if a direct rebuttal of his thoughts, a series of scattered staccato shots rang out from beyond the gate. From the gate-house someone called down. 'Cavalry. Look to your front.'

Holding his sheathed sword close to his side, Macdonell dashed across the yard and, ducking his tall head to enter, ran inside the gardener's house, curiously managing to notice in his haste the von Cutzems' half-finished plates of food still on the table. He climbed the small staircase to the upper storey and found four of his men sniping from the windows. Peered over a shoulder. There in the wood before them. Cavalry.

Green-coated chasseurs, using their free hand to take random shots with their carbines. As he looked the man standing next to him fired and dropped a French corporal from his horse.

'Well done, Kite.'

What a waste, though, he thought. Why were they using what would soon be valuable horsemen in what could now only be a fruitless attempt to seize the château? They were blindly following orders. No allowance for real initiative in the Emperor's army. That, he thought, would surely be its downfall.

More men scrambled up the stairs behind him, Gooch leading them, grinning, sword drawn. More muskets were brought to bear on the milling chasseurs. Two more fell. And another three. Four, including the officer, discernible by his gold lace, had been unhorsed and were taking cover behind a hedge which bordered the wood. Balls from their carbines struck the walls around the window embrasures; but none made it through to the Guards. The chasseurs began to look uncertain. A half dozen of them quickly decided that they at least would not meet their end in this futile and one-sided firefight. The Guards continued their sporadic fire, but the danger had passed. Descending slowly, Macdonell recovered his composure.

Walking out into the rain he resumed his tour of inspection.

'That's it, Dobinson,' he called out to a corporal from his own company. 'Like that. Have the men pile the timber up against the door. And Dobinson, once you've done that you had better get Sar'nt Miller and find those pioneers. I want fire steps along every wall.'

He would make this place impregnable. A fortress.

Passing the chapel, Macdonell reconnected with Moore and Elrington and walked back through the garden gate.

The formal garden was perhaps 200 yards in length and half as much wide. It was laid out in the classic French style with carefully trimmed calf-height hedged parterres flanking paths of gravel and in some places neatly cut turf. He gazed out across row upon row of greenery and colour, now at the height of its flowering and looking surreally beautiful, even in the rain which in the past few minutes had increased its ferocity. Thunder crashed out above their heads. Moore spoke.

'A hard night, sir.'

'Yes, Moore, but a harder day on the morrow.'

The three officers passed a group of sodden soldiers gathering wood to make a fire step, the rain running in rivulets down their now unbuttoned scarlet tunics. Recognizing Macdonell one called out, grinning: 'Just like Salamanca, sir, ain't it.'

Macdonell nodded and smiled back. There had indeed been a similarly violent thunderstorm the night before Wellington's great Spanish victory, almost exactly three years earlier. The man spoke again.

'We sent 'em running then, sir, and we'll do it again in the morning. So we will, sir.'

Through the rain he recognized Joe Graham, the sergeant's brother. County Monaghan born and just as huge a man, with the same Irish drawl. 'That we will, Graham. If I know you and your brother.'

He hoped to God that he would be proved right. The men would have to work through the night to get it done. Wellington would need to find them help.

'Moore. Find your horse and take yourself off to his Grace. Find an officer on the staff and ask if we might borrow some pioneers from elsewhere in the line. It is of the utmost urgency.'

How curious, he mused, to be strolling in such circumstances through this place of tranquillity. He imagined the garden as it might have been in happier times. Saw the owner and his guests taking the air after dinner. They must have walked a similar path. Must have remarked on the beauty of this flower or that. Laughed perhaps at the wit of a fellow guest.

The officers stopped together in the centre of the garden,

beside an elaborate ornamental fountain. Macdonell saw that the south and east sides were enclosed by a 6-foot-high brick wall and the rear by a stout hedge. Instinct and necessity brought him back to the present.

'Fire steps all along this wall, gentlemen, if you please. And be sure to knock loopholes in it. Every five paces will do nicely. At a height of three feet. And knock down those buttresses. You can use the stones elsewhere. Do not stop until the job is done. I shall return presently.'

At the far side of the garden they found the orchard, filled with the scarlet-clad troops of Saltoun's two light companies and what looked like a detachment of Dutch pioneers, clad in green and black. Huge men with white aprons slung over their tunics. Of the young colonel himself there was no sign. As they watched one of the soldiers reached up to pluck a cherry from a laden bough.

'That man.' Macdonell barked out the command. The cherry-picker dropped his hand. 'I don't know who you are, sir, but I would ask you to remember that this is not our property. We are accountable to its owners. His Grace is most specific on the matter and I will personally have any man shot whom is seen taking so much as a single cherry or apple from any of these trees. Is that clear?'

The men nodded. A sergeant shouted a command and whispered an oath and they returned to their duties. The cherries would wait.

By the time that he returned to the courtyard, Macdonell's boots were heavy with mud. He tried in vain to shake it off, stamping them on the cobbles behind the little chapel, and then walked through the driving rain round to the side entrance of the main house. He found Smith leaving the great barn, where with his customary ingenuity he had managed to find a stall and some straw for the colonel's horse. Macdonell gestured towards the château.

'I intend to see if I can find myself a dry billet in the house.

Inform anyone who wants me, Smith, that I shall be in the château. For precisely . . .' he took out his pocket watch, 'one hour.'

Stamping his boots again, Macdonell pushed at the door to the mansion and slowly it swung open. There was no light save that of the pale moon shining through the ground-floor windows. He was quickly aware, though, of the overpowering smell of damp and stale air. The smell of abandonment which carried with it memories of other times. A lingering odour of wax polish, candle-grease and long-dead cooking fires.

Feeling his way in the dark, Macdonell found a candle in a brass nightstick on a shelf. He struck the tinder box that lay alongside it and, as the interior sprang up before him in flickering shadow, was for a moment taken back to another darkened house. To Spain three years before and to another pair of civilians who had been even less fortunate than the gardener and his little daughter. To the stripped, mutilated and grotesquely animated bodies of a butchered Spanish peasant and his wife which so often haunted his waking thoughts as they did his dreams and which were here with him again as he walked through the half-light across the marble entrance hall of the empty château.

He tried in vain to suppress the image. Damn the war. Damn Bonaparte and all the French.

After a few paces he reached the foot of a sweeping stone staircase and began to climb. Lifting the candle higher he noticed on the walls the imprint of paler areas where paintings had clearly been removed by the chevalier or his tenant for safekeeping. Judging from the number of blanks it had been quite a collection. Close to the top of the staircase a particularly large space marked the absence of a full-length portrait. At last his mind moved to other things. To another country house, where his own portrait occupied precisely the same position. He had a particular fondness for the painting.

Recalled the hours of standing in the artist's studio. A freezing Edinburgh winter and Mr Raeburn's keen-eyed insistence on his holding the exact same pose. One hand on his belt, the other on his sword, eyes staring just so. How cleverly, though, the man had captured the youthful confidence of the hero of Maida. His younger self. And how well more recently the same artist, now so highly acclaimed, had caught his brother's likeness in that painting which now hung alongside his own. Macdonell thought too, though, how the difference between the two images reflected the characters of their subjects.

His brother. Alasdair Macdonell of Glengarry. That fearless fencible who had never fought a battle. Alasdair the great champion of Gaelic who in truth would rather have sheep on his land than those who spoke the native tongue and who even now was probably displacing his tenantry. He did not think that he should have done it that way. But it was not his concern. The estate was Alasdair's by right and he must manage it as he best thought fit. It was not his business. And wasn't his brother the very model of a great chief? The template surely for Waverley's Fergus McIvor? How he delighted his Highland neighbours with the tales of his brother's battles. What would he make, Macdonell wondered, of the encounter they were to face tomorrow? Whatever the outcome and whatever fate held in store, should he live or die, the battle, whatever it would be known as, would soon be the subject of another of Alasdair's anecdotes. Perhaps he would even command his piper to write a ballad. Or, as most assuredly he would were the colonel to meet his end here, a lament.

Reaching the first floor, Macdonell pushed open another door and walked across the dimly lit floor of what appeared to be a formal salon to a window where a simple wooden table was the sole remaining piece of furniture. He looked out into the night. The rain was heavier now, dripping from the roof and forming puddles on the cobbles below where the drenched redcoats splashed about by torchlight, their arms

159

filled with wooden planks and pieces of masonry, busily strengthening the position which tomorrow would be their only protection against the might of Napoleon's army.

A sudden clatter on the stairs and a murmur of voices made him spin round. 'James? Are you there? James?'

Candlelight filled the stairwell. A square-set figure appeared in the doorway. A familiar shock of curly black hair and, as the light grew in intensity, the coal-black eyes and that disarming, leonine smile.

'Dan?'

'James. You are here. Now we are complete.'

Behind the red-coated bulk of Colonel Daniel Mackinnon three other officers now came into view.

'Gentlemen. James, you know Ed Sumner, of course. And allow me to present Frederick Griffiths, newly arrived from England. And this,' with a theatrical gesture, 'is our doughty Lieutenant Drought of the glorious 13th. I found him outside, in the rain. Looking quite bedraggled.'

'I already have the pleasure, sir.'

'Indeed, Lieutenant.'

Macdonell nodded at the other two officers. Sumner he had also met before. One of Mackinnon's protégés. Griffiths was new to him. White-faced and every inch the terrified ensign. Both clearly worshipped Mackinnon and, just as obviously, had donated their precious personal provisions to what he had probably promised would be a convivial party.

From behind the party two Coldstream privates appeared, hats off, each one carrying a small hamper.

Mackinnon waved them in. 'Tonight we dine. For, gentlemen, it may be our last . . . Perkins.'

He summoned his soldier-servant, a weasel-faced individual who produced from his haversack a once-white tablecloth and with all the flourish of a footman at White's (which in fact in his younger days he had been), spread it across the table.

From one of the hampers the man now brought forth with

similar aplomb two silver candlesticks and candles, four napkins and silver knives and forks and spoons and a dozen short glasses. The other yielded a small piece of ham, a single Bologna sausage, a bottle of claret and one of brandy, what looked like a barrel of army-issue gin and a hunk of strong-smelling yellow cheese. It was a worthy last supper.

This, thought Macdonell (together, of course, with their exceptional fighting ability), was what marked the Guards apart from the common soldiery. What made them his family.

Mackinnon had been part of that family for the past eleven years. It had been he who had schooled Macdonell on his transfer from the 78th in the brigade's very particular ways and traditions. They were tied, too, by the bond of combat. Like Macdonell, Dan had seen action from Copenhagen to Salamanca. He was nothing less than a legend, in the regiment and throughout the army. A Highlander, like Macdonell, he was a Skye man and the son of the clan chief. But, for all their closeness, there the similarities ended. For while Macdonnell certainly enjoyed a joke as much as any man, Dan was a prankster without compare.

Had it not been Mackinnon who once, back in Portugal, had masqueraded as the Duke of York, Commander-in-Chief of the army, and who on another occasion had entered a Spanish convent dressed as a nun, only to find himself in-spected by Wellington? He was an expert juggler – with apples, oranges, or the regimental silver. Famously, on mess nights it was his custom to take wagers from fresh-faced new arrivals that he could not climb around the room like a monkey. He never lost. Mackinnon boasted too, not without foundation, of his friendship with Byron. He had brought the great poet and Lothario to the mess when the battalion had been encamped in Lisbon and ever since had prided himself on his ability to recite lengthy passages of Byron's verse. His *Childe Harold* in particular was not a performance which suited all tastes. But no one was going to argue with Dan Mackinnon.

And so Byron thundered out across mess, billet and camp with improbable regularity.

By God, thought Macdonell, as he watched Dan with scrupulous attention to detail supervising the laying of their meagre table, but this was soldiering. Mackinnon was the sort of man who could transform even the most godforsaken of billets into a life-enhancing evocation of the very soul of St James's. With his arrival they were no longer sitting in the damp and draughty salon of some deserted Belgian farm, but were almost transported back to the great rooms of White's, Almack's or Brooks'.

Macdonell smiled at his friend. Nodded his approval. He was confident that the defensive preparations were in hand. Wellington, he was certain, would send more pioneers, and his own men were well advanced in their work. He would not begrudge himself a half-hour for a last supper with dear Dan.

Mackinnon sank back against the rail of his chair and, balancing a glass of claret between thumb and forefinger, gazed into its red depths before speaking.

'Well, James? What price this? Here we are. It would seem that once again it has fallen to us to save the day. The Peer in his all-seeing wisdom has placed us in the weakest part of his line and has given us the chance to show the rest of the army, yet again, how His Majesty's Foot Guards make war.' He turned to the others. 'And I tell you, gentlemen, we shall have our work cut out for us. Where, you may ask, is the army of Spain? Eh? Gone, I tell you. Disbanded. Sailed away for "England, home and beauty". The Peer knows it. And we know it. Eh, James? What say you? D'you think we could win Salamanca again with this army? Vitoria? Bussaco? No. I think not. Belgians. Militia. Conscripted farmers. Men who only a year ago were fighting for Boney. And what of our own boys? Green as the corn and ripe for the cutter, I say.' He glanced at Griffiths, who had gone even paler. 'Oh, I do beg pardon, my dear chap. Present company excepted, naturally.'

He continued. 'The army's gone, I tell you, James, and in its place we've no more than ploughboys and thieves commanded by commissaries and quill-pushers. Why, only this morning I rode past an entire company of our own infantry drawn up at the roadside taking inventory of their equipment. *En route* of march, I tell you. I worry, gentlemen, for our fate tomorrow. Oh, there are men here, certainly. Men who can really fight. Certain troops. Certain regiments. Certain squadrons. The Inniskillings. The Highlanders. Others too. The dragoons, my dear Drought. But as for the rest. All we can do, James m'dear, is to fight our corner and hope that Boney throws his full might directly at us alone. At the Guards. For if he does not, then I am very much afraid, gentlemen, of . . . of I know not what. So, it lies with us alone, gentlemen. And, thank God, we are no ledger clerks. We are precisely what the army calls us, "gentlemen's sons". We fight in defence of freedom . . .'

As if on cue, immediately below their window a soldier, perhaps a fellow Scot, began to play a mournful, slow air on a fife. A lament: the 'Flowers of the Forest'.

Mackinnon, raising his voice slightly, rose to his feet. 'We fight for the freedom of our countrymen, gentlemen. And indeed, no less for our own freedom to live as gentlemen. We owe it to our country to preserve our birthright. For without us, surely, there would be no country. We, gentlemen, are England, and England us. And of course,' he added, with a smile to Macdonell, 'do not let us forget that we are also the north part of Britain.'

He looked at Drought.

'And God bless Ireland, Mr Drought, eh?'

He continued: 'But gentlemen, think on't. We are Britons. It is not only our privilege to defend Britannia's honour. But also our duty. It is the very mark of our rank.'

At length he paused. Griffiths, Sumner and Drought, hoping they might now begin to eat, raised a half-hearted 'Hear hear' and fell into an awkward silence. Mackinnon smiled and his eyes darted towards the window as outside the tempo of the music changed and the whistle-player struck up a jig. Macdonell knew what would follow. Sure enough, Mackinnon drained his glass, placed one foot on a chair and broke into rhyme:

> 'A lady of rank of Nankeen,
> Who was wife to a great Mandarine,
> Could not walk at all,
> Her feet were so small,
> So she rode on her arse, like a queen.'

It had the desired effect. Roaring with laughter, Drought, followed by the two junior Guards officers, thumped the table and begged him for another. Here then, thought Macdonell, was their promised evening. Here a last chance to lose troublesome thoughts of what tomorrow might bring. A chance to lose the ghost of that Spanish charnel-house. To lose, too, thoughts of home. A chance to lose yourself in friends and comrades. To become now, on the eve of battle, what you knew without doubt you must be tomorrow. Indivisible. Thinking and fighting as one. A foe without equal.

Macdonell stood at the window staring at the rain, half listening to the well-rehearsed Peninsular anecdote with which Mackinnon was now entertaining the small company. He flipped open his watch. It was half an hour after nine. Closing the lid, he replaced it in his pocket and turned back to the room. In the course of the last hour the party had increased as, hearing of Mackinnon's expedition to the château, five further Guards officers including George Bowles, attired at last in his own grey overall trousers, had braved the weather to wander down from the ridge. A dense fug of smoke from the small cigarillos which marked out the Peninsular officers from more recent recruits pervaded the room, whose walls were now hung with coats and cloaks, draped on hooks which had once held fine paintings and gilded sconces. In one corner stood two umbrellas.

Macdonell knew that it was now well past his time to leave these convivial surroundings. Time to return to reality. As he moved towards the door, other, junior officers began to follow his example. Two took their coats and slipped by him to the stairs. He turned to the room.

'Gentlemen, stay, I beg you. Finish your supper. I must make a tour of inspection. But stay. I'll say adieu to you, Dan. Until we meet tomorrow.'

Macdonell left and descended the staircase, passing on the way two slumbering soldiers who snapped to attention at the door. They had placed candles at intervals on the steps to light the way and he was able now to gather a clear impression of the house. It had evidently been until quite recently a place of moderate splendour. Coloured and carved panelling clad the walls, and where a chandelier would have hung only the gilded hook remained in the ceiling.

He collected his still sodden blue boat-cloak from the nail on which he had hung it earlier and walked out into the night. The rain was as heavy as ever. Around the yard groups of soldiers sat huddled over small fires, while others took their turn at the walls, hammering the defences into place. A huge bearded redcoat passed directly in front of Macdonell, almost knocking him down, dropped his burden of planks of wood, and swore to himself in German. A Hanoverian, thought Macdonell. So his request for further pioneers had reached High Command.

Huddled at the foot of the chapel wall he noticed Gooch. The boy was covered with mud and had contrived without much effect to wrap himself in a blanket. Leaving him to sleep for a few minutes more, Macdonell looked up at the château. A light still twinkled in the window of their improvised dining room and he could see Mackinnon again standing on the table. Was it another limerick? Or daring tales from Spain? Macdonell fancied that he could hear a favourite passage of Byron:

Each volley tells that thousands cease to breathe;
Death rides upon the sulphury Siroc,
Red Battle stamps his foot, and nations feel the shock.

In the dark of the courtyard, he shivered. He was not a superstitious man, but death, he knew, had a liking for the company of soldiers. Particularly in the dark watch before a battle. He had walked these twenty years in the shadow of his grim presence. But this place felt somehow different. It was as if he could actually smell something on the air. Death, he sensed, had marked this place for his own, and tomorrow he would claim his due. Was he himself to perish? And what of the others? What of Henry Gooch there in the shadows? And what of the Grahams, Dashwood, Wyndham, Henderson, Miller, Biddle? What of the unfortunate Monsieur van Cutzem and his little Marie? Could death claim them all?

Standing close by the south gate now, Macdonell heard voices drifting in on the rain from far into the wood. No distinct words. Merely murmured mutterings in a foreign tongue. It made him stop. And, as if to answer, fresh words began to ring in his head. Words he had heard spoken so often by Dan Mackinnon. Familiar words, which uttered by his friend could stir the feeblest heart to thoughts of glorious deeds. Yet here in the darkness he could derive no comfort from them. And not once through that long, wet, troubled night, either as he walked among the still-labouring men, or still later as he chased sleep in the château's echoing, empty salon, was he able, try as he might, to drive their ghastly truth from his mind:

Destruction cowers, to mark what deeds are done;
For on this morn three potent nations meet,
To shed before his shrine the blood he deems most sweet.

FIFTEEN

Chantelet farm, 9 p.m.
Ney

Gently, and with infinite patience, he picked the lumps of crusted mud from the tall collar of the thick blue coat, taking care to ensure that not an inch of the elaborately embroidered gold oak leaves or heavy bullion epaulettes should be obscured. He would be on show tomorrow. With the Emperor. Before the entire army.

Rollin had offered to help, but Ney preferred to clean his uniform himself. Took him back to the old days. To Sergeant-Major Michel Ney, 5th Hussars. Cleaning the mud from his boots after Jemappes, before the French army's triumphal entry into Brussels. November 1792. Curious, he thought, that so soon now he would be reliving that day. Leading another victorious army into that city.

Memories flooded his mind. Forgotten faces. Names of men. Names of horses, curiously. The smell of stables. The warm breath of the horses as you rubbed them down. The feel of the leather harness. Touching his sword belt, he tried to recapture it. Not the same. Never the same. We're all changed now.

He went back to working on the coat. It was all he could do now. Except eat and sleep, perhaps. And wait. He had personally seen to it that the last of the army was in its prescribed position. Had posted Reille's corps on the left wing, d'Erlon's on the right and, astride the great *chaussée* that ran up through the French lines, Lobau's corps and the Garde. One on either side of the road. Barely a mile away from Wellington. Certainly, after the confusion and bitterness of that morning he had no desire to spend this evening with the Emperor, even had he been given the invitation. Prince Jerome, Reille, Bachelu, Piré had taken rooms at Genappe, in the inn which on the previous evening had been occupied by the British staff. Jerome. Reille would keep him in check. He was brave enough for sure. Quatre-Bras had shown that. But Ney still worried about how he would react in the heat of what promised to be an altogether grander affair. Wondered too whether he might use his position as the Emperor's brother. Pull rank he didn't have. They would have to wait and see. Such thoughts did not make for sociability. Besides, Jerome was piss-poor company. Ney had preferred to look elsewhere for his lodging and had been fortunate to find a comfortable billet in this modest farm. Chantelet, they called it. It was exactly parallel with the Emperor's headquarters at the neighbouring farmhouse of Le Caillou, but separated by a distance of perhaps 1,200 metres and a small wood. He was also a good 2 kilometres back from the front line and away too from the generals in their mess at the village of Plancenoit, across a small stream to the north.

He guessed at the subject of their present conversation. The pursuit had been shambolic. The mud had done for them. The English cavalry had played hide-and-seek through the villages and the fields. And their horse artillery. How did they move their guns like that? So damned fast. Like birds of prey wheeling in the sky and then diving on their quarry before rising again, instantly out of reach.

It had not been made any easier of course, he thought, by that idiot Marbot mistaking the red-coated Garde lancers covering his flank for English cavalry. That had been a bloody, unnecessary mistake. Two troopers killed by their own side, two more and a sous-lieutenant wounded and three Hussars rendered *hors de combat*. But it was the sort of thing that happened when soldiers were nervous. And Ney knew that if the Emperor and his generals were nervous, the condition would run like plague through the army.

Of course the English must be pursued, but the Emperor's hysteria had put everyone on edge. Himself included. Now the army was boiling over with impatience to be at the enemy.

Thank God he'd found this place. Quiet and solitary. Away from the line. Just himself, the two aides and the fat cook and simple servant that the ever-resourceful Rollin had 'requisitioned' from the Emperor's own *service léger*. Smiling, Ney wondered whether they had yet been missed. Doubted it. Napoleon had other things on his mind.

He looked down to where, on the table, beside the white and gold cross of his Légion d'Honneur, he had placed the miniature portrait of Aglaé that he kept tucked inside his coat as he had through a dozen campaigns. She gazed up at him, her soft brown almond-shaped eyes catching his breath as if she had been there in person. Once more, my love, he told her, silently. Once more for France and for my Emperor. Then you and our darling boys shall have me entirely to yourselves.

He began again to hum the little piece of Mozart that always came into his mind with thoughts of his wife. From the small kitchen to the rear of the farmhouse came the smell of roasting mutton. For a moment it seemed a strangely domestic scene.

Rollin entered. 'Dinner, sire? We have a roast sheep.'

'Delicious. And I presume you have found some wine? You'll join me, Rollin? And find Heymes.'

Ney stood up, hung his cleaned coat on a hook on the wall, picked up a log and flung it on the fire. He paused in front of it to rub his hands together before sitting down in his shirtsleeves at the simple, scrubbed table. From a door opposite the kitchen the two aides appeared together, grinning, each holding two bottles of red wine.

'Liberating our host's cellars again, Heymes? Remember Friedland?'

'Oh yes, sir. What a night.'

'Yes, what a night. And what a victory.'

'It was magnificent. You were magnificent.'

Ney smiled at the compliment. Finished pouring himself a glass of wine. Took a swig and swallowed, loudly.

'Heymes. You don't think that I acted wrongly today? I was justified, wasn't I? I mean, how the devil could the Emperor have expected me to attack the entire Allied army?'

The food had arrived on the table. He hacked off a slice of the joint, cut it in two and stuffed half into his mouth. He did not need a reply. Had really asked the question of himself. Knew the answer. Nothing had been the same since he had rejoined the army four days ago. The Emperor he knew now was a changed man. All that had happened just compounded the worries he had felt since that night at Avesnes. Tomorrow, he thought, would come a chance to prove himself again. To win back the Emperor's confidence. Tomorrow, another chance to push for one last time at the boundaries of glory. Heymes was speaking.

'What? I'm sorry. I didn't hear you.'

The aide smiled. 'I was merely saying, sire, that no one can blame you for what you did or did not do. You did more than any man could. I'm quite sure that the Emperor is aware of that. He cannot expect the impossible.'

'Quite so.'

Ney pushed his chair away from the table. Stood up. 'Sorry. I need a breath of air. Excuse me, gentlemen.'

Not bothering to put on his coat, Ney threw his cloak over his billowing shirt and walked out into the rain. Close to the farm was a chapel. Its beautiful ornate façade seemed curiously out of place in this setting, directly opposite the gates of the simple, whitewashed farm.

From beyond the wood came the dull noise of the army.

171

Somewhere behind those trees were 70,000 men. And beyond them, he presumed, unless Wellington had cut and run, 70,000 more wearing different-coloured coats and speaking a different language. Different languages. English, Scots, Irish, Germans, Dutch and French-speaking Belgians. Near on 150,000 men, waiting to kill or be killed. Surely, Wellington would leave now. Would not be foolish enough to take on the Emperor without the Prussians. Their numbers were roughly equal. But the army encamped on the opposite ridge was a rag-bag. So very different from the men who had driven them from Spain.

Perhaps there would be no battle tomorrow. Perhaps the British would retreat to the coast. Would give up Brussels.

The Emperor would triumph again. There would be no more death. Ney sat down on the damp stone steps of the little chapel, rested his head in his palms and placed his elbows on his knees. No more war? Was that really what he wanted? Perhaps. Would he miss it? Almost certainly. Might there really not be a battle tomorrow? If there was, then surely it would be the greatest of battles. Did he, Michel Ney, the 'Bravest of the Brave', really want to miss that? The Emperor pitted against the finest that Britain had to send against him? The arrogant Irishman who had defeated Ney himself. Would he fight? They would only know in the morning. Ney got up. Pulled his cloak a little tighter. Shivered

He spoke softly. To himself. Barely audible. 'Oh my darling. Darling Aglaé. What fate has brought me to this place? This is not like any other battle. Surely this is not how it all begins? Alone here in the rain. Where is the Emperor? Where is the glory?'

The sharp sound of heavy boots made him stop. Heymes. 'Sire? Come in out of the rain.'

'Of course. Sorry. I was thinking. Do you think that Wellington will stand?'

'Without doubt, sire. He needs this battle as much as we do.'

172

'Yes. Of course. But what what Wellington needs and what he decides are not always one and the same. I don't know, Heymes. I'm not so sure.'

Silence. Both men knew what he meant. No one could be sure of anything any more. Wellington. The weather. Their army. Their Emperor.

'Come in, sire. You're tired. Have another glass of wine with us.'

'Yes ... Yes. More wine. Good idea. We'll know in the morning. Eh, Heymes? Tomorrow will tell.'

DAY FOUR

Sunday
18 June 1815

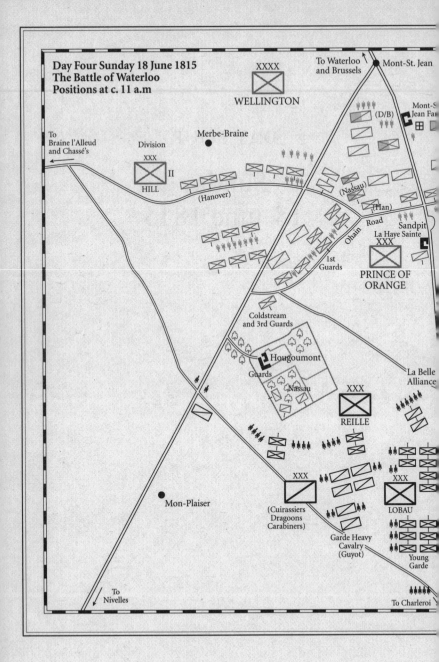

Day Four Sunday 18 June 1815
The Battle of Waterloo
Positions at c. 11 a.m

XXXX
WELLINGTON

To Waterloo
and Brussels

Mont-St. Jean

(D/B)

Mont-S
Jean Fa

Merbe-Braine

To
Braine l'Alleud
and Chassé's

Division

XXX
II
HILL

(Hanover)

(Nassau)

(Han)

Ohain Road

Sandpit

La Haye Sainte
XXX

1st
Guards

PRINCE OF
ORANGE

Coldstream
and 3rd Guards

La Belle
Alliance

Hougoumont

Guards

Nassau

XXX
REILLE

XXX
(Cuirassiers
Dragoons
Carabiners)

XXX

XXX
LOBAU

Mon-Plaisir

Garde Heavy
Cavalry
(Guyot)

Young
Garde

To
Nivelles

To Charleroi

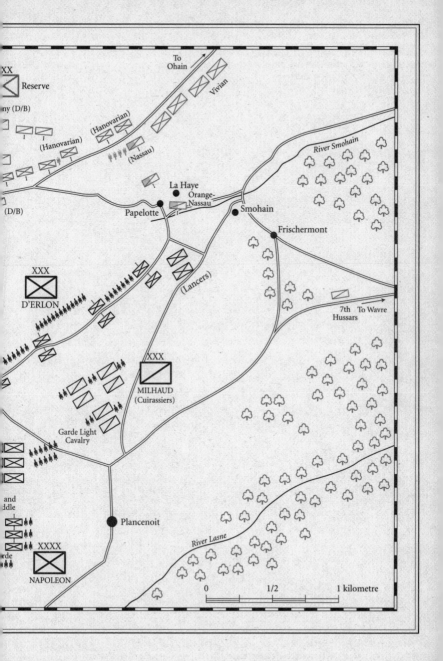

To Ohain

Vivian

XXX Reserve

ny (D/B)

(Hanovarian)

(Hanovarian)

(Nassau)

(D/B)

River Smohain

La Haye
Orange-
Nassau

Papelotte

Smohain

Frischermont

XXX
D'ERLON

(Lancers)

7th
Hussars

To Wavre

XXX
MILHAUD
(Cuirassiers)

Garde Light
Cavalry

and
ddle

rde

Plancenoit

River Lasne

NAPOLEON

0   1/2   1 kilometre

SIXTEEN

Mont St Jean, 8.15 a.m.
De Lancey

The mist, which had filled the valley for much of the night, had lifted now and the field was newly revealed to him. Holding the precious map in his hands, De Lancey sat, legs pulled up before him, his back against an old elm tree which grew a few yards in front of the crossroads. Above his head a solitary songbird was chattering in its branches. He was sitting almost directly at the centre of a long ridge which ran for three miles in a nearly straight line, from east to west. Along its length stretched the entire Allied army. Sixty-eight thousand men with twenty thousand horses and eight score of cannon. The smoke from their campfires spiralled into the leaden sky and De Lancey smiled as he recognized the familiar rattle and hum of an awakening army. As bugle calls and drumbeats summoned regiments and squadrons and troops, all about him the men stood to and blew on cold fingers.

To the right of where he sat, the ground sloped away gently to end in a flat-bottomed valley. To his left, though, he noted again that the contours were more complex. There were dips and gulleys here and there where it occurred to De Lancey that a man on a horse, perhaps a squadron or even an entire regiment of cavalry, could hide quite easily. Here in the centre, where the roads met, the Brussels highway was enclosed by a cutting, some ten or twelve feet deep. The road to Nivelles that ran off to his right was similarly sunken for a good hundred yards with what was in effect a natural defensive trench. To his left further cover was provided along the ridge by two holly hedges which flanked the road to the village of Ohain.

He looked to his front, across the apple trees and blue-tiled rooftops of a little walled farm, to the other side of the valley, where perhaps 1,000 yards away there rose a similar ridge. Originally Wellington had been of a mind to place his force along this line. But the two of them had concluded that their present position would be on the whole more advantageous. Now that opposite slope was filled with the French. Scores of them. Although there were not as many as he had supposed he might see. Indeed they appeared still to be arriving on the field, a steady flow up the road from the direction of Genappe. Napoleon seemed to be in no rush to meet his nemesis. Still De Lancey reckoned, there must be some 20,000 infantry and cavalry already assembled. The guns, also still being moved into position, were harder to count. It was a splendid sight. At once both impressive and intimidating. Raising his spyglass, he was able to discern among the dark blue masses a few of the more distinctive uniforms. The green of the mounted chasseurs, familiar from Spain, picked out with primrose yellow, bright pink and scarlet. The fluttering red and white pennants and glittering golden helmets that betrayed the presence of lancers and, even under this dull heaven, the momentary sparkle of light reflected from the breastplates of thousands of armoured cuirassiers.

He had risen at six in the billet he shared with Wellington in the village of Waterloo, two miles to the north, and had ridden here with the Peer and a few of the staff: Gordon, Somerset, Hervey and the foreign attachés including Müffling and Miguel d'Alava, all eager to reconnoitre the chosen ground in daylight. Passing the farm of Mont St Jean, slightly to the rear of the position, De Lancey had noticed that the surgeons had already transformed it into an aid post and were busy sharpening the tools of their grisly trade on grindstones set up in the courtyard by the cavalry blacksmiths.

After fifteen days of downpours the fields had been churned to mud by thousands of wagons and horses. Even the recently cobbled main road was sticky with the stuff. Although the rain had now stopped, the sky was again threatening and the air unseasonably cool.

He had sat in this spot since his arrival. In the same place that he had occupied for two hours the previous evening. It was a rare vantage point from which to weigh up the strength of the Allied position. And its weaknesses. And he thought now that at last he might have a notion of where Napoleon would make his push. There were two clear options.

The Allies were well protected on their left flank – to the east – by the marshy ground around the river Dyle and by a complex system of enclosed fields and copses that must be impenetrable to cavalry and horse artillery.

It occurred to him that in fact any attack across this country was going to be a feat of superhuman strength. For in the fields around him, apart from a few laid to clover, the rye and wheat grew full in ear, standing as high as a man above ponds, puddles and mud. To his right and just out of sight lay the château of Hougoumont, walled, wooded and secure. Beyond it, though, was open country. Napoleon might try there. For, apart from the château, their right flank was 'in the air'. Horribly exposed. If the French managed to manoeuvre men around the west side of Hougoumont and follow up with cavalry then they would simply roll up the Allied line. De Lancey knew this to be in Wellington's mind. Hadn't the Peer left a precious 15,000 men, a fifth of his force, over on the right at the village of Hal, ready to counter-attack just such a flanking march? This too surely was the reason why the bulk of their army was massed not in a central reserve, but towards their right. Yes. That was certainly their weakest point.

But in the course of the last few hours De Lancey had also become increasingly nervous of another target. Another Achilles' heel. Directly in front of him lay the farm of La Haye Sainte. A determined French assault might carry the farmhouse, and once they had that, once they were able to call up artillery and launch assaults from behind the cover of the buildings, another push would surely carry the day.

Right and centre. Their defence must somehow concentrate on both these areas. He wondered how the Peer would play that one. Doubtless he had already formed a plan in his mind. Of course he wouldn't tell them what it might be. That was not his way. And besides, as far as De Lancey could see, he had no real plan save to stand and fight, until Blücher arrived. Or until the French pushed him off his ridge.

De Lancey stood up. Shook his cramped legs back to life. Brushed the mud and the moss from his coat and turned towards the rear. Behind and below him, on the reverse slope, beyond the green-jacketed light infantry of the German Legion, stood thousands of dismounted cavalry. The red-coated heavy dragoons of the Household Brigade with the navy of the Blues and in the far distance the distinctive dark blue and silver helmets of the Belgian carabiniers. While officers and men went in search of what little breakfast was to be had, the sharp clang of metal on metal revealed that the farriers were busy replacing shoes cast on the previous day's retreat. The horses stood tied together in long lines, and behind them De Lancey could see the laden artillery trains and the supply wagons piled with such an assortment of baggage that they looked for all the world like a band of gypsies. Around them, chatting, laughing, washing, some half-naked, he could make out in their hundreds the camp followers, the women who followed their husbands and lovers to the field of battle just as they had in Spain and down through the generations before them through Flanders and across the German plains. There were children too. Soldiers' children who played incongruously between the cannon wheels and danced their rhymes round piles of muskets and barrels of powder. Closer to him stood other horses, the finer-boned, well-groomed mounts of the infantry's field officers, tethered to bayonets dug deep into the muddy ground. Their masters were gathered in groups about them, discussing the coming day and more trivial affairs. The matter of a wager. An unpaid mess bill. A woman. A wound. Some had found the necessaries for shaving and were dressing themselves for the French. Others clearly did not feel inclined to bother. De Lancey himself had attended to his own toilette before leaving the inn at Waterloo and thought that he now cut a not unreasonable dash. Not that it mattered one jot to the Peer. Providing his men could fight, Wellington was content. Word was that Sir Thomas Picton had arrived on the field in the same drab civilian clothes and top hat that he had worn to leave Brussels and that he was wielding an umbrella. Some said too, though, that he had been wounded at Quatre-Bras and kept the coat on principally lest he betray his hurt and be banished from the battle. It would certainly have been in character, thought De Lancey.

From all about him now came the pop of muskets discharging into the air as the infantry began to clear their barrels ready for the day's sport. The rain had continued throughout the night, ceasing only at around five o'clock, and a cold pan and damp powder would be of no use on this day of killing.

Yet again De Lancey had not slept well. Had still been working with the Duke at 2.30, writing orders and dispositions. They had received a message from Blücher an hour later, confirming that he would ride to their aid. The relief had been sufficient to persuade the Commander-in-Chief to take a few hours' rest, and De Lancey had thought to follow suit. But twenty minutes later he was watching the sunrise through the window of his little room. Magdalene haunted his mind. What would befall her should he be killed, or worse, if he were maimed, blinded or paralysed?

Now, as then, he began to contemplate what this battle really meant.

If they did not carry the day then they would, as far as he could tell, be plunged into another twenty years of bloody war. Should he survive the battle, however, whatever the outcome, it would undoubtedly mean advancement – social and financial. And what would that mean for his young wife? On the whole, renewed war would bring advantage. But peace must be preferred. He fancied their life together in London. Perhaps in one of the new townhouses being built in the village of Chelsea. The air was pleasant there, it was said, and it was but a short ride to Whitehall. They would live with no great pomp. A few servants and rooms enough in which to entertain and live in content. Children. Yes, there would be children. They had spoken of it, and certainly he felt a yearning. But for now he was content with Magdalene.

Oh, let him come through unhurt. He muttered the words in silent prayer. Let this be the last battle. Surely now, he thought. Now the time had come to settle down to the business of peace. Perhaps they would win this battle and he would return to a desk at the Horse Guards and the chance to grow old and fat, ending his days a Major-General signing orders to send other young men to death and glory. For in that place alone the pen was mightier than the sword.

A gentle cough brought him back to the present. Miguel d'Alava was standing behind him, resplendent in the elaborate white and gold uniform of a general of the Spanish army. Boots slipping on the muddy bank, De Lancey walked to greet his friend.

'Miguel. Here we are, as you predicted. And what now of our position?'

'The Peer has chosen well, William. He hides his men. Forces Napoleon to guess where his strength lies.'

'He is the master of the defensive position.'

'Of course. And so he has positioned his infantry behind

184

this ridge. Cavalry on the flanks and in the rear. And look how he puts the English, his finest troops, in the front line and sends the Belgians off to Hal.'

Of course d'Alava would have spotted that. And it did concern De Lancey. The men at Hal, Chasse's Dutch and Belgians, were untried. And the last time any had been in battle they had fought for Napoleon. If the French did turn the Allied flank, could they be counted on not to run or to desert to the enemy? Would they really march to rescue the position rather than retreat to Brussels? Naturally, he had said nothing to Wellington, but surely, he thought, a more dependable force would have been a better choice. A brigade of British line infantry perhaps, or the German Legion. But then, of course, should Napoleon ignore that flank they would simply be a waste of valuable veteran manpower.

'They are there for a reason, Miguel. Everything has its purpose.'

'What then, my friend, is the purpose of those?'

The Spaniard was pointing to a nearby troop of the Royal Horse Artillery who were assembling what looked like a number of 'A' framed tent poles. De Lancey winced.

'Ah. Yes. The rocket troop. You must remember them from Spain, Miguel. You know that they can be most effective against cavalry. The horses hate them.'

'No more than do your own men, William. You know as well as I that there is no telling where those infernal things will land.'

'You are quite wrong. It is such things as these and Shrapnel's deadly shells that will win this war and many after. You are too set in your ways, Miguel. Warfare is changing. It is not as you would have it. Something more than songs and banners and trust in God.'

The Spaniard shrugged. Turned away. De Lancey sensed that he had caused offence.

'Now, tell me. Have you inspected our strongpoints? There are but three.'

He passed d'Alava his spyglass.

'Over there to the left, you see, we have the farms of Papelotte and La Haye. Here below us is the farm of La Haye Sainte, and over there I think you may just discern the woods of the château farm of Hougoumont. A considerable complex with a mansion house, high walls, orchards and a wood to its front. It is the cornerstone of our line.'

D'Alava scanned the field. 'Yes. You are right. It is well chosen ground. Strong enough. But what of the human weaknesses, William? What of your allies? And what of the commanders? Where is our friend the Prince of Orange today?'

'The Prince rides with the Peer, Miguel, as you well know. And his brother has been, erm, honoured with command of the force at Hal.'

Both men smiled.

'Safely out of your way, you mean.' D'Alava laughed. Handed back the spyglass.

As the two men looked to their front, directly below them in the orchard of the farmhouse, they noticed an officer of British horse artillery, distinguished by his gold-braided navy-blue pelisse and extravagantly crested Tarleton helmet, smoking a cigar amid the remains of what appeared to have been a very merry breakfast party. As they watched he mounted his horse and, still puffing at the stub of his cigar, rode sharply up to their right on to the crest of the ridge. There, perfectly silhouetted against the sky, making himself a prime target for any bored French skirmisher, he took his time to make his own appreciation of the scene.

The Spaniard spoke.

'That, I believe, is a perfect example of what is called British phlegm.'

'We like to set the men a good example.'

'You like to die with honour.'

De Lancey snapped shut the telescope, replaced it in his saddle-bag, untethered his own horse and both men mounted

186

up. He was in the process of leaning over to talk to d'Alava when a commotion from behind made him turn round. A group of officers was riding towards them in uniforms of heraldic splendour. At their front and centre rode Wellington, clad in contrast to the rest of that brilliant company, as was De Lancey, in a simple, plain blue riding coat. The Peer's only decoration was worn on his hat. Four cockades, the colours of the allies in whose armies he carried the rank of Field Marshal: the black of Britain and Hanover, the orange of the United Netherlands, the white of Spain and Portugal's green. De Lancey noticed Picton beside the Duke, matching his asceticism in the much-derided civilian frock coat and old round hat. He was holding an umbrella.

The Peer was making a final tour of his army, collecting his officers as he went. Gordon rode closest to him, followed by young George Lennox and George Scovell. Then came Barnes, the fire-eating Adjutant-General, his high forehead betraying no hint of that infamous temper. After him was Fitzroy Somerset, his beak a miniature version of the Peer's own proboscis, and beside him the ever-affable George Cathcart and the rotund, black-coated figure of Blücher's exhausted liaison officer, General Müffling. Lord Uxbridge, commander of the cavalry and *pro bono* second-in-command, came next with his aide, Will Thornhill, and the commanders of the four brigades of Anglo-German cavalry, William Ponsonby, Edward Somerset, brother of Fitzroy, John Vandeleur and Hussey Vivian. With them rode their equivalent in the infantry: Daddy Hill, Generals Cooke, Alten and Clinton, and the Dutchmen Perponcher and Rebecque. And last came the Prince of Orange, clad as usual in his distinctive black pelisse.

Wellington spoke. 'Yes. This will do very nicely. Well done, De Lancey. Gentlemen. I shall make my headquarters at this elm. Mark it well. Although do not be surprised if you do not find me here. I shall be with the army. Now, De Lancey, guide me through the dispositions.'

'Your Grace, you will see that I have followed your directions to the letter. Over on the right you have the brigade of Guards under General Cooke; the light companies detached to Hougoumont and with them the Second Nassauers. Behind them I have placed the 23rd and to their rear General Adam's brigade with the light infantry and the German Legion, with the Brunswickers directly behind them. Next to them are General Halkett's men. Your old friends the 33rd and the 69th. Closest to us we have Colonel Ompteda's German troops, whose second light regiment has found the garrison of the farm, and between them and General Halkett lie the bulk of the Hanoverian militia. You will see, sir, that directly behind us is the Household Brigade and across the *chaussée* from them the Greys, the Royals and the Inniskillings. I have taken the step of placing General van Merlen's cavalry slightly to the rear of our own horse. I thought it prudent. They were somewhat mauled at Quatre-Bras.'

The Allies, Nassauers and Brunswickers, and the Hanoverian militia, had performed well in the fight at the crossroads, but De Lancey knew that like him the Peer remained unconvinced. He had placed most of them on his right, safely behind a strong front line of British regulars and the German Legion.

Wellington smiled. Turned to the Spaniard. 'You see, d'Alava, what De Lancey and I have done to render the army more effective. We have placed the raw troops among the veterans; the novices with the old salts. We have sandwiched farm boys between Spanish heroes. And should I suspect any trouble, we have the Hussars and the dragoons to push them back into the line. I will have no malingerers here today. We shall need every man we have. Pray continue.'

De Lancey resumed. 'If you look to the left, your Grace, you will find General Picton's brigade, the First of Foot, the Highlanders and beyond them the Hanoverians of Best and Vincke. The light cavalry under Generals Vivian and Vandeleur protects our flank, General Lambert is hastening up in support from Waterloo and the Dutch and the Nassauers are down there in the two farms, as you ordered.'

'Very good, De Lancey. Very good. That will do, I think.'

Without another word Wellington reined his horse round and led the company off along the ridge road to the right of the line. The battalions had deployed in 'column of companies'. Ten companies of some sixty men formed two ranks deep, the files standing a mere twenty-one inches apart, captains to the front of each company, sergeants and subalterns to the rear. They passed sergeants busy dressing their lines, officers brushing and preening, lost in contemplation or writing hasty last notes to loved ones back home. De Lancey himself had written a similar letter the previous evening and given it to Alexander Abercromby, his deputy, who had given his own note to De Lancey. There was no need for words. It was the old routine. What every soldier who could write scribbled before a battle. De Lancey wondered how many such notes had been written that morning and how many would be needed before the day was done. He looked at the faces of the men as they passed by.

Although they were redcoats mostly, he did not recognize their features as distinctively British. For the truth was that for most part they were not, but Hanoverians. Regulars and conscripts who gazed at this passing parade of pomp with blank indifference. It was only when Wellington arrived at the 73rd and the 30th, who were positioned directly in their path, astride the ridge-top road, that the sight of the Duke's figure drew smiles and scattered cheers. Next in line, the Guards: First, Coldstream and Scots, although somewhat battered after a battle and two days' marching, still made a passable and notably silent attempt at a 'present-arms' worthy of Horse Guards.

And then, barely five minutes after having left the elm, they were descending an incline, curving round to face the French. De Lancey saw the red-brick walls, gate and dark slate rooftops of Hougoumont. The Peer, he knew, had already visited the château that morning. The fact that it had been his first destination on reaching the field had made him realize at once the importance his commander placed on refusing it to the French.

As they entered through its north gate Wellington turned to him. 'You know whom I have placed in command here, William?'

'Colonel Macdonell, sir.'

'Yes. Macdonell. D'ye think he'll manage it? Can he hold this place for us?'

'If anyone can, he will, sir. He'll have hot work, though.'

'We'll all have hot work, William, before this day is out.'

It was in truth a good choice, thought De Lancey. And he had meant what he said. He knew the big Highlander well. They had served together in the 17th Light Dragoons on his return from India. December 1798. Macdonell, hungry for action, had been already three years with the regiment, transferred from the old 101st Foot. He had been rewarded with postings to Grenada and fierce fighting against the Maroons in the West Indies. De Lancey's uncle had been colonel of the 17th and his cousin John a major. He remembered Macdonell as an unlikely captain of dragoons. A giant on horseback. Remembered too the genteel society of Canterbury. The pretty young women at all those soirées, routs and assemblies. And all that interminable fencing practice. Macdonell's height had made him a formidable opponent.

He recognized the same Scotsman as the towering red-coated officer who approached him now with long-legged strides across the teeming courtyard.

Macdonell knew him too: 'Colonel De Lancey. I hear much of you. A knighthood. A bride. And she a Scot. You are a lucky man.'

'Thank you, Colonel. I am indeed fortunate. And through my dear wife I have developed a sincere love for your

190

countrymen that quite outdoes the respect and admiration with which I had learned to regard them in Spain. But you have a fight on your hands here today. Be sure, Macdonell, the Peer is depending upon you. All England is depending upon you. Scotland too.'

'Lord Wellington has no cause to worry, Colonel. My men are ready for all the French can throw at them.'

They were joined by Wellington. 'Ah, Macdonell. You have done well. No less than I expected. The defences look sound. But mark what I said to you earlier this morning. Yours will be the first position to be attacked. You must defend it to the last extremity. To the very last man. The last round. All depends upon you, Colonel. Do I make myself plain?'

'Quite plain, your Grace. You may depend upon the Guards. We shall not let them through.'

'You must hold the château to the last extremity, Macdonell. The last extremity.'

He turned to De Lancey. 'De Lancey, have the Nassauers move out of the woods now and into the château buildings. Macdonell, take the Coldstream's light company and join with the 3rd Guards on the west side of the garden. You are our right flank. That's where they'll try first. Hold them there as long as you can and then fall back within the walls. Do not risk lives. Be prudent. You cannot afford to lose a single man.'

Macdonell nodded. 'Your Grace.'

Wellington turned away and, followed by the staff, returned to where the horses were held by a Coldstream corporal. Having mounted, the small group rode out of the gate, but instead of returning whence they had come, up towards the Allied lines, the Commander-in-Chief surprised De Lancey by turning his horse to the left and trotting round the side of the great barn, towards the French. Fitzroy Somerset, his face riven with anxiety, rode to his side.

'Your Grace. D'you think this wise? You are well known,

sir. The French have voltigeurs beyond the woods. Perhaps in the trees. It would be rash.'

'Nonsense. The woods are ours, Somerset. The Nassauers have yet to leave them. Correct, De Lancey?'

'Quite correct, your Grace.'

'You see, Somerset. Not all my officers share your skittishness. I intend to take a look for myself.'

They arrived at the end of the wall. Ahead of them, beyond a large haystack, a dense wood stretched away towards the French lines. To their left rose the tall gatehouse and south gate of the château. Already Macdonell's men were beginning to file past them to take up their new positions.

De Lancey could see what the Duke had done. He had in effect divided the château complex into three independently defended sectors; one on the right under Macdonell, the buildings under the Nassauers and with them the woods containing their light and grenadier companies and some 200 picked Hanoverian marksmen. On the left the great orchard was held by the light companies of the First Guards under Lord Saltoun, another amiable Scot, who he knew held land close to that of Magdalene's parents at Dunglass.

'D'you see there, De Lancey?' Wellington raised his arm to point through the woods towards the French position, and as he did so a shot rang out. The ball scudded past De Lancey's face and perilously close to Wellington's. A French marksman. So Somerset's fears had not been groundless. They were firing at the Duke. A look of alarm crossed the Duke's face. But only for an instant. Then from the undergrowth a figure appeared, the muzzle of his musket still smoking. He was dressed not in blue but green and wore on his head a huge, red-trimmed bearskin hat. A Nassau grenadier. He was followed by an officer, similarly clad. The latter turned to De Lancey. Spoke in impeccable but clipped and halting English.

'I am most sorry, your honour. This man is very nervous.

The affair at Quatre-Bras was his first battle. He took your friend for a French officer.'

De Lancey raised his eyebrows. Wellington smiled. The Dutch officer, suddenly realizing at whom his trigger-happy private had loosed off a round, coloured and began to stammer.

'Oh. God. I ... Oh my good God. Your majesty. Please forgive me. I didn't realize. Sir. I ...'

Wellington waved his comments away. Addressed his companions. 'A simple mistake. My coat, d'you see. Blue. Fellow took me for a Frenchman.' And touched by the absurdity of such a thought, he laughed the extraordinary guffaw, unique to him, that some said resembled a horse with the croup. It was taken up, with less gusto, by the staff. Though not by Somerset.

It had the necessary effect upon the poor Nassau officer, who smiled, saluted briskly and, calling the shaken private to him, turned and trotted back into the wood.

Wellington took off his hat. Mopped his brow. 'By God, De Lancey. And they expect me to win a battle with men like that.'

Leaving the woods and riding past the château and on up the hill they soon regained the Allied lines. As they rode past the Welch Fusiliers and the Guards the officers saluted with swords and the men presented their muskets. When they reached the 33rd, however, the Duke's own old regiment, the men let out a cheer, throwing their caps high into the air. Their huzzahs were quickly taken up by the battered 69th and the German Legion. Other regiments began to join in. Even the Hanoverians.

Wellington turned to De Lancey. 'I don't think that we should encourage that sort of thing, do you? I hate all that. That cheering. If you allow soldiers to express themselves thus they may on some other occasion hiss you instead of cheer.' Nevertheless, he smiled back at the men as he passed and lifted his hat in recognition. Predictably, the cheering only became louder. Their path took them directly through the centre of the 73rd and, noticing a young ensign, barely more than sixteen, standing nervously with his regimental colour, Wellington waved his hat towards him.

'Good morning, Charles. A fine morning, is it not? See that you stay with your colour sar'nt today. I have promised your dear mother you'll come to no harm.'

He turned back to De Lancey. 'Well. I suppose it is better to be cheered than shot at. Ah. Here we are.'

De Lancey turned to find what the Duke had seen, and caught his breath. There, on the opposite ridge, where two hours ago there had been a few brigades of men and horses, there now stood the entire French army. Could there be, he wondered, perhaps 100,000? Could Napoleon have contrived to assemble his entire force against them? It certainly seemed so. This was something very different from the French he had known in Spain. They were putting on a display of arms. Parading their martial might as he had never, in twenty years of soldiering, seen before. This was what happened when an Emperor led his men to war. The endless blue columns stretched back up and along the ridge like the blue and white stratae of some exotic rock face. He put his hand in his pocket and felt the smooth pebble slip between his fingers. Thought of Magdalene. Of Scotland. Of history and warriors long dead. Of Marmion.

Shafts of sunlight began to pierce the cloud, catching the bronze eagles across the valley and the waving tricolour banners that fluttered beneath them. Surely, he thought, this is no modern battle. This is something much older. A clash of arms such as the ancients had seen. Or Henry at Agincourt.

Spattered with splashes of brilliant colour – orange, crimson, pink, primrose and saffron, purple, emerald green, turquoise – the regiments and squadrons seemed to him for a moment to take on the character of a knightly warrior army.

194

De Lancey unbuttoned his spyglass from its case and raised it to his eye. It was not only the colour that so astonished, but the texture. Glistening leather, sparkling brass, bronze and silver, gently waving crests and plumes of fur and feather.

But this chivalric fantasy was short-lived. Bringing his glass to the line of the enemy ridge De Lancey saw the evil-looking guns. Hundreds of them. Enough, it seemed, perhaps to destroy the entire Allied army by their firepower alone. And now came the sounds to equal the spectacle. To drag him back to bloody reality. The ragged tap and patter of a thousand drums drifted across the valley, followed by the full orchestral strains of the regimental bands as they played again the familiar tunes from Spain. 'Veillions salut à l'Empire' the 'Flag of Austerlitz'. For a moment, as spellbound as De Lancey, the entire staff stared at the unfolding splendour of their enemy.

Somerset broke the silence. 'The French, your Grace.'

'So it would seem, Somerset. So it would seem. Gentlemen. To your positions. What time have you, Gordon?'

'Thirty-five minutes after ten, your Grace.'

'And nightfall is expected?'

'At thirty minutes after nine o'clock this evening, your Grace. In eleven hours' time.'

'Then that is precisely how long we must survive. Unless old Blücher finds us first.'

All along the line the men were at prayer as regimental chaplains conducted hasty drumhead services. De Lancey heard the parting imprecation from the padre of the 73rd: '. . . And may God take pity on our poor bodies.' It sent a chill through his soul.

Wellington turned round to Müffling who, as the generals departed for their divisions, remained close behind him. 'Müffling, my dear fellow. I am very much afraid that I shall have to ask you for one last time to take a message to Feld-Marshal Blücher. Inform him, if you will, that I should be much obliged if he would make his primary attack in the rear of La Belle Alliance, directly into the enemy flank. It would be most expedient also if a secondary action might support the left of my line, around the farm of Papelotte. And do tell him that I await his arrival with anticipation.'

Müffling touched his hat in reply, but even as Wellington was making to ride away, his great round face already more flushed than ever, the Prussian spoke: 'My Lord. I am afraid that I must tell you my true feelings on this matter. I see what you intend, of course. And I understand too that you are counting on the Prussians. But Hougoumont, my Lord Wellington. Do you really think it wise? So few men. Barely 1,500 against what from here would seem to be an entire corps of the French army. Your men will be overrun for sure, sir. Obliterated. Blücher will not have time to reach you. You will lose the battle. You would do well, my Lord, to reconsider.'

Wellington smiled, nodded, then looked the fat Prussian straight in the eye. 'Yes, Müffling. Quite so. I do appreciate your concern. But those are no ordinary men down there. Those are the Guards. And what is more, my friend, you do not know Macdonell.'

SEVENTEEN

La Belle Alliance, 10.40 a.m.
Napoleon

Napoleon sat astride Marengo on the Brussels road beside the little coaching inn of La Belle Alliance. He had already passed through the Garde and Lobau's corps, and behind him the cheering seemed to be unstoppable. His spirits were higher now. The rain had gone, and with it the excruciating pain. Gone too were the troublesome generals.

He pulled his horse towards the left of the front line and rode along its rear, between the massed columns of infantry and Kellerman's heavy cavalry, drawn up in support.

Sunshine bathed his army in glory. Dwarfed by the carabiniers in their virginally bright white coats and the seemingly endless ranks of the huge cuirassiers, he kept his face to the front, feigning indifference to the frantic cries of adulation which left the throat of every man. They were standing in their stirrups now, throwing their black-crested helmets high in the air, whirling the gleaming, razor-edged swords high above their heads. Behind them he could glimpse the leopard-skin-draped helmets of the Garde dragoon regiment that bore the name of his dead wife and the towering forms of the 'Invincibles', the grenadiers à cheval, every one of them mounted on a huge black horse. He turned to Soult.

'Magnificent. It is nothing less, Soult. Magnificent. This will

197

shake the English and their friends, eh? And soon we shall honour them with a frontal assault. That will be the quickest way to finish this business. But first a bombardment from the grand battery of the like they've never seen. As soon as the army is in position the grand attack will commence to capture the village of Mont St Jean. D'Erlon and Ney will lead the way to victory, and we will push through the gap.'

He turned to the other remaining members of staff who had not as yet joined their corps or divisions. 'Gentlemen, if my orders are carried out to the letter, we shall all sleep in Brussels tonight.'

They grinned. Soult spoke. Quietly.

'You don't suppose, sire, that Prince Jerome's report might have had some truth in it? Sometimes serving girls are the best spies.'

'Soult. My dear Soult. You know as well as I that what he heard last night was gossip. Or perhaps even a ruse by Wellington to trick us. The Prussians and the English cannot possibly link up for another two days. Particularly after Blücher has suffered such a defeat as at Ligny and given the fact that he is being pursued by a considerable body of troops under Marshal Grouchy. For my part, I am only too happy that the English have decided to stay and fight here. I tell you, this battle will be the salvation of France and it will be celebrated in the annals of the world long after you and I are dead, Soult. Listen. This is how it will be. My artillery will fire. My cavalry will charge. Wellington will disclose his positions, and when I am quite certain where the English are I shall march straight at them at the head of my Garde.'

They had come to the end of the long line now, to where Piré's lancers formed the extremity of the left flank. Wheeling round to the right, Napoleon led the staff along the very front of the line. Past his brother's division first. The light infantry in their sombre blue coats. He was suddenly aware of movement in the woods to his left. The dense coppice before the farm that he intended to be the focus of his supporting attack. De la Bedoyere appeared at his side, with Gourgaud and Bertrand. All looked worried.

Gourgaud spoke. 'Sire. Do you not think that you are perhaps a little too close to the enemy? There are light infantry, sharpshooters in those woods. One shot alone would do, sire. You must move back.'

'I have survived such shots till now. Let me be, Gourgaud. My army must see me.'

Mustn't show fear. He pulled away from them and continued along the front. Clear of the woods now. Saw Reille and his staff ahead. Gestured recognition to him with a just perceptible nod of his head and the bare glimmer of a smile. The man was a fool.

Their breakfast conference at the farmhouse had been a farce. What had Reille thought he was doing, daring to suggest to him, the Emperor, that we should move around the British right flank? He himself had already decided that the only way to beat Wellington was by a direct attack to the front. Reille was jumpy. Unnerved to be confronted by his great Peninsular demon. So he had placed him here quite deliberately. Out of trouble on the left flank. A supporting action against Hougoumont. Nothing more. And his hot-headed brother would be contained there too. The real action would happen on the right. D'Erlon would lead the way, with Ney doing what he did best, shouting the men forward into battle.

The Imperial party crossed the Brussels road and from the corner of his eye, though without turning his head, Napoleon formed an impression of a line of redcoats drawn up on the opposite slope. Not many. A single line, perhaps eight battalions strong. There was some activity in the little white farm in the centre. But mostly what he saw on the slopes were cannon. Wellington was playing a game of hide-and-seek. Well, if that was what he wanted, let it be so. He would draw this monster out. There would be a flank attack. But not as

Reille had envisaged. A feint attack that would draw down Wellington's reserves from behind the ridge from the moment battle commenced and weaken his centre ready for the push. He turned to the right. Saw the mercurial, red-haired marshal next to Soult.

'Ney, Soult. We will not begin on the right after all. The assault will commence on the left. But it will be merely a diversionary attack. Look at his line. Tell me what you see? Well?'

'There are not many men, sire.'

'Quite. Not many men. He shows me nothing. But you and I know that behind that ridge he has an army. I need to draw in his reserves. Make him think we are going for his flank and weaken his centre. Then you go, Ney. Yes?'

'Yes, sire.'

'Well, note it then. Write it down.'

Soult handed Ney the orders dictated to him by the Emperor an hour earlier. Ney unbuttoned his saddle-bag. Found a pencil. Wrote with care a note against Soult's handwriting: 'Count d'Erlon will see that the attack will now commence by the left instead of the right. Inform General Reille of this.'

'We will not actually intend to take Hougoumont. We will merely use an apparent concentration of our forces there to pin down Wellington's flank. Make him nervous. Make him commit his reserves to the château. And then we will make it the centre of a great wheel. Down here. On the left.' Napoleon swept his right hand upwards, through the air. 'We will be a moving spoke of that wheel, advancing from the right and sweeping the English away along their ridge.'

They had crossed the road again and regained the line, moving slowly along the front of the right wing. Fourteen regiments drawn up in two battalion lines, each nine ranks deep. As battalion succeeded battalion the tricolour-hung eagles were dipped on the Emperor's approach. This was how it should be. The cheering now was thunderous. The entire army drunk with his presence.

Napoleon laughed. Turned to Soult and Ney. 'I told you earlier that there were ninety chances in our favour and ten against. I say it again, Wellington is a bad general. The English are bad soldiers. We will settle this matter by lunchtime.'

'I sincerely hope so, sire.'

Reaching the end of the line he decided not to descend into the valley where Jacquinot's light cavalry guarded the right flank. Turned right and as he did so could not fail to notice just on the crest of the ridge a mass of red-coated horsemen, forming up as if on a parade ground. How steadily they took the ground. How smoothly. Grey horses. He half-turned to the staff. 'Who are those beautiful horsemen?'

This time de la Bedoyere had the answer. 'They're Scottish dragoons, sire. We have not fought against them before. But it is said that they are among the finest horsemen in Europe. Their regiment fought under Marlborough.'

'Indeed? They are certainly fine horsemen. And brave too, I have no doubt. But believe me, de la Bedoyere, in half an hour I will have cut them to pieces.'

He was riding downhill now, across the right flank of Milhaud's 3,000-strong division of cuirassiers. They continued on towards the main road, along the front of the Garde light cavalry, the green-coated chasseurs first, their officers preening on the finest horses in the army. The cheering was louder than ever. He tightened his fist with emotion. Finally they passed the red lancers. As the grey coat and white horse moved along their line, the Dutchmen cheered just as loudly for their Emperor as had their French comrades. He wondered how many of their countrymen, those men in blue up there in Wellington's lines, still felt themselves to be soldiers in the French army, as they had been until last year. Wondered how many would change sides during the battle. How many would turn and run.

'You see, Ney, the effect I have on soldiers. When the battle begins I tell you one quarter of Wellington's army will run away and as many again will desert and fight again for me.'

Beyond the next crossroads, just before the roadside inn of Rossomme, midway between La Belle Alliance and Le Caillou, the staff of the Imperial household were awaiting his arrival. Napoleon pulled up Marengo and dismounted, his chest tight as he climbed to the top of the green mound. He sat down heavily in the armchair that had been brought out from the inn. The ground around it had been strewn with straw to prevent him slipping on the mud, and to the left a party of engineers was constructing a ramp to enable aides and couriers to deliver and collect despatches.

No sooner had he sat down than Napoleon got up again and walked across to the campaign table to which had been pinned his map. He looked straight ahead towards the Allied lines. Reached into his coat and found the eyeglass, opened it and surveyed the field he had just left. Here he was three quarters of a mile away from the front line and a good thirty feet higher. Surely it was a good vantage point. Why then could he still see no more of the enemy? He reached inside his coat. Withdrew his snuff-box, reached for a pinch and, uncharacteristically, inhaled. He sneezed and, as he did so, over to the right a church bell tolled. Napoleon looked up at Soult, who alone of the staff remained with him. The others, as was customary, sat, some ten paces to the rear.

'Plancenoit, sire. Eleven o'clock. Mass.'

Napoleon pulled out his handkerchief. Mopped his brow. Grasped the table with both hands. Spoke, without turning from the map. 'Is the grand battery in place, as I directed?'

Soult replied. 'Almost all the cannon, sire.'

'What is almost? Fifty? More?'

'Very nearly all eighty, sire.'

'Send word to St Maurice. Fifteen minutes more. Tell him that is all he has to get his guns in place. Fifteen minutes before he must open fire. And Soult.' He pointed to his right. 'Send

202

someone to find out what Marbot's Hussars have found in those woods. I want to know what's happening to the east. Remember, fifteen minutes. That's all, Soult. We have already delayed this affair far too long.'

EIGHTEEN

Hougoumont, 11.30 a.m.
Macdonell

He heard the cannon fire, but saw neither the ball, nor the smoke. It was followed by another shot and a third. The opening salvoes of a battle.

In their wake came a great noise. A sound like rolling thunder, yet quite unmistakably human. It was a cheer. But a cheer like none that he had heard in twenty years of soldiering.

Seventy thousand men were cheering their Emperor.

Macdonell, mounted on the grey mare, had taken up the new position as ordered, outside the walls to the west of the château in a narrow strip of kitchen garden, among downtrodden strings of vegetables. The light company of the 3rd Guards he had placed obliquely, along the line of the garden hedge, overlooking a field of ripe corn. From there they could mark the flank and that worrying little valley that skirted the west side of the farm and which could offer any attacking force considerable cover from the guns on the ridge. His own light company, the Coldstream, would face the French head on as they broke from the side of the wood. But he had decided already that should it grow too hot he would move them into the walls. He knew that he could not afford to lose a single man.

The horse kicked and splashed her hoof impatiently into the

thick clay which had channelled the night's water into dark puddles. At least the weather was in their favour. The rain would have made a hell of the ground for their attackers. Through such sticky, cloying mud they would now be able to advance at only half their normal pace. Under fire all the way, and moving out of the reassuring cover. Since early in the morning two companies of Nassauers, some 200 men under a Captain Büsgen, had occupied the château. They also held the formal garden, the great orchard and the wood, where they had been joined now by light troops from three Hanoverian regiments.

There were perhaps all told 1,000 Germans and Dutchmen in the complex. Plus his own 200 Guards. About to face God knew what lay out there. The cheering had become stronger now, as the French attackers began to gather momentum. Even Macdonell felt a surge of fear.

He looked down at his men as they strained to catch their first sight of the foe. All were unshaven. Many had torn their clothes during the previous night's exertions at building the defences. His eyes travelling along the line, he ran silently through the litany of their names: Robert Moore, Colour Sar'nt Biddle, the Graham brothers Joseph and James, Joshua Dobinson, Tom Henderson, Atkins, Beckey, McLaurence, Frost, Tarling, Withers, Muirhead. He knew their private fears and dreams and the fact that for the next few hours at least, or as long as it took, they would think only of the battle. Of killing Frenchmen. They were not fearless by any means. All had their terrors. Their particular nightmares. But they knew, as he did, that they were not here to worry. They were here to fight, to obey and to kill, as best they could.

One of the men began to cough. Looked up. Caught his eye. Macdonell felt the anxiety bore into him. Dismissed it. Smiled back.

'Don't worry, Frost. They're not aiming for you. It's me they're after.'

The man smiled. His comrades looked round. Macdonell addressed the rest of the line. 'Stand to, my lads. Make ready. Let's show them some British play.'

The French guns were firing heavier now. Five or six batteries, he reckoned. The five-pound hollow iron balls came flying over the woods, ahead of the advancing infantry, exploding just over the heads of the defenders, their heavy, red-hot shards, each a lethal missile, tearing at the trees and into the flesh of the men sheltering behind them. Roundshot too came crashing into the woods, but doing no real damage. Occasionally though a cannonball caught the corner of an outbuilding, knocking chips of brick in all directions. A guardsman cursed as a small piece of masonry hit him in the cheek.

Macdonell called out: 'Stay under cover. Kneel down. Stay close to the hedges.'

Smaller fragments of exploding shell began to fall in the garden, pattering down on the leaves like a weird, heavy rain. Occasionally one would strike home, bringing shock and an oath but few real wounds. From the woods, however, the pop of musketry now began to grow closer. It was clear that the Nassauers were falling back.

Come on, he thought. Come on, you buggers. Come to us. Let us see you. Let us kill you. What was it in battles that always took so damned long?

He realized that Gooch was standing beside him. 'How goes it, sir?'

'Gooch. How did you spend the night?'

'Well, I managed to get under cover, sir. My feet got quite damp though. Still are, to tell the truth. I hear that the First Guards up on the ridge have managed to find some ham and champagne for breakfast. Shall I see if I can beg some, sir?'

Macdonell managed a laugh. 'I think, Mr Gooch, that the time for breakfast is now past. D'you not? D'you hear that? That's the French, lad. They're coming.'

He could hear them in the woods now. Closer. The

crash of breaking branches and the ragged shouts of 'Vive l'Empéreur' were interrupted by the staccato hammer of muskets as the retiring Nassauers and Hanoverians strained to find their targets in the undergrowth.

Macdonell turned again to his line: 'Look to your front.' The words left him instinctively. Unnecessarily.

Colour Sergeant Biddle spoke to them under his breath. 'Here they come, my boys. Wait till you see 'em clearly now. You'll have enough time. Let 'em get nice and close. Wait for my word. Then you have my permission to send 'em to Hell. And be careful not to shoot any of them fellers in the green coats. Them's our allies, remember. Nassooers. Mustn't shoot them. Nosey would never forgive us.'

Macdonell could see the green coats now, falling back through the wood. Heard muffled cries of command in Flemish and German. Some of the Nassauers, mostly the big grenadiers, were pulling back slowly, in good order, their faces still to the enemy. Others though were running. Boys, pale with fear, panicked by the sight of so many of the enemy. He saw some fall, not to move again. Others gained the safety of the buildings. Crossed the thirty yards of open ground before the garden wall and spilled round the left side of the enclosure and into the cover of the orchard. With them came the Hanoverians, light troops in grey and dark green. Better trained than the Nassauers. Yet they too were pulling back. He was comforted by the knowledge that soon it would be the turn of the French to cross that same expanse of exposed grass. And then the defenders would not hold their fire.

He noticed Wyndham and Elrington beside him, momentarily detached for some reason from their commands, and wondered whether they had managed to make the champagne breakfast up on the ridge. Both officers saluted.

Elrington grinned at Gooch. Noticed he was frowning. 'Thinking of death, Gooch?'

'No, Elrington. Well, yes actually, I was.'

'Oh, don't worry. You'll probably end the day a field officer.'

The young ensign smiled. Turned to Macdonell. 'D'you think he's right, sir? D'you really think there's a chance that I'll get promoted in my first battle?'

Macdonell smiled back, but it was Wyndham who made the reply.

'He doesn't mean that they'll make you a major or a colonel, you young idiot. He means that you'll be an officer "beneath" the field. Under the sod, old boy. Dead.'

Gooch's face fell. He looked at the ground.

Macdonell spoke. 'Enough, gentlemen. We shall all survive this day if we only keep our wits as sharp as yours, Elrington. Eh, Gooch? And now to work. They are upon us, gentlemen. Take your posts, if you please.'

A sputtering volley of musket fire from the hedge to his right signalled that, as he had suspected, the French were attempting to outflank them. The sharpshooters of the 3rd Guards were picking off the skirmishing voltigeurs as they advanced along the valley through the cornfield and attempted with difficulty to climb its deceptively steep slope. Beyond them he glimpsed the flying pennants of accompanying French light cavalry. Lancers. It was a flanking move, sure enough. But this he knew was not the main attack. That would be a different thing entirely. The artillery fire had intensified and several of his men were now wounded. This, he thought, would be the time to remove at least part of his command into the relative safety of the château.

'Wyndham, bring your men into the buildings. Gooch, tell Dashwood to hold the kitchen garden for as long as he can and then follow us inside the walls.'

Reining his horse round, Macdonell trotted along the west wall and back into the farm through the north gate, dismounting outside the stable block. The Nassau commander, Captain Büsgen, approached him. He looked agitated.

'Colonel Macdonell. My men are being hard pressed. We cannot hold the wood much longer and I fear that the orchard will soon be lost also. What do you wish me to do, sir?'

'Captain, may I suggest that you take your men from the château and reinforce those at the garden wall. We shall occupy the buildings. I intend to close the north gate directly. Do not worry. I am sure that reinforcements will be with us in due course.'

With a nod of his head the nervous Nassauer departed, to be replaced by Sergeant Biddle.

'They've taken the woods, sir. The Germans have broke. There's Nassooers and 'Anaverians runnin' about all over the place. The Frogs is comin' on into the orchard too, sir. Shall we meet 'em there?'

Macdonell shook his head. 'No, Sar'nt. I intend to consolidate here. Inside the walls. But I am quite sure that our commander will already have assessed the situation. I'm willing to wager that we'll see Colonel Saltoun back here ere long.'

They were joined by Gooch. 'There are French in the field down by the kitchen garden, sir. Shall I go round to the side of the company? I could take a section, sir, and fire on them down the line.'

'No, Gooch. Don't do that. But it was a good idea. And it's called an "enfilade". Send word out to Colonel Dashwood if you would. Tell him to press a counter-attack into the wood and across the French left flank. We must contain them. And Gooch, it's the flank, not the side. Do try to remember, lad.'

He walked alone back to the north gate, climbed on to one of the improvised fire steps and peered over the wall. He could hear the French to his left and the crash of musketry. Ahead of him and a little off to the right of the approach road two long, red-coated columns were advancing down the hill. Saltoun, as he had guessed, commanded back to the orchard.

As he stood there, more Nassauers, singly and in small groups, began to come past him through the gate. A lieutenant saluted him hurriedly and attempted to regroup his small force. Many, Macdonell noticed, had been wounded.

'Sir. Colonel, sir.'

It was Gooch again. The boy needed a wet-nurse.

'Sir, the French are coming in on our right. They intend to take the farm, sir.'

'I am quite aware of their intentions, Mr Gooch. Have Colonel Dashwood fall back through the north gate directly. Go to it.'

So, they were throwing more men into the cauldron. Macdonell wondered for a moment whether this was really what Napoleon intended. It seemed foolhardy indeed to sacrifice so many men before the château walls. But perhaps Boney too knew that if he could take this place then he would carry the field. He sensed the impending crisis. Found Biddle by the gate.

'Sar'nt. See that Colonel Dashwood's men are admitted. Then close the gates.'

Drawn instinctively, as always, towards commotion, Macdonell walked back with haste towards the southern defences. Having pushed the Nassauers out, the French were indeed coming on in strength through the wood. He entered the gatehouse and climbed the stair into the upper room from which on the previous night he had seen Gooch's men drive off the French cavalry with such ease. Now the scene presented a very different picture. The woods below him were filled with French infantry. Blue coats as far as the eye could see through the white smoke, and beyond them the rising palls that betrayed the fury of the relentless artillery bombardment. The infantry were pushing on directly towards him. Drummers to the fore, their *rat-a-tat, rat-a-tat, rata-tata-tata-tat* almost overcome with the crash of the muskets. At their front the officers, in mud-bespattered white breeches, whirled round to spur them on. Swords cutting the air, shouting inaudible commands, they reached the edge of the wood. He looked at the first few ranks. All in blue. Some covered in brown or grey coats. Light infantry. Meeting like with like. They were voltigeurs mostly in this first wave, some with great yellow and red plumes that bobbed in the smoke as they sprang from the cover of the trees and, breaking into a run, rushed the wall.

They died in a hail of musket balls. Every man that Macdonell could see went down. Instantly, before the Frenchmen could think for themselves, their officers pushed the next three ranks forward. They moved instinctively, less quickly over the dead, but once in the open ground began to run, and suffered the same fate as their comrades. Yet still they came on. A bullet from a sharpshooter zinged through the open window and smacked into a beam behind him. Macdonell ducked, then looked out again through the smoke. More shots sang out towards the blue ranks. No point in volley fire. They all fell. He saw one man go down quite clearly. A French sergeant. Hit almost simultaneously by four of the three-quarter-inch musket balls, his legs just gave way beneath him. His face looked up directly at Macdonell's window with a curious, questioning expression. Beside him, another man, hit by as many balls again, was spun right round and came to rest with his eyes turned skywards, facing his own men. Another crumpled exactly like a child's rag doll. God, thought Macdonell, how easily human life is snuffed out. A guardsman on his right, no more than a boy, one of the new recruits (Valentine, was it?), turned grinning to Corporal Dobinson.

'I got 'im. Did you see 'im, Corp? Went and jumped up like a bleedin' hare, 'e did.'

The big Yorkshireman did not bother to turn to reply. Kept firing. 'Shut up, lad, and just shoot the buggers. Or it's you who'll be doin' the jumpin'.'

Macdonell looked back down into the clearing as it filled with bodies. The French were moving forward more slowly now. More of them tumbling at every pace. Behind them their comrades seemed even less keen for glory and the Emperor's

211

thanks. Still they walked on, though, pushing their way through the sticks and twigs. Pressing steadily closer. More shouting officers could be heard. A full colonel came into view, conspicuous on his fine white horse. He shouted a 'Vive l'Empéreur' and received a ball through the head for his trouble. He fell, but his foot caught in the stirrup and, panicked, his horse ran forward, dragging the dead man with it through the undergrowth until at length mount and corpse parted company.

Another mounted officer followed, his own exhortation, carried aloft on a gust of wind, was quite audible: '*L'Empéreur récompensera le premier qui avancera.*'

Of course the Emperor would reward the first to advance. But, as they could all now see, there were other, greater, eternal riches awaiting those foolhardy enough to venture out beyond the cover of the trees. In front of Macdonell the space between the wood and the garden wall had become a mass of dead and wounded Frenchmen. He tried to count the bodies and at length gave up. And all this in what? Ten minutes. How many rounds? Twenty-five, thirty a man. But they would have to make each shot count. Who was in command up here?

'Sar'nt Miller. Keep the men firing at will. But keep a close watch on your ammunition. We must not go short.'

Suddenly a lull. Less noise now. Yet still there was the crash of muskets as men continued to find targets at short range or fired blind into the wood. Then, for just a moment, no more Frenchmen came from the trees. They must have gone to ground, he thought. That was good.

He heard a noise from his right. Strained to look out of the window, but saw nothing. A musket ball struck the window embrasure and he tucked his head back in. He could see enough to realize that there was black smoke drifting over from the right. Heard the crackling of a fire. Something was wrong. Something, somewhere was ablaze. But which building?

It had puzzled him that the French had not opened up earlier with more of their artillery. The two howitzers incorporated into each of their batteries would surely have had enough combined firepower to flatten this brick-built château and farm, if not merely set it afire. Perhaps that was what had happened. If so then they must be doomed to abandon their stronghold. They would lose the battle. His heart pounding, Macdonell hurried past the still-firing guardsmen, down the wooden steps and out into the chaos of the courtyard. Men were running in all directions, slipping on cobbles slick with mud, water and blood; carrying ammunition, moving position, helping the wounded. The air was filled with oaths and commands in English, Flemish, German. White smoke billowed and drifted away from the firing platforms. Nowhere, though, could he see a building on fire. Neither was there, as he had feared, any sign of incoming shellfire. He leaned his back against a wall, placed his hands on his breeches and exhaled with relief. Looking up he was surprised to see three cannonballs sail high over his head. Relieved that they came, not from the French, but from the Allied guns up on the ridge. Seeing a flicker of flame on one of the balls, he realized that the gunners were using the explosive shrapnel shells unique to the Royal Artillery, sending them high into the air over the woods. Timed fuses fizzing, they burst in showers of death over the French infantry. From the flashes and cries that now came from that direction, they were clearly hitting their mark.

If only they could all keep this up, the French would surely die in droves. As long as the ammunition held out. Macdonell sensed that the orchard and the left flank would now most need his attention and began to walk away from the wall and past the gate into the formal garden which had predictably been swiftly reduced to a muddy mess. A cry from behind made him turn round.

Dashwood was running across the courtyard, his right arm pouring blood, his men streaming in after him, some being carried. Many were wounded.

'By God, sir, they're coming on thick out there. And there's thousands of them.'

'Yes, I believe that we are being attacked in some force.'

'And they've fired the haystack, sir.'

That, thought Macdonell, must explain the burning and the smoke. He looked at the young man's arm. 'You'd best get that seen to. Dr Whymper is plying his trade in the stable block.'

As the injured colonel walked slowly to the stables, Macdonell turned back towards the dozen or so men manning the north wall.

'Close the gates as soon as the last man is in.'

He moved towards them over the cobbles. A horseman appeared in the gate. A guardsman: Sergeant Fraser, ever the farmer's boy, balancing his musket over the saddle, came trotting in astride the blue-saddled mount of a French officer. Grinning, he dismounted and led the horse across to Macdonell.

'Took her off a French colonel, sir. She's a fine beast. Would you not agree?'

'Quite, Fraser. But I do think that matters of horse flesh might wait discussion until we have attended to the business of the moment. We are, in case it has escaped your attention, under attack.'

Fraser, still grinning, snapped to attention and led his new prize to the stable block. Macdonell shook his head. Grinned for a moment and caught sight of Wyndham.

'Close the gates, Henry. All your men inside, Dashwood?'

'I think so, sir. All that can be accounted for.'

'Close the gates then. Bar them. Quickly.'

He could hear the French on the other side. The cheers and shouts of 'En avant' and 'Vive l'Empéreur'. Two guardsmen lifted the great wooden crossbar and hefted it into place on one of the steel lugs. But instants before they could secure it, an axe blade came slicing in with lightning speed through the

214

tiny gap between the doors and with huge force cut the wooden stave clean in two. Instantly the gates sprang back under the force of numbers pressing from outside. And at the same time a volley of shots rang out from the French and came crashing through the timbers. A hundred yards in front of him Macdonell saw George Evelyn yell out as three musket balls tore open his arm from the elbow to the wrist. Staring down at the shattered limb, he sat straight down. His words came as a whisper: 'Please, help me.'

Macdonell pointed towards him. Yelled towards the barn. 'A surgeon. Find that officer a surgeon.'

And then they were in.

The gates fell away to either side of the entrance and a close-packed column of French infantry flowed through into the lower yard. Within seconds there were thirty, perhaps fifty Frenchmen in the yard. They were led by a giant of an officer. The huge lieutenant, an earring glinting gold in his right lobe, was quite Macdonell's equal in stature. He had no sword, but was wielding an axe, taken from a sapeur. Macdonell watched with horror as he cleft one of the Coldstream privates in two, through the shako, from head to abdomen, like some Highland Jacobite pole-axing one of Cope's dragoons.

He saw the boy Beckey go down and at the same moment was conscious that some of his men were already beginning to fall back to the barn before turning to shoot into the fighting. The sheer momentum of the French was carrying them forward. The young Nassau lieutenant who had saluted him an hour before found himself isolated now and pushed back towards the farmhouse. As he turned, he met the gaze of the huge French officer, who brought his axe down on the Dutchman's arm, severing his hand at the wrist before turning to find another victim.

There wasn't a moment to spare. Macdonell dashed across the yard, calling out as he went. 'Guards, to me. Re-form. To me.'

He reached the north wall of the château where a group of some thirty guardsmen were formed in two ranks, under the command of Colour Sergeant Biddle. Seeing Macdonell advance towards them they momentarily ceased firing. Macdonell found Biddle.

'Colour Sar'nt. We'll show them the steel, I think.'

Biddle smiled. Barked the order, emphasizing and prolonging the last syllable. 'Bayonets.'

The few men who had not yet fixed their bayonets now screwed them to the muzzles of their muskets.

Macdonell raised his sword. 'Coldstream Guards. Follow me.'

With a great roar the detachment burst at a run from the shadow of the wall upon the astounded French. The slight slope of the farmyard increased their momentum and carried them at full tilt into the front rank of the enemy. Every bayonet met its target. Blue coats tumbled to the ground. But the second rank of Frenchmen, mainly red-plumed grenadiers, were ready and began to push into the Guards. Now French steel found its mark. Macdonell levelled his blade and slid it deftly into the throat of a French corporal. Side-stepping the falling corpse, he noticed for the first time that two small haystacks to the right of the well had been set ablaze, presumably by shell fire. As he looked, a raft of burning hay fell over the face of a wounded man, a Nassauer he thought, lying at its base. His cries were pitiful. Macdonell turned back to the fight and saw that his charge had pushed the French as far as the gate. But more had now appeared in the space between the doors and were forcing an entry. Seeing a massive wooden beam lying on the cobbles, he picked it up. Ran towards the gates.

'To me, Guards. To me. Close the gates. Keep them out.'

He was aware that both Graham and his brother were running with him now as they neared the mêlée. And there, thank God, was Sar'nt Fraser. As they passed the well they were joined by McGregor and two other men of the 3rd Guards whom he did not recognize. To his left he glimpsed a knot of officers, momentarily motionless.

'Wyndham, Hervey, Gooch. Follow me. Light Company, form on me. Form on me, Guards. To the gates. Close the gates.'

He heard Fraser take up his cry: 'Shut the courtyard gates. Keep them out.'

Reaching the attackers, Macdonell pushed into the mêlée and cut down with his sword, severing a man's ear and half his shoulder. He dodged a bayonet and parried another before thrusting and hitting home deep into a Frenchman's side.

Smoke was everywhere now, stinging the eyes, making it hard to find friend or enemy. The acrid smell of powder filled his lungs and he coughed, almost retched. He felt metal on metal. Metal on wood. Metal slipping into flesh. Bayonets seemed to thrust wildly on all sides. There was the unmistakable sound of steel on bone. And other noises. The moans of the wounded. The animal grunts and shouts of men intent on killing each other with whatever came to hand. Bricks, clubs, bare fists.

A French officer appeared before him, smiled and thrust at him with a shining, straight-bladed infantry sword. Macdonell parried the thrust, but the Frenchman put up his white-gloved left hand and grasped the blade. Macdonell pulled hard and the officer, surprised at the Scot's strength, had no choice but to let the blade slide back through his hand, cutting it open.

'Merde.'

Macdonell heard his oath and, taking advantage of the man's shock, with a deft flick of his wrist encircled the officer's blade and penetrated his guard. The Frenchman side-stepped the attack and, placing his bloodied hand behind his back like a fencer in training, tried his luck again. But this time Macdonell had the measure of him. As the Frenchman's blade came towards his left breast he put up his own so that the two swords formed a cross and he was able to push his opponent's away to the side with ease. Continuing to move forward he now dropped his own point at the last moment and felt it slide firmly into the flesh within the tight blue tunic. The Frenchman, still staring into Macdonell's eyes, widened his own, opened his mouth, dropped his sword and grasped with both hands to staunch the fatal wound. Macdonell withdrew his bloody blade and turned away quickly, leaving the man to fall and die. It was no good when you saw their eyes. Not like that. Those faces stayed with you. Came back sometimes. Unexpectedly. Always the eyes. That stare of momentary surprise and then the horror as they understood the inevitable.

To his right he saw that McLaurence was locked in a desperate fight with a voltigeur. Macdonell was close enough to smell them now. He moved to help but his way was blocked by another Frenchman directly before him lunging with his musket. Macdonell prepared to take him on. But as he did so a shot went off close beside his right ear, causing momentary deafness.

A second later the Frenchman's face had vanished. Blown clean away at short range into a blackened mess. The half-decapitated body fell away in front of him and Macdonell pushed forward over it towards the gate. He was at it now. Found the filthy wood with his hands. Careful not to drop his sword, began to push against the sea of blue coats swelling through the gap. To his right the Graham brothers, both of whom had handed their muskets to the less well-built Wyndham, were doing the same. And there were two more men with him on the left. From the 3rd Guards, with Fraser and MacGregor. Other officers joined them, adding their weight to the mass of redcoats pushing at the wooden panels, and then, with a painful slowness that seemed to last an eternity, the great door began to move away from them. They pushed at it again. Did not let up. Harder now. It continued to move. Slowly. Slowly. Macdonell heard himself shouting, 'That's it, men. Keep pushing. Push, for God's sake. Push.'

They were still moving. Pushing against the French. Slowly. Slowly. And all the time muskets, bayonets, swords, men's arms were being thrust between the two doors as the French tried in desperation to keep them open. Musket balls hammered against the wood, a few penetrating. But the advantage was with the Guards. Macdonell looked up into the gap. Two feet to go. One and a half. A foot. Six inches. They were almost there.

'One last push, lads. Together now. Heave.'

With a splintering of wood the two doors met. One French musket broke in half as they banged together, its barrel and bayonet falling into the yard. And then Macdonell's men were pushing the thick crossbars into their iron lugs. Bracing them with anything that might help keep them in place. He stood beside them, drenched in sweat and filth. Wiped a hand across his dripping brow. Turned to his right. Saw Wyndham. 'We did it. Well done, Henry. Well done. Well done, Graham. Fraser. Well done, all of you. Thank God.'

There was no time to rest. Musket balls began to patter down into the yard. A few intrepid Frenchmen had climbed on to one another's shoulders and were firing over the wall down into the mass of heaving bodies in the yard. Macdonell saw a private of the 3rd Guards go down and noticed another voltigeur take careful aim at Wyndham. The lieutenant, though, had seen the sniper himself and, handing James Graham's musket back to its owner, stood coolly by as the keen-eyed corporal beat him to it and deftly put a ball clean through the Frenchman's brain.

Attempting to regain his composure, Macdonell turned back to face the yard and count his casualties and realized that it was far from finished. Ahead of him were forty Frenchmen, perhaps more, any one of whom was capable of reopening the gates. In their centre stood the big lieutenant, hatless now and covered in mud and blood, but still with his axe. Seeing the hopelessness of his position he flung the weapon down and was followed by his men as they let their muskets fall to the ground.

Macdonell raised his sword to his face in a salute.

'Sar'nt Fraser. Take these men prisoner. Have them fall back to the château.'

He turned back to the gates. By God. They were coming again. From outside another great shout announced a further assault. The gates moved under the sheer weight of bodies. Macdonell knew the moment was crucial.

'Keep at them, lads. Fire down on them. Don't let up.'

Men were running towards the north wall now. Climbing the fire steps. Squeezing into every available space to pour fire down on the heads of the French. A cry from behind made Macdonell turn round. He saw the boy, Wilby, fall to the ground clutching his side. Above him stood a French sergeant, his bayonet bloody. Great God. The prisoners had picked up their muskets again, were attacking them from the rear. It was against all the articles of war. Against honour. Desperation flared inside Macdonell. He turned to Fraser.

'Get them, for God's sake. Kill them. Kill them all.'

He heard the words leave his mouth. Basic, primeval, tribal command. The sergeant didn't need telling twice. Within seconds men were running from all directions, sending a deadly, close-range fire into the ragged square of French prisoners which had formed some twenty yards from the gate and was moving gradually towards the well. Their shots were returned with a disjointed fury. But it took only a few minutes before its ranks grew thin.

The Nassauers, seeing a moment when most of the French appeared to be reloading and incensed by their maimed lieutenant, his bleeding stump bound with a torn shirt, seized their chance and laid in upon them with no quarter. Bayonets rose and fell, muskets clubbed down mercilessly, spilling blood and brains on to the cobbles. Macdonell saw two Nassauers pick up a wounded Frenchman and fling him, screaming, on to one of the burning haystacks. Sickened, he turned away. And then it was over. More than twenty of the French lay dead. The others, all wounded, tried to drag their broken bodies across the yard. Some groaned. Called for water. Several just lay and twitched. The Nassauers walked round them, plunging bloody bayonets deep into dead and wounded alike. One corpse, Macdonald noticed, had soiled his trousers. Up against a wall a small boy of no more than twelve, a drummer in green and gold, pressed himself back against the bricks, his face an expression of pure terror. Macdonell held his hand out to the frightened child.

'*Venez, venez, mon brave. On ne va pas vous manger maintenant. Venez donc.*'

Cautiously the boy moved from his hiding place. Extended his own hand and folded it into Macdonell's as a child might into that of a comforting father. He was sobbing.

'Sar'nt Biddle. Take this young fellow away and see he's treated well. He's fought bravely. You might put him with the gardener's girl. They must be about the same age.'

Children, he thought. Just children. She must have been born the year of Austerlitz and Trafalgar, he only shortly before. They had not known peace. What would their future be? Perhaps, God willing, they might survive this great battle. And then? And what of himself? No. Don't wonder about that. Live for the moment. Take the day. Take the battle to the French.

They had done it. Had repelled the attack. Had shut the gate. Macdonell felt a surge of elation and almost as suddenly was conscious of a sharp pain in his cheek. He put up his hand and felt warm blood. Damn. He pressed at the wound to see how deep it was and how long. Looked at his palm. It wasn't so bad. Must have been that officer. The fencer. He spotted Gooch, bewildered by the skirmish, looking around himself distractedly. In need of orders.

'Gooch. Take twelve men up to the highest room in the château. Tell me what you see.'

One more push, he thought. One push and they'll do it. And I do not have the men.

He climbed up on top of a pigsty and peered over the north wall.

Through the smoke he was able to make out a column advancing directly towards the gate. Infantry with mounted officers. Oh God, he thought. They have come round to the rear in force. There must be 300 of them. He rubbed his eyes. Looked again. Searched for the eagle, the drummers. Saw only red. Their coats were red. British red. He could make out columns now, three companies. And as they grew closer he was able to see their distinctive oilskin shako covers. British Guards. Reinforcements from the ridge, with three mounted officers. He recognized Edward Acheson on his bay mare. Another on a familiar grey. Dan Mackinnon with the grenadier company. And Colonel Woodford.

The French saw them too. Began to turn. But such an about-face was clumsy at the best of times, and it was too late now. Bayonets glinting, the first ranks of the British smashed into their disordered flank. The French turned in a rabble to the left and rushed pell-mell back the way they'd come. A lone officer, trying to rally them, was shot from his horse. At the corner of the wall a small knot of voltigeurs turned to fire. Their effort was not concerted, but Macdonell saw a dozen holes appear in the Guards' ranks. Acheson's horse was shot from under him and he watched horrified as Mackinnon's horse too was brought down and threw its rider. The redcoats came on, bayonets fixed. Number Four Company first, followed by the grenadiers and Number One Company. Macdonell watched as Mackinnon, his leg bleeding from the knee, struggled to his feet. Leaning on a corporal, he urged the grenadiers on against the French. A few of the voltigeurs managed to get in another shot at close range. Macdonell saw one of the captains, young John Blackman, popular with the men, shot clean through the head. And then came the bayonets. The

222

fight lasted barely a minute. Most of the French took flight as the rear column pushed through the grenadiers and smashed into them. Some surrendered. Not always with success. Macdonell watched as Blackman's furious sergeant pushed aside the praying hands of a kneeling voltigeur and spitted him clean through the chest with seventeen inches of steel. Conscious that the danger was not yet over, Macdonell called over to the men on the wall: 'Open the gates. Let them in.'

Hands worked at the improvised barrier and the great wooden gates were heaved open. Outside the path was strewn with dead Frenchmen. There were 100 at least, maybe 200. Some of the bodies had been badly trampled and were almost unrecognizable under the mud. As the two leading companies of Coldstreamers continued to pursue the French into the wood, the rear column marched into the château over this carpet of corpses. Macdonell ran towards Mackinnon, who was limping with his corporal through the gate.

'Dan, how good to see you. And not a moment too soon, by God. You're hurt.'

'The cap of my knee. A musket ball, by God. It really is quite excruciating. But James. What of you? You're alive. They had you encircled. We thought for a minute you were overrun. Hard to see through the smoke.'

Their words were almost drowned by the cheering that erupted from the tired defenders as another hundred men filed in through the gate. Woodford rode up. Swung a gleaming boot over his saddle and jumped down. Macdonell saluted.

'Colonel Woodford, sir, how very pleasant to see you. Am I to suppose that I should now hand over command, sir?'

'Indeed not, Macdonell. I can perceive no earthly reason to relieve a man of command when he appears to be doing such an excellent job. The château is yours, sir. Consider me merely as . . . an equal. We shall command together, *n'est-ce pas*? Now, acquaint me properly with your position and place these lads where they're most needed.'

He noticed Macdonell's bloody face. 'You, uh, appear to have cut yourself . . . in shaving.' He laughed at his feeble joke. Then caught sight of Mackinnon's more serious wound. 'Dan, what's this? Get to the surgeon, man.'

'It's merely a touch, sir. You see. No more than a graze.'

'Touch or no, you'll see Dr Whymper.'

The others were filing in now and with them, having detached himself from Number Seven Company up on the ridge protecting the colours, rode George Bowles – clean-shaven, coat spotless, boots polished and buffed by his soldier-servant to a glass-like sheen. Macdonell applauded. Mackinnon grinned.

'George. Bravo. Off to a review?'

Bowles laughed. 'Come to offer you a hand, James. Colonel Woodford says to us, "Macdonell's done for, boys," he says. "Who's for helpin' the poor old Jock?" Well, James, you know that I can never resist a call to arms. Besides, you didn't think I'd miss this scrap, did you? But, gad, you've had hot work here, eh?'

'You could say that, George. It has been damned hot work. Though I've a feeling that it's about to get a good deal hotter.'

NINETEEN

The ridge of Mont St Jean, 1.40 p.m.
De Lancey

The cannonball hit the man at a height of around five feet, four inches, travelling at 800 miles an hour. It took off his head. Or rather, it smashed it to a bloody pulp and, covered with his brains, went on to hit the man directly behind him square in the chest. Passing through him like a knife through butter, it entered the third rank man to his rear, disembowelling him before crushing the groin of the unfortunate ensign who happened to be standing at the rear of the company. Now slightly deflected by its collision with bone, it continued to travel away from the screaming officer before finding a home in the next battalion, where it fell on the head of a sheltering drummer boy, crushing it quite flat, before rolling away into the mud, its mischievous force finally spent.

It was not the most destructive roundshot that De Lancey had ever seen. A cannonball at Salamanca had passed high over his own saddle before killing and wounding no less than twenty men of the 27th in a similarly bloody fashion. The added effectiveness then had been due to the gunners' ability to exploit the fact that on hard ground roundshot would bounce like a giant cricket ball. Here though, thankfully, the mud had annulled such a technique. Nevertheless the shots were still telling. He looked at the bloody swathe the missile had left in its wake. At the headless and eviscerated corpses. At the whimpering, pitifully emasculated young officer who had now been picked up by four soldiers and was being carried with due deference to the field hospital at Mont St Jean farm. As De Lancey watched, the dead were hauled out of the ranks and the files closed up as if nothing had happened. The regimental sergeant-major, granite-faced, muttered just one word: 'Steady.'

De Lancey turned back to face the enemy.

For ten minutes now the French cannon had been belching smoke and flame across the valley. It was a display of artillery power whose like he had never seen. Eighty guns – six, eight, twelve pounders – lined along a small spur on the eastern side of the battlefield. A battery of such prodigious firepower that its smoke now not only obscured the army assembled behind it, but also seemed to threaten to blot out the very sun itself. He turned to Basil Jackson.

'Damn this fire. How much longer will they keep it up? Look at the men. Our lads can take it. But have you seen the Hanoverians? D'you think they can stand much more?'

'The Peer seems cool enough about it, De Lancey.'

'The Peer always seems cool, Basil. But what he shows to us and what he really feels are quite different.'

Ahead of him and slightly to the left, Wellington sat astride Copenhagen, his eyeglass pressed close to his cheek. Lowering it, he turned to De Lancey.

'I think we might expect something now, De Lancey. D'you see how they are moving their caissons aside. I believe they mean to attack us.'

De Lancey raised his own telescope. Wellington was right. There was something happening behind the extended gun line. The hundreds of ammunition caissons which had hitherto been parked in three long lines behind the guns were being moved together into long columns. Columns which would allow bodies of troops to pass between them in single file. Wellington continued:

'Tell Picton to be ready to meet them. But tell him to keep his men lying down until the last possible moment. Or until the guns cease. And have him move those Dutch and Belgians back from the lower slope. They've taken enough of a pounding.'

It was true. They had all watched in horrid anticipation as shortly after midday the French had begun to lug the great cannon into place on the rising ground. Such a battery was one of Napoleon's favourite tactics. And always the prelude to an attack in force. It had taken over an hour before the battery was ready. The guns were extraordinarily close to the Allied lines, he thought. No more than 700 yards. Close enough for him to observe quite clearly, with an almost clinical objectivity, the individual gunners as after each shot they laboured to move the great ton-heavy cannon back into position, before sponging out the barrels, reloading and taking aim. Then he was able to follow the arc of the ball as it flew from the smoking mouth of the gun towards the ridge, sometimes for a full two seconds before it struck.

Here on the right of the line, save for the regiments positioned directly behind the farm, chiefly the German Legion, they had not yet suffered too badly. On the left, where Picton's division supported the Hanoverians, the toll appeared to be heavier. It was hard, though, to tell the dead from the living, for all were lying down. It was a trick that Wellington had used much in Spain and of whose effectiveness the late round-shot had just proven a grizzly reminder. Yet for the most part the cannonballs were flying too high to make their mark. The majority of the casualties were being caused by French shells which, bursting over the heads of the recumbent infantry, sent down a lethal rain of red-hot metal. Such had been the disturbed nature of the night that often the exhausted men were simply dying in their sleep, apparently unaware that they had been hit. De Lancey turned in the saddle. Found Will Cameron.

'William, ride to Sir Thomas Picton. Tell him that his Grace believes that the French are about to attack. He should make ready. Tell him to keep his men in cover until the last possible moment. And ask him to move Bylandt's men beyond the crest.'

As the young officer sped off, De Lancey turned back to Wellington and, with the rest of the entourage, followed him as he began to make his way along the ridge towards what he perceived would be the focus of the coming attack.

They passed a battery of British artillery. Its commander, a ruddy-faced young captain, rode up to the Duke.

'Your Grace. I beg you, allow the artillery to engage the enemy batteries. Our men are suffering horribly.'

'I have specifically ordered, sir, that our cannon should not exchange fire with the French. Such a duel is ineffective and costly. We will reserve our ammunition for the infantry, when they come. I'm very much afraid that the men will simply have to bear it.'

Almost as he spoke a shell burst above their heads, thirty yards over to their right. All save Wellington ducked. De Lancey watched a larger than average piece of the exploding iron ball fly from the sky and cut a company sergeant-major clean in half.

At the same instant a shout came from directly behind them. Turning round he saw that another shot had hit a large tree and cut it through, causing the tip to fall on top of a first aid post which two surgeons had recently established beneath its boughs. They were now attempting to extricate themselves from the fallen branches. What a farcical contrast, he thought, to the carnage all around them. But that surely was what a battlefield was about. A place whose very essence was absurd, which in turn invited episodes of absurdity. It was clear from the effect on the tree that the French had raised their angle of fire. And that could mean only one thing. Instants later De Lancey began to make out the small black dots of men emerging from the landscape before him to the left of the *chaussée*

directly opposite Picton's line. French tirailleurs and voltigeurs. Skirmishers advancing ahead of the main force. He
watched as they approached the comparatively sparse Allied
skirmish line. As the puffs of smoke marked individual dramas
where men stood or fell. Then, while the rifles continued
to fire, he saw the blue-coated Belgian skirmishers turn
away from the advancing French. Watched as French light
troops approached the farmhouse of La Haye Sainte, engaging
Baring's German Legion riflemen in the buildings.

And then quite suddenly the cacophany, which for half an
hour had rent the air, just stopped. He could still hear the
popping of the skirmishers' muskets. But as one, the cannon
had fallen silent. A new sound now took the place of their vile
roar. An insistent, rhythmic beat which seemed to come from
the very base of the valley. He knew it instantly.

Rum dum, rum dum, rummadum, rummadum, rum dum.
Again.

Rum dum, rum dum, rummadum, rummadum, rum dum.
The *pas de charge*. The heart-stopping sound that the veterans called 'old trousers'. The familiar Peninsular tattoo of
French infantry making their approach march. Two hundred
drummers beating out the death knell. De Lancey felt his
stomach tighten into a knot; his throat grow dry. Now he
could see the columns quite clearly. The sun glinting off sixteen
eagles bobbing with their standards high above the blue
masses. Quickly he counted them. Two hundred men wide;
perhaps twenty deep. He saw officers dancing round and
round in front of the men; urging them on. Drummers lifting
and lowering their sticks. Men hurling shakos into the air. The
very glory of France, it seemed, was marching towards him. It
did not take the columns long to descend the slope. And once
they were beneath the crest, the guns above began again. The
balls came in high and fast, at the height of a cavalryman or
mounted officer. Tellingly, one made contact with the outer
edge of the Duke's staff, carrying away the upper torso of a

teenage bugler seconded from the dragoons, along with the front portion of his horse's head.

De Lancey concentrated on the sight to his front. How slowly they are coming on, he thought. It is the mud.

An officer of horse artillery rode up. Saluted Wellington. 'Your Grace. Napoleon and his staff are in range. I have a clear view, sir. May I have your permission to try a shot?'

'Certainly not. I will not allow it. It is not the business of commanders to fire upon each other.'

'Are they trying to frighten us from the field?'

It was d'Alava. Wellington touched his hat to the Spaniard. 'My dear Count. I have never left a battlefield on account of the noise and I do not intend to do so now.' He turned to the commander of the allied artillery, Augustus Frazer. 'You may have the artillery give fire now, Frazer. At the infantry, mark you.'

Wellington caught De Lancey's eye. 'This one's going to need careful timing.'

Three minutes later, all along the Allied ridge, thirteen batteries – seventy guns – opened fire.

There was cheering from the furthest advanced of the Allied infantry.

'De Lancey. With me.'

Wellington was galloping eastwards. As De Lancey caught up with him, he began to issue orders: 'Tell Colonel Ompteda to send the First Light Battalion across the highway in support of the rifles. And have the Prince of Orange order down a battalion of Hanoverians to reinforce La Haye Sainte. Be sure to tell him to watch out for cavalry.'

No sooner had De Lancey despatched Abercromby with the Duke's instructions than they were reining in their horses behind a low hedge close to the 79th – the Cameron Highlanders. The regiment's huge colour of green silk with its distinctive central garter and saltire fluttered above them alongside the Union flag. For although the men were lying down as ordered, above them, enclosed by a ring of pipers, their colour party still stood, while the ancient regimental tune, the 'Cabar Feidh', skirled out over their heads. It provided an accompaniment for the unsettling vignette which now greeted De Lancey as he looked back towards the Allied right wing, across the Brussels road.

The Prince of Orange, distinctive in his black and sky blue, was in the process of delivering an order. His second-in-command, the respected veteran Constant-Rebecque, appeared to be arguing with his master. There was an outburst. De Lancey saw a rider being sent down the ridge towards Kielmansegge's Hanoverians. Seconds later the battalion was advancing down the slope towards the farm. And there it halted. In column. What the deuce was the Prince up to? De Lancey looked to Wellington. But the Duke was preoccupied with developments on the left flank. Neither he nor Kielmansegge saw the mass of French infantry approaching the farmhouse, or the cuirassiers protecting their flank. Nor presumably, lacking the height of his position, could the Hanoverians themselves. Yet if they did not form square they would be cut to pieces. And, tied as he was to the Commander-in-Chief, there was absolutely nothing De Lancey could do about it. He looked for an aide but found no one. A commotion made him turn round in the saddle, back towards Picton's line. Hundreds of blue-coated Belgians and Dutch were walking towards him back up the hill, towards the rear. Some hideously wounded. This was Bylandt's brigade, which, positioned on the forward slope, had borne the brunt of the fire. Men whom only last year, he pondered, had been loyal to the man who now commanded on the other side of the valley. Even more worryingly, though, with them came the green-jackets of the 95th, forced from their strongpoint in a roadside sandpit by sheer weight of numbers. Further left he was able to see that one of the French columns was now engaged in a firefight with the remaining line of Bylandt's men.

And then the Dutch broke. Turned and fled back through the gap between Kempt and Pack. A single Belgian battalion remained alone on the crest to hold back the rising blue tide. A great cheer went up from the advancing French. To them, De Lancey supposed, the ridge must seem almost deserted now. He peered down the line of British regiments. Along the hedge, to where Picton's men, the Peninsular veterans of Kempt's and Pack's brigades, who two days ago had suffered so at Quatre-Bras – the Highlanders, the 28th (the 'Slashers'), the Royal Scots – still lay in the shoulder-high corn. Waiting with stoic patience for the command.

The Allied artillery had now switched their load to canister. Eighty-five one and a half ounce solid iron balls, packed tightly into a tin cylinder, primed to explode in an expanding cone of destruction. They were tearing bleeding holes in the French columns. But still the eagles came on. He could hear the drum beats closer now and quite clearly the cries of 'Vive l'Empéreur'. All along the line British and Allied artillerymen began to run back from their guns to the shelter of the battalions.

De Lancey turned to Wellington. 'Here they come, your Grace. But I think we shall have them.'

'Indeed, De Lancey. That would seem to be the case.'

De Lancey could feel the ground tremble under the feet of the 16,000 men advancing up the slope directly towards him. His horse pawed nervously at the mud.

Wellington turned to Kempt: 'What d'you say to this, Sir James?'

'We'll see them off, your Grace.'

'Up with your men then. Have them rise up.'

All around him officers and sergeants barked the command.

'Rise up the 32nd.'

'28th, stand up.'

'Make ready.'

And from the ground, like an army of spectres, 3,000 redcoats rose as one, formed rank and, on the order, presented their muskets.

The French, having crested the hill on the tail of the fleeing Dutch, stopped still. Their complete surprise at being confronted by a line of British infantry was palpable.

'Fire!'

The echoing command ran down the line of Kempt's brigade like quicksilver. Every musket crashed out. The French columns froze, and from further east another massive volley echoed the first as Pack's brigade opened up. As the smoke cleared De Lancey could see the extent of the carnage. The entire French front rank had crumpled to the ground. Bodies lay everywhere. He saw officers retrieving eagles from fallen colour-bearers; wounded and dying men clawing at the earth in their agony. The second rank was attempting to load. Desperate hands fumbling with priming pan, flint and cartridge. Men dropping ramrods. Trying to find the space to present. All too late. For in the densely packed columns, even in this new formation, the fronts were just too short. A mere 500 able to fire against the thousands that now opposed them. Again the British muskets crashed out, and above them now came another sound, as the pipers of the three regiments of kilted Highlanders, the Camerons, the Gordons and the Black Watch, took up the high-pitched wail of their regimental battle tunes.

Now, thought De Lancey. Now we will finish them with the bayonet.

To his left he heard Sir Thomas Picton's great bellowing voice take up his thoughts as he shouted through the cacophany, waving his furled umbrella in the air, like a great black sword. 'Charge, boys. Hurrah! Hurrah!'

De Lancey saw the Welsh commander motion to his aide, Horace Seymour, to give the order to advance.

Picton looked about. Found Kempt. Shouted. 'Rally the Highlanders.'

His face set, he twisted again to face the enemy and suddenly started up in the saddle as a musket ball tore open the crown of his black top hat. De Lancey watched the general's lifeless body slump forward and fall from his horse.

Wellington's voice, apparently oblivious to the tragedy, drew him back to his senses. 'I am needed, De Lancey. The 79th.'

The Duke swept past to the left and De Lancey followed, towards where the Cameron Highlanders had advanced and were trading fire with a French battalion which had formed up across the road at a range of a mere twenty yards. For once the French appeared to be having the better of it. Wellington made sure that enough of the shaken Highlanders could see him before shouting a general command. 'Now, 79th. Give them a volley. Go to it.'

The Peer's presence, thought De Lancey, was enough to turn the faintest heart. All thought of flight now gone, the Camerons loaded at a furious pace and sent their fire into the French ranks. As the blue column recoiled, Wellington smiled.

'That will do.'

He turned Copenhagen towards the right flank and cantered away across the highway, pursued by the staff. As they reached the elm tree behind the farm, De Lancey pulled up his horse.

To the right of the farmhouse the ground at the foot of the ridge was speckled with red-coated German corpses, while up the hill streamed the unformed rabble of the men sent down on the Duke's orders by the Prince of Orange. With them scrambled what was left of the green-coated battalion of the German Legion that had gone to their aid. Through the smoke De Lancey could see the remainder of Ompteda's and Kielmansegge's battalions formed up on the ridge in squares. The majority of the fugitives seemed to have found refuge in their ranks. Down in the orchard of the farmhouse he could also make out dozens of figures in blue and white. The French had taken the gardens, surrounded the buildings and were attempting to climb the walls.

Wellington looked to the left and right. 'Uxbridge? Where is the man?'

Resplendent in the uniform of a Hussar colonel, the commander of the Allied cavalry cantered up to the staff. 'Your Grace?'

'Ah, Paget.' Wellington addressed his second-in-command incorrectly, by the name he had used before succeeding his father to the Earldom. De Lancey knew this slight to be deliberate, and the reason for it. Famously, the Duke had not yet forgiven the flamboyant cavalryman for eloping six years ago with his sister Charlotte, and relished every available opportunity to irritate him.

'Paget. Find Lord Edward Somerset. Take the Household Brigade and attack the French cavalry to the right of the farm.'

Uxbridge grinned with smug satisfaction. 'I have just left General Somerset, your Grace. With those precise orders.'

'Have you, by God. Well then you had better return and help him see them off. You must push back the infantry as well. If you are able.'

'Your Grace.' Uxbridge turned to the group of horsemen gathered around the Duke. Found three of his own aides. 'Thornhill, Seymour, Wildman. Care for some sport?' He turned his horse and pushed her back along the right of the line, towards Somerset. 'View halloo!'

As the three officers hurried after their general, Wellington raised an eyebrow. 'De Lancey. Ride and tell General Ponsonby that he must charge the French infantry to the east of the *chaussée*. The fate of the battle now rests with him. He must push them off the ridge. And tell him to mind to go no further than the slope on our own side of the valley. On no account must he either advance into the valley or attempt to attack the guns. Is that clear?'

'Your Grace.'

235

De Lancey spurred his horse across the road and down the reverse slope towards where, behind the embattled infantry, the red-coated cavalry of the Union Brigade awaited the order to attack. He found Ponsonby in conversation with Arthur Clifton, the commanding officer of the leading regiment, the Royals. The general saw him approach.

'Ah, De Lancey. D'you see them? The French? Now's our time, surely? Have we the order to advance?'

'You judge your moment well, Sir William. You are to take your brigade immediately and attack the infantry. But do not advance into the valley. The Peer was most adamant on that point.'

Ponsonby smiled. 'Rest assured, De Lancey. My boys'll send 'em to the devil. Clifton, you heard the command. Form your men. Now's our time.' He turned to his aide. 'Braithwaite, m'boy. Wave yer hat in the air. The colonels know what to do. The brigade will advance. Come along, boys. To Paris!'

As Uxbridge and Seymour rode back across the main road, anxious not to miss out on accompanying Somerset, De Lancey pulled his own horse away from the flank of the Royals and watched the young lieutenant raise his hat three times to send the dragoons on their way. Watched as the magnificent horsemen began to climb the hill, fanning out for the attack, the Greys moving to the left and the centre being taken by the Inniskilling Dragoons – 400 brawny Irishmen splendidly mounted on tall, jet-black horses. And as they advanced De Lancey glimpsed perhaps the most bizarre spectacle yet in a day that was proving more curious by the minute. From behind a hedge on the reverse slope there appeared a man and a boy clad in civilian dress. The former, whom he recognized as the shock-headed Duke of Richmond, raised his top hat and cheered the cavalry as they passed as if he were waving on a Newmarket winner: 'On, my brave boys. On to victory.'

Bemused but not wanting to become distracted, De Lancey rode back up the hill, parallel with the leading squadrons of the dragoons. He heard the buglers sound the 'advance' and then, somewhat absurdly, the 'charge': its distinctive blasts rising to a crescendo in 'G'. For such was the mud that there was no chance of their advancing at anything more than a canter. Reaching the crest of the hill, the horsemen began to negotiate their way through the lines of British infantry behind the hedgerow. He saw the Royals split in two and pass between the three regiments of Kempt's brigade.

The move was well executed, but nothing could prevent it from being at any more than a canter that most of them finally broke against the front rank of the French infantry. De Lancey stationed himself at the crossroads, directly behind the re-formed rifles, and watched entranced as along the line of the ridge the cavalry caught the blue-coated infantry completely by surprise, in the middle of a manoeuvre which, had it been completed, he perceived, might, with their greater numbers, quite easily have gone the way of the French. As it was, half-way between column and line, the infantry were now rendered doubly helpless as the heavy horses and their cheering, vengeful riders careered straight into them.

He watched the great flat swords, their edges cut deliberately with ugly notches, scythe down mercilessly into the ranks. Saw a French colonel mounted on a beautiful white horse attempt to engage one of the Irish dragoons, only to have his puny sword smashed in two by the weight of the other's blade. Watched as a second cut cleaved the colonel's nose from his face, leaving it hanging down across his mouth on a flap of skin. The man put up one hand to staunch the flow of blood and with the other turned his horse back into the mêlée, attempting to regain his lines. Then horse and rider vanished from sight. They did not rise again.

Closer to De Lancey, although a few of the French on the crest of the ridge had managed to get in a volley before the cavalry closed about them, the Royals were enjoying similar success. Panic had seized the French and they were streaming back into the valley away from the dragoons, discarding as they went anything that might slow them down. Packs, haversacks, muskets and shakos lay strewn across the hillside with the dead and wounded. Some men lay down and allowed the cavalry to ride over them before leaping up and running for their lives. The fighting seemed particularly fierce in one spot some 200 yards down the ridge. At length De Lancey saw the reason for the fury as a corporal emerged carrying across his horse's neck a flagpole topped with an eagle. An eagle! Only two had been taken in Spain. The lone horseman, his helmet lost in the struggle, left the press of men and rode towards the Brussels road, clearly searching for Wellington's position. De Lancey was about to guide him towards the Duke, whom he could see was positioned directly beneath the elm tree, when a flash of red caught his eye through the smoke and he realized that the dragoons had ridden on, beyond their objective.

Had they not heard him? The Peer had distinctly commanded that they should not enter the floor of the valley. Yet there they were, galloping through the French infantry and on towards the opposite slope. He strained to see through the smoke whether the other regiments had also disobeyed the order. With horror he saw that they had. Far off on the left wing the grey horses of the Scots betrayed their presence, too deep in the valley. Four, perhaps five hundred yards ahead of the Allied lines.

De Lancey headed towards the elm.

'Your Grace. Believe me. I conveyed your wishes directly. Made it quite plain. They should not attack the guns.'

'Of course, De Lancey. I am quite convinced that you gave the correct order. But you see now the old problem with the cavalry. They simply become too inebriated with the charge. It's the same trouble we had in Spain. They will go galloping at everything. It's just not done. It will quite finish them.'

'We might recall them yet, sir. If we sent a messenger. There is still time.'

Wellington raised his glass again. Paused. Then lowered it, slowly. 'I think not.'

De Lancey withdrew his own telescope from his saddle-bag and put it to his eye. He could see the red-coated cavalry quite plainly now, still hacking at the fleeing infantry and sabring the gunners too as they rode across the great battery. And then his attention was drawn by something else. Over to the left. Fluttering pennants. Lancers in green coats and shining helmets were bearing down on the exposed flank of the Scottish cavalry. He watched in horror as the trapped Greys began to realize what had happened. Watched, compelled, as the individual tragedies unfolded. As one by one the French picked them off, pushing the dismembered regiment along the valley in a heap of destruction. He scanned towards the right and saw officers and NCOs attempting to reform the Inniskillings. To make an orderly withdrawal. But now they too were being counter-attacked. Hundreds of cuirassiers, fresh to the battle, were riding down on them from the ridge. Meanwhile directly below him the Royals were turning back, pursued in turn by their own armour-plated nemesis. They were mixed together now with troopers of the Life Guards, Somerset's men, some of whom had charged down the main road. The whole disordered rabble were riding hell-for-leather for the British lines, up past the farm.

De Lancey lowered his glass. Turned to Wellington. 'Oh God, sir. What have we done?'

Wellington looked at him blankly. 'We, sir, have destroyed and disordered an entire corps of the French army and put a number of their cannon out of action.'

'But at what price, sir? We have lost the heavy cavalry.'

Looking about him, De Lancey now realized that he was also missing a number of his staff. He saw Basil Jackson, his face deathly white.

'Basil. Where the devil are the rest of you? Where's Will?'

'Wounded, sir. Gone to the rear. Rotten luck too. A ball took most of his right arm clean off.'

De Lancey grimaced. 'Fitzgerald? Beckwith? Dawson?'

'Fitzgerald's wounded too, sir. And Beckwith. Hit very bad. In the leg. I haven't seen George for a half-hour.'

De Lancey shook his head. His family was being torn to pieces.

Wellington saw his distress. Shouted across the road: 'A brave show, Edward. Well done.'

His words were directed towards the approaching figure of Lord Edward Somerset who was riding towards them, bare-headed and covered in mud. In his wake came the first of the Life Guards to regain the ridge. The Duke doffed his hat to them: 'Life Guards. I thank you.'

From the rear of his entourage d'Alava emerged with the portly Austrian attaché Baron Vincent in his distinctive white coat and the Russian commissioner, the Corsican emigré Count Pozzo di Borgo. All three wore wide smiles. D'Alava held his hands before him in adulation.

'Your Grace. I believe that you have carried the day. Never have I seen cavalry used to such effect. You have routed the enemy.'

'Thank you, d'Alava. But you will observe that we are far from victorious. This has been merely the first attempt. He will come at us again, soon, and in greater force. Do not rejoice too soon, gentlemen.'

As he spoke, past them, down the main road to where the rye still stood shoulder-high, rode a troop of horse artillery carrying what looked like bundles of sticks stuffed into buckets. Russian and Austrian looked equally puzzled.

D'Alava, smiling at De Lancey, endeavoured to explain. 'Rockets. The British . . . secret weapon.'

Wellington, although secretly in agreement, ignored the Spaniard's mischievously facetious remark. 'De Lancey, I do believe that we shall have to take greater care now. The great thief of Europe may have lost the first roll of the dice. But he's far from done with us.'

Looking to his left, through the smoke to the now re-formed left wing, De Lancey saw a steady stream of wounded – unhorsed dragoons, Highlanders and line infantry – limping back to the aid station. Along the Ohain road a lone horseman was approaching them at speed. As the man grew closer it became clear that he was a British hussar. He reached De Lancey at a gallop. Pulled up his horse. Saluted the Commander-in-Chief.

'Your Grace. Compliments of Captain Taylor of the Tenth, sir. He reports, sir, cavalry to the east. Prussians, your Grace. He is quite certain of it.'

For once Wellington's face became animated. 'Blücher. Where are they? How far from here?'

'We sighted them close to Chapelle St Lambert, your Grace. Some five miles distant.'

Five miles, thought de Lancey. If Prussian cavalry had been spotted only five miles away, surely the remainder of the army could not be very far behind? He spoke for both of them: 'It is all we hoped for, your Grace. Blücher has come across from Wavre. The Prussians are but five miles away.'

'Five miles, De Lancey. But it might as well be 500 miles if they cannot reach us soon. Look.'

De Lancey raised his telescope and peered out across the valley. There on the opposite ridge he could see the French guns being re-crewed. Gunners were cleaning out the great bronze barrels, infantrymen bringing up fresh shot. He could make out the artillery riders whipping their horses as they drove the huge ammunition caissons back into line. Wellington was right. Pray God the Prussians would reach them quickly. For he knew that in a few moments, once again, the gates of Hell were about to open.

TWENTY

Hougoumont, 2.50 p.m.
Macdonell

Alexander Saltoun rode up the slope of the ridge at the head of his men, back towards the main position where, above the red battalions, squares of blue and crimson silk flapped ragged in the gale of battle. Macdonell watched them go, the wounded supporting each other, some being carried. Watched as four guardsmen gently bore in a plain, grey blanket the lifeless body of an ensign. He had known him as Ed Pardoe, just turned nineteen, who last night had left Mackinnon's soirée early, passing Macdonell on the stairs in his haste to rejoin his unit. Unlucky that, they said. Passing on the stairs. Luck. It was anyone's guess who had it on this field. Macdonell watched, and wondered.

Over the last three hours Saltoun's command had suffered a savage mauling in its defence of the orchard. The first French assault had come in at around a quarter after one o'clock. The next an hour later. Macdonell admired the bold, some would say reckless, courage of his fellow Scot, whom someone had told him had already had four horses shot under him today. Watching from the kitchen garden, Macdonell had half an hour earlier seen Saltoun personally lead a direct charge at a French howitzer which had been brought up with the clear intention of setting the buildings afire. Mounted on his fourth

242

horse, Saltoun had pushed forward at the head of what was left of the light companies of the First Guards, a few of their grenadiers and a handful of the remaining Hanoverians. Of course it had been no use. Barely 200 men taking on three brigades of Frenchmen. Beaten back through the apple and cherry trees, the Guards had taken refuge in the cover of the sunken lane, and now at last Saltoun, after licking his wounds for half an hour, had been given the order to withdraw. Macdonell tried to count the men of the First Guards as they climbed the hill. Could hardly believe his eyes. Saltoun had come down from the ridge at noon with 150 men, all ranks. Now they were retracing their steps with barely fifty still able to fight. A third of his original force.

Macdonell looked around the courtyard. His men had hardly fared better. But they still held this place. Everywhere wounded men sat against the battered walls; cradled their heads in their hands; bound improvised bandages around wounds of greater and lesser severity.

Peering again over the wall he saw now that Saltoun's survivors were being passed by their relieving force. Eight hundred fresh guardsmen, the remainder of the Third, under Francis Hepburn. Peninsular man, hero of Vitoria. An altogether pleasant sort of person.

Macdonell tried to calculate what was left of his own command. Here, in the buildings, which he held in the joint command of Colonel Woodford, was almost the entire strength of the Coldstream and the remainder of the Nassauers. Perhaps 1,700 men in all, excluding casualties. Beyond the walls he knew now that they were opposed by an entire French division. Perhaps 12,000 infantry with five batteries of cannon and a considerable force of light cavalry protecting the flank.

Biddle doubled towards him, across the yard. 'Here they come again, sir.'

Muskets cracked as with another cheer the French advanced against the south side of the château. How many times was that now, he wondered. Five? Ten? Macdonell walked across the yard towards the attack. Heard the captains and NCOs repeating their orders above the irregular volleys: 'Present. Fire. Present. Fire. Fire at will.' Heard too the dreadful shrieks as the attackers went down. Again and again. The endless, unholy litany of the battlefield: 'Fire. Fire. Fire at will.'

Again the howitzers in the wood opened up and, as he neared the gardener's house, two shells flew high over the buildings and into the yard. One landed on the cobbles and sputtered to a pathetic stop without exploding. The other, though, seemed to spin as Macdonell looked up at it and then almost to stop in mid-air at precisely the moment that Henderson, the corporal in whose charge he had placed the gardener's daughter and the French drummer boy, stepped out of the building. It burst directly above the man and, as he looked up in surprise, a four-inch-long splinter of solid iron took him on the shoulder, just below the neck. He collapsed on the cobbles in a fountain of blood and was dead within seconds. Transfixed for a moment, Macdonell stared at the partly decapitated body and noticed that in his hand Henderson was still holding a small piece of wood. Looking more closely, he saw it to be a small, hand-carved toy soldier, a guardsman. He supposed that Henderson must have been making it for the children. Mustn't let them see this. He looked for help. Found a corporal.

'Robinson. Remove this man. Quickly. You there. You two men. Help him.'

Macdonell looked about for a replacement child-minder. Spotted the bugler, George Flinchley. 'Flinchley. Go into that house and take care of the two children. The girl and the drummer boy. And take this with you.'

He bent down and, as the three guardsmen lifted Henderson's corpse with due care, mindful lest the dangling head should become detached, prised open the dead man's fingers, removed the tiny figure and gave it to the bugler. 'Can you make this sort of thing?'

'No, sir.'

'No matter.'

The boy looked crestfallen. 'But I could give the kids a tune on the tin whistle.'

'Yes. That would be nice.'

Strange, thought Macdonell, the things that men did in the very midst of battle. How somehow, amid all the death, there was yet a place for humanity. He turned to John Biddle.

'Colour Sar'nt. What's our strength?'

'We've taken thirty-two casualties in the Light Company, sir. Six is dead, sir, and there's some as is hurt real bad. Joe Graham's hit mortal, I reckon, sir. We've put 'em in the barn.'

'Officers?'

'Mr Montagu's been shot, sir. He'll live, though. And Captain Moore. Mr Wyndham's taken a scratch too, sir. Mr Blackman's dead, of course, and Mr Vane's been hit. Colonel Mackinnon you know about, sir. They're in the big house. And Colonel Acheson's missing, sir.'

'What of the rest. D'you know?'

'I reckon as there's another 140 hit of the Coldstream, sir. Perhaps forty dead and dying. Dr Whymper's cussing and blindin' in there, sir. Says he's got no light and precious little brandy or gin. He's puttin' powder on the stumps, sir.'

'Dear God. I'm sure he knows his business. So what is our strength on the walls?'

'I reckon we're down to 700 able-bodied men, sir, and another fifty wounded but as can still hold a musket.'

Of nigh-on 1,000 Guards now in the château, one in six were already casualties and more than a third of those dead or dying. Macdonell wondered how many Frenchmen lay dead outside the walls.

Wondered too what was happening elsewhere on the battle-field. He was quite isolated in this place. Might as well be in another country or on a far-distant planet. For all they knew the battle might be won already. Or lost, God help them.

Colonel Woodford approached him across the yard. 'Splendid garden, Macdonell, eh? Pity we have to ruin it. Thing of real beauty, if you want my opinion. Not quite up to my own, of course. Too many trees, eh? Don't you think?'

'I dare say so, Colonel.'

The colonel continued. 'Poor Dan, eh? No more monkey business for him in the mess, eh, Macdonell? Shot in the knee, uh? Got his Byron's limp at last. That'll tickle him. Still, could have been worse. Could have been a few inches higher, eh? And then no business with the ladies, James. No business at all. If you do dare say so. No business at all.'

As he chortled at his joke a great shout went up from the orchard. Hepburn was leading the Third Guards through the trees to retake it from the French. Macdonell turned to Gooch.

'Gooch. Take your men and reinforce the upper storey of the main house. See if you can fire down on the heads. And if you can, pick off the gunners before that infernal battery sets fire to the buildings. I'll give any man a shilling who kills a gunner. See to it.'

The ensign and his men began to double across the courtyard.

Macdonell called to Gooch. 'Henry. One moment.' He spoke quietly. 'Position yourself by the door to the upper room. They're sure to shell the house soon and I want you to keep the men in there until the fire is as hot as Hades. You understand? But for God's sake be careful not to lose any.'

'Sir.'

As Colonel Woodford opened his mouth to impart some fresh wisdom, a cannon shot came crashing through the south gate, splintering the cross-beam and pushing the door wide open. The French outside did not lose a moment. Within seconds a score of red-plumed grenadiers were pushing their way into the inner archway.

Macdonell saw them just in time. 'To me, Guards. Form line. Ready. Present. Fire.'

A dozen soldiers ran to him, half instinctively dropping to one knee to provide a kneeling front rank. The improvised volley crashed out from their ready-loaded muskets and immediately the twelve Coldstreamers followed up with the bayonet towards the wounded and dying Frenchmen. In a flurry of steel and crashing musket butts, they closed the gate. Kept their shoulders at it while Frazer hurried up with two other men carrying a long wooden plank as a replacement crossbar.

The French, pinned down by harrowing fire from the gatehouse, were reluctant to contest the struggle.

Macdonell walked back to his station beside the main house. Saw one of the guardsmen march a freshly captured drummer boy towards the stable in which the wounded of both sides had been placed together. He shouted to the man. Couldn't see who it was. 'You there. Chosen man now. Guard that archway. See that if another shot breaks it you are ready to repair the damage.'

Turning, he shouted up to the highest window of the château. 'Mister Gooch. If you please. I think that we might deal with that cannon now. As soon as you like. And a shilling for every man who brings down a gunner.'

'Sir.'

Shots rang out from the upper floors and as they did, as if in reply, two shells came screaming in from the wood and punched great holes in the roof. Within seconds it was alight. It was as he had feared. The French gunners had raised their trajectory and switched to carcass shot, an oblong canvas box secured with steel hoops and containing a mix of turpentine, tallow and sulphur. Once ignited by its charge it was almost impossible to put out and on contact was sure to ignite any flammable material. Now they were really in trouble. Macdonell watched as the flames began to lick

247

upwards through the exposed roof timbers. Even as he looked it became clear that the French cannon were firing more heavily. A mixture of projectiles: carcass for the buildings, shell for casualties, and roundshot directly at the brickwork. A terrible crash made him spin round. A French ball had smashed into the gatehouse, leaving a great hole in both walls before passing out and into the courtyard. In the process it had carried away with it not only bricks but the bodies of four guardsmen. Their bloody remains now lay half tumbled out of the ragged hole. Macdonell shouted towards a group of Coldstreamers standing up on the pigsty, reloading their muskets, ready to fire down on the advancing French.

'Someone move those bodies up there. Bring them down. Secure the position. You four up there. Now. Elrington. You take the gate. Keep alert. We must not let them in.'

Smoke now filled the compound, hanging in acrid clouds that choked and stung the throat. Macdonell placed his hand over his mouth to breathe and as he did so a shell exploded ten yards over to his right, tossing a guardsman into the air like a child's rag-doll. A burning fragment from the shot, tumbling wickedly to the ground, fell into a barrel of gunpowder being manhandled by two more redcoats. They were blown to atoms. Another man who had been standing close by turned to Macdonell, his face a mass of blood. Macdonell did not know the man. Could not make out the features, yet saw the bloody mouth open wide in agony.

'Oh God, help me. Oh help. I can't see. My eyes. Oh dear God, my eyes.'

Macdonell rushed to support the man as he collapsed to the ground. 'A surgeon. Where's Dr Whymper? Someone find a surgeon. Help this man.'

Two redcoats came to his aid. Helped the blinded man to his feet.

Macdonell turned back to the gatehouse but as he did so the roof of the cart-house adjacent to the barn shot up in a sheet of flame. Instantly, from within came a terrible, animal screaming.

'The horses. Save the horses.'

Macdonell watched in despair as his servant Smith ran with three others to rescue the officers' mounts, all of which had been quartered in the cart-house. One man emerged dragging a whinnying mare. Another followed, but as they came from the door a shell fell in front of them and the horse, terrified, backed again into the stable. The man let go her rein and she was gone. Smith emerged empty-handed, his face and arms blackened by smoke, crying pathetically. That was it, then. All but one of the horses burned to death.

Macdonell was aware of an officer walking towards him from the north gate. Recognized him as Francis Home of the 3rd Guards. He offered Macdonell something in his hand.

'A note, Macdonell. From the Commander-in-Chief, by way of Major Hamilton.'

Macdonell took the message, written on a piece of cured mule skin. Read the orders.

I see that the fire has communicated from the haystack to the roof of the château. You must however still keep your men in those parts to which the fire does not reach. Take care that no men are lost by the falling in of the roof or floors. After both have fallen in occupy the ruined walls inside of the garden; particularly if it should be possible for the enemy to pass through the embers in the inside of the house.

He turned to Biddle. 'Come with me.'

Together they entered the main door of the château and climbed the stairs. How different it was now from the previous evening. The walls were black from smoke, and timbers from the upper floors had fallen in across the staircase. Here and there a hole in the wall showed where a French shot had made its target, but it was the heat that struck him most. As they went higher it grew still more intense. In the great saloon lay the officer casualties: George Evelyn with his shattered arm, Montagu, Moore, Vane, his wrist in a sling. Macdonell noticed that Surgeon Whymper was carefully re-dressing Dan Mackinnon's leg. Three other ranks were helping the wounded officers to beer from their canteens. Macdonell paused in the doorway.

'Gentlemen. May I respectfully suggest that you get yourselves out of here with some haste. The roof is liable to fall in at any moment. Corporal. You bandsmen. Help them. And Doctor, with all respect to Colonel Mackinnon, I think that you might find rather more pressing work across in the barn. There are close on sixty men there who need your help. And do remember please to make sure that the French are comfortable too.'

Walking back to the staircase, he climbed, with the colour sergeant close behind him, up to the attic storey, and there, among the hissing, smoke-filled eaves found Gooch and his chosen men still, without much evident success, attempting to pick off at long range the gunners of the irritating howitzer battery.

Above them flames licked around the gables and roof timbers, several of which had already given way and were lying, charred, white and red-hot across the room at crazy angles.

'Gooch, I think the time has come to abandon the house. You've done all you can. We need you in the courtyard.'

Visibly relieved, the handful of sharpshooters lost no time in abandoning the holes they had broken in the roof and began to file down the stairs.

Gooch smiled. 'I'm afraid we didn't have much luck, sir. Although you do owe a shilling to Private Clay, I believe. At least he claimed one shot, and Phillips attested to his story.'

'Then I shall honour the debt, Henry.'

Macdonell made to leave, but on a whim turned back and

peered out of a hole in the tiles. 'By God, but that's a view.'

Below him, through the smoke he could make out the grounds of the château sweeping away to the south. There was what remained of the garden, filled with redcoats again, and beyond it the woods, crammed with the blue-coated French. As the smoke drifted away he was just able to glimpse, to the left, what must be an entire wing of the French army. For an instant the sun managed to break through the blanket of cloud, and Macdonell gasped. For its rays had caught the shining steel breastplates of fully 5,000 cuirassiers. He had never before seen such a spectacle. And they were on the move. All of them. Advancing at a slow trot, directly, it seemed, for him.

He turned to Gooch. 'I . . . Gooch. D'you see? There. Good God, man. Look there. How can we hope . . . ? Surely we cannot withstand that. And look.'

He pointed now as the sun broke through again and shed more light on the fields beyond the red-tiled roof of La Belle Alliance. 'Look there, man. Yet more cavalry. Cannon too. And fresh battalions. But surely the Peer must know. He must have a plan. We can only trust in him now, Gooch.'

'And in ourselves, sir.'

'And indeed in ourselves, Henry. Yes. The hope of all humanity rests with us.'

TWENTY-ONE

Mont St Jean crossroads, 3.15 p.m. De Lancey

For almost half an hour they had sat here, enduring the deadly storm of shot that came in over the ridge from the thundering French cannon. All around him the ground around was strewn with bodies and parts of bodies; broken and abandoned weapons and pieces of uniform; trinkets and scraps of paper. De Lancey wondered whether perhaps he was making of himself too obvious a target. True, he could not see the enemy guns, nor they him, but it was common practice to draw your range on the enemy's standards and he had only just realized that directly to his right, not ten yards away, stood the colour party of the 73rd. He cast them a glance. How young they seemed. Two ensigns, perhaps sixteen and seventeen years apiece, and a drummer boy of how old? No more than fifteen. On their flanks stood a sergeant and a colour sergeant. Seasoned veterans both. De Lancey could see the old salts muttering whispered words of encouragement to their pallid officers. And even as he watched a French roundshot came bounding in from the valley, bounced up from the earth before the redcoats and tore off the head of the drummer boy, still in its shako, spattering the men around him with his brains. One of the ensigns threw up. The other looked aghast. Said simply:

'Oh! How extremely disgusting.'

The men about him burst into peals of laughter, but they stopped when moments later another cannonball came flying in and took off six bayonets in a row. It was swiftly followed by a third which, glancing off the cross-belt of one of the sergeants, threw the man to the ground. Bending over his writhing form a corporal looked up towards the commanding officer, who had now ridden over.

'His breast bone's broke, sir.'

The noise of the man's screams took De Lancey back to the Peninsula. He was not the only member of their party to have been so affected by the little tragedy played out before them.

Wellington spoke: 'Gentlemen. I think that perhaps we are a little thick on the ground. Would it do for us to disperse a little? Gordon. Would you ride over to the right flank and have General Chassé bring his division across from Merbe Braine. Have him take up position behind General Adam.' He paused. Produced a piece of muleskin from his valise and scribbled another note. 'Canning. Take this order to Colonel Olfermann. Have his Brunswickers move up towards Hougoumont. But do remember to tell him to keep them out of sight of the French guns.' He turned to his right. 'Somerset?'

'Your Grace?'

'The entire line will fall back behind the ridge. And have the men lie down again.'

De Lancey turned to Wellington. 'He may commit his cavalry, sir. Do you not think? If he were to come at us with merely half of those cuirassiers, your Grace, supported by the infantry that we can see held in reserve and merely a battery of horse guns, then we should really have something of a struggle on our hands. Or do you suppose that he might bring on the Garde, sir?'

'No, De Lancey. I know enough of this man to guess that he will keep the Garde under his personal command until he is absolutely certain of the day. Either that or until he feels himself in crisis. And it would go against all the rules of war to attempt an assault with cavalry alone. Bonaparte is fully aware of the strength of a square against even the most formidable of cavalry. No, I believe that he intends to pound us once more and to keep on pounding. That, it would appear, is his way.'

De Lancey nodded his agreement. Although he did not in truth share Wellington's unremitting faith in the power of the square, it was without doubt the only formation in which infantry might resist cavalry. Who did not know of the fate of John Colborne's brigade at Albuera – rolled up and annihilated by a cavalry attack in the flank? Almost 80 per cent killed and wounded, and five of six of their colours taken. But it was itself horribly vulnerable to close-range artillery and small-arms fire. And it was not, as they all knew full well, 100 per cent reliable. A square was only as strong as the men who formed it. It depended upon psychology. Upon mutual dependence. You might be the handiest lad in the army with the bayonet, or the sharpest shot. But with thousands of cavalry bearing down upon you it was all too easy for your skills to desert you. A square would only survive on the absolute faith of each man in the ability of the next man to hold firm. Only then did it work. And even then, should even the smallest breach be made in its side, the cavalry might pour in and break upon the defenders from the rear. All it took was for a dying horse to crash into two or three ranks of men. Then it would be over in a moment. Broken squares lived on in infamy: the Austrians at Wagram; the French themselves at Garcia Hernandez. And should the square not happen to be quite completed when the cavalry broke upon it – it was a complex manoeuvre at any time – then once again the enemy cavalry might pour in and turn the ranks into a bloody butcher's shop. Why, at Quatre-Bras only two days ago a hasty order given in the course of the manoeuvre had propelled the 69th to disaster and the loss of their colour. The 42nd had narrowly escaped the same fate. Yes, thought De Lancey. Wellington was right. To attack with cavalry alone went against all the principles of war. But Napoleon had never played by the rules. And, if he were to use his cavalry *en masse* here, every Allied square must be watertight and supremely confident. He looked across the right wing of the Allied army, at the columns of Brunswickers, Nassauers and Hanoverians falling back down the ridge, and for the first time began to have grave doubts. If they could only discover what Napoleon intended. Perhaps now, thought De Lancey, now was his moment. Somehow now he might absolve himself of the blame for the débâcle at Quatre-Bras and the embarrassing confusion of the promise to Blücher. Perhaps Wellington would at length forgive him. He must at all costs be seen to make himself useful. Must do his job to the utmost. What would Murray have done? He turned to the Duke.

'Your Grace, I think that perhaps I should take a closer look at the situation. We must ascertain what Bonaparte intends.'

'Indeed, De Lancey. If you believe that to be possible. The master plays his cards damned close. But do be quick about it. I cannot afford to lose another of you. You in particular, De Lancey. We shall follow you.'

Calling George Scovell to accompany him, along with Charles Lennox, the Earl of March and a young cornet of the Blues, De Lancey turned his horse and cantered for the crest of the ridge, back towards the elm tree which for so much of that day had been their mustering point.

Within minutes the four men had reached the brow of the hill, close to where Christian Ompteda's Germans, along with the farmhouse and the château, marked the farthest, most advanced position of the Allied line. As he crested the ridge the air about him changed. While previously he had been conscious of the great cannonballs screaming into their midst out of the smoke, here it seemed that the very atmosphere itself had taken on a new substance. Was alive with thousands of particles of flying lead and iron. The noise was bizarre. Like a gigantic swarm of bees.

Wellington was right. It was getting devilish hot. Too hot. He would have to find some other opportunity to make his peace with the Peer. To remain here or to advance any further was madness. De Lancey decided that they would leave. Return to their former position. He pulled his horse round. And it was then, from the corner of his left eye, that he noticed a brilliant flash away on the left to the front of the French line. Perhaps 200 yards distant. As the smoke cleared he was better able to trace the source of the now evident explosions. Although the farm was still held by the German Legion, the French had brought up a battery of horse artillery to just behind the orchard of La Haye Sainte and had started to open up at close range. Canister and ball. He turned his horse towards Scovell and March. Then, noticing Wellington and the staff closing fast upon them, shouted across to the Duke: 'Your Grace. A battery. Close up, on our left. I think it would perhaps be prudent were we to withdraw.'

Too late, he realized that his voice would not carry. Could not possibly be heard. He watched in horror as a canister case flew past his horse's head and exploded directly in front of March, whose arm was shattered instantly by several of the small iron balls. The boy fell from his horse. De Lancey turned in the saddle towards the Allied line and had just begun to call for aid when, at the same moment, he felt a tremendous smack on his back as, for an instant, he imagined it might feel if one were to be hit with the flat of a cricket bat. He instinctively went to turn to the left. To find out what had happened. And as he did so . . . everything changed.

For, rather than turning, he found himself falling. It seemed to be happening so slowly. He was aware of flying over the head of his horse – a curious and for a moment not entirely unpleasant sensation. In mid-air he became conscious too of a curious taste in his mouth. Warm. Sweet. Blood. A red mist invaded his vision. He was no longer looking at poor March now, but down the length of the Allied line. At the pretty silk flags fluttering; at soldiers turning like automatons, in succession of ranks, and moving back, according to the Peer's orders, behind the ridge.

And then something else flew across his line of sight. Half a horse. And a nameless, bloody thing in a blue coat that a few seconds ago had been the upper portion of Cornet Wilson.

De Lancey's head hit the ground with a sickening thud. And then. Pain. Suddenly too it seemed that the sky had become solid. For an instant he wondered where he was. Then understood. Not sky but earth. Mud. He was lying in mud. Face down. But where exactly? At home? In Scotland? Pain again.

He remembered. The battle. But could hear nothing. Another pain now. More acute. In his lower back. He tried rising. Tried to move. Could not.

He opened his eyes. Earth. Red earth; mud; stones; blood. Tried again to lift himself. Body so very heavy. To his surprise he managed to gain his feet. Now then. I shall just straighten up. And again he was falling. Falling. Damn. Damn. Bugger.

He hit the ground. But the pain of the impact was nothing compared to that in his back. Tried again to move. Pointless. Opened his eyes. Saw . . . stones.

He tried to move his right arm. Reach inside his pocket. Touch the stone. Her stone. Magdalene. Tried to say her name. Closed his eyes. Saw more stones. Rocks. Eternal stones. The cliff face at Dunglass. Waves lapping against the shore. Waves like pain. Pain like waves. Lapping. Crushing. Wave upon wave. Red-hot pain upon pain. Relentless. Timeless.

And suddenly, with the imploding whoosh of a thousand oceans, sound re-entered his world. Awful sound. Screaming. Who the devil was that screaming? He tried to raise his head. To say something. Come on, man. Come on. Stop that noise. Noise like a serving girl tupped for the first time. Like a Spanish whore being raped. Who the hell was making that bloody noise? Then, horribly, recognized the voice as his own. The pain came crashing in again. Wave upon wave.

He heard someone speak. Far away, above him: 'Oh God. Good God, sir.'

Another voice now. George Scovell. 'It was *en ricochet*, d'you see. Bounced up from the ground. Caught him clean on the back.'

Oh, he thought. Yes. I do see now. So is this how it is then? Is this how it begins? I am dying, am I not?

He tried to signal but could not move his arm. Leave me here. Please leave me here to die. I will never leave you. Never leave. I will never leave here. This field. These stones. This earth.

He opened his eyes and discovered that somehow, magically, his world had become microscopic so that while above him everything was no more than a blur, down here on the earth all was crystal clear. He saw now, for the first time, every particle of earth, every tiny stone, every blade of grass with disarming clarity. Tiny insects on the ground. So many tiny specks. Men or insects? Men as insects. No more. Must remember to tell Magdalene's father of his discovery. Man no bigger than an insect. The world spinning. Us clinging to it, lest we fall off. He had fallen off. Was trying now to cling to the earth. Grasped at it with his left hand. Desperate not to fall into oblivion.

He heard a voice. 'Look, your Grace. He's still alive. He's moving.'

He tried to raise his head. Managed it briefly and fell back. Saw the legs of a horse. Black horse. Heard voices drifting in and out.

'Help him, someone.'

'Oh God. De Lancey. Poor chap.'

Then Wellington's voice. 'I had known him since we were boys almost, you know. Poor, poor De Lancey.'

So am I dead then? You speak of me as if I am dead. I am not dead. He tried to speak. Tasted more blood in his mouth.

Blood and earth. Four men picked him up. Turned him over. He saw a face. George Scovell.

'George?'

He heard the word leave him. Scovell's eyes brightened.

'Sir William?'

'George.'

He could speak. At last.

'It is mortal. I feel it, George. You must tell them to leave me. Let me die in peace.'

'Nonsense, De Lancey. It is no more than a graze.'

He tried to laugh. But only vomited. Puke and blood. Saw it lying in a pool on the road as the four redcoats lifted him on to a blanket. Saw beside it his papers. The orders of battle. The map. Letters. Must save them. Tried to speak. More pain now. Wave upon wave.

They placed him gently into the tumbril. He was aware of the straw beside his lips. Tried to bite on it. Stop the pain.

He was acutely aware of every movement as the men began to wheel the little cart along the road. Sensitive to the rise and fall of every cobblestone. So many fresh agonies. God, but his back was on fire. He clutched at the side of the filthy farm wagon. Spewed again. Tasted blood and vomit. So much blood. Where was he hit? His back, they'd said. His lungs? His kidneys? Spleen?

After what seemed an eternity the ghastly motion stopped. De Lancey could see only the sky and the side of the wagon. Carefully they pulled him from his warm straw bed and, taking the strain of his weight, began to bear him in the blood-sodden blanket through an arched gateway.

He managed to speak again: 'Carry me gently, lads. I'm not dead yet.'

He seemed to recognize this place. A farm. The casualty clearing station. Mont St Jean. Doctors here. Well, they would either mend or do for him.

He tried to turn his head. Failed. Saw soldiers standing

about clutching gaping, bloody wounds. Others were sitting on the ground. Some lying. He saw a few, faces numb with shock, nursing freshly bandaged stumps. As they bore him through the door of a barn he noticed, piled up against the wall, a pyramid of amputated limbs. Arms and legs, feet and hands. Some still wet. How many, he wondered? How many cripples have we made today? Knew that was probably the best he could hope for now. Poor cripple. Bent double. Paralysed. Useless. Not a man at all. He said her name out loud.

'Magdalene.'

He closed his eyes as they laid him on the stone floor. Moved his lips but spoke with no sound.

Oh my darling. I am sorry to cause you such pain.

Through the red mist in his head he saw their little church, its yard strewn with apple blossom. The giggling girls in white. The laughing officers. And saw himself. Striding across to his bride. Laughing. Someone was talking to him.

'Sir William, isnt it. Don't worry, sir, we'll soon have you fixed up.'

He opened his eyes. Saw the surgeon, bloody hands, standing over him. Smiling.

Fixed up? Fixed up into what? A twisted stump of humanity? A cripple? Oh, I am so sorry, Magdalene. What will we do? What can you do? I shall never leave you. But how shall I live with you? How can I? Yet how can I live without you?

Slowly, each small movement bringing more pain, he inched his hand towards what had been his waistcoat pocket. To his surprise he found the stone; slick with his blood. And in the still shadows of the barn, surrounded by the gentle sobbing of the wounded, he felt the tears begin to chase each other down his cheeks. And then the pain came in again. Rolling in. Wave upon wave. Crashing against the rocks of his existence. And gently, silently, De Lancey allowed himself at last to slide into unconsciousness.

TWENTY-TWO

La Belle Alliance, 3.45 p.m.
Napoleon

The attack had failed. Of that there was no doubt. As the smoke cleared, Napoleon was able to see quite clearly that the farmhouse was still in the hands of the British. Peering through the drifting grey and white clouds, his eyes dwelt on the empty field, littered with the corpses of men and horses. To the left the château was in flames. That was good. Soon the British would be driven out and then, with the flank secured, Reille's men could begin to sweep up Wellington's line. The heavy cavalry too were only waiting for the command. The struggle had drawn in most of Reille's corps. Every division save that of Bachelu. And what of it? If that was what it took to collapse the Allied flank, then let it be so.

The right wing, though, was more worrying. D'Erlon's men he knew had not yet recovered from their mauling by the British cavalry. Two eagles lost. And again only one division, Quiot's, was left unscathed. And now, led by Ney in a lightning attack, that too had been beaten back from the farm. La Haye Sainte. The centre of the Allied line and the key to Wellington's position. He noticed though that the marshal had succeeded in placing, for a while at least, a battery of horse artillery on the left of the farmhouse. That must have hurt the British sorely. But it had been forced to withdraw with the infantry.

261

If only there was some way of keeping his guns up there at close range. He turned his head upwards to the sky. Closed his eyes. Then opened them. Perhaps it could be done. He turned to Soult. Smiled.

'They were very brave, those men on grey horses, eh? Very brave. They did well, Soult, don't you think? Very well. But we cut them to pieces all the same. Did you see it? I believe that we've seen off the best of his cavalry. He's left himself wide open, you know. Quite exposed.'

He looked across to his right. Over there, somewhere to the east, beyond the woods, the Prussians were coming. He knew it for certain now. Had sent Lobau's corps, 10,000 men, thirty cannon, to engage them. With orders to fall back on Plancenoit, to defend the village house by house. That at least would buy him enough time to win against this arrogant Englishman. He had sent a despatch to Grouchy an hour earlier ordering him to march to their aid. If the marshal moved with sufficient speed he might even catch von Bülow's Prussians in the rear on the march as he attempted to join Wellington. He turned back to Soult. And as he did so a salvo of shots from a British battery on the ridge came screaming in dangerously close to the Imperial entourage. It landed beside the tethered horses, just at the moment that the Garde artillery general Jean Desvaux de Saint Maurice rode up. Soult's horse shied as one of the cannonballs flew over its mane and a split second later another roundshot hit St Maurice at waist height, cutting him in half. His severed torso toppled to the ground. But his legs, still gripping the saddle, were carried away by his panic-stricken yet miraculously unharmed horse towards the centre of the battlefield. One of the junior aides threw up.

For a moment Napoleon, who had turned towards the noise, gazed, wide-eyed, at the bloody remains of his artillery commander. He fumbled in his pocket for the scented handkerchief. Held it to his nose. Looked away.

Gourgaud spoke: 'Moline. Clear up that mess. Quickly.'

Within seconds all trace of the unfortunate general had been removed. Recovering his composure, the Emperor tucked away his handkerchief and scanned the Allied position before him. He must attack without delay. A bold frontal assault with cavalry would take Wellington completely by surprise.

It was not, of course what he would have chosen to do when a younger man. The sensible thing to do now would be to regroup. To wait for Grouchy's 30,000 reinforcements. But there was no time. Blücher, part of his army at least, he knew now must be in the woods to his right. How long until he came? One hour? Less? D'Erlon's corps had been decimated. Two thousand men taken prisoner; herded into the British lines. God knew how many more lay out on the field dead and dying. He had been forced too to order d'Erlon to release further infantrymen to replace the massacred gunners of the grand battery. Had to keep up the bombardment. Must give the British no relief. There was still a good chance. Still a chance. He paced up and down. Bit his lip. Crossed his hands behind his back and ground the fingers together tightly. At least he was feeling better now. The pain in his arse had gone. Dr Lameau's miraculous ointment. But still the tiredness would not lift. He rubbed at his eyes.

Soult spoke: 'Sire. It would be sensible to withdraw. If we were simply to pull back the infantry behind the cavalry. Form a screen. Use Lobeau as a rearguard. We might summon Marshal Grouchy and consolidate. Then we could attack again. But now, sire, the men are exhausted. The ground. We cannot move. And the Prussians . . .'

'The Prussians? Why do you worry so about the Prussians, Soult? They are exhausted. We beat them at Ligny. They do not want a fight. Lobeau will deal with them. And we have the Garde. I do not have time to consolidate. And we will do it, Soult. Look there. The farmhouse will soon be ours. The château too. See how it burns. They cannot hold on much longer. Now is the time to attack. When they are at their weakest. Look up there. On the ridge. What do you see? Wellington is pulling his men back. He needs time to reorganize. We are tearing holes in him with our cannon. All that we need to do now is to attack in force and those holes will open wider. And then we will have him, Soult. We need to reinforce the front line.'

He paused. Frowned. 'Order the Young Garde to move across to the right. They will take up position on the forward slope in the space formerly held by d'Erlon.'

The Chief of Staff summoned a messenger. Gave him a hastily scribbled order.

Napoleon continued. Caught up now in his own rhetoric. 'Remember Eylau, Soult? Does anything similar strike you about this battle? There by mid-afternoon we had lost one corps. It looked hopeless. And what did I do?' He used his hands to demonstrate. 'While you were holding the left, here, I sent Murat into the centre with 10,000 cavalry. The entire reserve – cuirassiers, dragoons – and behind them all the cavalry of the Garde. You remember, Bertrand, Gourgaud? De la Bedoyere?'

'I was not there, sire.'

'Mm? Yes. Of course. But you remember, Soult? What happened?' He punched a fist into his palm. 'We smashed the centre of the line. Split the Russian army in two. Took how many colours? Fifteen? Twenty?'

'Sixteen, sire.'

'Sixteen. Sixteen Russian colours to hang on the walls of the Tuileries. Cavalry, Soult. Cavalry. And we can do it again. Wellington cannot match us. We have broken his dragoons and his infantry are exhausted.'

'But they will form square, sire. It would be madness. In Spain we –.'

Napoleon raised his eyebrows. Raised his hands in mock supplication. Mimicked his Chief of Staff in high falsetto. 'In Spain we were defeated, sire. The British infantry, sire. We couldn't break their squares, sire.' He resumed his normal tone. 'Spain, Soult? This is not Spain. I was not with you in Spain. At Eylau we smashed the squares. Remember? We carried them before us. Why are you so afraid now? Is it Wellington? He's not a god, you know. He's only a man. I tell you we will smash his infantry today just as we smashed the Russians at Eylau.' He crossed his hands behind his back. 'Find General Milhaud. Tell him I need his cuirassiers. Now. All eight regiments. Three thousand men. The entire corps. He is going to have the honour of destroying Wellington's army. He will lead my army over that hill, to victory. To Brussels.'

Yes. Brussels was the key. He closed his eyes and without warning the pain began again. He ground his hands tighter together. No. Not now. Not when I most need to be here. When I must be able to command. Please, no. One last chance. Do not let me be sick.

But he knew it to be useless. The pain had already begun to grow in intensity, clawing at his insides with sickening regularity. He must divert his thoughts. Brussels. Brussels was the key to the campaign. To the war. Take Brussels and the coalition collapses. The war is over. He would defeat Wellington and take Brussels. He tried to picture how the attack would be. A frontal attack with cavalry. Old style. With the cuirassiers. An unstoppable wave of horsemen that would sweep up the hill and carry everything before them. Milhaud could do it. One division would do. Delort's men. Second strongest in the army. Fresh to the fight. Of course Milhaud himself should go with them. Lead them in. Or maybe . . .

Napoleon placed his forehead in his intertwined fingers and slowly pulled his hands down over his face. He opened his eyes. No. Not only Milhaud. The blow would be delivered by the one man, next to Murat, who was truly capable of leading such a charge. The man whose example in Russia had earned him the title, Prince de la Moskowa. Napoleon summoned de la Bedoyere.

'Where's Ney?'

'Forward, by the farmhouse, sire. At La Haye Sainte. With General Quiot.'

'Go and find him. Tell him that I need him now. Tell him that I'm giving him the cavalry. The cuirassiers. Delort. The 14th Division. Milhaud. Tell Ney that he's going to take Delort's cuirassiers and drive the British off their hill. Tell him he's going to win me the battle.'

TWENTY-THREE

The valley, 4 p.m.
Ney

They moved across the field, from east to west, through the clamour of battle in their own bizarre silence. No cheers and huzzahs marked the stately progress of Napoleon's cuirassiers, merely the jingle of their polished brass and leather harness, the hollow clank of empty scabbard against top-boot and the rhythmic clatter of thousands of steel breastplates. The ultimate shock troops, the Emperor's 'Gros Frères', were on the move.

Each man stood almost two metres tall. Combined with his horse, weighed in at over 300 pounds. Black horsehair manes flew behind their gleaming helmets, and on their shoulders they wore the red epaulettes of the élite. Second in status only to the Garde, for twenty years the Imperial cuirassiers had struck fear into all the armies of Europe. And now Ney was about to lead them into battle.

The Emperor had sent word to him twenty minutes ago. Had pulled him out of the fight for La Haye Sainte, beside whose devastated orchard he had been urging on Quiot's exhausted infantry. It was the key to the field. But how were they to take it? Napoleon's orders, delivered in person by Bertrand, had been a little vague, but simple enough. He had admittedly been a little surprised, particularly after the series of rebukes he had suffered over the last three days.

He was, it seemed, to take Milhaud's entire cavalry corps and press the Allied line to the left of La Haye Sainte. A grand cavalry charge which would clear the centre of the line ready for the artillery to move in at close range. And then, he presumed, would come the *coup de grâce*, delivered by the Garde with Napoleon at its head.

Not doubting the Emperor's word, Ney had ridden straight to Delort, the closest to him of Milhaud's two divisional commanders. But the general had not believed him. An unsupported cavalry attack? It was unthinkable. Suicide. Ney had shouted down his protestations. Had turned his horse and gone directly to Milhaud. He of course had not dared to doubt the marshal's authority, and so here they all were, Delort included, riding at the head of the mightiest force of heavy cavalry assembled in Europe for three summers. Ney laughed. Turned to his aide-de-camp.

'Well, Heymes. Here we go at last, old friend. Look around you. Have you seen the like? Not since the Moskowa, I'll bet. And we can do it again.'

Heymes smiled. Nodded.

Ney swivelled to his left. 'Eh, Rollin? Don't you think so? We'll make them run.'

'Of course, sire. You will do it. No one else.'

Ney looked around. Searched for familiar faces in these awful, stomach-churning moments that always came in the calm before the attack. 'Milhaud?'

The armour-clad cuirassier general drew closer. 'Sire?'

'Remember Eylau, Milhaud?'

'Of course, sire.'

'We did it then, Milhaud. Didn't we? What a slaughter that day.'

They had done it then. He had done it. Done what he had always done best. Michel Ney, the young hussar. Marshal

Michel Ney, Prince of the Moskowa, daring leader of the cavalry charge.

Peering through the smoke, he scanned the hill before them. Of the redcoats there was no sign whatsoever. The guns, with their blue-clad crews, were still firing at them from the forward slope, sending shots ploughing through the ranks of d'Erlon's decimated infantry who had now re-formed on the ridge behind the grand battery. But their fire seemed to him as nothing compared to the cacophanous bombardment maintained by the hundreds of French cannon. Who would want to stand under that?

Perhaps Wellington really had gone. But if that were the case then surely he would have made some attempt to evacuate the château and the farm where the battle still raged. The good general would never abandon his troops. Particularly the Guards who garrisoned the château.

Ney rode in the centre of the line, at the front and centre of the 5th Cuirassiers, Armand Grobert's men. Their ranks filled with the veterans of Austerlitz, Wagram, Borodino, Leipzig. They were brigaded with the 10th under Pierre Lahuberdière, similarly experienced. On their left rode the 6th and the 9th commanded by Baron Vial and over on the right the 13th Division with the 12th and 7th under Travers and Dubois' 4th and 1st, not yet recovered from their efforts at helping to repulse the British heavy dragoons. Almost 3,000 men and horses, crossing the bloody field in column of march.

He was enveloped in a comforting smell of damp horse and fresh manure. They passed La Belle Alliance. The little inn was awash with staff officers and aides. Of the Emperor, though, Ney could see nothing. Perhaps he was resting. Back up the hill at Le Caillou. Moving on to the left wing, directly astride the road leading from the inn towards the ridge, they began to fan out into their designated attacking formations.

They would go in with maximum impact. Eight regimental columns, each with a frontage of between thirty and forty men, drawn up in two ranks. Invincible, irresistible and still absolutely, resolutely silent. Waiting to hear the word of command.

To his left Hougoumont burned ever brighter, columns of flame reaching up from her rooftops, thick black smoke belching from the windows. On the right stood La Haye Sainte, doggedly holding out. These were their markers. The left and right of their small world. And in between stretched the valley, funnelling them up the slope. Two dozen trumpet calls rang out, drawing the regiments into place. Swords drawn and tucked squarely into their shoulders, the troopers man-oeuvered with balletic precision around the fluttering, eagle-topped guidons.

'Walk forward.'

Ney looked over his left shoulder. The slowly moving line shimmered in the dim sunlight like a single rippling entity. Four hundred troopers, riding almost knee to knee. An endless wave of steel. In front of every squadron rode five officers. Why did the British never learn, he wondered. The only way to control your cavalry was to place at least half of the officers to the front. If only Wellington had done that with those brave men on the grey horses. Perhaps by now the day would have had a different story to tell.

They had advanced almost forty paces when the collective silence was suddenly broken. Eight colonels spoke almost in unison. 'Advance. At the trot. Forward.'

From the eight regiments the commands rang out across the field. Slowly the great horses began to move into the valley. The first artillery rounds came smashing into the cuirassiers before they had crossed ten yards, carving channels of blood through their tall ranks, claiming man and horse alike. They closed up without need of an order. Their progress was horribly slow.

'Canter.'

They moved on. Passed the shattered orchard to the east of Hougoumont. Ney saw puffs of white smoke as the British defenders loosed off sporadic shots at the passing cavalry. And there was something else. Looking down the line towards the château he noticed that the cavalry on the farthest left of the charge were not cuirassiers but dolman-clad chasseurs. The chasseurs of the Garde. What were the Garde cavalry doing with them? He had not ordered them to charge. Who had given the order? The Emperor? It must have been the Emperor himself. They would answer to no one else. Well then. They would go in together. This would really finish the British. And their German friends. He wondered whether the Garde lancers were with them too, but, caught up in the rhythm of the charge, could not turn to see. Thought, if I can just lead them into the enemy now. Can just push on. Can only make it to the hill.

'Gallop.'

The ground was shaking. Their hooves beating a relentless thunder as close on 5,000 horsemen speeded up into the attack. Ney could feel his heart pounding, paying back the rhythm of the hoofbeats.

'Heymes. Milhaud. Travers.' He screamed their names. 'With me now. For France. For the Empire.'

From the guns to their front, the deadly rounds came crashing in, parting the wave of men. They were answered now, though, by a barrage of shots from their own artillery, stationed on the incline above the valley. The French cannonballs sailed high over Ney's head, to vanish deep in the reverse of the Allied position. The cavalry made the foot of the slope at a canter and carried on at the same pace up the firmer ground of the hill.

Only 100 paces away from the crest. Buglers calling again now. Willing them forward. The shrill, insistent notes of the '*charge à la sauvage*'.

He looked to his right. Could see nothing but steel, steaming horses and the long, black horsehair manes of the cuirassiers' helmets, flying in the wind.

And then they were silent no longer.

'Vive l'Empéreur! Avancez!'

The cry was everywhere, not least on Ney's own lips as, wild-eyed, grinning, he pushed his horse forward. The thick scent of sweat and gunpowder caught his nostrils. He shrieked, to no one in particular: 'Follow me. Follow me, to glory. For France. For the Emperor.'

Mounting the lower slope, some of the horsemen pushed on in textbook style. The front rank held their sabres forward, arm fully extended, the great, flat, four-foot blade pointed straight at head height, tip inclined slightly downwards. Behind, the second rank held their swords high in the air, over their heads. The regular, well-dressed lines had long since gone and the officers had fallen back in line with the men. But for Ney it was as good a charge as he had ever seen, the short width of the front maintaining a semblance of the packed formation. And so it was that, carried forward by the impetus of their attack, at the canter, they crashed over the top of the hill. The Allied artillery were sending shells up now, shrapnel. All along the line men were hurled from the saddle, cut to ribbons by iron fragments, while smaller pieces came down like pattering hail on their breastplates and helmets.

Ney was not certain exactly what he had expected to see as they crested the ridge. The Allies in retreat? He had never really thought so. But nothing had prepared him for what met them. The cannon he knew would be there but not, he had thought, in such force. As the French closed on them, at twenty yards they opened up and the cuirassiers were hurled back by the hammer-blow force of the grape and canister shot, double-loaded. He watched them go down in scores. Before every Allied gun, with each discharge of canister, four or five cuirassiers collapsed upon one another, men and horses killed together; a single heap of mangled flesh. Their job done, the gunners deserted their cannons and ran for the rear.

It was only a moment before Ney saw what they were

running to. Riding beyond the smoke, it became instantly clear to him that the entire Allied army had pulled back 100 yards. It was arrayed before them in a series of thirteen perfectly formed hollow squares and oblongs, set in chequerboard pattern, some composed, to judge from the many standards and drums assembled in their centres, of two regiments. The infantry stood in three ranks, the nearest kneeling down, bayonets fixed, pointing upwards. And most of them were redcoats. No, he thought. This was not Eylau. But something very different. Something deadly. He knew, though, that there was no alternative for the French cavalry but to charge straight at the serried ranks of steel.

Across the hilltop, as the cavalry moved in, disciplined volleys began to erupt from the rear two ranks of each of the Allied formations. Around him Ney saw comrades topple from the saddle; shot horses throwing their armoured riders before collapsing themselves. Milhaud went down, his horse shot from under him. The cuirassiers barely had time to switch from a canter to a gallop before they impacted on the first of the squares.

Ney tried to bark a command. 'Shoot at them. Use your pistols. For God's sake shoot them.'

But he knew in his heart that, at least for this moment, God had forsaken them.

He saw a huge cuirassier launch himself against a square of redcoats, only to receive a bayonet thrust from the ground, deep into his horse's stomach. The animal reared and threw the cavalryman who, once on the ground, was helpless to raise himself. The man scrabbled around. Tried to find his carbine. Grasped his sword. Attempted to rise. Fell again. All around him Ney saw similar stories unfolding.

He rode through a gap between two of the squares of redcoats, caught up in the irresistible flow of the attack. Glancing momentarily to his right, he saw quite clearly for an instant, in the centre of one of the squares, the unmistakable figure of

Wellington, in his distinctive blue coat and simple black hat. Such was his surprise that, hesitating momentarily, Ney found himself again being carried bodily along by the force of the other horsemen. Sweeping round the rear face of the square, caught in the crossfire, he glimpsed yet more squares formed up below them, on the reverse slope of the ridge. Black Brunswickers, three battalions of them. And beyond them a vast body of light cavalry, British Hussars and light dragoons, poised to deliver a counter-attack.

Oh God, he thought. This is no retreat. We have played into Wellington's hands. This is exactly what he hoped that I would do. Riding on, over to the left, he saw two more columns. Infantry – Dutch, by the look of them, advancing to strengthen the Allied right wing.

There, in the rear of the enemy's front line, only five paces away from Ney, Travers fell from his horse, as three shots penetrated his breastplate at point-blank range. Colonel Thurot of the 12th led a troop against a side of the square. Threw himself on to it. Three bayonets sank deep into his horse's chest, bringing it down on the men below. Thrown, Thurot struggled to his feet. Ney lost sight of him. And then once again the marshal was being pushed around the edge of the square and back towards the French lines. They must regroup. Must attack again. It was the only way to win now, of that he was certain. By smashing these squares. He knew it to be possible. Hadn't he done it himself before? It was their only hope.

Ney realized that he had been carried far over to the left. Close to where the chasseurs of the Garde had closed with the Allied line and were riding helplessly round and round two squares of Brunswick infantry.

As Ney approached he saw an officer and five chasseurs fall like dolls, taken with the same volley.

He passed the Red Lancers of the Garde on his left. So they too had joined the fight. Saw Colbert leading his men in, his left arm, wounded at Quatre-Bras, tied up in a sling.

Ney called over to him. Tried to make himself heard. 'Colbert. Colbert.'

The colonel saw him, smiled, nodded, shrugged in resignation and turned back into the mêlée.

Their three-metre-long lances had given Colbert's men an initial advantage, allowing them to stab down over the hedge of bayonets. But now, having left the weapons in the bodies of the dead Allied infantry, most had changed to swords and, caught up against two squares of the British Guards, were receiving volley after disciplined volley. He watched as three of the furious lancers hurled their weapons like javelins into the square before drawing sabres and going to meet their deaths, impaled on the line of steel.

It was useless. Slaughter. The sweat pouring off him, Ney tried to push through the milling throng. To regain the French lines. Perhaps if he could bring in more men. Kellerman's cuirassiers and dragoons. Men and horses fresh to the fight. The carabiniers too.

He rode back down the slope, and as he did so he was aware of roundshot flying past him from the rear. How could this be? Surely they had taken the Allied cannon? Had they not disabled them? Driven a spike into the touch-hole? Confirming his fears, a shell burst close by, sending a large fragment into his horse's stomach. The animal reared for an instant and then plunged down upon its front legs, throwing Ney over its head. He hit the ground hard. Sat up. Shook his head. Reached to find his sword. Two cuirassiers dismounted. Helped him to his feet. One gave him his own horse. All around them cannon-balls were ploughing into the mud, finding targets among the regrouping cavalrymen. It must be true, he thought. As soon as the cavalry left the ridge, the British gunners were coming out of their squares and retrieving their cannon. Firing again. They had to spike those guns. And perhaps they could move a battery of horse artillery up to the slope. Then there would be a real chance of success. Above all they must attack again. As Ney began to mount, Milhaud came cantering up on a fresh horse, his black bicorn hat riddled with bullet holes, his breastplate dented and muddy.

'Sire, are you hurt? Your breeches.'

Ney looked down. Saw that the right thigh of his breeches had been slightly torn in the fall. He had lost a gold button too, from his filthy coat.

'It's nothing. I'm fine. But, Milhaud. We must try again.'

'Yes, sire. But it's murder up there. Where is the artillery? We need artillery.'

'It's coming. I've requested it. The Emperor knows what you're doing. He's very proud of us. He's sending the guns.'

Well. Why not lie if it helped? For all Ney knew there were cannon on their way.

He moved to the foot of the slope, where the bewildered, frustrated cuirassiers were attempting to re-form. Made out one regiment from their bright orange collar facings, the 5th, their numbers horribly depleted. Five hundred men, three squadrons, reduced now to perhaps half that number. Their commanding officer was still with them. Charles Grobert, his face covered in blood. Beside them, similarly dazed, stood all that was left of the 10th, and next to them the 6th. Both units seemed to lack officers, for now at least. Hatless, Ney made sure that they could see his red hair. Shouted: 'That's it. Re-group. Reform your squadrons. Follow me. I'm Ney. Marshal of France. Come with me. Regroup.'

Finding himself at the head of a ragged group of perhaps 300 cuirassiers of various units, he called out to a wounded captain, the highest ranking officer, save Grobert, that he could see. 'Come on. We're going in again. Follow me.' And then to the rest of the men: 'Avancez! For France. Here. Up this hill. Charge with me now. Charge for the keys of freedom.'

They managed a ragged cheer. Began to advance up the slope against the storm of fire from the Allied artillery. But the guns ceased as they neared the crest and again they saw the gunners taking cover. Two of the British artillerymen attempted, too late, to feign death beneath their gun carriage. They were cut down by three cuirassiers.

Ney led his force towards the nearest square. The surprise was gone now. At thirty yards out the British opened up with a volley. To his left three men fell and two horses. The same and more over on the right. A score of cuirassiers trotted up to the square. Attempted to fire into it with their pistols. Another half-troop, led by a maddened sergeant, took a path between two squares, slashing down with their sabres on both sides and, although constantly losing men, rode away with as much calm dignity as if they were on exercise in the Bois de Boulogne. Ney watched, mesmerized for a moment, as one of the huge cavalrymen, seeing a gap in the line, reached in and deftly lopped off the head of a huge redcoat sergeant. Another man he saw set his horse before a square and cut down three men of its second rank with the considered precision of a butcher, before himself being taken down by a volley of close-range musketry that left his corpse scorched and smoking. Moving further down the slope towards the Allied second line, Ney found Delort lying under his horse, struggling to get free. A cuirassier reined up, jumped down and helped lift the dead beast aside, before being shot through the temple. The general had taken a musket ball in the upper leg. He struggled to his feet, helped by another cuirassier. Began to shout at Ney. 'This is madness, Ney. Madness. I told you we'd all be killed. It's madness. What are we doing? We need infantry. Where are the infantry?'

Ney just stared at him. Turned away. Sought out another square. Nassauers, this one. He trotted towards them. Shots flew past his head. Mere youngsters, mostly. Some barely older than his own eldest son. Putting aside the thought, he leaned down and cut viciously into their ranks with his sabre. Sliced halfway through a musket, severing all the fingers of its owner.

But he could not reach any further, in beyond the bayonets. A bearskinned Nassau sergeant grabbed at his harness. Tried to pull him down on to the lethal steel skewers. Ney, used to the trick, twisted away. Then tried to make his horse rear in the air. To kick the kneeling front rank. He saw a green-coated officer take aim at him with a pistol. Turned away quickly and rode as fast as he could, feeling his horse slipping on the bloody cuirasses and bodies, alive and dead, beneath her hooves. Knew now that there was only one thing to do. They needed more men. Infantry. Cannon and infantry. And more cavalry.

He found one of Milhaud's junior officers. 'Press the attack. Don't stop. I'm going to find Kellerman. Keep at them. Go on.'

Managing to extricate himself, Ney headed once again for the French lines. Had begun to ride down the slope when, advancing towards him, he saw a mass of cuirassiers in perfect order, and to their left two regiments of green-coated dragoons. The Emperor, it seemed, had second-guessed his thoughts. Not infantry then, but fresh cavalry at least. He spotted the corps commander with his staff. Galloped across.

'Kellerman. Quickly. We need your men. Quick, man. France is counting on you.'

The general motioned to his officers and, as Ney watched, the regimental buglers began to sound the charge. He swung into rank, to join the advance, as the sea of cuirassiers and dragoons attempted to move faster now, through the quagmire of mud and corpses. Of the carabiniers there was as yet no sign. No matter. They would be a third wave. Better that way. On the right, passing the château, he could see the distinctive bearskins of the grenadiers à cheval of the Garde, and there too were the Empress Dragoons. So the Emperor had finally sent them in. Now, truly, there was a chance. He pushed his horse to the left, towards where the 11th Cuirassiers were moving up to a canter. Found their colonel.

'All right, Courtier?'

'Never better, sire.'

Milhaud's battered squadrons were racing back through them now, and down the hill towards the rear. Ney shouted to them as they passed. 'Regroup. Regroup in the valley. Form up. You must go again. Regroup. You must regroup.'

He dug his spurs deep into his horse's sweating flanks. Waved his sword above his head. Moved to the very front of the charging cuirassiers. 'Charge. With me, men of the 11th. Remember Jena. Leipzig. Remember the Moskowa. Charge with me. Look, I'm Ney. Charge to glory. Follow me to glory. For France. For the Emperor.'

As they reached the top of the hill another blizzard of shot flew into them. Again, as if by a miracle, Ney was unhurt, but through the smoke he was horribly aware of the devastation all around him. He watched as L'Heritier, leading his division, was touched by a cannonball which passed across his stomach and carried away the pommel of his saddle before bisecting the torso of his aide-de-camp. Weaving his way through the mêlée and the maddened, circling horses, Ney tried to move across to the right. Glimpsed Picquet, the dragoons' commander, as he too was hit by a musket ball, and watched as he fell, slowly, leaning far back in the saddle, and was carried off into the centre of the fighting. Riding on along the left side of a square of Hanoverians, he was aware of a force of cavalry approaching fast from the rear of the Allied lines. A counter-charge. Light blue uniforms. Hussars. Belgians? Dutch? He pulled his horse round to the left and found himself riding along the front of two squares of Nassauers who took pot-shots at him and straight towards a smaller group of Brunswickers. Avoiding them, he almost careered into the flank of another counter-charge. Dutch carabiniers this time. He swung away and found himself facing the French lines. Cantering through a battery of unmanned British cannon, he emerged at the top of the hill beside a square of British riflemen. God. Was there no end to their infernal squares? All

279

around him Kellerman's cuirassiers were stabbing with futile fury at the bayonets. Trying to force a passage into the ranks.

A lieutenant of the 8th rode up, bearing a tattered white standard emblazoned with the arms of Hanover.

'Sire. Sire. We have taken a colour. May I have your permission to convey it to the Emperor?'

Ney grinned. Clapped the young officer on the back. 'Of course, boy. Of course you must. Well done.'

He turned to Milhaud. 'D'you see? We will win. We can do it. They are weakening.'

Where was Heymes? Dead? Probably. In his place Ney grabbed the arm of a passing cuirassier sous-lieutenant.

'Quick. Ride to the Emperor. Go with that captured colour. Tell him the news. Tell him we're winning.'

Ney looked back to the squares. Saw at once just how hollow his words were. The hopelessness of their position. Of course they were not winning. But how had it come to this? The finest cavalry in the world were being sacrificed. Broken against squares of steel. Yet what could he do but carry on? Perhaps just one last push might break some of the squares. And if one or two collapsed, then, their morale weakened, perhaps others would run. Perhaps. He would rally Milhaud again. Would find the carabiniers. He hurried on past the rifles, through a squadron of the 3rd Cuirassiers and into the flank of the attacking grenadiers à cheval, 'the Gods', who were attempting to engage a square of British light infantry. Ney spotted their commander, General Jamin, imprisoned within their tightly packed ranks, alongside his gaudy trumpeter. The huge man was standing high in his stirrups, screaming, his mouth wide open and his sword whistling around his head. And then quite suddenly he wasn't there. Ney had no idea where he had gone. He just seemed to disappear into the crowd of humanity and horseflesh. Determined now to find the carabiniers, Ney turned past the grenadiers and rode along the tall hedges of the château's orchard. At last Reille had moved up a battery to the edge of the compound and was sending roundshot over the heads of the cavalry deep into the infantry squares.

Just beyond the guns, taking cover in a slight dip in the ground, he found the carabiniers. Two regiments of them, pristine in their white and sky-blue tunics, bright red crests and shining, brass armour. The strutting peacocks of the heavy cavalry. Their commanders were deep in conversation. Were for a moment unaware of Ney's arrival. Their ignorance was shortlived.

'Blancard, Rogé? What the hell are you doing here? Who ordered you to stay here? What do you think you're doing. Can't you see? We're attacking. Look, man. Look up there.' He pointed, his arm shaking, up towards the ridge.

'We were ordered, sire. General Kellerman specifically ordered us to remain here in reserve.'

'And here, Blancard, here I speak for the Emperor. I am his orders. Come on. Come with me all of you. We have them beaten. Forward. For the honour of the eagles!'

Strangely, given the debris littered across the field, they seemed to reach the crest of the hill more easily than before. Or perhaps it was merely that he had grown used to it. Used to riding over the faces and shattered bodies of the dead and dying troopers. Ney spurred forward. All about him wounded, wide-eyed and unhorsed cuirassiers, chasseurs, red lancers and dragoons were trailing back towards the rear. An equal number of riderless horses, maddened by blood and destruction, galloped through their ranks in all directions. Ney spurred on his horse, the third of the day. Turned to Blancard.

'Charge. Sound the charge. We have them.'

Picking their way over the mounds of dead cuirassiers, the 800 carabiniers were barely able to manage a trot. Yet the British held their fire. Ney brought them to thirty paces from the square. Recognized the men as foot guards. Waited for the impact. Twenty paces. Fifteen. At twelve paces the redcoats opened up. The leading squadron of the carabiniers, men and horses, just seemed to melt away. Ney closed his eyes for an instant. Blinked them open. Shook his head. Then, still unhurt, led in the second line. Incensed by their impotence, he cut down blindly, three times. Sensed that his blade had touched flesh, metal. But did not look to see the maimed, the dead. At last his sword stuck fast in something. He turned away. How, he wondered, does this happen? How can we be beaten? Are they so very good? So much better than us? How can they hold out? How do they do it? Faces flashed past him. Expressions of horror and hate. Seeing the marshal without a sword, a cuirassier officer offered his own. Ney took it. Felt whole again. Prepared to return to the fight, but, swept round now by the force of his own men, found himself once again heading towards the French lines.

As he passed the most advanced of the Allied squares, a wall of musketry opened up against the French flank and he felt his horse begin to drop to the ground. Holding tight to the new sword, he threw himself away from her. Must not be trapped. Rolling to safety through the mud, he found himself lying beneath an abandoned British gun. Abandoned but not disabled. Ney pulled himself up by its wheel spokes. Dead British gunners lay all around him, along with redcoated infantry killed earlier in the day and his own cavalry. One man, a British regular by the look of him, lay, eyes wild, staring, propped against the wheel of the cannon, where he had evidently dragged himself to die. A few yards away to his left a cuirassier with a gaping hole straight through his breastplate – canister – moaned and gurgled blood as his life ebbed away. Ney looked about for something to drive into the cannon's touch hole. A spike. A simple nail would do. Anything that could stop the gun from firing at them again when a fresh crew emerged from the shelter of the squares, as he knew they surely would. There had to be something here. Something.

Ney knelt on the ground. Desperately scrabbled about in the earth, raked at it with his hands. At length he picked up a bayonet. Stood up. Attempted to jam the length of steel into the cannon's touch hole. Shouted at it. 'In. Get in, God damn you. In. Get in.' But the socket of the blade merely rasped hard against his hand, cutting open his palm. He wiped away the blood. Tried again. 'Shit. Shit. Get in. Damn. Damn. Bugger it.'

Unable to force the blade to stay in the gaping touch hole, he hurled the useless weapon down the hill. Looking at the ground again he saw the hilt of his sword. The blade had snapped in the fall from his horse. Ney picked it up. Leaned against the heavy bronze barrel. Noticed the royal cipher of King George. Slowly, deliberately, he began to smash the pommel of the sword hard down against the gun, increasing the force until his hand started to ache and the blood ran freely between his fingers.

'Sire. Are you all right? Sire?'

Ney looked up. It was Rollin, miraculously still alive and still mounted, leaning down towards him. He was holding the reins of another horse, a tall black charger. The mount, he realized, of a cuirassier officer, of the 5th.

'Rollin. You're alive?'

'Yes, sire. And Heymes. A fresh horse, sire?'

Ney said nothing. Looked back at the gun. Shut his eyes. Dropped the shattered sword and buried his head in his hands. When he raised it again and at last found the words, they came through a mask of bitter tears.

'Rollin. We have to regroup. Find Milhaud. General Kellerman. Tell them we're going to re-form. Tell them to find as many of their men as they can. Tell them . . . tell them we're going in again.'

TWENTY-FOUR

Hougoumont, 5 p.m.
Macdonell

Standing fifty yards away, despite the drifting smoke, he could see the hands as they reached in through the holes in the long, red-brick wall. Clawing, desperate, they closed around the barrels of the guards' muskets, some of them red hot from incessant firing, and naturally, as they did so, most let go. But some held on. Braving the searing heat, attempting to wrench the weapons away from their owners. Eventually, though, their hands burnt and bloody, even the most determined fell away. Occasionally the point of a bayonet was poked through the gap, only to be beaten back by the defenders, who were working in pairs now, two men to a hole, the one loading while the other fired.

As Macdonell watched, he saw, to his astonishment, one of the Frenchmen vault from his comrade's shoulders, and, one of his feet connecting with the top of the wall, spring over the heads of the defenders to drop behind them on the grass. A hand flung his musket after him and, as the man grasped it, Macdonell saw that more of the attackers were attempting the same stunt, with varying degrees of success. Some of the defenders, alerted to this new danger, turned from their firing posts at the wall and in doing so momentarily exposed themselves to fire from outside. Unopposed now, French muskets poked in through the holes. Fired. He saw several of the guards go down.

He rushed towards them, bareheaded, slipping on the sodden grass and gravel, all that remained of the once elegant garden. 'To me. Form on me. Stop them. You men at the wall. Back to your stations. Don't let them over the wall.'

From left and right guardsmen ran to his call. Ten, fifteen, a score of them now, men of all three regiments, running with him, towards the intruders. He spotted a familiar face.

'Sar'nt Miller.'

'Sir.'

'With me.'

Quickly they closed upon the small group of intrepid Frenchmen, the half a dozen who had followed their athletic comrade into the formal garden and were now standing back to back against a section of the wall.

'Make ready.' Miller barked the command.

At twenty paces the guardsmen halted, raised their loaded weapons. The French, waiting for them, let loose a desultory volley. Two of the guards fell wounded.

'Fire.'

There was no contest. As the smoke cleared, Macdonell saw that only one Frenchman remained standing. Hands above his head, he called for quarter. Two of his comrades lay moaning on the ground. The others were dead.

'Take him prisoner. And help the wounded.'

From the left a great cheer announced a counter-attack through the orchard. It was Hepburn's men, who a quarter of an hour ago had been pushed back to the sunken lane by this latest French attack. They were pouring through the trees now. Bayonets gleaming, they smashed into the front and right flank of the French, hurling them back through the orchard and against the thick hedge that marked its boundary with the lane. It took barely three minutes.

Macdonell relaxed. 'Hold your fire. Stand down.' He turned

to Miller. 'But keep watch, Miller. They're sure to come again.'

He turned and, feeling his boot hit something soft, looked down and found himself staring at the body of a Frenchman. One of the storming party. He glanced at the shako. Third regiment of the line. Good soldiers, these. No parade ground dummies, for all their Emperor's pomp, but simple foot-sloggers. Plain bloody infantry. You could not fail to admire the devotion of these Frenchmen. Very different from Britain's infantry. Not the Guards, of course. Nor the Highlanders. But the bulk of Wellington's army – listed for gin. The French flocked to their Emperor out of pure adoration. It puzzled him still, after so many years. How a nation could have cut off its king's head, only to take as its new leader a despotic gutter-snipe a thousand times more powerful and ruthless. What had the Revolution been about? What had they wanted? How had it come to this? He was more aware than ever now that, were they to prevail today, this battle would represent not only the end of Napoleon, but the death of a process that had begun back in 1789, on the streets of Paris. He looked down at the shako again. The corpse grinned back at him. Who had he been, he wondered? Had he known anything of the principles of the Revolution. *The Rights of Man?* The Jacobins? No. This man had been seduced, like so many thousand others, by something far more dangerous. By the concept of imperial glory. The sweetness of sacrifice. The honour of a hero's death. Honour, yes, of course. They all fought for honour. But glory? Macdonell looked around the garden. Saw the reality of glory lying dead in its ruins.

Walking to the north end of the wall, he pushed his way through a gap in the adjoining hedge and entered the orchard. Fragments of apple and cherry trees, blasted from their trunks by shellfire, lay strewn across the grass, the fallen fruit ground into sticky mush. Beside the cherries lay the dead. Frenchmen, mostly. He walked across the orchard past guardsmen helping wounded friends. He pushed back the hair from his sweating brow and was trying to recall where he might have lost his shako, when he was suddenly aware of another rhythm added to the thrum of the battle. A strange change in the earth. It was vibrating. Something was happening beyond the trees. Hurrying now, Macdonell crossed the last few yards. Found himself standing beside a sergeant of the 3rd. Both men froze. Stopped dead by the sight before them.

The sergeant spoke: 'By the Lord above. Jesus, Mary and the bloody Devil. Would you look at that.'

As the smoke blew across the open field beyond the wall, Macdonell was able to make out through its drifting white mist the tall forms of thousands of cavalrymen. Cuirassiers, green-coated dragoons, and the bearskin-clad giants of the Garde cavalry. As he watched their pace increased, a trot giving way to a canter. On the wind, above the low boom of the guns, dozens of trumpeters sounded the unmistakable notes of the charge. It was, he knew, the most splendid sight he had seen in a lifetime of soldiering. And it was as mad as it was glorious. Looking up the hill to the left he could see white smoke rising over the crest of the ridge, and as he looked hundreds more French cavalrymen, cuirassiers, lancers, chasseurs tumbled pell-mell down the slope. Others on foot slipped and tumbled through the mud. Riderless horses ran in all directions.

Macdonell stared, incredulous. While they had been preoccupied with defending the château, the French had attacked with a vast force of massed cavalry. Driving straight up the muddy slope into the very heart of Wellington's position. If the Allied infantry had formed square, then the cavalry, however many there were, must surely be impotent. This he presumed might explain the retreating mass on the hill. But why then was Napoleon sending more of them in? It was as mad as it was spectacular. The new wave swept past him, barely thirty yards away. He was galvanized into action.

'Any man who can do so, shoot at their horses. Bring down as many as you can.'

The hedge was lined with redcoats now, drawn as he had been to this dramatic sideshow. They began to loose off shots into the flank of the attacking cavalry.

Macdonell walked away, back through the trees and into the garden. Found Colour Sergeant Biddle gathering ammunition pouches from the dead Frenchmen. The sergeant rose to his feet.

'Colour Sar'nt.'

'Sir?'

'How are we for ammunition?'

'Precious little, sir. We're running low.'

Macdonell saw a passing officer, moving towards the orchard. Called to him. 'You there? Who are you, sir?'

'Drummond, sir. Ensign, 3rd Guards. Gazetted acting Battalion-Major.'

Macdonell had him now. William Drummond. Clever boy. Peninsular veteran. 'Ah, yes. Major Drummond. Take yourself on a run up the hill, if you would. Find someone on the staff. No matter who. Tell them that we need ammunition. That Colonel Macdonell requests ammunition. That we're damn near out of ammunition.'

'Sir.'

The lieutenant went scurrying off, back towards the sunken lane. Well, thought Macdonell, he has a better chance than many. He saw Gooch, agitated, running towards them, down the garden path from the château.

'I think you had better come, sir.'

He did not need to ask why. As the three men walked towards the château it seemed as if the entire complex must be alight. Thick, black smoke spewed from the windows and cinders flew through the air, stinging their faces as they entered through the garden gate. Macdonell put a hand over his mouth and walked through the smoke towards where the flames looked their fiercest, over by the great barn. Badly burned, wounded men, those able to walk, were staggering from the blazing building. The stench was indescribable. Burning timber and human flesh, gunpowder and filth. From deep within the crackling, hissing din of the fire came the awful screams of men burning alive. He found that Woodford was with him. Both men walked slowly towards the door of the barn, only to be beaten back by the heat. Woodford coughed, then spoke.

'Macdonell. What on earth can we do? The wounded. It's impossible. They're burning to death. Poor beggars. Dear God.'

A soldier snapped to attention before him. 'Sir. Permission to fall out.' James Graham.

'What on earth for, Graham? Why now, man?'

'My brother, sir. He's in there, sir. In the stables and if I don't get him out then he'll burn, sir. With respect, sir.'

'Then for God's sake go and help him. Quick, man. You've no time to lose.'

They watched as, apparently impervious to the heat, Graham fought his way through the smoke and flames.

Macdonell shouted across the yard: 'Put out the fires. Get anything. Your kettles. Canteens. Find water anywhere.'

He knew that the farm's pond, its main water supply, lay outside the gates and that any concerted attempt to carry water from there was liable to provoke a French attack. They would have to make do with what they could find. But he knew too that the canteens were precious. That all the men must have the terrible thirst always brought on by smoke and gunpowder and fear. A man of the 1st Guards ran up to him.

'Sir. The chapel's on fire, sir. And there's wounded inside.'

'Then get them out, man. Hurry. Soak your blankets. Piss on them if you can't find water. Wrap them around the worst burned.'

His defensive position was fast being reduced to little more than a pile of ash. A huge roof beam crashed down from the top storey of the château, narrowly missing Macdonell's leg. He noticed Private Williams grinning at him.

'I wouldn't stand there, sir. You're likely to get hurt.'

'Thank you for that useful warning, Williams. And mind your tongue in future. Now get these fires out.'

In truth there was no safe place in the yard. They were carrying some of the wounded away from the barn now. Laying them on the cobbles by the well. He recognized most of them. Saw Edward Mann, one of the most recent recruits. Too obsequious. Irritating habit of saying 'sir' after every second sentence. His face was ashen. Macdonell walked over to him. Noticed a wound on the side of his head. Ear half torn off. Still, he'd seen worse. Then to his horror he saw that Mann's legs had been burned quite black. Beneath the crust, the skin was peeling off in strips. Strangely, he did not seem to be in any pain and was quite lucid:

'I think we did well, sir, didn't we?'

'Very well, Mann. We did very well.'

'Rotten night though, weren't it, sir. Real wet it was.'

'Yes, Mann. Very wet.'

'Sorry, sir. Can't hear very well, sir. On account of my ear, sir. Being in part shot away, sir. Rotten bloody shoes. Sorry, sir. But rotten shoes is full of holes, sir. Rotten bloody wet last night, sir.'

Macdonell nodded. Smiled. 'We'll soon have you out of here, Mann. Thank you.'

He moved on. Around the corner of the chapel Henry Wyndham came clattering over the cobbles. Breathless, filthy with soot and mud.

'We've fallen back, sir. They've taken the orchard again.'

Macdonell pushed past him and back through the garden gate. Together they ran straight down the main path, for the east wall. The men were back in position. Firing down into the orchard.

'Form a line along the wall. Close up. Use the fire steps.'

Macdonell climbed on to a wooden fire step and at once could see the extent of their peril. Hepburn's men had fallen back through the orchard to the hollow way and were desperately holding off the swarm of French who were now charging across the grass.

'Steady.' Macdonell called out to the men standing behind the wall and those already on the fire steps. 'Fire down on them. Aim for the officers if you can. You two. Find more wood. We need more platforms.'

He jumped down. Called across the yard. 'More men over here. Defend the wall. Fire at will. Keep them pinned down.'

The muskets were pouring a furious fire down on the heads of the attacking French. Macdonell turned to Biddle. 'How much ammunition have we?'

'Wouldn't really like to say, sir. Perhaps we should just hope Colonel Hepburn pushes 'em back again, quick.'

One of the Coldstreamers, a man from Number 2 Company he thought, called down from the fire step. 'Colonel Macdonell, sir. They're running. They're retreating, sir.'

'What's going on? Tell me, man.'

'Frogs is running away, sir. Only there's none of our officers left, sir. They've all gone.'

Macdonell hauled himself up on to a scrap of firing step. Peered over the wall. It was true. Hepburn's men were advancing back into the orchard. Pushing the French back, inch by bloody inch. A sergeant of the 3rd Guards was leading the counter-attack, followed by two companies. The French were fleeing before them, back to the far hedge. Looking to his left, Macdonell saw that the field was littered with red-coated bodies, several of them officers. Beyond the orchard he could hear what could only be the noise of another great cavalry attack. How long could any one of them last? This battle was sucking them dry. Leaching away their men. Bleeding them into defeat.

He climbed down into the garden and, followed closely by

Biddle, made his way back towards the buildings. Entering the yard, he walked round the side of the burning house to where the wounded lay. Walked past Mann. The boy was dead. Macdonell noticed his feet. The holes in his shoes. The wet wouldn't bother him now.

To the left of Mann's corpse, Tom Tarling, the company clown, was sitting up against the well, his right arm wrapped in what looked like a piece of shirt. He was covered in blood. 'He's dead, sir. Just now. Poor lad.' Tarling winced with pain.

'You should have that seen to, Tarling. Can you make it back up the hill? There's a dressing station behind the lines.'

'Sure, sir. Thank you kindly for your concern. But ye see, if ye send me back up there it's certain the bloody surgeons will have me ruddy arm off before I can blink. No thank you, sir. I'll stay here and take my chances. It saves them the trouble, you see.'

Macdonell smiled. Turning away, he fancied that he could hear a child crying. Looking about he found the gardener's daughter standing before the broken windows of her father's house, one of the only buildings not yet afire. She was sobbing uncontrollably. Corporal Robinson was attempting to comfort her. Macdonell walked up to them.

'I've tried to help her, sir. But she just don't seem to understand English. I can't find her father nowhere.'

Macdonell looked the boy in the eye. Raised his eyebrows.

'I swear it weren't my fault, sir. Piece of shell just flew in the window. Killed the boy stone dead.'

Macdonell walked past the girl and peered into the room where Robinson had been looking after her and the two captured French drummer boys. Of one there was no sign. The other, though, was sitting at the table, his back taut against a chair, his face staring in wide-eyed surprise. From his chest there protruded a large piece of shell. Before him on the table lay the carved toy soldier and a penny whistle. Macdonell walked back to the girl.

'All right, Robinson, I'll deal with her. *Alors, calmez vous, ma petite. Ne vous dérangez pas. Je vous conduisez au arrière avec un de mes serjeants. Votre père vous attenderez maintenant. Sans doute.*'

Recognizing the words, the girl stopped her sobs. Looked at Macdonell with puzzled eyes.

He turned to the corporal. 'Find Sergeant Lloyd. Get him to take her to the rear. Quickly through the gate and up the hill and through the lines to the forest. This is no place for her now. Where's her father?'

'Don't know, sir. Last I saw he was helping with the fires.'

'Well, find him too then and, if you can, persuade him to go with her. And see if you can find her something to eat. A few biscuits, at least.'

A furious hammering at the gate. Surely the French hadn't got round to the north again? Expecting another attack, Macdonell ran across the yard. Found Biddle.

'Keep them out. Keep the gates shut. Guards, to me.'

A guardsman on the wall shouted down to him. 'It's not the French, sir. It's our lads. An officer, sir, and ammunition. A wagon-load of it.'

'Then let them in. Open the gates. Quickly. Get them inside.'

The great gates creaked open and in rolled a horse-drawn tumbril packed with barrels of powder and shot. Driving it was a man of the royal wagon train. Beside him sat Francis Drummond, grinning hugely. The Guards cheered them through the gate.

Biddle sighed. 'God be praised.'

'Are you all right, Sar'nt?'

'Well in truth, sir, I wasn't sure how to tell you before. But we're down to three rounds a man, Colonel. Two minutes more and we'd have been at them with nothing but the bayonet.'

Macdonell smirked. Turned back to the gate. 'Close the gates. And get that ammuntion unloaded and distributed. Biddle, you take charge.'

Looking up the hill he could just see the distant figures of Sergeant Lloyd and the van Cutzem girl, as they reached the first of the British lines. She at least would be safe now. One less soul for death to claim in this charnel house.

Her father, he realized, was not with them. Macdonell wondered where the man could be. Still helping with the futile attempt to control the fires? Attempting to rescue some precious fragments of his own property? He walked across to the south gate. Musketry snapped all around him, mingled with the staccato crackle of the flames. He shouted to the upper storey. 'That's it, Gooch. Keep up your fire.'

Turning the corner behind the chapel, Macdonell came upon the gardener. The man was kneeling on the ground, eyes tight shut, before the outside wall of the burning building. His hands were pressed together in silent prayer. He made an odd sight amid the frenzy which otherwise filled the courtyard. For a moment Macdonell watched him, careful lest he should disturb his devotions. Then he turned away. Stared blankly at the dead bodies littering the cobbles and tried to make sense of the two images. Was there yet a place for God in this hell? Was van Cutzem praying for his own salvation or for the souls of the dead? Or was he perhaps, as Macdonell had often done himself, simply asking 'why'?

TWENTY-FIVE

Ohain, 6.00 p.m.
Ziethen

Ziethen was intrigued. Never before had he seen an English-man quite so agitated, so utterly detached from that legendary coolness. Something was very wrong. Again he listened to the red-coated colonel, whose face now almost matched the colour of his uniform. Had his aide translate the hurried speech.

'General von Ziethen, sir. I appreciate your need to adhere to your orders, but the fact of the matter is that the Duke of Wellington is urgently in need of your assistance. I beg of you, sir. You must send reinforcements. I implore you. However few you may have to spare. A mere 3,000 men. A single battalion. General, you are less than two miles from our lines. Listen to the guns, sir. How can you not march to help us?'

He felt truly sorry for this man. It was a fact. They could hear the sound of the guns more clearly now than they had all day. They had marched through the sound of cannon fire. Now from Wavre, now from Wellington's battle. There was no doubt as to whose were now the loudest. But were they British or French guns? Throughout the long day as they cut their way through the heavy country the reports had continued to come in. Napoleon had won. Ney had broken through with cavalry. Wellington had been killed. The Prince of Orange too. And now this English gentleman, this Colonel Freemantle, was telling him that none of it was true. That Napoleon was far from being victorious. That Wellington could still hold on, but for only an hour longer. This English officer was trying to persuade him, a general in the Prussian army, that he should disobey his orders. That he should go against everything in which he believed. Discipline. Obedience. Strict, unquestioning faith in his commander. That he should march not to reinforce Blücher, but Wellington. It was only half an hour since his new orders had come to turn away from his original line of march directly into Wellington's flank and move south to assist Blücher at Plancenoit. In fact the plan to reinforce Wellington's left flank had only ever been half-hearted.

'March slowly,' Gneisenau had told him. Clearly the Chief of Staff had not forgiven Wellington for withholding reinforcements from Ligny and was intent now on returning the compliment. He had qualified his instructions: 'Of course we need to save the British, General von Ziethen, but not too soon. Pace yourself. Just in time will be fine.'

Plancenoit, Gneisenau had said, was the key. Not Wellington. Take the village and we cut the French line of retreat. Catch them like rats. Then we shall carry the field for Prussia. Ziethen was not to have any part in the victory. The Second and Fourth Corps would do it. He recalled Gneisenau's smug expression. 'Don't trouble yourself, Ziethen. Go and help Wellington. Bülow and Pirch will manage Plancenoit.'

Now, though, it seemed that Blücher was of a contrary opinion. He was needed after all, at Plancenoit. For once Ziethen was relieved. He thought of Ligny. Thirteen thousand of his men dead. Where had the British been then? Where was Wellington's promised support? So now he would march to help Blücher, and the British would have to take their punishment. Just as his own men had at Ligny. He shook his head.

'I am so sorry, Colonel Freemantle. You must understand. I would dearly love to help your Duke. But I cannot commit my corps against the enemy in small groups. Piecemeal, as you say. They would simply be defeated in detail. Believe me, as soon as I have assembled the majority of my men I will send some to help you. You must understand. My orders have been changed by immediate command of the Feldmarschall. You have met Major von Scharnhorst. He comes direct from Feldmarschall Blücher. He brings me explicit orders to turn south, towards Frischermont and Plancenoit. You see, surely, that I cannot go against them.'

Freemantle shook his head. Closed his eyes.

Ziethen shrugged.

A Prussian officer rode up. Sweating, breathless. Ziethen couldn't quite place him.

'General. Sir. Wellington is retreating. He's running. His army is in rout. I've seen it.'

Von Scharnhorst glanced at him. Smiled at Freemantle. Spoke with confidence.

'It is precisely as I told you, Herr General. I saw it myelf. The Allies are running away.'

Freemantle looked aghast.

'Impossible. British infantry commanded by Wellington would never run. Did you see any redcoats among them?'

'Well, yes. Only a few. But there were definitely redcoats.'

'Hanoverians, I'll be bound. Deserters. Take my word for it, General von Ziethen. There is no retreat. Wellington will stand, I tell you. You must ride to our aid, General.'

'I am sorry, Colonel Freemantle. It is decided. We march on Plancenoit. I am afraid that Lord Wellington will have to wait.'

Freemantle stared at him. 'Then, sir, you have just lost us the battle.' The Englishman saluted, turned his horse and, summoning his escort of German Legion hussars, cantered away down the tree-covered lane, towards the sound of the cannon.

His parting words hung in Ziethen's mind. Sent a chill through his soul. 'Lost us the battle'. He turned his own horse to the left, and began to trot down another lane of the crossroads, leading towards Plancenoit. He said nothing. Scharnhorst rode at his side. Orders shouted to their rear and the familiar jingle and clank of an army on the move indicated that the corps was following.

God, this was awful country. Great defiles cut through with tracks and lined to either side with impassable woods. At some places – crossing the Lasne – they had been forced into single file. How long, for God's sake, would it take them to reach Plancenoit?

They had gone barely half a mile when a shout from the rear brought Ziethen to a halt. Turning in the saddle, he saw two horsemen approaching. Prussian staff officers. Von Reiche and with him Müffling, the fat liaison officer on Wellington's staff. What did they want now? This would hold up his advance.

Von Reiche spoke first. 'Sir. You must not continue on this route. We must turn back.'

Scharnhorst, glaring hard at Ziethen's Chief of Staff, was the first to speak. 'What is the meaning of this, Oberstlieutenant von Reiche? Feldmarschall Blücher's orders state clearly that the First Corps must turn south. It is needed in the battle for Plancenoit.'

Von Reiche ignored him. Spoke directly to Ziethen. 'Sir. You must listen to me. General Müffling has important news.'

Müffling mopped his brow. 'General von Ziethen. You must turn about. You must ride to Wellington's aid.'

Ziethen smiled. 'My dear Müffling. All this time with the British army has turned your head. Captain von Scharnhorst assures me that it is already too late. Wellington is in retreat. Our only hope is to take Napoleon in the flank. At Plancenoit.'

Von Reiche spoke again. 'That, sir, with the greatest respect, is where you, and Captain von Scharnhorst, are wrong. Wellington is not beaten. He is standing. His infantry has beaten off 15,000 French cavalry and destroyed an entire infantry corps. He is holding hard on to his hill. But, sir, he cannot hold it much longer. Unless you ride to help him. You are his only hope. You will win the battle. If not, if the First Corps does not go to the Duke's aid, then I am afraid that the battle is lost. And with it Europe, and civilization.'

Scharnhorst's face was quite white. He spoke calmly. Matter-of-fact. 'General von Ziethen. May I remind you that if you do not obey my direct orders from the High Command you and Oberstlieutenant von Reiche will both be held personally responsible.'

Ziethen looked at him. Saw in his face the years of blind obedience. And, for once, felt uncertain. He was torn in two. His military training, everything he had been taught to believe in, told him that he must obey the orders. His instinct told him otherwise.

Ziethen unbuttoned his saddle-bag and took out his spyglass. Put it to his eye. Tried to train it towards the north, to find the Allied lines. It was almost impossible from here to make out anything through the smoke. He could see the farm – Papelotte – up on the hill, enveloped in smoke. Blue-coated figures thronged its walls. But French or Dutch? It was hard to tell. His mind was quickly made up by the appearance of a squadron of lancers. French. He saw them entering the farmyard. So the farm that had protected Wellington's left was now in French hands. He swept the telescope further to his right and doing so could see, quite plainly, scores of green and blue-coated infantry, Nassauers and Dutch this time, in open retreat from the farm. Perhaps Scharnhorst was right. Perhaps the British had gone. He continued his sweep and then he saw it. A little further away along the ridge. A solid line of redcoats. Two lines now. More. A square. A battalion of Highlanders. It was as Freemantle had said. Wellington was still there. Holding on. They were right. This was the crucial moment. If the French now succeeded in pushing forward from the captured farm of Papelotte they would be able to just roll up Wellington's line. And that would be an end to it. In that instant there was no longer any doubt in his mind. He closed the telescope. Put it away. Spoke quietly.

'Müffling. Ride to Lord Wellington. Tell him that we're coming. We're all coming. First Corps. Five thousand men. We'll be as quick as we possibly can. Tell him to hold on. At all costs.'

Against all he had been taught. Against his orders. Against his commanders and the Prussian military machine, Ziethen was marching to help the British.

Von Scharnhorst narrowed his eyes. Spoke equally softly. 'In my opinion, General Ziethen, this is a very bad move. Bad for the army and bad for you. You are making a very serious mistake.'

Ziethen turned towards him. Looked him straight in the eye. 'I do not need your opinion, Captain von Scharnhorst. This is my decision alone. I accept full responsibility. Unless you wish to be disciplined for insubordination, I strongly advise you to take yourself immediately back to General von Gneisenau. Tell him that I have gone to help Wellington. Tell him that I intend to defeat the French.'

As von Scharnhorst turned his horse and galloped off, Ziethen turned to von Reiche. Glimpsed the huge smile. Tried hard not to return it.

'Oberstlieutenant von Reiche. Order the corps to about-turn. Inform the divisional commanders we're taking the road to Mont St Jean. We're going to save the Duke of Wellington.'

TWENTY-SIX

Near La Belle Alliance, 6.45 p.m.
Napoleon

Standing in front of the little inn, he watched blank-faced as the remnants of his cavalry returned through the valley. Watched the broken men and the bleeding horses. Saw the torn and bloody uniforms, the shattered weapons, the staring eyes, and knew that, up there, beyond the crest of the ridge, the British still held on. They had not been routed. Were not even in retreat. Wellington had tricked him – had tricked Ney – into squandering the finest cavalry in the world on a madman's dream of victory. The realization left a bitter taste. This was not as it should be. To be thus outwitted. This was not at all what he had planned. Napoleon bit his lip. Stared wide-eyed at the ground. What had Ney thought he was doing? It had been all too soon. Much too soon. He turned to Soult.

'It was too soon, Soult. To attack like that with all the cavalry. Too soon. Don't you agree? How did Ney think that such an action would achieve the results I ordered? What did he think he was at?'

The marshal, clearly aware that it had been Napoleon who had precipitated the attack, said nothing. 'It's just as it was at Jena, sire. Ney has compromised us again. He has concentrated everything on one flank. He must realize now that we have to face not one enemy, or one point, but so many at the same time.'

Napoleon glared at him. 'Don't ever tell me again about the Prussians. Don't say the word. Grouchy will deal with them, I tell you. We still have enough time here to finish this business.'

He looked across to his left. To where, above the shattered trees, the burning mass of Hougoumont spoke of its agony. Thrusting out his arm, he pointed towards Jerome's division entangled in its smoke-shrouded woods and orchards.

'And as for that idiot.'

'Idiot, sire?'

'My brother, Soult. My brother, Prince Jerome. This is the second time in two days he has compromised France. Compromised me. What did he think he was doing, committing an entire corps to what was never . . . had never been intended to be anything more than a diversionary attack? And what the hell was General Reille thinking? Could he not see what was happening? Surely he could have countermanded the order. He is the corps commander, is he not? Is he not? Not my dear brother.'

'He is, sire.'

'Well then, tell me what the hell he was doing? How could Reille allow Jerome to do that? How could you allow him to do it, Soult? A corps. How?' He thought for a moment. 'No. No, that was unfair of me. You could not have stopped him.' Napoleon smiled, indulgently. Then frowned. 'But what have they done? The fools. A corps wasted.'

As both men stared at the burning building, a carabinier, his armour dented with bullet-holes, rode past them along the *chaussée*, towards the rear. Napoleon noticed that the man's right arm had been almost severed at the elbow. He was holding the bones together. Behind him came perhaps a dozen cuirassiers, on foot. Most were wounded, some blinded, one missing his nose. Only two wore helmets. All were without weapons. Seeing the Emperor, they managed a cheer. He acknowledged them. Nodded his head and then, blinking back tears, looked again at Hougoumont. How could the British still hold the château? What kind of men were there inside that burning hell? He crossed his hands behind his back. Picked at his thumb. Paced right and left. Spoke aloud. To no one.

'What could I have done?'

He coughed. Took out the perfumed handkerchief. Closed his eyes. Opened them and saw Soult, smiling. He rubbed at his eyes. A voice by his elbow.

'Sire?'

Pierron, the majordomo of the imperial headquarters, had come forward from Le Caillou in a little barouche with a hamper of provisions. He offered the Emperor a glass of Chambertin, cut with water, just as he liked it. Without a word, Napoleon waved it away. Turned to Soult.

'The attack had started. You saw. We had no other option but to sustain it. That's right? Yes? That's right. I had to order Kellerman to charge. You see, Soult, don't you? I had no choice.'

Soult said nothing.

An aide came galloping towards them from the valley floor, his face ecstatic. 'Your Imperial Majesty. Sire. The farm has fallen. We have taken the farmhouse. La Haye Sainte is ours, sire. The English, the Germans, all the defenders are wiped out.'

Now they had a chance. A foothold close to the Allied line. Now if only he could punch through the centre of the line. It was weaker now. The British cannonballs were falling in fewer numbers. Wellington had been too caught up in repelling the cavalry. Had concentrated on his right. The centre was falling apart. He spun round on one foot, eyes darting at the huddle of staff who had been poring over Pierron's welcome hamper. They snapped to attention.

'Where's Ney?'

'At the farmhouse, sire. He's taken the farm.'

'Well, tell him to attack again. Bertrand, ride to Ney. Tell him to push home his victory. Attack the centre. Now. Go now.' He turned to Soult and Gourgaud. 'If Ney can break the centre, we can win. Wellington is weak. I know the Prussians. The Prussians are too occupied with Plancenoit. They want all the glory for themselves. They do not trust the British. They will not send anyone to help Wellington. He is abandoned, and now we have him. They do not trust him, Soult.'

'Sire?'

'The Prussians. They do not trust Wellington. You agree?'

'Of course, sire.'

Ney would do it. He would break the centre, and they would win. The Prussians had not yet assembled sufficient men to take the field. They had only one corps. He turned to Soult. Excited. Flushed. He spoke in a rush.

'Blücher has only one corps in the village. One corps. They cannot hold on with one corps. Lobau will match them. We can reinforce him. Keep the Prussians out while we finish Wellington.'

Ney would break the centre. Then the tables would really be turned on 'Papa' Blücher. He would be the one caught in the trap. Caught between him and Grouchy. He laughed. Clapped Soult on the back. 'We've won. We've done it. Ney will smash the centre and I shall lead in the Garde.'

A horseman was approaching them from the east. A hussar. One of Marbot's men. He reined in and dismounted. Saluted the Emperor. 'Sire. I come from Plancenoit. The Prussians have brought up cannon. We are being cut down. General Lobau has occupied the churchyard, sire. His men are dug in. But he begs me to tell you that he cannot hold forever, sire. He implores you to send support to the village.'

Napoleon nodded. 'Very well. Here it is. Flahault. Find General Duhesme. Have him take the Young Garde to Plancenoit. He must retake the village. Throw the Prussians out and hold both the village and the woods. Understand?'

That would stop them. Four thousand élite veterans. And Ney would smash the centre.

As he was congratulating himself on his foresight, Napoleon's attention was caught by a figure in a vivid red hussar uniform who had dismounted ten paces away and was walking towards him. Heymes. Ney's aide-de-camp.

'So, Heymes. Have you triumphed already? How is the worker of miracles? Where is Ney?'

'Sire. Marshal Ney is at La Haye Sainte. He asks me to inform you that he has weakened the centre of the Allied line with artillery fire from the farm and that the enemy are giving, sire. He has opened a gap. But he needs more men, sire. With more troops we will surely break them.'

Napoleon furrowed his brow. Shrugged. 'More troops? Why does he need more troops. He has a corps, doesn't he? D'Erlon's corps. Isn't that enough?'

'General D'Erlon's corps is unformed, sire. Marshal Ney has but one division. He needs more troops, sire.'

Napoleon's eyes widened. He tensed. Clenched his fists together and crossed them behind the shabby grey coat. 'More troops? How can he ask for more troops? Where, my dear colonel, do you suggest I get them from?' He laughed. Scowled. Pushed his face uncomfortably close to Heymes. 'Do you want me to make them? Look around. What do you see? More troops? Can you really see more troops?'

'But sire, with only a few more men we can advance from the farm. We can smash the centre. The moment is here.'

Napoleon raised his voice. 'The moment is here? Who are you to tell me "the moment is here"? The moment is here when I make it, and I have not yet decided when that will be. When I do so I shall order in more men. And only then.' But Napoleon knew it to be true.

Heymes did not move.

Soult broke the silence: 'You still have the Old Garde, sire.'

Napoleon looked at him in disbelief. 'What? Commit the

305

Garde? Commit my *masse de décision*? Place them in the hands of Ney? After what has just happened up there? Are you mad?'

He turned away. This would not have happened at Eylau. At Borodino. They would not have asked him before. Would never have had the temerity. What was happening? He had to rest.

'Pierron. Find me a chair.'

The valet came rushing forward. Arranged the folding chair. Napoleon sat. Placed his feet on a drum and, with Heymes still standing in incredulous silence beside Soult, closed his eyes.

The shellfire brought him to his senses. Soult and Gourgaud stood before him. Of Heymes there was no sign. How long had he been here? Had he been asleep? Another artillery round came crashing into the inn, passing through the roof, sending the red tiles flying. Soult spoke.

'Sire. It would be wise to take cover.'

Napoleon ignored him. Watched with no concern for his personal safety as more cannonballs came thundering in. Noticed they were coming from the right. Not British, but Prussian guns. Blücher. But how had he come so close? What about Duhesme's men?

'Sire. You must take cover. Shelter, sire. I beg you.'

Napoleon waved him away. Stood up. 'The men must know that I'm still here. Without me there is no army. Who's that?' He had spotted a courier. A lieutenant of lancers, standing close to the wall of the inn. He beckoned the man to him. 'Yes? What news?'

The young man saluted.

'Sire. Plancenoit has fallen The Young Garde has been pushed back, sire. Out of the village. They are re-forming. General Duhesme requests –'

Napoleon cut him off. 'I know what General Duhesme wants. And he shall have it. Soult, deploy the Old and Middle

Gardes. Two regiments only. General Pelet will take the 2nd Grenadiers, General Morand the 2nd Chasseurs. They will retake Plancenoit. You hear? They must recapture the village. At all costs. But they are to do so without firing a single shot. They will recapture it *à la baïonnette*. Understand? Not a shot.'

That would really give the Prussians something to think about. He knew that the Germans would run at the mere sight of his Garde. There would be no need to fire. When they saw those bearskins they would assume that behind them were all 10,000 men of the Garde. Two battalions would be sufficient to create the right impression. Quicker that way, too. And they would inspire the Young Garde and Lobau's men. Very soon his right flank would be restored. But what of Ney? He looked for a familiar face.

'Gourgaud. What is Ney doing? Where is he? Why isn't he here?'

'He's attacking, sire. By the farmhouse.'

Napoleon pulled out his spyglass. Rested it on Gourgaud's shoulder. Tried to see through the smoke to the farm. What was he doing? What men did he have? Should he have given him the Garde?

Flahault, the handsome aide-de-camp, rode up. He was grinning. 'Sire. General Durutte reports that the redcoats engaging him at Papelotte are being attacked in the rear. The Hanoverians are being attacked in the rear, sire. It can only be Grouchy. Grouchy is here.'

Napoleon nodded, sagely. So Grouchy had done it. Now surely the right flank was secure. Perhaps now the moment had come. Perhaps it was the time to go to Ney's side. But not with any infantry. He, Napoleon, would take the men of his Old Garde straight into Wellington's centre. It was the moment.

'De la Bedoyere, Gourgaud, send runners. Broadcast the news. Let my army know. Grouchy is here. Grouchy has come

307

across from Wavre. He is attacking the British in the rear. Go on. Tell them. Tell everyone. We are winning the battle. Flahault, find General Drouot. Tell him to bring the nine remaining battalions of my Garde. Here. Right here. And Flahault. Tell him to keep them in formation.'

He gazed towards the ridge. The sun, having spent most of the day obscured by cloud, was nearing the horizon, pouring its light over the ghastly field. Napoleon folded his arms and, looking straight across the valley, tried to estimate how long it might be until nightfall. An hour, perhaps an hour and a half. That, he thought, is all I have. One hour and a half. If I can win the battle in that time, then I will win the war.

TWENTY-SEVEN

Mont St Jean farm, 7 p.m.
De Lancey

The surgeon stooped low over De Lancey. Smiled down into his face, adjusted his spectacles and cleared his throat. He smelt of brandy, carbolic soap, sweat and blood.

'Now, Colonel, I'm just going to turn you over on to your side. It may hurt a little.'

As the two orderlies grasped hold of him, De Lancey closed his eyes. At least he knew this physician. John Gunning. Deputy Inspector of Medical Services, no less. Officer commanding at the field hospital of Mont St Jean.

He felt hands around his shoulders and waist. Slowly the two men began to lift.

Despite his best intentions, he was unable to stifle a groan. The pain cut through him. It was in his back. In his side. Everywhere. A raw, deep, burning pain that pierced his very soul. He bit deep into his lip. If only they would allow him to lie still. Only when he lay motionless did the agony leave him. But with the slightest movement it returned. If only they would let him be. He tried to speak. Managed a hoarse whisper: 'Doctor Gunning. You're wasting your time. You should have let me die in peace. On the field.'

'Nonsense, my dear chap. You're not going to die. You've been damned lucky. The ball appears to have only broken a few ribs. Granted, you are badly bruised. And it's hard to tell any internal damage. But in my professional opinion, you'll live.'

De Lancey knew it to be untrue. He had seen just such an injury before. At Salamanca. A young captain of the Blues. Musgrave, wasn't it? Seconded to the staff. De Lancey had been sitting close by him at the moment that he had been hit by a ricocheting roundshot. He too had been thrown from his horse. Had suffered a bloody back and eight broken ribs. The surgeons had bound him up. Had bled him frequently. Had talked for five days of his imminent recovery. On the sixth day the boy had died. De Lancey would not survive. He knew it. He did not care for himself. He had had a good life. A soldier's life. But Magdalene. Magdalene troubled his every thought.

Through the red mist of his pain De Lancey heard Gunning call now to an officer across on the other side of the room.

'Doctor Hume. An opinion if you will.'

He saw John Hume turn round from binding up the freshly amputated leg stump of an infantry colonel. Hume was Wellington's favoured doctor. The Duke had made him his personal physician. He was famously charming. He walked up to De Lancey, wiping his blood-covered hands on a piece of flannel. Smiled. 'Oh, I say. De Lancey, isn't it? My dear chap. I am sorry. How perfectly dreadful. Gunning?'

'Sir William received a cannonball on his back. More precisely a cannonball *en ricochet*, which glanced off his back. You will observe the contusions. The impact, though not severe, has I fear broken several of his ribs. But as to the extent of the internal damage we can merely guess. Nevertheless, he does seem in good humour, as I'm sure you will agree. I find the prognosis favourable on the whole. Your thoughts?'

Hume pondered. Gazed for a while at De Lancey's back. Still the orderlies held him on his side. How much longer? De Lancey wondered. How long could they take to decide whether a man was to live or die. A simple question to which in his own mind he already had a simple answer. The awful pain was beginning to drain him. He felt faint. Made a conscious effort. Must hold on. Dignity. Example.

Hume wandered away. Beckoned Gunning. De Lancey watched them confer in private and, after what seemed an eternity, return to him. Hume spoke.

'Well, Sir William, I am quite satisfied that you are in no immediate danger. We shall, however, have to try to find somewhere rather more comfortable to put you, in due course. But do not concern yourself as to your condition. I believe you'll live.' And then, almost as an afterthought, he added: 'Have you any next of kin?'

'My wife. Magdalene. She's in Antwerp.'

'Best to inform her then.'

'Oblige me then, if you will, sir. I need to find an officer. My cousin, Colonel De Lancey Barclay, of the Foot Guards. He is Assistant Adjutant-General. Could you possibly find him for me?'

'Of course, Sir William. Rest easy. We shall find your cousin. And, I pray you, do not worry. You will not die.'

Lying on his front, his head supported on a filthy coat, he was able now to observe his surroundings more closely. This small, gloomy room must he guessed, have been the farm's kitchen. The stone-flagged floor, strewn with straw, was now discoloured with blood. The whitewashed walls, the same. The principal furnishings consisted of a plain deal table and chairs and a dresser. Other pieces of furniture, more elaborate, stood scattered about. Incongruous here, he thought. Brought in to act as beds. Around the walls, on shelves and hanging from hooks, the medical orderlies had placed torches of tallow which now, as the day slowly began to draw to its close, cast a flickering light over the gruesome scene, giving it the appearance of some dramatic performance. Shakespeare perhaps, he thought. The last act of a bloody tragedy. Finale. He tried to laugh. Found it hard to move his head. Then, through a process of counting the number of coughs emanating with irritating regularity from the improvised cots that surrounded him, he was able to reckon, after a few minutes, that he shared this unholy billet with perhaps a dozen other men, most probably all officers. Aside from the coughing, the sound of quiet groaning provided a constant undertone, punctuated by the occasional scream. Words came in staccato bursts. Oaths or imprecations mostly. One man in the far corner called feebly for his mother. De Lancey fixed his gaze on the wall nearest the window and the door. As he watched, a new patient was brought into the room. A colonel of hussars. His ashen face wore a blank expression. De Lancey looked with interest to see where he had been hurt. His left leg was hanging, half-severed, suspended by only a few shiny, white muscles. The skin hung down in strips from the bone which had splintered into jagged shards, like the remains of a shattered tree-stump.

A doctor walked up to the hussar. Appeared to know him. The two men exchanged pleasantries. De Lancey heard the word 'amputate'. The colonel nodded grimly and rested his head. Two redcoats arrived bearing a rustic door, ripped from some outhouse. On it they placed the wounded man. As they picked him up he turned to De Lancey and managed a pathetic smile. And then they were gone.

He had no idea how much time had elapsed when his cousin arrived and woke him with a loud cough.

'William. I say. You poor chap. Are they looking after you? This is a hell-hole. And the stench. Poor wretches. You know, I've just seen the most amusing thing. Farmer's wife, d'you see. Refused to leave her precious home. This house, as it were. She's been here all day, William. Up in the damned attic. Balls falling all round her. And now she's blaming us. Not only for the destruction of her precious house, but the slaughter of her livestock. Naturally, they've all been blown to atoms. D'you

312

know I actually saw her arguing with the adjutant of the ordnance. Out there, in the yard. All quite comical.' He laughed to himself. 'Really most amusing. I say, William. Your poor back does look bad. How can I help?'

De Lancey loved his cousin dearly. But he was in no mood for laughter. He called him closer. Whispered instructions. 'Barclay. I would be much obliged if you would convey a note to my wife. To Magdalene. In Antwerp. Be a kind fellow. Break to her the news of my passing in person. And gently. Tell her that I love her. I shall always love her.'

'Your passing? But the doctors assure me that you will recover. What nonsense, William.'

'I tell you, Barclay, I know that I shall die. I only wish they had left me on the field. To perish with honour. Instead they have brought me . . . to this stinking hole.'

'Well, that's one thing we can arrange right away. I'm going to have you moved. Wait there, William. Don't move. Ah. I'm sorry. Of course you are unable . . . Wait. I shall return instantly. And then I shall fetch Magdalene.'

De Lancey tried to rise. To stop him. Too late. Thought, she must never see me like this. Must never see this place of putrefaction. He must order Barclay to keep her away. For just as long as it took him to die. Better to lie to her. Better to say he were dead already.

He saw Barclay re-enter the room. So soon?

'William. It seems that the farm is to be evacuated. The French have taken La Haye Sainte. A swift attack now and they will be here. Gunning has been ordered to move the wounded back to the village and thence to Waterloo. We must get you to Brussels. I shall ride to Magdalene. She can join you there. Do not worry. Prince Blücher has come across. Boney may have the upper hand for the moment, William, but he is hard pressed. They say that the day will yet be ours. What would you have me do?'

'I beg you, do not fetch Magdalene. Tell her only that I died

313

on the field. There is a letter for her. A letter in my valise. But I do not know where it might be.'

He thought for a moment. Began to try to reach down into his clothes. 'Here. Take this.' His hand scrabbled desperately beneath his chest, pressed down against the table top by the weight of his immobile body. Tried to locate his waistcoat pocket. Could not. 'Here, Barclay. Reach down here. Into my pocket. There's a stone.'

His cousin fumbled with the bloody buttons. At last managed to find the hole in the ragged cloth. Probed with his fingers. Grasped.

'There. There. You have it.'

De Lancey gazed at the pebble. At its smooth coolness, shining in the half-light. Barclay stared at it too. He wore a quizzical expression.

'Yes. I see. But, I can't think what . . .'

'Take it to Magdalene, Barclay. Tell her not to mourn me. That I shall be always with her. Be sure to tell her that she is free.'

'William. This is nonsense. You will not die.'

'Do this, Barclay. For me. Take it. I beseech you.'

'Very well. I shall do as you ask. But I cannot tell her you are dead.'

He turned towards the door. Barked a command to two orderlies who were loafing in the doorway. 'You men there. Move the colonel on to a board. Carry him further up the *chaussée*. Into the village. There are two houses at the junction of the roads. Place him in one of them. And be sure to do it gently. And then one of you, see if you can find his servant. He'll be with the General Staff.'

He turned back to De Lancey. 'Well, William, adieu then. I shall inform the doctors where they are taking you. Someone is sure to attend you. Good luck.'

The two reluctant stretcher-bearers lifted De Lancey with surprisingly less pain than previously and laid him on a door covered with a grey blanket, which they wrapped around him. On this they carried him from the room, out into the yard and on to the Charleroi road. It was a scene of chaos and human devastation. Everywhere wounded men walked or crawled in the direction of Brussels. The lucky few had been piled into tumbrils. At the same time reinforcements, cavalry mostly, were making for the battle, regardless of who stood in their way. Twice De Lancey's party was forced off the cobbles and on to the verge beside the ditch. The noise was indescribable. The roar of cannon and musketry. Shouts and screams. Orders, in English and German, shouted from all points. Bugle calls, drums and fifes. Bagpipes. Horses. De Lancey looked up at the sky. Cannonballs flew high above his head. Seemingly in every direction. Slowly they moved from the ridge and down into the village of Mont St Jean. After having gone he estimated perhaps 300 yards, they entered a small house on the south side of the junction of the main highway and the Nivelles road. It was as simple a peasant's cottage as he had ever seen. It seemed surprisingly deserted, save for a kilted Highlander, quite dead, slumped in one of the corners in a pool of his own blood.

The men laid him down, still on his door, on top of the kitchen table. One of them, an Irishman, spoke in a thick brogue.

'We'll leave you here then, sir, if you please. Good day to you, and good luck, Colonel.'

De Lancey smiled. Thanked them as best he could and positioned his head so that he might see out of the room's single window.

He had just watched incredulously as an entire squadron of Hanoverian cavalry streamed past his view in the direction of Brussels, apparently in retreat, when a man entered the room.

'Colonel de Lancey? James Powell. Surgeon.'

Barclay had been as good as his word.

'I am instructed by Dr Hume to bleed you, sir. Now we'll just have to make you a little more comfortable.'

De Lancey noticed that Powell was accompanied by three orderlies.

'I'm rather afraid that it may hurt a little. May I have your permission, sir?'

De Lancey nodded. Sighed, closed his eyes. Thought of the captain of the Blues. Five days of agony. As he felt the orderlies' cold hands begin to raise him on to his side, he whispered a silent prayer. Please, dear God, let me die now. How long, for pity's sake, could it take a man to die?

TWENTY-EIGHT

Above Hougoumont, 7.15 p.m.
Macdonell

Out of the falling twilight they came in through the shattered north gate. Black-coated soldiers with great, plumed shakos and short, braided coats. A battalion of Brunswick light infantry. In the Peninsula the redcoats had joked that these Germans ate anything they could find – rats, hedgehogs. They would even, it was said, steal the officers' pet dogs. These men though, he saw only too clearly, were hardly the bloodthirsty dog-eaters of Spain. They were no more than boys. But they were reinforcements, and at this present moment Macdonell would have gratefully welcomed in the Prince of Orange himself to help him defend what was left of the château.

The house itself was now no more than a burnt-out wreck, in which huge flames crackled and leaped up twenty, thirty feet. The fire had spread to the little chapel but, miraculously, had stopped abruptly at the feet of the life-size crucifix that hung on the back wall. The men had called it a miracle. James Graham, the devout Irishman, had solemnly declared that the place was blessed.

That wasn't the word that Macdonell would have used. He looked around the courtyard. At the exhausted men, their white faces coloured matt black from the soot of incessant musket fire. All had one thing in common. Their eyes.

317

Bloodshot, red-rimmed, they stared blankly from their sunken sockets with the fatigue that came only with battle. Those men who could still do so stood to at the walls. The lightly wounded sat around the blazing courtyard, unable to move. The worst cases had been crowded into the tiny gardener's house, which of all the buildings was the least damaged. The dead lay piled in the ruins of the great barn. Macdonell tapped the blade of his sword on the slippery cobbles, in between which the blood had mixed with mud in small pools.

'Hold to the last extremity.' Those had been Wellington's words. To the last man. The last round. For eight hours now they had been holding. Soon they would be down to but a few rounds per man. They were nearing the last extremity.

As three guardsmen slammed the gates shut after the Brunswickers, Macdonell sensed a momentary lull in the ebb and flow of the fighting which all but surrounded the stronghold. Best use this, he thought. Take stock.

He found Biddle by the burnt-out stable block, attempting to staunch a splinter-cut in his neck with a length of torn white shirting. Seeing his superior, the sergeant dropped the bloody rag and snapped to attention.

'Sar'nt Biddle. What's our state?'

'By my reckoning, sir, we have close on 700 men fit for duty. Then there's the Nassauers, what's left of them. Those black Germans as have just come in; nigh on 500 of them, sir.'

'How many of our men are wounded?'

'Hard to say, sir. There's some as have died, and others is back on the walls. But it must be close on 200.'

'And the French?'

'We've got one officer, minus his hand. A sergeant, perhaps a score of men and two drummers, sir.'

'Thank you, Biddle. You'd better see to that cut.'

So that was it. He had perhaps 1,500 men and no hope, he guessed, of further reinforcements. Fifteen hundred to face the dogged French army corps of possibly ten times that number that all day had thrown itself against the walls. It would have to do. Macdonell knew that the remainder of the brigade, Hepburn's Scots, save the companies left with the colours, were now gathered on the edge of the orchard, along with Saltoun's light companies of the First Guards. How they were faring, though, was anyone's guess.

He turned to Colonel Woodford, who was gazing down distractedly at the body of his horse, whose neck had been almost severed by a shard of falling shell.

'Sir. I wonder if we shouldn't give the men a tot of the rum that came in with the ammunition cart. It's unorthodox, I know. But it might do them some good.'

The colonel continued to stare at the dead mare. Seemed not to have heard.

'Rum, sir. A small tot might do the men some good.'

'What. No, no. Can't you see? The beast's dead, man. Stone dead.'

'The men, sir. The rum ration. Now might be a good time.'

'Oh. Yes. As you will, James.'

Macdonell found Henry Wyndham attempting to steady the ragged defenders of the west wall.

'Henry. The colonel and I thought that it might be a good idea if we were to give the men a portion of their rum ration. That barrel that Drummond found. Might put a bit of fire into them, eh?'

Wyndham smiled. 'I'll see to it. Sar'nt Miller.'

'Sir.'

'Rum ration. Now.'

'Rum, sir? Now, sir?'

'Now, sir. Rum, Sar'nt. Colonel's orders. Half rations. That barrel there. By the well. Start with those men. In sixes. Number off.'

The sergeant saluted and walked across to a group of wounded. 'All right, you lovely boys. It's your lucky day. Odd numbers first. Colonel Macdonell's orders. Rum ration. And

319

you'd better come and get it quick before the Frenchies have it out of you. And it's all we have. Better make the most of it.'

Macdonell watched as a corporal broached the barrel with his bayonet and lowered in his own tin cup, from which he then filled the men's. They formed before him six at a time, while others took their place at the walls. Miller stood to one side, watching to see that equal measures were served. Still there was nothing to suggest that another attack was about to be unleashed, although from time to time a shell burst over the compound, causing the small queue to duck in unison. One man, Cotterill, did not move from his position by the north wall. Miller called across to him, raising his voice above the din.

'Cotterill. Come and get yer rum, lad.'

'No thanks, Sarge. Never did like the stuff.'

Robert Jones, an old Peninsular sweat, sidled up to Miller, innocent-eyed. 'I'll have his, Sergeant.'

'Yes, Jones. I do believe you would. Half-rations, the colonel said. Not double. Now get back to the wall.'

Macdonell smirked and walked back to Woodford, who was still standing, staring silently at the body of his horse. 'Sir, the French appear to be taking a rest. I wondered whether I should have a look in the orchard. See what the rest of the brigade was up to.'

The colonel smiled, bemusedly. 'Damn shame. Damn fine horse. Yes. Very well, Macdonell. Best take an escort. Damn shame.'

Calling to him the six guardsmen he had just seen at the rum barrel, Macdonell led them through the garden gate and across what had once been a lawn, now strewn with bodies. Making their way through the remains of the formal garden, the little party turned obliquely to the north and ran in a diagonal towards the orchard wall. To the south Macdonell could hear the sounds of renewed fighting. Another small attack. There was no time to lose or they would be cut off in here. They were near the wall now. He clambered on to a fire step. Tried to look through the trees. Turned to a corporal.

'Robinson. It's no good. I can't see a damn thing. Come with me. The rest of you, wait here.'

Skirting the wall, the two men advanced deep into the orchard. The dead lay everywhere. French, mostly, but here and there a lifeless body in a red or a green jacket told of the ferocity of the fighting. Cannonfire had shorn the trees of their branches, as if cut back by some demonic gardener, and by the time they were half way across not only could Macdonell see the reassuring ranks of Hepburn's and Saltoun's redcoats formed up fifty yards to his left and preparing it seemed to move back into the orchard, but he also found that he had a relatively unobscured view directly into the bottom of the valley.

He stopped and squinted. Robinson waited behind him. Macdonell looked hard through the drifting smoke. He wasn't quite sure what he expected to see. More French cavalry, perhaps? Though that seemed unlikely, given the recent carnage. Another massive flanking attack, perhaps, from the light infantry who had been their opponents throughout this endless day? He prayed not. Perhaps, please God, he might see the Prussians. Here at last, sweeping across the field, driving all before them. Surely Blücher must come soon?

He peered into the dusk. Searching for hope or for some new horror. Nothing, he thought, would surprise him now. But there he was wrong. For what met his gaze stopped him dead.

TWENTY-NINE

The valley, 7.30 p.m.
Ney

He saw them come. A dark blue mass. Felt the weight of their numbers. The Garde. Five battalions, three of chasseurs, with their distinctive black bearskins, two of grenadiers, their own bearskin hats fronted by curved copper plates embossed with the imperial eagle. At the head of each battalion rode no less than a general. Old friends. Friant, Poret, Harlet, Michel, Mallet, Henrion. Behind them three more battalions in a second line of attack. And in front of them all, surrounded by the blue, red and gold of the Imperial General Staff, rode the Emperor.

They came on in column, muskets shouldered straight, bayonets fixed. Each battalion of around 600 men. And between each of them came two horse-drawn cannons with bearskinned gunners resplendent in their own still recognizable red, blue and gold. On his right Ney could see what was left of Donzelot's men, and next to them the battered ranks of Bachelu's division. Most of what now remained of d'Erlon's corps. Men who had already done so much that day and in the days before. In all he supposed there were 10,000. Ney stood with Heymes beside the ruined orchard of La Haye Sainte, surrounded by the bloody remains of the two divisions who had died taking the farm where the tricolour now flapped triumphantly, and together they waited for the Garde.

To his left, beyond Hougoumont, the setting sun appeared at last from behind the cloud which had hidden it throughout the day. But its rays were obscured and diffused by the clouds of acrid, sulphurous smoke which hung about the field, while from the blazing château sheets of flame rose to meet it in the sky. It was a vision of hell. What time must it be? He had lost his watch up there on the ridge, among the cavalry. He supposed it might be shortly after seven o'clock.

He heard their music now. A band was playing. The full band of the Old Garde grenadiers and chasseurs – 150 men – as if they were on parade at Fontainebleau. Playing the triumphant marches of the Carrousel. He caught 'La Victoire est à nous', from Grétry's Egyptian opera, a favourite of Napoleon's. Hard to make it out in the noise. As they came closer it became another melody, a tune written so long ago it seemed in another world. The Emperor's own march for the Garde: 'La Marche des bonnets à poil'.

As the Garde advanced towards him Ney began to think forward, to what would now happen. How he would join them. Would take them up the hill. Guide them in. To victory – or to nemesis. He deliberately slowed his breathing. Must slow himself down now, regain composure. Relax the pounding heart that seemed to be about to burst from his chest. Ney spat on his hands and rubbed at his face. They came away black with soot and gunpowder. He wiped them on his breeches and attempted to fasten his tunic with the one remaining gold button. To at least make himself look like a Marshal of France about to receive command of the Garde from his Emperor. He half closed his eyes and attempted, for one last time before what he knew must come, to put his mind far away from this place of death. To Aglaé and his boys. To the orchard at Coudreaux. To the cherry trees. To his garden. To Aglaé. The roses. The boys. They will be proud of me. I will die a Marshal of France. I only wish . . . one more time. He saw their smiles. Felt his hands running through their hair. Muttered their names. Mostly he thought of Aglaé. Was she thinking of him? Even with the din of battle and the march of the Garde, he caught echoes of Mozart drifting into his mind.

'*Lá ci da-rem la ma-no, la mi di-rai di si.*'

Could she somehow see him standing here, in this charnel house? Could she ever know what he had seen? No. Don't think it. You must never think of that. He opened his eyes. There was Heymes. Dependable Heymes, in his bright red uniform. Remarkably unhurt. Smiling. Telling him something.

'Sire. You are to take the Garde, sire. The Emperor's orders.'

'Heymes.'

'Sire?'

'How's your girl?'

'Suzanne? She's fine, sire. Just fine.'

'Will you tell her about all this? Anything of this?'

'No, sire. It's magnificent, isn't it? But I do not think . . .'

'No. You're right. This is only for us. There is no place for love here, and love should never know anything of this.'

No place for love. Only one love here. Glory. France. Death. Love for all three boiling up inside him now. About to over-flow. Even amid the constant crash of the guns, he could hear the music. Louder now. Closer. He felt the tread of their steps. Saw the gleam of the gilded bronze eagles, the flash of the sulphurous evening sun on the bayonets. Saw Mallet turn to an aide at his side, mouth open in a grin, before turning his horse away to his own command. The aide was laughing. Some coarse joke. Wonder what. Whores, drink, money? He knew Mallet's tastes. Ney looked at the Emperor, grim-faced, almost enveloped by his staff. The drab grey figure. From his side a horseman broke away. It was de la Bedoyere. He too was smiling. Laughing.

'Sire. The Emperor begs to inform you that Marshal Grouchy has arrived on your right. Grouchy is here, sire. Grouchy.'

Ecstatic, de la Bedoyere galloped his chestnut mare across the front of the entire army, towards the remnants of d'Erlon's corps, bare-headed now, shouting to the officers. Ney heard his cries diminish.

'It's Grouchy. Grouchy is here. It's Grouchy. He's here.'

It was, Ney knew now, a lie. Napoleon's final ruse. A desperate attempt to raise morale. He was tricking his own men. To the marshal the reality was only too evident. Looking to the east Ney could certainly discern the black shapes of masses of men, marching it seemed directly for him. But also, in front of them, came masses of civilians, camp followers and French officers and men, all of them making their way, apparently, away from these newly arrived French reinforcements. Colonel Levasseur rode up.

'What is happening, sire? Do I ride to Grouchy? What are we to think?'

Ney closed his eyes and stroked his forehead. 'You stand, Colonel. You stand with the men.'

Perplexed, the colonel turned his horse and rode back to the staff. Ney began to get ready. Heymes had brought him a new horse, his fifth of the day, its leopardskin shabraque proclaiming it to have recently belonged to a, now presumably dead, officer of Garde chasseurs à cheval. Ney climbed into the saddle. From the battalions he could hear the cries now of the officers and sergeants as they formed their men ready for the attack. With one beautiful movement – parade-ground precision – the columns became eight open squares, each one 150 men wide on each side, three ranks deep, with drummers in the centre. They were going in alone. Without skirmishers. Without cavalry. Napoleon approached him. Reined in. For an instant, the two men stared at one another. Knew what must be done. Knew what would happen.

'Ney. You must take them. You must lead them.'

'Of course, sire.'

He wanted to say something. One last thing at this last

325

moment. One last word to explain everything. Love. Glory. France. You. Just once. Now.

'They insist, Ney.' Napoleon gestured to the staff. 'I . . . I have been ordered. I have been commanded, Ney. Not to go with them. With you.'

He gazed at Ney with rheumy eyes. Uncertain, this master of men. The man who had defined the concept of glory. Forbidden now to lead his children to that glory and to death. Unable to savour that fatal inevitability. Ney wanted suddenly to touch him. Went to bend forward. One last word. One moment.

'You must do it, Ney. Take them. Take the Garde.'

And then it was too late. For anything. Napoleon turned Marengo and rode back towards the lines, his staff closing again around him. Ney was silent. He watched the Emperor go and reined his own horse in at the head of the column. Stood high in his stirrups. Drew his sword. Raised it in the air. Turned to the waiting blue ranks. Smiled.

'Follow me.'

Heymes was up with him. Grinning. Together they rode to join Friant.

'Ney. Did we lay down a cannonade? I was away from the brigade. Did you see anything? You know what they have there? Did you see? You must have seen when you were up with the cavalry. What do you think? Are we ready?'

Ney did not reply. Turned his head. Shouted – to the air, with measured interval.

'For France. For Glory. For the Emperor.'

On the crescendo of his command, his horse reared and, using its forward movement, he led the advance up the now familiar slope. The gentle slope. The killing ground of crop fields, turned to mire by rain and cannonballs and the fresh harvest of human flotsam. Around him commands rang out and the drumbeat grew in volume. Ney looked straight ahead. Steadied his nervous mount as it shied and stumbled over the heaps of dead. Sensed the ranks part slightly as they avoided a pile of corpses. And now he felt it once again. That familiar emptiness in the pit of his stomach that always came with the first advance into fire. Old feeling. Good feeling. Tight chest. Mouth dry. So dry. He licked his lips. Tasted the gunpowder. Swallowed. Looked at Heymes. Smiled. Saw a corporal of grenadiers cross himself.

At 500 yards out he saw the flash of the guns. The balls screamed in fast and high. He looked straight ahead. Don't look to left and right. Old wisdom. Eyes on the smoking enemy. Ignore the falling bodies of your men. He heard their cries. Felt the rush of air as the first flood of canister hit the blue wall and swept away three ranks. They did not falter.

'Steady. Keep steady.'

The sergeants were controlling the rolling tide of the great blue mass. A hail of shot took his own horse from under him and, as he landed, it collapsed on top of him, blood gushing, frothing, screaming in agony. Unhurt, Ney pushed his way out from under the dying animal, scrambled to his feet, grabbed his sword and began to march at the head of the nearest column. He looked around to see who was still with him. Friant and Poret, both also on foot now, and behind them the 3rd Grenadiers. Still intact. Still coming. Close up. Keep together.

The shot was getting denser now. Like hailstones. Beside him a mustachioed grenadier fell to the ground, clutching his side, blood pumping through useless fingers, desperate to keep in the life. Yelling curses, keeping their ranks, the big men made their way over the piles of dead. Such an assortment of uniforms, thought Ney, looking around him. Fabulous. Glorious. Here, judging by their green feathers, were the Hanoverians he had seen cut down by Dubois' men earlier that day. And not far from them lay the bodies of the cuirassiers themselves, shattered a few hours later in their futile charge at the British guns.

Quickly, he began to realize that the columns were not keeping to their allotted routes. That only his own and that of the 4th Grenadiers still marched as ordered. The others were veering towards the left. Towards the strongpoint of Wellington's army. Into the vortex. At 100 yards out from the Allied lines the French horse artillery unlimbered and quickly opened fire. Through the smoke Ney saw the red coats appear to thin. He looked around. Heymes had gone. He had not noticed it. Did not know when. Friant was down now, blood pouring from a mangled hand; stumbling, being helped to the rear. But the general was still smiling. Still shouting: 'All is well. All is well.'

Ney looked to his left. Saw the beginnings of hesitation. 'Dress your ranks.'

His words rang out. Instinct. A hundred battles. Officers echoed the command and the great blue mass closed the gaps – the horrid gashes of red which seconds earlier had been men. Harlet rode up to him. He was holding his side, traces of red showing through his fingers.

'This is the stuff, Ney. Eh? We'll have him now. This stinking Spanish hero.'

Ney gestured behind him. 'We are marching, dear Harlet, at the head of the finest infantry in the world. What can stop us?'

He wondered himself. Knew that there was a chance – if they made it to the crest. If Wellington had made mistakes. If they had managed to find a weakness in his line. If they could concentrate in one place. There was a chance. The drums had changed their beat now. The 'Grenardière', the Guards' own, distinctive, insistent rhythm of the assault:

Patapata patapata patapata panpan.
Patapata patapata pan.

Now he remembered again. Bussaco. How he had argued then against a frontal assault on the ridge. Then the final yards into the attack and the line of redcoats coming up from behind

328

the crest. The terrible fire, ten paces out, of that single battalion of British light infantry. The shattered blue columns tumbling back down the hill. The bayonets. The terrible screams echoing, echoing to reach him across the valley.

He was at a hedge now – shattered remains of a hedge. Crossed it, and then they were only a few yards from them. He understood now exactly what was going to happen. On his right, facing Donzelot, Ney saw ranks of the black-clad Brunswickers. Black and yellow and blue, death's-head badges gleaming. Levelled muskets. Then they saw the Garde. Began to inch away from the advancing masses. Young men, he thought. And beyond them he saw green coats. Same patchwork army. A Nassau battalion. But a single volley of flame and smoke had Donzelot's exhausted men in flight. Ney saw the green ranks rush forward in pursuit, shouting wildly, then stop and turn and themselves retreat as they saw that beyond Donzelot's dazed battalions stood two squadrons of French cuirassiers.

His own juggernaut column of veterans continued its ordered advance. Halted by command yards before the right-hand square of a red-coated brigade. Waited for what they knew would come. Seemed to brace themselves as one. Raised their loaded muskets and as they did so took the fire of a well-ordered volley. British, he thought. Veterans themselves, most likely. Good troops. Good men. Spanish War veterans. Perhaps he had met them before. And then all around him the world exploded in flame and white smoke, as the grenadiers returned their fire. He saw men in red go down. Saw their comrades stand. Close up. Reloading now, as his own column did the same, seconds behind. Could see their officer now, standing close to his men. Coolly elegant in all this mud and blackness. Young man. Half his own age. Saw the colour, ragged green square, flapping. The ensign in his teens. His eldest boy's age. White face. Ashen white. Sergeant holding him steady. The flash and smoke again. Around him men doubled over. And then again the reply. Saw the colour tumble. Glimpsed the ensign's bloody face. No face. Saw the flag rise up. To his right a company of French guardsmen had charged home into a British battery.

Ney saw the gunners go down, bayoneted as they fought desperately with ramrods, sticks, buckets. Their helmeted officer fired a pistol and was spitted on his horse by a giant of a grenadier. Open mouth, horror-stricken eyes, as he pushed at the long piece of steel, trying to deny its presence, deep inside his body. His scream was high and never-ending. My God. We are winning, Ney thought. We will do it. Napoleon will do it. Has timed it right. How could he have doubted? It was Eylau again – when the prospect of defeat in the morning had been turned by the evening, with Murat's great cavalry charge and his own sweeping offensive, into one of the Emperor's greatest victories. It was masterly. Wellington was beaten. There was nothing left before them. Brussels would be theirs. Ney looked behind him. Lines of men. Grim-faced. The finest soldiers in the finest army in all the world.

As he turned to his front again Ney was stopped by another crash of fire, and when the smoke drifted he saw that he was left alone – officers gone. Rank behind gone. Then he saw the gleam of bayonets. Saw the green flag move towards him, the officer's mouth open and close in an impossible to hear command. Looked about him and saw the Garde begin to fall back. Slowly at first, and now faster. Moving backwards down the hill. Still in order – mostly. But moving back – around him. Ney steadied his nerve. Best to go with them. Rally out of musket range. Try again. And even as the thought came to him he saw the red troops turn in perfect order and march back towards their own lines. They don't have the men to follow up. They need to retire. They are exhausted. The French guns opened up again, scythed great furrows through the backs of the British ranks. Ney looked about him.

Fifty cavalry. Give me fifty horsemen. A single squadron of

cuirassiers and I shall take the day. He saw the opportunity open up. The line was adrift. The gap visible now. Wide. The confusion palpable. He saw mounted British officers trying to preserve order among the two, no, three regiments which had become one confused mass making its way back up the slope to its position.

'Cavalry!'

He caught himself shouting the word. But no one heard. No one came. Where in hell's name were the cavalry? Ney looked around. Looked down, and saw at his feet where they were. He was standing on the cavalry. In them. Treading the lifeless bodies of men who, only two hours before, he himself had led up this same slope. Carabiniers, cuirassiers, lancers, chasseurs, strewn before him in grotesque attitudes and crumpled heaps. Gorgeous uniforms, twisted metal, parts of men and horses together in piles of bright red meat. There was no cavalry. Only a single squadron of cuirassiers near the farm, which had now become entangled in Donzelot's fleeing division. They could not be reached. There was no one else. No one left. And, as quickly as it had come, the moment vanished. Ahead of him Ney saw the British line close up; the red-coated men turn and re-form.

The Garde was suddenly immobile. Could not move. And then the red ranks fired again. Men fell around him. And he knew. And they began to fall back. Slowly, still facing the enemy. Edging backwards. Incredibly, the Garde began to retreat. In square. Still a unit. Ney did not attempt to stop them. They were the Garde. Knew what they were doing, and he went with them. And then, from behind the redcoats there came other troops, running now towards the French. Men in blue. Belgians. Dutch. Furious faces. Bayonets fixed. Some threw their hats in the air as they descended the slope at double time, their officers galloping at the front. And Ney began to run too, to his left, through the ranks of his own column. And even as he went he saw it disintegrate. Saw the unthinkable.

331

Saw the grenadiers turn and run. He pushed through the mass. Gained the shelter of a battery still firing into the red ranks from lower ground and then he was safe, inside another square of the Garde. Chasseurs now. Here was Michel, and there Malet. Both hatless and horseless. Swords in their hands. Their men were still advancing. Muskets at the port. He heard shouting. Words of command in English. The clear ring of officers' voices, carrying across the ridge. He could not see their owners at first. And then, in front of him, not thirty paces away, the ground appeared to rise up. From nowhere a mass of men appeared. Red coats, black shakos. Muskets to their shoulders. Three ranks, he reckoned quickly. Perhaps 2,000 men.

Brilliant, he thought. Spain was no chance opportunity. No luck. This was generalship. This was soldiering. This was all that he had feared. This was Bussaco again. Wellington had kept his single strongest battalion in reserve and now revealed it, fresh to the fight. He saw the guns spit. Felt the scud of the balls as they passed around him. Heard the dull thwack as they thudded into the men behind. He half turned. Saw the lines of still-advancing men lower their heads, as if walking into a strong wind. Tried to speak as the front two ranks of the 3rd Regiment of chasseurs just melted away in a sea of agony. He saw officers go down. Michel, Cardinal, Angelet. Others, whose names he did not know, had not known. And then they stopped. Without an order, the French advance just came to a halt.

'Line. Form line.'

He heard a junior officer shout the words before seeing him hurled round by a musket ball and, desperately, the square began to go through the manoeuvre, the chasseurs helplessly exposed, defenceless. Halfway through the change from square to line the British opened up again. More shot struck the men in blue coats, and the manoeuvre just fell apart. The French began to huddle together in natural groups. Tried to deliver small volleys. Anything to stop the slaughter, as the three red ranks in front of them rose and fell in unceasing fire. Ney knew those men now, with their fluttering crimson standard. Saw the gleam of gold and silver on their tunics, the beauty of the officers' uniforms. Gentlemen's uniforms. Guards. English foot guards. Wellington had matched him with the best. Had made his finest troops lie down behind the ridge until Napoleon's own Garde was at the very crest, and then, only then, had he ordered them to stand up and inflict this devastating fire. Through it all the enemy cannon continued to send in its storms of canister.

A huge grenadier sergeant fell across Ney's left thigh, right arm severed by cannon shot, face split with musket fire. Ney expected to be hit now. The tightness in his stomach was long gone. Replaced by a hollow feeling. A deep emptiness. Why wasn't he hit? Surely one shot would find its mark? We must re-form, he thought. Must fall back from all this. It was surely too much to bear. We will all die here. But already it was too late. With a great shout the redcoats came rushing towards him, and what was left of his square turned and ran.

Again Ney looked to his left and saw, again, one solitary square of tall blue-coated men. Stumbling over fallen chasseurs, he found its side. The men, some recognizing him, parted to allow him in. Once inside, Ney caught his breath and looked out at the wreck of the attack. Saw the unimaginable. The Garde in retreat. Yet the square which was now his home continued to advance towards the red ranks. Steady. He heard himself shout an order but could not make out the words. Instinct was taking over. Careful. Walking forward now. Into the fire. On his left there was a sudden commotion. A huge force pushed against the ranks. Forced him physically away from it. In front of him a drummer fell, shot in the back. Ney ran to the left of the square and found carnage. In front of him part of the great red wall of men in tall black shakos – English light infantry- had somehow come towards them. Had wheeled outwards and down the hill, in perfect order, to deliver one more terrible, crashing, thousand-musket volley into the left of the square.

'Close up.'

Hearing the sergeants, those that were left, he joined the call. 'Close your ranks. Close up.'

What remained of the left side of the square moved together. 'Present arms. Fire.'

The chasseurs replied with their own volley. Nicely done, thought Ney. We can still do it. Can make them hurt. He saw men in red double over in their scores. Their officers were shouting. Replacements came from the rear ranks. Prepared to fire again. Spat flame. Ney winced at the impact of the volley. He was not hit. How could it be? All around him men were falling. A great smack of air to his right, and another ten men were down. He saw Malet fall too. He did not get up. Shot through the head. And Major Agnes, riddled with at least five musket balls.

And so it happened.

The last square began to break up. Began to fall back. Across the field. Over the bodies. Towards the burning château. They were close to the orchard now, and in front of them the red mass seemed to grow. Volley after volley crashed into them. For one eternal, suspended moment the redcoats seemed to pause. A break in the volleys, and Ney could not hear. Then a ringing in his ears. And after it a new noise. Like a wave crashing against sand, as gradually a cheer unfurled along the red line and over the hill came column after column, line after line. Flags flying loose in the wind, blue, yellow, green. British music now. The old marches. And so, with the tunes of the Spanish War, on they came.

And with them, passing through the red ranks, came the rushing blue of the cavalry. Hussars and light dragoons in a whooping charge of blue and yellow, slashing at the retreating bearskins with hungry, razor-sharp sabres. And so, the rout began.

'*Sauve qui peut.*'

Ney heard the cry. Found himself caught up in it. Felt the tears chasing down his face. Mingling with the blood from the earlier sabre cut, re-opened now. Wild-eyed boys rushed past him, desperate to escape the merciless hissing of the sabres they knew to be just behind. And still he would not join them. He crossed the battlefield. Half in, half out of reality. Near La Haye Sainte he caught sight of d'Erlon, himself attempting to rally scattered elements of his own divisions. Made his way towards him.

'D'Erlon. What are you doing? Go back. Don't you want to die in glory?'

The general stopped. Just gazed at him. 'I intend to fight. I came here to fight. Not to die.'

Ney smiled. 'You know, d'Erlon. If you and I ever get out of this alive, you know what they'll do to us? They'll hang us both, for sure.'

The general turned away without a word. Continued his impossible task. Ney found a new, unbroken square, yet still in steady retreat. Saw that they were the 95th Line, Garnier's men. Their commander, though, was nowhere to be seen. They had managed to keep their eagle and the tatters of its tricolour. A big sergeant seemed to be in command. Ney stared at them wildly.

'Stop. Stop. I command you.'

To his surprise, they stopped. Recognized him, despite the blackened face; the blood. His tunic was open, all the buttons gone, the braid ripped away. One of his epaulettes too. He addressed them:

'Follow me. Come with me and see how a Marshal of France dies.'

Again, to his surprise, they followed. Walking slowly back up the muddy slope, boots slipping on the mire, Ney led the few last remnants of the 95th in a pitiful attack which never stood a chance of reaching the enemy. Turning, right and left he saw them falling. Boys, just folding in half. And still no shot came for him. He called, silently it seemed, to the survivors to fall back and stumbled blindly down the slope into the valley, past the rear walls of La Haye Sainte, where the tricolour still flew. And there, beside the orchard he had left barely thirty minutes earlier, he found the last three squares of the attack.

They had never come forward. Had witnessed the carnage and remained intact. And now the order came to retreat. Ney moved inside one of the squares where the maimed remains of the Garde now sheltered in bloody chaos. He found a familiar face. Jean-Jacques Pelet – his companion on the retreat from Moscow. Then a colonel of infantry, now a brigade commander of the Garde. Together, less than three years ago, they had taken 5,500 men across the frozen river Dnieper, escaping the Russians. Then too they had been retreating in square.

'Pelet, dear friend. What next? What are we doing? Where is the Emperor?'

'It's hopeless. The Prussians are everywhere. We tried to hold them in Plancenoit but there are too many. Ney. We must retreat. Regroup. Fight again. We can do it again, Ney. We did it in Russia. We can do it again.'

But, even as he spoke, Ney noticed the tears coursing down the officer's cheeks. He looked out from the ranks, back up at the slope above the farmhouse, and through the smoke he could see the entire Allied army advancing towards them across the field. Their artillery was still firing, and as the square continued to fall back it was losing more men with every step. Ney wiped at his eyes. Looked at Pelet's eager, pleading, trusting face and just shook his head.

Ney walked away. Deep into the square. Over the bodies of the dead. Past the outstretched hands of the wounded and dying, reaching up to touch him. To touch Ney. Merely to touch, one last time, the 'bravest of the brave'. This then, he thought, was how it all ended. Here, on this sodden, bloody field. Not in his death. Worse than that. In the death of a dream. The death of the Garde, and with it the death of the Empire. The death of France. The end of the world.

THIRTY

Between Papelotte farm and Mont St Jean, 8.00 p.m. Ziethen

He saw the four men ride out from the blue-coated ranks. Officers. Two with drawn sabres. Aides, presumably, and in front of them two more men. One, he thought, must be their colonel. Perhaps a more senior officer. He did not immediately recognize the uniform, though. Line infantry? Light? Or perhaps some more obscure French unit? Undoubtedly the commander wanted to parlay. A truce. Surrender. They had been firing on each other for some five minutes now and it was clear that the French were getting the worst of it. Steinmetz's scouts had spotted them first. Around 2,000 men, moving steadily towards Wellington's flank, away from the farm of Papelotte. It appeared that he had arrived just in time to prevent a massacre. The Prussian jager had opened fire immediately on the rear ranks of the blue column, which had of course to turn and re-form before returning a volley. Naturally, in the course of the manoeuvre the Prussians had taken their toll. Now the French were hemmed in by woods and hedges on either side and, formed as they were in close order, they were falling fast to the accurate fire of the two leading Prussian regiments.

As the man rode closer Ziethen signalled to an aide.

'Ride quickly to General-Major Steinmetz. Have the men cease fire. In particular don't shoot those officers. Let them through.'

He would be merciful in these last moments of France's shattered glory. Would allow this Frenchman to plead for his men. What chance did they have against even his battered corps? Even now Pirch's brigade was joining Steinmetz on the battlefield. Jagow and Schutter, he knew, were close behind. Five thousand men to shore up Wellington's flank.

Ziethen drew out his telescope from his valise and putting it to his eye scanned the enemy infantry. Blue coats and white trousers. But what colour were their facings? They looked orange. What the French called 'aurore', the colour of the rising dawn. That could only make them infantry of the Garde. But they did not behave like veterans. More like conscripts. Their volleys were ragged and irregular. He saw that they too had now stopped firing. The horsemen were almost with him now. Ziethen could see their faces quite clearly. Three of them blank; the fourth, the commander, a mask of rage and indignation. Rage?

The officer approached him. Shouted as he came. In perfect German. 'What the devil d'you think you're doing?'

Ziethen waited until there was no need to shout. 'I am firing on your men, sir. Would you kindly explain to me what is wrong with that? But I have ordered my men to cease firing and we will be happy to accept your surrender.'

'Surrender? Surrender? What business would I have in surrendering to you? You are Prussian, are you not?'

'General-Lieutenant Hans von Ziethen at your service, sir. And this,' he gestured, 'as you so astutely observe, is the First Corps of the Prussian Army of the Lower Rhine. And you are?'

'We're Germans, you fool. The Royal Regiment of Orange-Nassau. Can't you see our uniforms? Don't you recognize your own allies, man?'

Ziethen bristled. 'It is not my fault, sir, if your men are dressed like Frenchmen.'

He turned to von Reiche. 'See that the order to cease firing reaches every regiment. Every battalion. Make sure that the men know.'

He turned back to the distressed German officer. 'And whom do I have the honour of addressing?'

Von Reiche intervened quickly before the officer had time to speak. 'Herr General. May I introduce his Grace Prince Bernhard of Saxe-Weimar.'

Ziethen saluted. 'Excuse me, your Grace. My apologies. But you must understand it was a simple mistake.'

'Simple, yes. But a mistake which has cost the lives of dozens of my men, Herr General.'

Saxe-Weimar paused. Looked away for a moment. Regained his composure and looked Ziethen straight in the eye. 'Still, General von Ziethen, you're here. Thank God for that. And Blücher?'

'Yes, your Grace. Prince Blücher is at Plancenoit with the Second and Fourth Corps. We are all here.'

Saxe-Weimar rode closer. Extended his hand. Ziethen took it. The Prince spoke.

'Then we have him at last, this Corsican upstart. And this time, by the grace of God and the will of the German peoples, he will not escape.'

As he watched the Prince return, jubilant, to his command, Ziethen pondered his decision to go against Gneisenau's orders. He had no doubt now that he had done the right thing. But would the High Command see that? He had broken the cardinal rule. Disobeyed a field order given in battle. It was a hanging offence. A court-martial at least. Even with his family's reputation among the military. But he had no doubt that it had been the right thing. He would bear the responsibility. Prince Bernhard had informed him that an entire French division was positioned to the rear of Papelotte farm and another brigade in Smohain, poised as they spoke to attack the Allied left wing. Well, they were in for a surprise. His men might have mistaken the Nassauers for their enemy, but, thank God, his gamble had been right. It was as he had supposed. They had arrived in the nick of time.

He scanned the scene directly to his front, beyond the tangle of woods and small farms. Saw only smoke and the flicker of far-distant flames. The noise was incredible. An Armageddon. Ziethen wondered just what had taken place down there in the valley over the past few hours. Soon, no doubt, they would know. Now there was work to be done. He found von Reiche again.

'We need to regroup. Concentrate to our left. Order the reserve cavalry to ride to the English lines. Run the cannon, all three batteries, along the ridge and take up position as close as you can to Wellington's flank. Let's give these Frenchmen a last taste of Prussian roundshot.'

Reiche smiled and saluted before whipping his horse into a gallop.

Ziethen turned to his assistant Chief of Staff, von Dedenroth. 'It's not over yet. We've got a fight on our hands. Find Steinmetz. Send the fusilier battalions of the 12th and the 24th directly against Smohain. Clear it of the French. Then have him follow up with the musketeers. And be quick about it. There's no time to lose. And Dedenroth, tell Major Laurens to let me know the moment he makes contact with the English. We've come this far. Let's at least make sure they know we're here.'

THIRTY-ONE

Near La Belle Alliance, 8.30 p.m.
Napoleon

It was over.

He watched the blue columns stream past him in retreat. The men cowering to hide their faces, lest they meet the gaze of their Emperor. On both sides of the inn and along the cobbled *chaussée*, his army hurried away from the battle. To his front, through the smoke and the rising mist that came with sunset, he could see the red-coated ranks advancing steadily down the hill. Moving at last off the ridge from which all day he had been trying to push them. Looking to his right, he saw more blue-coated infantry. His men. Lobau. The Young Garde. And behind them, almost on top of them, the oncoming black of the Prussian cavalry. Dark masses of hussars and lancers, and beyond them the thick columns of their infantry. From the ridge above the village, muzzle flashes announced that the German artillery had taken the high ground. He saw the cannonballs fly high over the field and land among the moving masses of the retreating 6th Corps.

How, he wondered, had it come to this? His horse paced upon the stones, its hooves casting up splashes of muddy water. It had been the mud, yes, certainly the mud, in part. If only I could have started the battle two hours, even one hour earlier, he thought. Then I would have crushed Wellington.

But he knew too that it was more than the mud. What use was it to have soldiers who fought like madmen, tooth and nail, for your honour, when you were surrounded by fools for generals? Soult. Jerome. Ney. And finally, that idiot Durutte.

They had not been Grouchy's men that Durutte had seen up by Papelotte, but Prussian imbeciles, firing in error upon their own Dutch allies. This was Ziethen's corps, not Grouchy's. Fresh to the battle, it had taken him completely by surprise. Once they had realized their error, the Prussians had turned and swept away all that remained of D'Erlon's men like an unstoppable wave. Then they had smashed into Lobau's left flank, driving a great scythe through the centre of the French line. Within minutes the right flank of Napoleon's army had ceased to exist.

Silently, bitterly, he cursed them: Durutte, Soult, Jerome, Ney.

'Ney.'

He spoke the word aloud. The generals looked at him, puzzled.

Ney. 'Le Rougeaud'. That ruddy-faced, red-haired war god.

It was Ney's fault. Of course. Ney and Grouchy. He had been betrayed. First by Ney at Quatre-Bras, and now by Grouchy. The army was full of traitors and turncoats. They had shown their true colours. Ney, though, would never betray him, surely? Yet what about his promise to King Louis? That 'iron cage'. Had he meant it after all? Perhaps the whole thing, this whole campaign had been an elaborate bluff. A bluff to trick him, Napoleon, the greatest general who had ever lived, into losing. Had his enemies realized at last that having one, perhaps even two traitors among his own generals was the only way in which to defeat him? Perhaps there were other traitors, even now. He stole a nervous glance at the men who surrounded him. De la Bedoyere, Gourgaud, Bertrand, Soult.

Soult. Yes. He certainly had been in the pay of the Bourbons. Perhaps Soult, then. His own Chief of Staff. And what of his predecessor, the indispensable Berthier? Berthier, whose brilliant administration had carried them through so many campaigns. How had Berthier come to fall to his death?

He began to sweat. Put his hand in his pocket for his handkerchief. Failed to find it. Tried another. Looked for a page. Called into the throng. 'Pierron. A handkerchief. Bring me a handkerchief.'

But the valet had gone, and the Emperor had to content himself with mopping his dripping forehead on his coat sleeve. The air was thick with heat. His mind was filled with visions of the dead and dying. Men running away from the battle. He could sense a force pressing in on him through the darkness, from all directions. Thousands of men, seething with hate. Aiming for him. Directly at him.

His horse whinnied, smelling the fear that drifted across the battlefield. They were getting closer now. He heard new music. Not the Garde. A hymn. But not one he recognized. Tried to make out the distant words. Called over to Soult.

'What's that?'

'Prussians, sire. A hymn of victory. "Herr Gott die loben wir." They're thanking God.'

He managed a broken smile. Well, then, of course it would be unfamiliar. A hymn to a Prussian victory? A hymn to the Prussian God. Where now, he wondered, was his God?

A helmeted lancer came cantering by. Did not notice his Emperor, but yelled in the general direction of the group of officers. 'The Prussians. We are betrayed. Save yourselves. The Prussians are coming.'

Before anyone could detain him, the man was gone. Galloping up the crowded road – back to Charleroi and France.

Napoleon found Bertrand at his side.

'Sire. He's right. It's true. They're here. Blücher is here. You must save yourself. For the future of France, I beg you, sire. Retire.'

Napoleon stared at him. 'The future of France? What

future? What future has France now, do you suppose, my dear Bertrand?'

Soult approached. 'Sire, it is still possible. We have Grouchy. We do not know what has happened to him. He has 30,000 men, sire. And there's the Army of the South. We could muster more men. But you must save yourself. Without you we are nothing. France is nothing.'

Of course he was right. They still had Grouchy. And, more importantly, at least another 150,000 soldiers under arms. There was Suchet's Army of the Alps, all 25,000 of them, just south of Lyons. Add to that Rapp's seasoned veterans of the Army of the Rhine, another 25,000 men, even now marching on the Marne. The three observation corps of the Jura, Gironde and Var – totalling 35,000. And in the Loire General Lamarque with the 15,000 men of the Army of the West. There were also, he knew, 500 field guns in Paris, along with 36,000 men of the National Guard and another 80,000 volunteers under Davout. They would strip the royal arsenals again. Rearm the militia.

Yes. It was possible. He must not despair. They could fortify Paris. Push back the Prussians. Drive a wedge between the British and the Austrians. Just as soon as he was back in Paris he would start to mobilize again. All possible units. Conscription. For the good of the nation. There must still be some boys left. A few young 'Marie-Louises' who would be proud to come to the aid of their Emperor as their brothers had done after the horrendous losses in Russia. He smiled. Clapped the marshal on the back.

'Yes, Soult. I do believe that you are right. We can re-mobilize and rearm. Yes. It's not too late. Come. All of you. We should ride for the border. Regroup.'

They turned and trotted up the *chaussée*, the imperial escort of Garde chasseurs clearing their way with the flats of their sabres. The road was clogged with walking wounded and men of all regiments and all arms. Men without weapons, dazed and leaderless. Horseless cuirassiers who threw off their armour in order to run more quickly. Artillery drivers who had cut the traces of their harnesses and leapt on dray horses to gallop from the field. At Rossomme the Emperor's party found the perfectly formed square of the First Grenadiers of the Garde. Standing to attention, precisely where he had left them. Their ranks parted and the imperial staff trotted in. Napoleon turned his horse and surveyed the scene again. Fires licked the evening skies as, to the west, Hougoumont burned. Up on the ridge he could make out the glow of thousands of new campfires, as the Allies prepared to enjoy a rest that no Frenchman would know this night.

Above the cacophany of the dying battle, another sound drifted to him on the evening breeze. A curiously thin drumming. A uniquely Prussian sound. The haunting hollowness of the Pomeranian drum.

'They're coming, Soult. D'you hear them? They're coming for me.'

'Sire, you cannot remain here. You must fall back again.'

Quickly they left the square and galloped further up the road towards Le Caillou. The farmhouse was in chaos. Valets and imperial servants were loading private papers and as many of the Emperor's possessions as they could carry into a single carriage. Beside him the First Garde chasseurs under Durring had formed a column of route and were preparing to accompany their Emperor on his journey back to France. De la Bedoyere found him.

'Sire. If you intend to ride to Charleroi it would be wise to take a remount. Take a fresh horse.'

Reluctantly, Napoleon dismounted from Desirée, handed her to a servant and grasped the saddle of a troop horse of the chasseurs, offered him by the page, Gudin. As he was about to place his foot into the stirrup, his eye was caught by something beneath his feet. Something of value. The imperial travelling library had been dropped on the cobbles and its leather-bound volumes on war, diplomacy and philosophy were being trampled into the mud. One book, he noticed, Caesar on war, lay open. He picked it up. Its pages were bent back at a passage warning of the dangers of forming up in a defensive position with a wood to your rear. Napoleon let it fall, smiled and heaved himself up with difficulty on to the unfamiliar, nervous troop horse. He should not be riding. Should be in his carriage. The pain was beginning again. His body was on fire. He stared for one last time back towards the ridge. Perhaps it was the Prussians who were to blame. Perhaps if they had not diverted him. Ney had taken the cavalry too early. An hour too soon. If only he had stopped that. If only he had delayed. Then a grand push with the cavalry and directly behind them the Garde. Not as it had happened. This was not the way. And this was not the way that it would end. He would rise again.

The men continued to stream past him. He spoke out loud, but to no one in particular. 'Have we any news of Grouchy?'

'None, sire.'

'De la Bedoyere, send someone to find Grouchy. Tell him that we're pulling back. Tell him he must take care not to be caught between the Allied armies. Gourgaud, have the artillery fire one more round. Then abandon the guns.'

He turned. 'Petit, order a general retreat. But you remain here with the grenadiers. Form a rearguard. We shall regroup at . . . Genappe. We shall halt the Prussians there. If not there, then at Philippeville.' Thinking, he bit his lower lip. Looked at Gourgaud, who was staring at him with a look of incredulity. Scowled. 'Well? What are you looking at? What are you waiting for? Get on with it.'

With difficulty he turned the unseasoned horse to face south along the *chaussée*, moved his aching buttocks along the saddle and prepared for what he knew in his heart was likely to be a very long ride. Then, as an afterthought, he turned back to Petit, his eyes wide. Staring. His words were taut, terse, bitter.

'Petit. If you should happen to see him, inform Marshal Ney

that I shall be waiting for him in Paris. This is not the end, you know. We may have lost this battle, but we keep on with the war. Be sure to tell him that, Petit. This is not the end. The war starts here.'

THIRTY-TWO

Before Hougoumont, 9.30 p.m.
Macdonell

The redcoats moved through the woods with careful step, in a futile attempt to stop their feet treading on the bodies of dead Frenchmen which formed a new and ghastly undergrowth. Between the trees lay shapes, indistinct in the twilight, which had once been living men – or parts of men. There were dead horses, too, shot from beneath their officers. And everywhere lay discarded weapons, clothes, packs and scraps of paper. Most of the trees had been splintered by cannon shot and it was proving difficult to push between the sagging boughs without snagging upon a branch. Curses in a dozen different English accents rang out across the darkness. A few shots greeted them. A handful of French skirmishers attempting to cover their retreat. For retreat it was. It was a good hour since the Allied army had begun to pour down the hill after the Garde. Macdonell had watched them go and yet had bided his time before requesting Colonel Woodford's permission to take a party out into the woods. They had been preceded by the Hanoverians and the Brunswickers who, with perhaps rather more ardour than Macdonell might himself have exercised, had finally routed, killed or in a few, rare cases taken prisoner the scattered survivors of the French corps whose battle had become a personal struggle with the defenders of the château.

He had almost made it through the trees now. At the southern boundary of the great wood they began to pass abandoned cannon, their dead gunners slumped over shattered carriages. And then, quite abruptly, the tree stumps fell away and ahead of Macdonell and his men stretched the rolling plain which only a few hours before had served as a parade ground for the flower of France's military might. Now the fields were littered with motionless lumps. Bodies lay as far as his eye could see. Shots still rang out. Cannon mostly, but with an intermittent crackle of musketry from far across the valley which suggested that gradually any remaining pockets of resistance were being extinguished. Far away in the distance he could hear the unmistakable sound of an army in pursuit.

The axis of the action had changed now from north–south to east–west as from the left the Prussians poured on in their tens of thousands, rolling up the battlefield like a giant map, driving what remained of the French army fleeing before them. The crowds of blue-coated infantry were running pell-mell through the valley and close to the wood, their weapons and packs discarded in their haste to find safety.

They didn't have a chance. Macdonell and his men watched as a small group of maybe thirty men, leaderless and bewildered, turned to face their pursuers, the black-coated Prussian Hussars, their shakos proudly emblazoned with a white-metal skull and crossbones. Some of the Frenchmen raised their hands in surrender above their heads. Others sank to their knees. Prayed for salvation. It made no difference. He continued to stare, fascinated, as the cavalry closed in on them. Saw the great silver sabres rise up in the air and whistle down fast upon the defenceless men, their razor-sharp blades sliding effortlessly through flesh and cloth. He heard the screams and watched the Frenchmen die. From his right a motley group of French cavalry – cuirassiers, chasseurs and lancers – galloped towards the scene, swords raised, shouting obscenities. The Prussians, their horses splashing in puddles of French blood, left their butchery and turned calmly to face this new and equally useless gesture. The French, exhausted and outpaced on winded horses, made easy sport for the vengeful Hussars. Again he saw the blades rise and fall. Watched as one of the Germans turned his horse with a single expert tug on the reins, swung his sword high and severed both the weapon and the hand that held it from his opponent's right arm before recovering his blade with ease, to place the point at the wounded man's throat and push it hard through his neck. From deep within the mêlée he saw a cuirassier's helmet fly up and through the air with the trooper's head still inside it, while the man's horse set off back across the field, the headless torso still upright in the saddle.

It was quickly over. As the Hussars continued to ride around, slashing down to make sure of their work, Macdonell turned away, unable to watch any more. Surely now, he thought, the killing could stop. Now at least, dear God, he prayed, give us this one night of peace. Ahead of him and across to the left the entire French army was in headlong rout. There was no need to stay here any longer. His job was done. Turning back into the wood, he found Sergeant Miller.

'Bloody business, sir. If I may say so.'

'Bloody, Miller. Yes. Bloody enough by any reckoning. But we were victorious.'

'We were that, sir. I reckon as any man that fought here today and has lived to tell it will count himself lucky, sir. I know that I do. Wouldn't have missed it. Not for all your Spanish scraps, sir. We've finished with Boney now, I reckon.'

Macdonell looked into Miller's grinning face. Saw the honesty smiling through the soot and sweat.

'Yes, Miller. I do believe we have.'

He paused. Frowned, looked out at the battlefield and spoke again: 'Immortality, Miller. D'you know what that is? That's what you and I and the rest of them have achieved today. Immortality. A story to tell to your grandchildren.'

The sergeant looked bemused. 'Right you are, sir.'

Macdonell looked again towards the south, at the retreating army and the dark landscape with its piles of dead and dying men. Occasional shapes moved among them now. Dots of light that marked a hundred lanterns. The looters had come. There were few things uglier, he thought, than the killing fields after a battle.

'You may take the men back through the woods now, Miller. They'll need a rest.'

They entered the château by the south gate, its double doors wide open now. Inside, amid the carnage and desolation, the victors sat in groups huddled around fires that sprang from within the embers of the buildings. Some were eating. Sausage, cheese, flat bread and hard biscuit. Anything they could find, most of it plundered from within the knapsacks of dead Frenchmen. Macdonell noticed one soldier, a private of the 3rd Guards, sitting by what appeared to be a full mess tin of stew which had congealed beneath a glistening film of fat.

'No appetite?'

The soldier struggled to his feet. Attempted to salute. Macdonell nodded.

'No, sir. That is, I was going to eat, sir. There's a fine fire burning by the barn, sir. And the meat's cooked nice. It's just that. Well. It is the fire, sir. Doesn't really make you feel very hungry.'

Wondering what the man could mean, Macdonell followed the soldier's gaze. Wandered over to the blazing timbers at the side of the barn on whose flame two other, older redcoats, a private and a corporal of the 1st Guards, one wearing the long-service stripes of a Peninsular man, were cooking their own meagre supper. Seeing him, the two veterans snapped to attention and stood away from the flames. Macdonell nodded to them and looked into the fire. His curious gaze was returned from within the embers by the hollow grin of a charred human head. So that was it. The source of the fuel for the cooking fire, intended or accidental, was the burning bodies of the fallen. For once, Macdonell felt an unusual nausea in the pit of his stomach. Surely now this must be the final act of a drama played out in Hell? Looking about him in the fast-falling darkness, he watched the light of the other fires across the courtyard as they lit up the faces of its defenders, giving the appearance of so many demons rather than His Majesty's Foot Guards.

Walking away from the fire, he moved towards the garden and noticed the scores of bodies that lay heaped in curious attitudes. With the objectivity that came only with years of soldiering, he began, as a matter of instinct, to calculate their last movements. Here, just behind what had until recently been the wall of a building, was a man, a guardsman who, wounded and placed inside for his safety, must have been burned alive along with the house. Close by, half inside the remains of a doorway, lay another corpse. The man's head and upper torso were perfectly recognizable. Macdonell placed him as a private of No. 2 Company. He had a nasty gunshot wound to the upper arm. His legs and feet though, and all from the waist downward, had been burned almost to ash. Evidently he had managed to crawl so far before his strength had run out and the fire had claimed him.

Macdonell pressed a hand across his grimy forehead. Rubbed his eyes clear of smuts and cinders. The smell in the courtyard was indescribable. A vile, sweet stench that caught the back of the throat and lingered on the clothes. Burning wood and well-done pork. He swallowed hard. This was slaughter of a scale and ferocity he had not seen since Badajoz. This surely would be a final end to these long years of war? Napoleon was beaten. Routed from the field. Surely he could not hope to recover? This must then be an end to it. Let there be no more killing. No more death like this. Yet almost as he heard the prayer form in his mind, he knew it to be futile.

353

Knew that men would continue to do these things to each other. That other men would come. Other Napoleons with their ambition, their glory, their death. And he knew too that there would always be men ready to stop them. Men like Graham, Miller and Gooch. Men like poor, dead Blackman, and Dobinson and Frost. Men like him.

No. This was not an end to war. Merely an entr'acte between the bloody dramas that made up real life. The only life he knew. Would ever know.

As the darkness grew deeper, he crossed the yard and found his servant. The man's face wore a look of deep concern.

'Trouble, Smith?'

'It's your valise, sir. Appears to have been, erm, misplaced in the battle, sir. Can't say as I know where it can be at all.'

Macdonell sighed. 'Burnt to a cinder, I've no doubt. Still, Smith. No matter. What's needed now is a horse. You must find me a horse before daybreak. I'll wager there are a good few on this field and of no bad quality. D'you think you can manage it?'

The man looked relieved. 'Oh yes, sir. You can rely on me. I'll be sure to get a good one, Colonel. A general's horse, sir. A marshal's horse. Boney's very own nag.'

Macdonell shook his head. 'Just a horse, Smith. Don't over-reach yourself. A colonel's horse would do very nicely.'

He spotted Biddle. He was leaning against the parapet, polishing a gilded copper eagle prised from a Garde grenadier's bearskin. A trophy.

'Got your booty, Sar'nt?'

'Sorry, sir. Didn't see you there, sir. Didn't I find this lying behind the wall? And you know that its owner has no further use for it. So I just thought I'd give it a bit of a shine. Take it back to the missus, sir. And now, if you'll excuse me, sir, I was just away to see that the men were fed and watered. Or perhaps I should have them stand to, sir?'

'No, Sar'nt. Not tonight. We're to leave the Prussians to

354

chase the Frogs. We've done our bit. You can tell the men to bivouac where best they can. They deserve to rest. And why don't you see if you can find any more of that rum? Colonel Wyndham's in command. I intend to find Colonel Mackinnon. I understand he's been taken to the dressing station. Can't have him there on his own. He'll fleece all the army's junior officers of their back pay before they know what he's at.'

Biddle smiled.

'And be sure to look after yourself, Biddle. You've all earned it.'

'I may have to agree with you there, sir. That was a real day, and no mistake. Such a day as we'll not see again. I did hear one of the lads say as some of the Frogs had filled their canteens with brandy. Now that's something I do like, sir. A nip or two of fine French conn-yak would suit me just fine right now, sir. If I might have your permission?'

Macdonell laughed. Nodded his head. Turned and walked past the dead, towards the garden.

So Biddle would have his brandy and Dan Mackinnon would win the annual pay of ten subalterns at whist or macao and once again all would be right with the world.

He walked through a small doorway and into what had been the garden. Men were attempting to restore order to what in the course of the day had been transformed into a bloody wilderness. By the light of the blazing château he could see Henry Wyndham supervising a party of men clearing bodies from around the perimeter. Others were sorting the packs and weapons of the dead into separate piles.

He turned and walked alone towards the Allied position, through the trampled parterres and muddied walkways. At length he reached the hedge which marked the northernmost boundary of the garden and which throughout the day had been the refuge of Saltoun's men. British bodies, guardsmen mostly, lay tumbled in the ditch where they had fallen or crawled in the agonies of death. A burial party had already

355

begun the business of sorting them into dead and wounded, officers and other ranks. Those with any chance of recovery were lifted and dragged to higher ground – the officers placed in wagons. The corpses, though, were left to lie till morning. No one had either the energy or the inclination to offer them a burial this night.

Walking round the trees and across the track he began to ascend the slope towards the position occupied by the regimental colour party. It was hard going. The mud had been churned to a thick, clinging paste. The easiest thing would have been to have walked on the bodies that lay strewn so thickly that one might have stepped from one to another with each pace. But Macdonell, unable to bring himself to do so, took care to place his feet on the patches of ground between the corpses, using them only to steady himself as the mud caught at his legs. It seemed that every sort of soldier was here and every rank. British infantry, cavalry and artillerymen of all varieties lay alongside their French counterparts. Cuirassiers with hussars and lancers; tall grenadiers and skinny drummer-boys, their bodies contorted into impossible positions. And death was never neat or logical. Men lay blown apart, eviscerated or with half a head. Body parts littered the ground. Yet still in death it was possible to detect the vital indicators which a few hours earlier had branded these men, now united in eternity, mortal enemies. The green jackets of the Nassauers and the black of Brunswick were mixed indiscriminately with redcoats and French blue. He could see entire ranks of bearskinned French Garde grenadiers and chasseurs lying dead in formation where they had been cut down by cannon fire and musketry. And everywhere the bulky forms of thousands of dead horses transformed the contours of the ground into a new and terrible landscape.

Towards the crest of the ridge he began to encounter groups of Allied soldiers, sitting down in small groups wherever they could, making camp for the night among the dead. Many had already fallen into an exhausted sleep, making it almost impossible at times to tell the living from the dead. They propped their heads against anything they could find: a greatcoat, a discarded blanket, a corpse.

Macdonell paused and looked back down the hill. Took in the extent of the carnage and the rubbish that battle forever left in its wake. Clay pipes, buttons, musket flints, cartridge papers, thousands of musketballs lay strewn around. And scattered among the dead and dying were thousands of personal possessions. Things once invested with a private meaning, now meaningless. Blown, like their owners, to oblivion. Letters, snuff boxes, playing cards, coins, a sewing kit, miniature portraits of wives, lovers, children. The very stuff of life.

On the ridge he found a single, decimated platoon of his regiment. They looked up and the corporal, whose name he could not bring to mind, recognizing him, rose to his feet and saluted. The others made to follow, but Macdonell motioned them back down. Realized that some words might be required.

'Well done, all of you. Well done. You have more than done your duty today. You have made history. Get what rest you can, lads.'

Amid the murmured thanks, he walked on and began to wonder if, like him, they were aware that this had been a battle unlike any other they had ever fought. That in the course of these nine hours not only their own lives but their whole world had been changed. A little further along the track, beside another group of guardsmen, he made out a familiar figure. George Bowles was struggling to squeeze himself into a pair of grey overalls. Macdonell approached him.

'So, George, that's it then. I say, found your overalls?'

'No, damn it, James. Not mine at all. Came off some fellow in the 52nd. Damned if a sergeant of artillery didn't just sell them to me for three guineas. Swore they'd fit me like a glove. Well, look at me, James. Do they fit?'

357

'After a fashion, George. But does it matter? You are alive. We are alive. The battle is won. Bonaparte is beaten. The war is over.'

Bowles gave up attempting to fasten the buttons of the undersized trousers, which had in fact belonged to a now dead, diminutive fifteen-year-old ensign half his height. He finally managed to secure them with his belt and fell to adjusting his coat and cuffs in an attempt to cut some sort of a dash.

'Quite so, James. It's over. And a bloodier business I never knew. And damned costly.'

Macdonell, surprised, nodded gravely and was about to offer a suitably profound reply when Bowles spoke again: 'I tell you, James, not only have I lost my valise, but my damn sword's broke too and me hat's gone. Damned tailors. Damned Frogs.'

Macdonell smiled. Turned to take a last, lingering look out across the devastated battlefield and back down on the smoking ruin of Hougoumont. Then, walking over to Bowles, he patted him gently on the back.

'Come along, George. Let's see if we can find you a new sword.'

POSTSCRIPT

At around 9.20 in the evening Wellington and Blücher meet on the road near Le Caillou. The Allied army retires for the night and the Prussians take up the pursuit of the French. At Genappe they find Napoleon's imperial coach and within it the Emperor's medals and a set of diamonds which will later be worked into the Prussian crown jewels.

Dawn brings a new horror to the battlefield. In and around an area no larger than three square miles, close on 50,000 soldiers lie dead and wounded. Wellington has lost 17,000 men, around a quarter of his force. Of the Allied officers almost a third have become casualties. Blücher's losses amount to 7,000 dead, wounded and missing. Napoleon's army has suffered 25,000 men killed and wounded out of a total of over 40,000 casualties including prisoners and deserters: 50 per cent of the French forces. With the exception of a few officers, taken to Waterloo and Brussels, the bodies of the dead are buried over the next few days in mass graves on the battlefield, or burned in giant funeral pyres.

Back in Paris by 21 June, two days later Napoleon abdicates for a second time. On 7 July the Prussians enter the city, which is occupied by a joint Allied force for the next three years.

In the newly Bourbon France a 'White Terror' reigns in

which some 300 French Waterloo veterans of all ranks and other Bonapartists are hunted down and killed.

For the victors of the British army, the end of the war brings mixed fortunes. All soldiers who have fought at Waterloo, whatever their rank, receive a specially struck medal, the first of its kind in the British army, bearing on one face a winged victory, on the other the head of the Prince Regent.

However, while officers are lauded, decorated and promoted, many of the other ranks, discharged by reason of their wounds or on the reduction of the army, are left without employment and reduced to begging on the streets. Two years after the battle, every soldier of the British army who served at Waterloo is presented with prize money. A general receives £1,275; a colonel £433. Privates receive just £2 each.

While the French attempt to christen the battle after the name of their objective of Mont St Jean and the Prussians after the inn of La Belle Alliance, it is its British name, the village that was location of Wellington's headquarters, which sticks in the public mind.

Waterloo will become the most written about battle in the history of warfare.

BIOGRAPHICAL NOTES

The French

Maréchal de Camp Comte Charles-Angelique de la Bedoyere is arrested in France by the Royalists, tried for treason and shot by firing squad on 26 August 1815, leaving a widow and a small son. Refusing to wear a blindfold, his last words are: 'Above all, do not miss me.' He is twenty-nine.

Jean-Baptiste Drouet, Comte d'Erlon flees to Munich and on to Bayreuth and is condemned to death by a French court *in absentia*. In 1825 he receives a pardon and takes a post in the French army, at Nantes. Between 1834 and 1835 he is Governor of Algeria and in 1843 is created a Marshal of France. He dies in 1844, aged seventy-nine.

Auguste Charles, Comte de Flahault, Napoleon's favourite aide-de-camp, holds Napoleon up in the saddle as they flee the battlefield and goes with him to Paris. It is de Flahault who tells Napoleon at the end of June that he must leave France. Protected by his natural father, Talleyrand, he is exiled and moves to London. On 19 June 1817 he marries the Scottish heiress and friend of Byron the Hon. Margaret Elphinstone at St Andrew's Church in Edinburgh. The daughter of the British admiral, Lord Keith, she is disinherited. The couple move to Paris. Central to the coup which enthrones Louis Napoleon, de Flahault dies in 1870, aged eighty-five, the day before the French surrender to the Prussians at Sedan. The couple have one daughter who goes on to marry the 4th Marquis of Lansdowne.

Maréchal de Camp Gaspard Gourgaud accompanies the Emperor to St Helena where he keeps a journal recording the conversations of his master. He returns to France in 1818 and is made a general by Louis-Philippe. He dies in 1852.

The Emperor, Napoleon Bonaparte flees to Paris. On 23 June he abdicates for a second time and by 3 July is in Rochefort, planning his escape to America. Blockaded by the Royal Navy, he surrenders to the British on 15 July. He is exiled to St Helena, in the South Atlantic. His gaoler is Sir Hudson Lowe, who in 1816 marries Susan de Lancey, sister of the late Sir William de Lancey. Napoleon spends the rest of his life writing his memoirs, in which he manipulates the truth about Waterloo, laying most of the blame on Ney, d'Erlon, Soult and Grouchy. He never again sees his son, the King of Rome. He dies on 5 May 1821, aged fifty-two. Research published in 2001 suggests that the cause was not, as had long been supposed, stomach cancer, but slow poisoning by arsenic. The source remains unclear.

Marshal Michel Ney arrives back in Paris on 20 June. Ignoring advice to leave France, he is arrested by the restored Bourbon regime and court-martialled for treason. Army officers refuse to try him and he is convicted and sentenced to death by the Chamber of Peers. He is executed by firing squad against a wall of the Luxembourg Gardens in Paris on 7 December 1815, leaving a widow and four sons. Refusing to wear a blindfold, he dies in civilian dress. He is shot eleven times, six times in the chest, three in the head, once in the neck and once in the right arm. One of his executioners fires into the wall above his head. Ney is forty-six years old. His final words are: 'Soldiers of France. This is the last order I shall give you. Fire!' He has no monument on the field of Waterloo.

General de Division Comte Honoré Charles Michel Reille remains in the French army and in 1847 is created Marshal of France by Louis-Philippe. He dies in 1860, at the age of eighty-five.

Marshal Nicholas Jean de Dieu Soult takes the remnants of Napoleon's shattered army and, joining with Grouchy, fights a brave rearguard action against the Prussians. Going into exile in Düsseldorf, he is pardoned in 1819 and serves as France's Minister of War from 1830 to 1834. In 1838 he represents France at the coronation of Queen Victoria in London. From 1832 to 1836 and from 1839 to 1840 he is Prime Minister of France. In 1847 he is created Marshal-General of France. He dies in 1851, aged eighty-two.

The Allies
Captain George Bowles is knighted and made Commander-in-Chief of the First West India Regiment and Lieutenant of the Tower of London. From 1845 to 1851 he is Master of the Household to the Queen. He dies in London in May 1876.

Lieutenant-Colonel Charles Dashwood remains in the army and in 1822 marries Caroline, the daughter of Sir Robert Barlow. He is retired by 1830 and dies in April 1832.

Captain George Evelyn leaves the army before 1824 and marries in Ireland. He dies in 1829.

Sergeant Ralph Fraser is awarded a medal for his gallantry at

Hougoumont and is discharged from the army in 1818 'in consequence of long service and being worn out'. He confounds this description and becomes a bedesman at Westminster Abbey. He lives until 1862, dying peacefully at the age of eighty.

Lieutenant Henry Gooch is promoted captain in the Coldstream Guards in October 1819. He leaves the army as a lieutenant-colonel in June 1841.

Corporal James Graham, having rescued his brother from the flames at Hougoumont, sees him die of his wounds some days after the battle. He is later nominated for an annuity from the Rector of Framlingham for being 'the most deserving soldier at Waterloo'. He retires from the army in 1816 and dies at Kilmainham in April 1843.

August Graf von Gneisenau goes on to have an illustrious military career in the Prussian army and becomes Governor of Berlin. In 1830 he is given command of a Prussian punitive expedition to suppress a Polish rebellion. He dies of cholera later that year, aged seventy-one.

Sir William Howe De Lancey dies in the arms of his wife, Magdalene, in a small house at Mont St Jean on 26 June. He is buried at the Protestant cemetery of St Josse Ten Noode in Brussels. In 1887 his remains are removed to the new Waterloo memorial at Evere cemetery in North Brussels where they lie today, alongside those of James, Lord Hay and Wellington's aide-de-camp Sir Alexander Gordon.

Magdalene De Lancey leaves Belgium after the death of her husband and returns to Scotland. In 1816 she writes an account of her experience of the Waterloo campaign, of which nine copies are known to have existed. It is praised by her friend Walter Scott and reduces Charles Dickens to tears. Although consumed by grief, she marries again, in March 1819, Henry Harvey, an officer in the Indian army. The couple tour Europe, return to Edinburgh and settle in Worcester. They have three children, but in July 1822 Magdalene dies, aged only twenty-two. Dunglass is sold by the Hall family in 1915 and the house is demolished in the 1950s.

Sergeant Brice Macgregor is discharged from the Scots Guards in 1821 with a full pension. He becomes a Yeoman of the Guard and dies in November 1846.

Fitzroy Somerset, having lost his arm at Waterloo, goes on to enjoy a successful military career in the British army. He is chiefly remembered today as Lord Raglan, the Commander-in-Chief of the British army in the Crimea, who ordered the charge of the Light Brigade at Balaclava in 1854. He dies of dysentery in the course of the war, later that year.

Captain Edward Sumner dies of his wounds in Brussels on 26 June 1815.

Lieutenant-Colonel James Macdonell is created Companion of the Bath for his services at Hougoumont. At the end of the war he is named by Wellington 'the bravest man in the British Army', a title which he hates. He does not welcome the £500 which accompanies it, giving half to his old sergeant, Ralph Fraser. Macdonell continues to serve with the Coldstream Guards and in 1825 becomes its colonel. In 1830 he is made major general and commands the English forces in Ireland between 1831 and 1838. Later he becomes British commander in Canada and in 1838 is made a Knight Commander of the Bath (KCB). He becomes colonel of the 79th (Cameron) Highlanders and then of the 71st Highland Light Infantry. In 1841 he is promoted to lieutenant-general and in 1854 to general of the army. In 1855 he is made Knight Grand Cross of the Most Noble Order of the Bath (GCB). He dies, unmarried, in London in May 1857 at the age of seventy-nine.

Lieutenant-Colonel Daniel Mackinnon recovers from his leg wound and continues with the Coldstream Guards. He becomes colonel of a battalion of the Coldstream in 1826. He marries and writes the first regimental history of the Coldstream Guards. He dies in 1836.

Lieutenant-Colonel Alexander Lord Saltoun rises to become a lieutenant-general and Colonel-in-Chief of the 2nd Regiment of Foot. He commands a brigade in China in 1842 and is created a Knight of the Thistle and Knight Commander of the Bath. He marries and dies in 1853, near Rothes.

Arthur Wellesley, First Duke of Wellington, returns from the battlefield to the village of Waterloo on the evening of 18 June and spends the night seated at his desk writing his despatch of the battle, his bed being occupied by his dying friend and aide-de-camp, Alexander Gordon.

In Britain a grateful nation presents Wellington with a grand country estate, Stratfield Saye. He remains with the army of occupation in France until 1818, and on his return to Britain enters politics with a Cabinet post. Under George IV he is appointed Lord High Constable and in 1827 Commander-in-Chief of the Army. In January 1828 Wellington becomes Prime Minister. He opposes the 1830 Reform Bill and plummets in popularity. Nothing, though, can challenge his lasting reputation as the victor of Waterloo. Foreign Secretary under William IV, in 1846 Wellington retires. He dies in 1852 at Walmer Castle in Kent. One and a half million people line the route of his funeral cortège through the streets of London.

Alexander Woodford is created Companion of the Bath for

his role in the defence of Hougoumont. In 1842 he becomes Colonel-in-Chief of the 40th Foot and in 1861 transfers to the Scots Guards. He dies in 1870.

Hans Ernst Graf von Ziethen is rewarded for his part in the Waterloo campaign with the post of Commander of the Prussian Army of Occupation in France. In 1835 he is promoted to Feld-Marschall. He dies in 1848 at the age of seventy-eight.

AUTHOR'S NOTE

This book is a novel. It does not pretend to be a history of the Waterloo campaign. It was written in an attempt to see inside the minds of a few men who took part in a battle which decided the fate of the western world.

Almost every character in the book is based on an actual person. Where possible I have used what information I have been able to find about each man, particularly in the case of the officers and men of the Light Company, 2nd, Coldstream Guards. Wherever possible, where I have found individual memoirs, the characters speak as they did then. Students of language and manners may not always agree with the sentiments and expressions of the characters. I can only ask for a little interpretive licence, without which it would have been impossible to tell, in human terms, the story of those momentous four days.

In the course of researching the book I consulted some 300 published works and numerous first-hand accounts. I am endebted for their help to the staff at the library of the National Army Museum, the Public Record Office at Kew and the reading room of the National Library of Scotland in Edinburgh. My thanks also to the present-day tenant of the farm of Hougoumont, who allowed me to walk at liberty on several

368

occasions around the site of some of the book's key moments in the months before the structure became too unsafe for public access.

I must thank Patrick Barty, Seamus Collins and Ben Whitworth for taking the trouble to read all or part of the manuscript and offer invaluable comments. I am also indebted to Denis Critchley Salmonson for his notes on his ancestor Henry Hardinge and to Rollo Wilson.

I owe a huge debt of gratitude to the late Giles Gordon for his enthusiasm in the early stages of this book, which he was tragically unable to see through to publication.

I am also, of course, indebted to my long-suffering wife Sarah and my children Alexander, Ruaridh and India, who, having endured my 'Waterloo-mania' with varying degrees of enthusiasm, have never ceased to provide their own particular brands of unstinting support.

Finally, thanks to my parents, with whom it all began when, unwittingly, some thirty years ago, they agreed to take a detour on the journey home from France and visit a muddy Belgian battlefield.

For those who wish to go further into the facts behind the book I can only point them in the direction of Mark Adkin's superb *Waterloo Companion*. Peter Hofschröer's controversial works on the German perspective of the campaign and the workings of the Prussian army also proved invaluable, as was David Miller's highly readable life of William and Magdalene De Lancey.

While the portrait of Alisdair Macdonell of Glengarry is now one of the best known works in the National Gallery of Scotland, Edinburgh, I have been unable to trace the whereabouts of Raeburn's portrait of James Macdonell, which I have only seen in reproduction. I would be grateful for any information which would assist in my ongoing search.